Praise for Susan Wiggs and the Bella Vista Chronicles

The Apple Orchard

"Wiggs tells a layered, powerful story of love, loss, hope and redemption."

—*Kirkus Reviews*, starred review

"This brilliant and epic family drama...fills the senses...courtesy of Wiggs's amazing narrative and supreme skill as a writer."
—*RT Book Reviews*, Top Pick!

"A tale with universal appeal."

—*Booklist*

"This is classic Wiggs, with its emphasis on the strength of family and friends, and a landscape integral to the plot."

—*Publishers Weekly*

The Beekeeper's Ball

"Wiggs' carefully detailed plotlines, one contemporary and one historical, with their candid look at relationships and their long-term effects, are sure to captivate readers."

—*Booklist*, starred review

"A dazzling intergenerational tale."

—*Publishers Weekly*

"A satisfying, engaging read."

—*Kirkus Reviews*

"Highly recommended."

—*Library Journal*

Also by Susan Wiggs

CONTEMPORARY ROMANCES

Home Before Dark
The Ocean Between Us
Summer by the Sea
Table for Five
Lakeside Cottage
Just Breathe
The Goodbye Quilt

The Bella Vista Chronicles

The Apple Orchard
The Beekeeper's Ball

The Lakeshore Chronicles

Summer at Willow Lake
The Winter Lodge
Dockside
Snowfall at Willow Lake
Fireside
Lakeshore Christmas
The Summer Hideaway
Marrying Daisy Bellamy
Return to Willow Lake
Starlight on Willow Lake

HISTORICAL ROMANCES

The Lightkeeper
The Drifter
The Mistress of Normandy
The Maiden of Ireland

The Tudor Rose Trilogy

At the King's Command
The Maiden's Hand
At the Queen's Summons

Chicago Fire Trilogy

The Hostage
The Mistress
The Firebrand

Calhoun Chronicles

The Charm School
The Horsemaster's Daughter
Halfway to Heaven
Enchanted Afternoon
A Summer Affair

For a complete list of all titles by Susan Wiggs,
visit www.susanwiggs.com.

SUSAN WIGGS

The APPLE ORCHARD

mira™

ISBN-13: 978-0-7783-0506-4

The Apple Orchard

Mira
22 Adelaide St. West, 40th Floor
Toronto, Ontario M5H 4E3, Canada
BookClubbish.com

Printed in U.S.A.

For my mother and father, Lu and Nick Klist, with deepest love. All I know in the world of love and passion, hard work and dedication, and the sturdy resilience of the human heart, I learned from my parents. You are, and have always been, my inspiration.

The APPLE ORCHARD

PART ONE

Stay me with flagons, comfort me with apples:
for I am sick of love.

—The Song of Solomon, 2:5

··· • ···

Apples are iconic and convey so much—home, comfort,
wholesomeness, health, wisdom, beauty, simplicity, sensuality,
seduction…and sin. The Gravenstein apple (Danish: Gråsten-
Æble) comes from Gråsten in South Jutland, Denmark. The
fruit ranges in color from yellow-green to crimson and has a
tart flavor, perfect for cooking and making apple cider. This
is an ephemeral variety that doesn't keep well, so it should be
enjoyed fresh from the orchard.

ÆBLE KAGE
(DANISH APPLE PIE)

Before they taste this, people wonder at the lack of spices. If lovely fresh apples are used, the spices won't be missed.

1 egg

¾ cup sugar

½ cup flour

1 teaspoon baking powder

dash of salt

½ teaspoon vanilla

2 cups diced apples, peeled and sautéed in 1 tablespoon butter until soft

½ cup chopped walnuts

Beat the egg, gradually adding the sugar and vanilla. Then add flour, baking powder and salt to create a smooth batter. Fold in sautéed apples and nuts, then pour into a buttered and floured 8-inch-square glass pan. Bake for about 30 minutes at 350 degrees F.

Cut into squares and serve with caramel topping, ice cream or both.

CARAMEL APPLE TOPPING

....

This is one of the simplest and most delicious ways to prepare fresh apples. Keep a jar on hand to serve over cake, ice cream, pound cake or yogurt, with your morning granola or straight out of the jar with a spoon at two in the morning, when you find yourself alone and hungry.

4 sliced apples; no need to peel

4 tablespoons butter (no substitute)

a pinch of nutmeg

1 teaspoon cinnamon

1 cup walnuts

1 cup brown sugar

1 cup cream or buttermilk

Melt the butter in a heavy pan. Add the sugar and swirl until melted. Add the spices and apples and sauté until the apples are tender. Add the walnuts and stir. Turn off the heat, and slowly stir in the cream. Serve immediately over ice cream or cake, and keep the leftovers in a jar in the fridge.

(Source: Traditional)

PROLOGUE

Archangel, California

The air smelled of apples, and the orchard hummed with
the sound of bees hovering over the bushels of harvested
fruit. The trees were in prime condition, waiting for the harvest workers to arrive. The branches had been pruned in
readiness for the ladders, the last pesky groundhog had been
trapped and carted away; the roads between the trees had
been graded smooth so the fruit wouldn't be jostled in transport. The morning was cool with a mist hanging among the
branches. The sun, ripe on the eastern horizon of the rolling hills, offered the promise of warmth later in the day. The
pickers would be here soon.

Magnus Johansen balanced on the picking ladder, feeling
as steady as a man a quarter his age. Isabel would scold him
if she saw; his granddaughter would call him an old fool for

working alone instead of waiting for the pickers to arrive. But Magnus liked the early solitude; he liked having the whole orchard to himself in the muted hush of the warming morning. He was in his eighth decade of life; God only knew how many more harvests he would see.

Isabel worried so much about him these days. She tended to hover, like a honeybee in the milkweed that surrounded the orchard. Magnus wished she wouldn't fret. She should know he had already survived the best and worst life had to offer.

Truth be told, he worried about Isabel far more than she worried about him. It was the things she *didn't* know that weighed upon him this morning. He couldn't keep her in the dark forever. The letter on the desk in his study confirmed his worst fear—unless a miracle occurred, all of Bella Vista would be lost.

Magnus did his best to set aside the troubles for the moment. He had risen early to don his denim and boots, knowing today was the day. Over the years, he had learned to judge the moment of maturity for the fruit. Too early, and you had to deal with the inefficiencies of spot picking. Too late, and you risked having fruit that was senescent, breaking down from old age.

Some mornings he felt his own kind of senescence deep in the marrow of his bones. Not today, though. Today, he felt a surge of energy, and his fruit was at the peak of perfection. He'd performed the starch iodine test, of course, but more importantly, he'd bitten into an apple, knowing by its firmness, sweetness and crunch that the time had come. Over the next few days, the orchard would be as busy as a beehive. He would send his fruit to market in the waiting boxes, each with a bright Bella Vista Orchards label.

A trio cluster of glossy, crimson-striped Gravensteins hung several feet out on a branch above his head. Hard-to-reach limbs were usually pruned, but this one was productive. Carefully aware of the extent of his reach, he leaned forward to pick a trio of apples and add them to his basket. These days, most of the workers preferred the long bags, which made two-handed picking easier, but Magnus was old school. He was old, period. Yet even now, the land sustained him; there was something about the rhythm of the seasons, the yearly renewal, that kept him as vigorous as a much younger man. He had much to be thankful for.

Much to regret, as well.

As he captured the apples on the high limb, his ladder wobbled a bit. Chastened, he left the rest of the branch for the gleaners and climbed down.

As he moved his picking ladder to another tree, he heard the frantic whir of a bee in distress in the milkweed. A honeybee, greedy for the abundant nectar of the tangled blossoms, was trapped in the flowers, a common occurrence. Magnus often found their desiccated bodies enmeshed by the sticky seedpods. Modern farmers tried to eradicate the milkweed, but Magnus allowed it to flourish along the borders of the orchard, a habitat for bees and monarch butterflies, finches and ladybugs.

Feeling charitable, he liberated a trapped and furiously buzzing bee from the sticky down, releasing a flurry of seeds parachuted by feathery umbrellas. With no notion that the sweetness was deadly, the bee immediately dove back into the hedge and returned to sipping nectar, the risk of getting caught obliterated by its hunger.

Magnus moved on with a philosophical shrug. When nature drew a creature to sweetness, there could be no stopping it. He moved his ladder to the next tree, positioning it for maximum efficiency, and climbed to a lofty perch. There, his head above the branches, he inhaled the glory of the morning—the redolence of the air, the quality of light filtering through the mist, the contours of the land and the distant haze of the ocean.

A sense of nostalgia swept through him, borne along on a wave of memories. As though it were yesterday he could see the sun-flooded landscape, with Eva down at the collection bins, smiling up at him as she supervised the harvest—his war bride, starting a new life in America with him. They had built Bella Vista together. It was a terrible shame that the bank was about to take it away.

Despite the successes and tragedies, the secrets and lies, Magnus had an abundance of blessings. He had made a life with a woman he loved, and that was more than many poor souls could count. They had created a world together, spending their days close to nature, eating crisp apples, fresh home-made bread slathered with honey from their own hives, sharing the bounty with workers and neighbors… Yet those blessings had come at a cost, one that would be reckoned by a power greater than himself.

His pocket phone chirped, disturbing the quiet of the morning. Isabel insisted that he carry a phone in his pocket at all times; his was one of the simple ones that sent and received calls without all the other functions that would only confuse him.

The ladder teetered again as he reached into the pocket of his plaid shirt. He didn't recognize the number that came up.

"This is Magnus," he said, his customary greeting.

"It's Annelise."

His heart stumbled. Her voice sounded thin, older, but, oh, so familiar, despite the passage of decades. Beneath the thin, wavery tones, he recognized the sound of a far younger woman, one he had loved in a much different way than he'd loved Eva.

His grip tightened on the phone. "How the devil did you get this number?"

"I take it you received my letter," she said, lapsing into their native Danish, probably without even realizing it.

"I did, and you are absolutely right," he said, though he felt his heart speed up at the admission. "It's time to tell them everything."

"Have you done it?" she asked. "Magnus, it's a simple enough conversation."

"Yes, but Isabel…she's… I don't like to upset her." Isabel—beautiful and fragile, so damaged by life at such a young age.

"And what about Theresa? She's your granddaughter, too. Would you rather the news come from you, or from some un-designated stranger? We're not getting any younger, you and I. If you don't do something right away, I will."

"Fine, then." He felt a flash of hatred for the phone, this little electronic intruder turning a bright day dark. "I will take care of it. I always do. And if by some miracle they for-give us—"

"Of course they will. Don't ever stop expecting a miracle, Magnus. You of all people should know better."

"Don't call me again," he said, his heart lurching in his chest. "Please don't call me again." He put away his cell phone. The wind swept through the trees, and the powerful scent of apples surrounded him. Wheeling hawks kettled overhead, and one of them loosed a plaintive cry. Magnus reached for one more apple, a lush beauty dangling at arm's length, the shine on its cheek so bright he could see his reflection.

The reach unbalanced the ladder. He grabbed at a branch but missed, and then there was nothing to hold on to but the misty air. Despite the brutal swiftness of the accident, Magnus felt eerily aware of every second, as though it was happening to someone else. Yet he was not afraid for himself—he was far too old for that, and life had taught him long ago that fear and happiness could not coexist.

PART TWO

Millions saw the apple fall, but Newton was the one who asked why.

—Bernard M. Baruch

··· • ···

APPLE CHUTNEY

This is a nice accompaniment to spiced pork, roasted chicken or grilled salmon.

3 tart cooking apples, cored and diced (no need to peel)

½ cup chopped white onion

1 tablespoon minced ginger root

½ cup orange juice

1/3 cup cider vinegar

½ cup brown sugar

1 teaspoon grainy mustard

¼ teaspoon hot pepper flakes

½ teaspoon salt

½ cup raisins or currants

Combine all ingredients except the raisins in a heavy saucepan. Bring to a boil, stirring constantly, then reduce to simmer and stir occasionally until most of the liquid has evaporated; about 45 minutes. Remove from heat and add the raisins. Store in the refrigerator or can using traditional methods.

(Source: Adapted from a recipe by the Washington State Apple Commission)

ONE

San Francisco

Tess Delaney's to-do list was stacked invisibly over her head like the air traffic over O'Hare. She had clients waiting to hear from her, associates hounding her for reports and a make-or-break meeting with the owner of the firm. She pushed back at the pressing anxiety and focused on the task at hand—restoring a treasure to its rightful owner.

The current mission brought her to an overfurnished apartment in Alamo Square. Miss Annelise Winther, still spry at eighty, ushered her into a cozy place with thready lace curtains, dust-ruffled chairs and a glorious scent of something baking. Tess wasted no time in presenting the treasure.

Miss Winther's hands, freckled by age, the joints knotted with arthritis, shook as she held the antique lavaliere. Beneath a pink knitted shawl, her bony shoulders trembled.

"This necklace belonged to my mother," she said, her voice breaking over the word. "I haven't seen it since the spring of 1941." She lifted her gaze to Tess, who sat across the scrubbed pine kitchen table from her. There were stories in the woman's eyes, winking like the facets of a jewel. "I have no words to thank you for bringing this to me."

"It's my pleasure," said Tess. "Moments like this—they're the best part of my job." The sense of pride and accomplishment helped her ignore the insistent buzz of her phone, signaling yet another incoming message.

Annelise Winther was Tess's favorite kind of client. She was unassuming, a woman of modest means, judging by the decrepit condition of her apartment, in one of the city's rambling Victorians that had seen better days. Two cats, whom the woman had introduced as Golden and Prince, lazed in the late-afternoon autumn sunshine spilling through a bumped-out bay window. A homey-looking needlepoint piece hung on the wall, bearing the slogan Live This Day.

Miss Winther took off her glasses, polished them and put them back on. Glancing again at Tess's business card, she said, "Tess Delaney, Provenance Specialist, Sheffield Auction House. Well, Ms. Delaney. I'm extremely glad you found me, too. You've done well for yourself."

Her voice had a subtle tinge of an accent. "I saw that History Channel special about the Kraków Museum. You won an award last month in Poland."

"You saw that?" Tess asked, startled to know the woman had recognized her.

"Indeed I did. You were given a citation for restoring the rosary of Queen Maria Leszczynska. It had been stolen by Nazi looters and was missing for decades."

"It was...a moment." Tess had felt so proud that night. The only trouble was, she'd been in a room full of strangers.

No one was present to witness her triumph. Her mother had promised to come but had to cancel at the last minute, so Tess had accepted the accolades in front of a small camera crew and a cultural minister with sweaty hands.

"The very second I saw your face, I knew you would be the one to find my treasure." Miss Winther's words were slightly startling. "And I'm so pleased that it's you. I specifically requested you."

"Why?"

A pause. Miss Winther's face softened. Perhaps she'd lost her train of thought. Then she said, "Because you're the best. Aren't you?"

"I try my best," Tess assured her. She thought the conversation odd, but in this business, she was accustomed to quirky clients. "This piece was with a group of recovered objects from World War II." Tess fell quiet as she thought of the other pieces—jewelry and art and collectibles. The majority of objects remained in limbo, their original owners long gone. She tried not to imagine the terrible sense of violation so many families had suffered, with Nazis invading their homes, plundering their treasures and probably sending many of the family members off to die. Restoring lost treasures seemed a small thing, but the look on Miss Winther's face was its own reward.

"You've made a miracle happen," she declared. "I was just telling a friend on the phone that we're never too old to appreciate a true miracle."

For a miracle, Tess reflected, the task had entailed a lot of hard work. But the expression on the woman's face made all the research, travel and red tape worthwhile. At her own expense, Tess had paid an expert to meticulously clean every link, baguette and facet of the lavaliere. "This is a copy of the provenance report." She slid the document across the table.

"It's basically a history of the piece from its creation to the present, as near as I could trace it to its origins in Russia."

"It's amazing that you were able to find this. When I first contacted your firm, I thought…" Her voice trailed off. "How on earth did you do it?"

Working backward through the provenance report, Tess explained the progress of her research. "This piece was found with a collection of treasures seized in Copenhagen. The lavaliere is pink topaz, with gold filigree embellishments. The chain and clasp are original. It was made by a Finnish designer by the name of August Holmstrom. He was the principal jeweler for the house of Fabergé."

Miss Winther's eyebrows lifted. "*The* Fabergé?"

"The very one." Taking out her loupe, Tess pointed out a tiny spot on the piece. "This is Holmstrom's hallmark, right here, his initials between a double-headed Imperial eagle. He designed it specifically to foil counterfeiters. This particular piece was first mentioned in his design catalog of 1916 and produced for a fashionable shop in St. Petersburg. It was bought by a member of the Danish diplomatic corps."

"My father. He brought the necklace home from a business trip to Russia, and my mother was seldom without it. Besides her wedding ring, it was her favorite piece of jewelry. He gave it to her to celebrate my birth. Though she never said so, I suspect she couldn't have more children after me." Her eyes took on a faraway look, and Tess wondered what she was seeing—her handsome father? Her mother, wearing the jewel against her heart?

The stories behind the treasures were always so intriguing, though often bittersweet. The sad ones were particularly hard to bear. There were some cruelties that were simply inconceivable to normal people, some injustices too big to grasp.

Miss Winther must have been tiny when her world was ripped apart. How scared she must have been, how confused.

"I wish I could do more than simply restore this object," said Tess. "It wound up with a number of other pieces in a repository in the basement of an abandoned government building. I spent the past year researching the archives. The Gestapo claimed they kept objects for safekeeping. It was a common ploy. The one helpful thing they did was to keep meticulous records of the things they seized."

Here was where things got dicey. How much information did Miss Winther really need? Did she have to know what had likely happened to her parents?

There were facts Tess had no intention of sharing, such as the evidence that Hilde Winther had been seized without authority by a corrupt officer, and probably treated like a sex slave for months before she was put to death. This was the trouble with uncovering the mysteries of the past. Sometimes you ended up discovering things better left buried. Was it preferable to expose the truth at any cost or to protect someone from troubling matters they had no power to change?

"This piece was taken from your mother after she was arrested on suspicion of hiding spies, saboteurs and resistance fighters at Bispebjerg Hospital. According to the arrest report, she was accused of pretending her patients were extremely ill, and she would tend to them until they conveniently disappeared."

Miss Winther caught her breath, then nodded. "That sounds like Mama. She was so very brave. She told me she was a hospital volunteer, but I always knew she was doing something important." Behind her spectacles, the old lady's eyes took on a cold glaze of anger. "My mother was dragged away on a beautiful spring afternoon while I watched."

Tess felt an unbidden shudder of sympathy for the little girl

Miss Winther had once been. "I'm so sorry. No child should have to witness that."

Miss Winther held out the necklace, the facets of the large pink topaz catching the light. "Could you...put it on me?" she asked.

"Of course." Tess came around behind her and fastened the clasp of the necklace, feeling the old woman's delicate bone structure. Her hair smelled of lavender, and her dress under the pink shawl was threadbare and faded. Tess felt a surge of emotion. This find was going to change Miss Winther's life. In a single transaction, the old woman could find herself living in the lap of luxury.

Miss Winther reached up, cradling the jewel between her palms. "She was wearing it that day. Even as they were taking her away, she ordered me to run for my life, and that is just what I did. I was very lucky in that moment, or perhaps there had been a tip-off. A boy who was with the Holger Danske—the Danish resistance—spirited me to safety. Such a hero he was, like the Scarlet Pimpernel in the French Revolution, only he was quite real. I wouldn't be here today if not for him. None of us would."

None of us...? Tess wondered who she was referring to. Ghosts from the woman's sad past, probably. She didn't ask, though; she had other appointments on her schedule and couldn't spare the time. And knowing the human cost of the tragedy made Tess feel vulnerable. Still, she was taken by the old lady's sweetness and the air of nostalgia that softened her features when she touched the reclaimed treasure around her neck.

We're both all alone, we two, thought Tess. Had Miss Winther always been alone? *Will I always be?*

"Well, I'm certainly glad you're here." The old lady's smile was soft and strangely intimate.

"This is the appraisal on the piece. I think you'll be very pleased."

The old lady stared at the document. "It says my mother's lavaliere is worth $800,000."

"It's an estimate. Depending on how the bidding goes, it could vary by about ten percent up or down."

Miss Winther fanned herself. "That's a fortune," she said. "It's more money than I ever dreamed of having."

"And not nearly enough to replace your loss, but it's quite a find. I'm really happy for you." Tess felt a glow of accomplishment and pleasure for Miss Winther. In her frayed shawl, surrounded by old things, she didn't look like a wealthy woman, but soon, she would be.

All the painstaking work of restitution had led to this moment. Tess spread a multipage contract on the table. "Here's the agreement with Sheffield Auction House, my firm. It's standard, but you'll want to go over it with a contracts expert."

A timer dinged, and Miss Winther got up from the table. "The scones are ready. My favorites—I make them with lavender sugar. It's an old Danish recipe for autumn. You sit tight, dear, and I'll fix the tea."

Tess pressed her teeth together and tried not to seem impatient, though she had more appointments and work to do at the office. Honestly, she didn't want a scone, with or without lavender sugar. She didn't want tea. Coffee and a cigarette were more to her taste and definitely more suited to the pace of her life. She'd been running since she'd rocketed out of grad school five years before, and she was in a hurry now. The quicker she brought the signed agreement to her firm, the quicker she earned her bonus and could move on to the next transaction.

However, the nature of her profession often called for forbearance. People became attached to their things, and sometimes letting go took time. Miss Winther had gone to a lot of trouble to make scones. Knowing what she knew about the Winther family, Tess wondered what the woman felt when she reminisced about the old days—fear and privation? Or happier times, when her family had been intact?

As she bustled around her old-fashioned kitchen, Miss Winther would pause every so often in front of a little framed mirror by the door, gazing at the necklace with a faraway look in her eyes. Tess wondered what she saw there—her pretty, adored mother? An innocent girl who had no idea her entire world was about to be snatched away?

"Tell me about what you do," Miss Winther urged her, pouring tea into a pair of china cups. "I would love to hear about your life."

"I guess you could say finding treasure is in my blood."

Miss Winther gave a soft gasp, as though Tess's statement surprised her. "Really?"

"My mother is a museum acquisitions expert. My grandmother had an antiques salon in Dublin."

"So you come from a line of independent women."

Nicely put, thought Tess. Her gaze skated away. She wasn't one to chat up a client for the sake of making a deal, but she genuinely liked Miss Winther, perhaps because the woman seemed truly interested in her. "Neither my mother nor my grandmother ever married," she explained. "I'll probably carry on that tradition, as well. My life is too busy for a serious relationship." *Gah, Tess, listen to yourself,* she thought. *Say it often enough and you'll believe it.*

"Well. I suspect that's only because the right person hasn't come along...yet. Pretty girl like you, with all that gorgeous red hair. I'm surprised some man hasn't swept you off your feet."

Tess shook her head. "My feet are planted firmly on the ground."

"I never married, either." A wistful expression misted her eyes. "I was in love with a man right after the war, but he married someone else." She paused to admire the stone once again. "It must be so exciting, the work of a treasure hunter."

"It takes a lot of research, which most people would find tedious. So many dead ends and disappointments," said Tess. "Most of my time is spent combing archives and old records and catalogs. It can be frustrating. But so worthwhile when I get to make a restitution like this. And every once in a great while, I might find myself peeling away a worthless canvas to find a Vermeer beneath. Or unearthing a fortune under a shepherd's hut in a field somewhere. Sometimes it's a bit macabre. The plunder might be stashed in a casket."

Miss Winther shuddered. "That's ghoulish."

"When people have something to hide, they tend to put it where no one would want to look. Your piece wasn't stored in a dramatic hiding place. It was tagged and neatly cataloged, along with dozens of other illegally seized pieces."

Miss Winther arranged the scones just so with a crisp linen napkin in a basket, and brought them to the table.

Tess took a warm scone, just to be polite.

"It sounds as though you like your work," Miss Winther said.

"Very much. It's everything to me." As she said the words aloud, Tess felt a wave of excitement. The business was fast-paced and unpredictable, and each day might bring an adrenaline rush—or crushing disappointment. Tess was having a banner year; her accomplishments were bringing her closer to the things she craved like air and water—recognition and security.

"That sounds just wonderful. I'm certain you'll get exactly what you're looking for."

"In this business, I'm not always sure what that is." Tess sneaked another glance at the clock on the stove.

Miss Winther noticed. "You have time to finish your tea."

Tess smiled, liking this woman almost in spite of herself. "All right. Would you like me to leave the contract with you or—"

"That's not necessary," the old lady said, touching the faceted pink topaz. "I won't be selling this."

Tess blinked, shook her head a little. "I'm sorry, what?"

"My mother's lavaliere." She pressed the piece against her bosom. "It's not for sale."

Tess's heart plummeted. "With this piece, you could have total security for the rest of your life."

"Every last shred of security was stripped from me forever by the Nazis," Miss Winther pointed out. "And yet I survived. You've given me back my mother's favorite thing."

"As you say, it's a thing. An object you could turn into comfort and peace of mind for the rest of your days."

"I'm comfortable and secure now. And if you don't believe memories are worth more than money, then perhaps you've not made the right kind of memories." She regarded Tess with knowing sympathy.

Tess tried not to dwell on all the hours she'd spent combing through records and poring over research in order to make the restitution. If she thought about it too much, she'd probably tear out her hair in frustration. She tended to protect herself from memories, because memories made a person vulnerable.

"You must think I'm being a sentimental old fool." Miss Winther nodded. "I am. It's a privilege of old age. I have no debt, no responsibilities. Just me and the cats. We like our life exactly as it is."

Tess took a sip of strong tea, nearly wincing at its bitterness.

"Oh! The sugar bowl. I forgot," said Miss Winther. "It's in the pantry, dear. Would you mind getting it?"

The pantry contained a collection of dusty cans and jars, its walls and shelves cluttered with collectibles, many of them still bearing handwritten garage sale stickers.

"It's just to the right there," said Miss Winther. "On the spice shelf."

Tess picked up the small, footed bowl. Almost instantly, a tingle of awareness passed through her. One of the first things she'd learned in her profession was to tune into something known as the "heft" or "feel" of the piece. Something that was real and authentic simply had more substance than a fake or knockoff.

She set the tarnished bowl on the table and tried to keep a poker face as she studied the object. The sweep of the handles and the effortless swell of the bowl were unmistakable. Even the smoky streaks of age couldn't conceal the fact that the piece was sterling, not plate.

"Tell me about this sugar bowl," she said, using the small tongs to pick up a cube. Sugar tongs. They were even more rare than the bowl.

"It's handsome, isn't it?" Miss Winther said. "But the very devil to keep clean. I was not in a terribly practical frame of mind when I picked it up at a church rummage sale long ago. It's been decades. Rummage sales have always been a weakness of mine. I'm afraid I've brought home any number of bright, pretty things that just happened to catch my eye. Once I get something home, though, it's anyone's guess whether or not I'll actually use it."

"This is quite a find," Tess said, holding it up to check the bottom, and seeing the expected hallmark there.

"In what way?"

Could she really not know? "Miss Winther, this bowl is a Tiffany, and it appears to be genuine."

"Goodness, you don't say."

"There's a style known as the Empire set, very rare, produced in a limited edition. I'd have to do more research, but my sense is, this could be extremely valuable." Not that it would matter to the old lady, who preferred her artifacts to cash. "It's a lovely piece, regardless," Tess conceded.

"What a surprising aspect of your job," Miss Winther said, clasping her hands in delight. "Sometimes you stumble across a treasure when you're looking for something else entirely."

Tess watched the sugar cube dissolve in her cup. "It keeps my job interesting."

"Tell me, is this something your firm would sell?" asked Miss Winther.

"It's possible, though even with the sugar tongs, a single piece—"

"I didn't mean just the bowl. I meant the entire set."

Tess dropped her spoon on the table with a clatter. "There's a *set?*"

TWO

Seated at a view table in San Francisco's best bar, Tess was drinking a dirty martini, salty with olive brine. The olives were the closest thing she'd have to dinner. As always, she had worked right up until happy hour.

She worked. That was who she was and what she did with herself. *She worked*...and she counted herself lucky to have a job she loved. Yet meeting Miss Winther, seeing the old lady all alone with her cats, had unsettled Tess. The encounter tapped into her most secret fear—that she would go through life alone and end up surrounded by treasures with no one to share them with. Working kept her from thinking too hard about how alone she was.

Backing away from the thought, she reminded herself of today's accomplishment and of the fact that she had good friends to celebrate with. She and her friends had a standing happy hour at the Top of the Mark, crowning the historic Mark

Hopkins Hotel perched at the pinnacle of Russian Hill. It was a San Francisco landmark, ultra-touristy, but known locally for its stunning views, well-made martinis and live music.

Thanks to her peripatetic childhood, she'd grown up with very little in the way of friends and family. Yet here in the heart of San Francisco, she'd made her own family, a small and convivial tribe of people like her—young professionals who were independent and ambitious. And fun—gypsies and geniuses, hard workers who also remembered to kick back.

There was Lydia, an interior designer who was a constant source of client referrals for Tess. She found things like Duncan Phyfe sofas and Stickley tables stashed in people's attics and storage units. She understood the adrenaline surge of a treasure hunt better than anyone Tess knew. The third member of their trio was Neelie, a wine broker who sometimes did business with Sheffield House. She had brought a new guy along tonight, Russell, who couldn't keep his eyes off her boobs. Neelie kept sending secret text messages to Tess's phone: Well? What do you think of him?

He can't keep his eyes off your boobs.

You say that like it's a bad thing.

The two of them grinned at one another and lifted their glasses.

"You two look like you're up to something," said Jude Lockhart, a guy Tess worked with at Sheffield.

"That's because we are," she said, patting the seat beside her.

Jude gave each of them a kiss and shook hands with Nathan, who was Lydia's steady boyfriend. Neelie introduced him to Russell, her date.

Tess loved the ease and charm of her friends; she loved that they were all still young and fun enough to meet and hang out after work. She especially loved that tonight, she had something to celebrate and friends with whom to share her news.

"I hit the jackpot today," she said.

"Ooh, spill," said Neelie. She turned to her date and explained, "Tess is a professional treasure hunter—really. She's like a modern-day Indiana Jones."

"Not exactly," said Tess. "I didn't have to fight off any snakes today." She told them about finding the Tiffany service at Miss Winther's. "It turns out she used to be a garage sale addict and a bit of a hoarder. Most of the things she had were junk, but I found some other pieces, too." She described the set of Ludwig Moser cordial glasses, a smallish woodcut image, pencil-signed by Charles H. Richert, and a jade cuff from pre-war China. With no particular sentimental attachment to any of the pieces, Miss Winther had cheerfully agreed to consign them to Sheffield House.

"Damn, girl," said Neelie, lifting her green apple martini. "Good work."

Everyone around the lounge table raised their glasses. "If you don't watch out, you're going to get yourself promoted," said Jude.

Tess felt a thrill of nervousness. She knew she was being considered for a position in New York City, a big move in more ways than one. It would represent a huge leap for her, vaulting her to the top of her profession. Jude regarded her with a combination of respect and envy. Somehow, they'd managed to be associates without becoming rivals.

When Tess had first met Jude at an auction in London, she'd developed a severe crush on him. After all, it wasn't every day you met a guy with an Oxford education and the face of a matinee idol. The crush hadn't lasted, though. She quickly discovered they were too much alike—skittish about relationships, mystified by people who flung themselves into crazy love and ended up getting hurt. Eventually, the two of them had settled into a comfortable friendship. They were work colleagues, drinking buddies, and sometimes during the lonely times of the year—like the holidays—they pretended together that the loneliness didn't matter.

"Leave it to Tess to find a fortune in some old lady's pantry," said Lydia, snuggling close to Nathan. The two of them shared a private look, then Nathan gestured at a passing waiter.

Jude nodded. "Tess seems to have a thing with little old ladies. My favorite is that time she found the program from a Giants game, signed by Willie Mays, in a client's piano bench along with her sheet music."

"She remembered he was 'such a nice young man,'" Tess said, smiling at the memory. "She had no idea she was sitting on a treasure every time she sat down at the piano to play 'You'll Never Walk Alone.'"

"I swear, you have the Midas touch," said Neelie.

She laughed. "Hey, don't put *that* on me. Remember, Midas was the guy who turned everything to gold, including his little kid."

"I thought you didn't like kids," Jude pointed out.

"But I like Cheetos. What would happen if all my Cheetos turned to gold?"

"The world would come to an end," said Lydia. "Besides, you do too like kids, Tess. You just don't want to admit it and seem uncool."

"I like kids and I'm totally cool," Neelie pointed out. "And you'll come around, Tess. Even people who don't like kids fall in love when they have their own."

"Hey, speak for yourself," Jude protested. "Watch it, Russell, my man. That ticking sound you hear? That's her biological clock."

Russell put his arm around his date. "I think I can handle her."

"I don't need handling," Neelie protested. "Cuddling, yes. Handling, not so much."

Tess's phone vibrated, signaling an incoming call, and she paused to check it. Not recognizing the number, she let it go to voice mail. *There,* she thought. *I'm not* all *work and no play. I can resist a buzzing phone.*

"Speaking of things that are great..." Nathan gestured at the waiter, who had just showed up with a bottle of Cristal and a tableside bucket.

"Cristal?" said Tess. "I didn't realize my work story was *that* awesome."

"There's more awesome news." He stood up as two older couples entered the bar area, a few younger people trailing behind.

"What's going on?" Jude asked.

With obvious excitement, Nathan introduced everyone to his and Lydia's parents, and various brothers and sisters. Family resemblances were fascinating to Tess. Lydia's two sisters looked like slightly skewed versions of Lydia herself, sharing her nut-brown hair and button nose. Nathan's dad was tall and gangly like his son. An air of excitement swirled around them.

Families were the ultimate mystery. As much as they fascinated her, they also struck her as messy and complicated. Yet she couldn't stop herself from wondering what it must feel like to be surrounded by people you were connected to by blood and history.

Her friends were her family, her job was her life, and she had a dream for her future. But every once in a while, an intense yearning slipped in, sharp as a slender blade.

"Lydia and I wanted to get everyone together tonight," Nathan was saying. "Our families and our closest friends. We have an announcement."

"No way." Neelie clasped her hands over her mouth, and her eyes sparkled with delight.

Tess's heart sped up, because she suddenly knew what was coming next.

Nathan smiled with a glow of happiness so intense, Tess imagined she could feel the warmth of it. "Mom and Dad, Barb and Ed, we're engaged!" Lydia took a small green box from her pocket and placed the diamond solitaire on her finger.

Lydia's mother squealed—*squealed*—and the two of them shared a hug, their eyes closing blissfully. The sisters joined the group, and the two families comingled. Hugs and handshakes made the rounds. Neelie, ever the organizer, immediately took charge of finding out the date, the venue, the wedding party, the wine list.

Watching the happy couple, Tess was surprised to feel the burn of tears behind her eyes and a lump in her throat. "Congratulations, my friend," she said to Lydia. "I'm so, so happy for you."

Lydia clasped Tess's hands. "I couldn't wait to tell you. Can you believe it, me, getting married?"

Tess laughed past her tears. "We used to swear marriage was for girls who have no imagination." She recalled the late-night dorm-room drunk-a-logues they used to indulge in when they were roommates just out of school. Whatever happened to those girls? Tess didn't miss the drinking, but she did miss the camaraderie. Even as she felt a surge of happiness for her friend, there was another feeling tucked away in a dark corner of her heart. She felt the tiniest twinge of envy.

"That was before I learned what this kind of love felt like." Lydia gazed adoringly at Nathan, who had abandoned his glowing-with-happiness look and was now chugging a beer, oblivious to the female sentiment. "Now I'm unbearable. Lately all I dream about doing is keeping house and making babies." She giggled at Tess's aghast expression. "Don't worry. It's not contagious."

"I'm not worried. Just promise me you'll talk about other things, too."

"Of course we will. No talk of domesticity until it's your turn."

Tess admired the ring, a brilliant marquise cut diamond in a platinum setting. It was remarkable, seeing her friend so proudly displaying it, a glittery symbol declaring to the world that someone loved her, that she was no longer going it alone. "Don't hold your breath," Tess said. "I don't actually want a turn."

"You say that now. Just wait until you've met Prince Charming."

"If I spot him, feel free to give him my number."

Lydia went to show off her ring to her sisters and in-laws-to-be. Neelie was already taking down dress sizes for the bridal party. Still a bit startled by the emotion that sneaked up on her, Tess dabbed at her eyes with a cocktail napkin.

"I completely agree," Jude said, moving next to her. "This is a tragic turn of events."

"Don't be mean. Look how happy they are." She watched as Lydia's family gathered around her—mom, dad, two look-alike sisters—and felt a lump in her throat again.

"Look at you, swept up in the romance of it all," Jude said, studying the happy couple. Lydia and Nathan couldn't keep their eyes off each other.

She sighed. "Yeah. I guess I am."

"Come on, Delaney. You just said not to hold my breath until it's your turn. Don't go all soft and mushy on me."

"Why not? Lots of people like things that are soft and mushy."

"People in old-age homes, maybe."

"Be nice."

"I'm always nice."

"Then pour me another drink. I'm celebrating tonight, too," she reminded him.

He refilled her champagne flute. "Ah, yes. We're celebrating the fact that you've done the firm out of a Holmstrom original."

"Don't be bitter. We're getting a mint condition Tiffany service, right down to the sugar tongs. The other things, as well."

"I'd rather have it all. What was the old lady thinking, that hanging on to the necklace is going to bring her mother back from a Nazi death camp?"

"Gee, how about I ask her exactly that?" Tess drank more champagne.

"Okay, sorry. I'm sure you tried your best."

"She's a nice lady. Kind, filled with stories. I wish I had more time to spend with her. Do me a favor, and get a ton of money for her Tiffany."

"Of course. I'll send over our best appraiser. By the way, Nathan's brother is checking you out." He glanced over her shoulder.

"And?"

"And, are you available?"

"If you mean, am I seeing someone at the moment, the answer is no."

"What happened to Motorcycle Dude?"

"Rode off into the sunset without me," she confessed.

"And Popeye the Sailor Man?"

She laughed. "The navy guy, you mean. Eldon sailed off into the sunset. What is it with guys and sunsets?"

"You seem heartbroken."

"Not." In order to have her heart broken, she had to give it into someone's care, and she simply wasn't willing to do that.

Too dangerous, and men were too careless. Both her mother and her grandmother were proof of that. Tess was determined not to become a third-generation loser. Tess knew what she was good at—primarily, her work. In that arena, she was in control; she had been raised to keep a firm grip on things. Matters of the heart, however, were impossible to control. She found intimacy unsettling, especially in light of her friends' defection to marriage and even starting families.

"I'm going to stop trying to keep track of the men you date," said Jude. "None of them stick around long enough for me to remember their names, anyway."

"Ouch," she said. "Touché."

"Do you secretly hate men?" he inquired. "Could that be the problem?"

"God, *no*. I love men," she said. She broke eye contact and turned to stare out the window. Night lay over the city in a blanket of gold stars. "I'm just not very good at keeping them around."

"You want to get a room, make wild monkey love for a while?" Jude suggested, lightly running his finger from her shoulder down to her elbow.

She gave his arm a smack. "Don't be a creep."

"Just being practical. We're the only ones here who aren't coupled up, so I thought—"

"What, us? We would destroy each other."

"You're no fun, Sister Mary Theresa. When are you going to give in to my charms?"

"How about never?" She tossed back the last of her champagne. "Does never work for you?"

"You're killing me. Fine, I'm going on safari to soothe my poor, rejected ego." Bending down, he gave her a peck on the cheek, then smiled at her with fond familiarity. "Later, Gorgeous. I've got a one-night stand to organize."

"Okay, that's depressing."

"No. Going home alone is depressing." He moved toward the moodily lit bar, where young women were lined up like ducks in a shooting gallery.

Tess had no doubt he'd make a conquest. Jude always made an outstanding first impression. Not only did he look as though he'd stepped out of an Armani ad; he had a way of gazing at a woman that made her feel as though she'd instantly become the center of his world.

Tess saw straight through him, though. In his own way, he was as lonely and damaged as she was.

She set down her champagne flute and went to look out the window. San Francisco on a clear night was pure magic, the city lights like a necklace of diamonds around the bay, the sky as soft as black velvet. The bridges were swagged by golden chains formed by their cables. Boats of every size glided back and forth in the water. The skyscrapers lined up like gold bars of varying heights. Even the traffic in the streets below moved along in ruby-studded chains of gold. Tess had visited dozens of the world's cities—Paris, Johannesburg, Mumbai, Shanghai—but San Francisco was her favorite. It was the kind of city where being independent was valued, not pitied or regarded as a problem to be rectified by well-meaning friends.

She approached the newly engaged couple to say her goodbyes. Watching her friends together, flushed and smiling, joy shining from their eyes, Tess felt a twinge of bittersweetness. Lydia was one of those people who made love look easy. She wasn't naive enough to regard Nathan as perfect. Instead, she simply trusted him with her heart. Tess wondered if that was a learned skill, or if you had to be born with it.

"I'm taking off," she said, giving Lydia a hug. "Call me."

"Of course. Be careful going home."

Tess left the bar and stepped into the elevator. The angled

mirrors of the car were oddly placed, so that her image grew smaller and smaller, into infinity. She studied that image—pale skin and freckles, wavy red hair, a Burberry trench coat she'd bought in Hong Kong for a fraction of its price in the U.S.

She stared at her image for so long that she began to look like a stranger to herself. How was that possible?

For no reason she could discern, her heart sped up, hammering against her breastbone. Good God, how much had she had to drink? Her breathing grew shallow in her upper chest, and her throat felt tight. She gripped the handrail, trying to steady herself against a wave of dizziness.

Maybe she was coming down with something, she thought as the sensations persisted, accompanying her all the way down to the opulent lobby of the hotel. No. She didn't have time to come down with something. It was out of the question.

There were mirrors in the lobby as well, and a glance told Tess she didn't look like a woman who was about to collapse. But she felt like one, and the feeling chased her out the door. She dashed outside, into the night, heading toward the Lower Nob Hill neighborhood where she lived. No need for a taxi. The brisk walk might do her good.

Her heels clicked nervously on the pavement. The metallic squeal of a streetcar pierced her eardrums. Her vision blurred in and out of sharpness as though she were peering through binoculars and adjusting the focus. Her heart was still racing, breathing still rapid and shallow. Maybe it was the champagne, she thought.

If she had a doctor, she would ask him. But she didn't have a doctor. She was twenty-nine years old, for Pete's sake. Doctors were for sick people. She wasn't sick. She just had the occasional feeling her head was going to explode.

She took out her phone and dialed her mother without much hope of getting her. Shannon Delaney was traveling somewhere in the Lot Valley in France, an area famed for its history, its wines and scenery—and notorious for its lack of cell phone signals.

"Hey, it's me, checking in," she said. "Call me when you get a chance. Let's see, Lydia and Nathan are getting married, but you don't care about that because you don't know Lydia and Nathan. I found a complete set of Tiffany today. And some other stuff. Call me."

She put the phone away, wondering when the jittery feelings would abate. A cigarette, that was what she needed. Yes, she was a smoker, having fallen thoughtlessly into the habit on her first major business trip to France. She knew the horrific health effects as well as the next person. And naturally, she intended to quit one day. Soon. Just not tonight.

Stepping into the shelter of the darkened doorway, she rummaged in her bag for the red-and-white package. Then the challenge—a match. As always, her bag was a mess, a repository of makeup, receipts, ticket stubs, notes to herself, bits of information about things she was working on, business cards of people whose faces she'd forgotten. She also carried tools of her trade, like a jeweler's loupe and a penlight. There was even a small bag filled with lavender scones from Miss Winther, who had insisted on sending Tess home with a supply.

Finally, she hit pay dirt—a box of matches from Fuego, a trendy bistro where she'd gone on a date with someone. A guy who, for whatever reason, hadn't called her again. She couldn't remember who, but she recalled that the salad made with Bosc pears and Point Reyes blue cheese was amazing. Maybe that was why they hadn't gone out again; he was not as memorable as the cheese.

Flipping open the box, she discovered she was down to her last cigarette. No matter. Maybe tomorrow she would quit.

Putting the filter between her lips, she struck a match, but it flamed out in the breeze. She took out another match.

"Excuse me." A woman pushing a battered shopping cart uphill stopped on the sidewalk near Tess. The cart was piled high with plastic bags filled with cans, a rolled-up sleeping bag, bundled clothing, a hand-lettered cardboard sign. In the front of the cart was a small, scruffy dog. Its beady eyes caught the yellowish glow of the streetlamp as the woman angled the cart cross on the hill.

Tess was trapped in the doorway. She couldn't very well keep walking, couldn't avert her eyes and pretend she hadn't seen.

"Spare a smoke?" the woman asked in a voice that sounded both polite yet exhausted, slightly breathless from the uphill climb.

"This is my last one."

"I only want one."

Resigned, Tess put the cigarette back in its box and handed it over. "Here you go."

"Thanks," said the woman. "Gotta light?"

"You bet." She gave her the box of matches.

The woman's hands shook with a tremor as she tucked away the cigarette box and matches.

"How about some homemade scones?" asked Tess, holding out the bag from Miss Winther.

"Sure, thanks." The woman took one out and bit into it. "Did you make them yourself?"

"No, I'm useless in the kitchen. They were made by a—" Friend? "A client." She tried not to dwell on the fact that she had more clients than friends.

"Well, it's mighty tasty." She gave a morsel to the dog, who acted as though it was manna from heaven. "Jeroboam thinks so, too," the woman said, chuckling with delight as the dog stretched out to lick her chin. "Take care." She angled her cart down the hill. "And God bless."

Tess watched her go, pondering the irony of the homeless woman's words. *Take care.*

She felt a fresh thrum of discomfort in her chest, rolling back through her with new vigor, and she started walking quickly, nearly running, to…where? And why the hurry?

"Take it easy," she whispered in time with her breathing. She repeated the phrase like a mantra, but it didn't seem to help. She fled to the door of her walk-up, fumbling with the key at the top of the stairs. Her hand shook as she unlocked the door and rushed inside, up another flight of steps through the faint smells of cooking and furniture polish.

"You're home," she said, ducking into her apartment and looking around her messy, familiar domain. There were suitcases and bags in various stages of unpacking, laundry in transition, piles of reading material, crossword puzzles and work documents. Busy with travel and work, she was seldom home long enough to neaten things up.

Still, she loved her home. She loved old things. The brown-brick place was a survivor of the 1906 earthquake and fire, and proudly bore a plaque from the historical society. The building had a haunted history—it was the site of a crime of passion—but Tess didn't mind. She'd never been superstitious.

The apartment was filled with items she'd collected through the years, simply because she liked them or was intrigued by them. There was a balance between heirloom and kitsch. The common thread seemed to be that each object had a story, like a pottery jug with a bas-relief love story told in pictures, in which she'd found a note reading, "Long may we run. — Gilbert." Or the antique clock on the living room wall, each of its carved figures modeled after one of the clockmaker's twelve children. She favored the unusual, so long as it appeared to have been treasured by someone, once upon a time. Her mail spilled from an antique box containing a pigeon-racing counter with a brass plate engraved from a father to a son. She hung her huge handbag on a wrought iron finial from a town library that had burned and been rebuilt in a matter of weeks by an entire community.

Other people's treasures captivated her. They always had, steeped in hidden history, bearing the nicks and gouges and fingerprints of previous owners. She'd probably developed the affinity from spending so much of her childhood in her grandmother's antiques shop. Having so little in the way of family herself, she used to imagine what it might be like to have siblings, aunts and uncles…a father.

Tonight, she found no comfort in her collected treasures. She paced back and forth, wishing she hadn't had that extra glass of champagne, wishing she hadn't given away her last cigarette, wishing she could call Neelie or Lydia, her best friends. But Lydia was busy being engaged and Neelie had a new boyfriend; Tess couldn't interrupt their happy evening with a ridiculous cry for help.

"Yes, ridiculous, that's what you're being," she said to her image in the mirror. "You don't have a single thing to worry about. What if you were really in trouble? What if you were like the Winthers in Nazi-occupied Denmark? Now, *there's* something to fret about."

Then Tess thought about the panhandler, who probably had her worries as well, yet she seemed to face the world with weary acceptance. She seemed content with her scones and her dog. *Maybe I should get a dog,* thought Tess. But no. She traveled too much to take responsibility for even an air fern, let alone a dog.

Yet no matter how much she tried to ignore the hammering in her chest, she couldn't escape it. That was the one thing she'd never figured out how to run from—herself.

PART THREE

My dear, have some lavender, or you'd best have a thimble full of wine, your spirits are quite down, my sweeting.

—John O'Keeffe, *A Beggar on Horseback*, 1798

··· • ···

LAVENDER SCONES

....

2 cups flour

½ cup rolled oats

1 tablespoon baking powder

½ teaspoon baking soda

½ teaspoon sea salt

¼ cup butter

1½ tablespoons lavender flowers, fresh or dried

1 egg, beaten

⅓ cup honey

½ cup buttermilk

1 teaspoon vanilla

Preheat oven to 400 degrees. Combine flour, oats, baking powder, baking soda and salt. Cut in butter and add lavender. Make a well in the center of the flour mixture. Pour in the egg, honey, buttermilk and vanilla. Stir just until combined. With floured hands, pat the dough into a round about 1 inch thick and cut into eight wedges. Bake scones for 12 to 15 minutes, or until lightly browned. Serve with butter and honey.

(Source: Adapted from *Herb Companion Magazine*)

THREE

Archangel, California

"Ifound him wandering down the highway," said Bob Kro-kower, indicating the gangly shepherd-mix dog strug-gling at the end of the leash. "Fay and I thought Charlie would be a nice companion for us in our retirement, but...uh...turns out it's not exactly a match made in heaven."

Dominic Rossi eyed the huge paws and mischievous eyes of the overgrown pup. Then he turned to Bob, a friend and client at the bank, who had yanked the dog across the field and over Angel Creek, which ran between their homes. "I've already got two dogs," he said. "Iggy and the Dude." Both were also rescues, a crazy little Italian greyhound who'd sur-vived a puppy mill, and another dog of such mixed heritage, sometimes Dominic wasn't even sure he was a dog.

"We can't keep him. Leaving this morning for a weekend

with the grandkids. He's real social," said Bob, adjusting his baseball cap. "Here's a big bag of dog food. He'll get along fine with your other dogs. With your kids, too. He loves kids. Just...not retired folks."

Dominic had a list a mile long of things he had to do today, including picking up the kids from his ex-wife's, but there was nothing on the list about rescuing a stray dog. He'd risen early as usual, starting the day with a walk through his vineyards. Growing grapes and making wine was a passion, but at this point, it was far from a living. He had to fit it in between his day job and his duties as a single father, rushing around between roles.

"Listen," said Bob, "if you can't take him, I guess I could drive him down to the shelter in Healdsburg...."

Dominic looked into the young dog's liquid brown eyes. Once you looked into a dog's innocent eyes, it was all over. "Leave him. I'll figure out something to do with him."

Bob shoved the leash into his hand. "You're real good with dogs and people. I'm sure he'll do just fine with you. Thanks a bunch, Dominic."

Dominic watched him amble away, confident that the big pup was in good hands. Bob knew him too well. He knew Dominic Rossi had a hell of a time with the word *no*. "Charlie, eh?" Dominic said to the dog. "You look like a handful, but I'll find a new home for you. The Wagners need a housewarming gift, come to think of it." Kurt Wagner had just qualified for a mortgage under a program Dominic had instituted at the bank enabling military veterans to buy homes; maybe Kurt would be willing to give the dog a home. Doubtful, though. Kurt's wife had a baby on the way, so a half-grown dog would probably be too much.

Checking to see that the leash was secure, Dominic looked across the rolling hills at the Johansen spread, the apple trees of Bella Vista in craggy rows along a distant ridge that abutted

Dominic's place. The pickers should be in full swing by now, but Magnus's orchard was curiously silent, with no one in sight.

The thought of work reminded him he'd better get going. He paused for a few seconds more, taking a big breath of morning and telling himself to be grateful for the life he had, even though it wasn't the life he'd planned out for himself. His career as a navy pilot had ended when a mission had resulted in a mishap. Now he was a single dad here in Archangel where he'd grown up amid the sun-seared fields and vineyards, a place for dreamers and bohemians, farmers and families. The landscape, wild and dry, was crisscrossed by roads lined with twisted old oak trees leading down to a postcard-perfect town filled with shops and cafés. It wasn't exactly torture, being back here. He was growing grapes and making wine, something he'd always dreamed of doing, even though there weren't enough hours in the day to do it right. Life was good—mostly—so long as he focused on the things he had rather than the things he lacked.

Charlie gave a noisy yawn and licked his chops.

"I know, buddy. Let's figure out what we're going to do with you." He thought again of Magnus and his granddaughter Isabel. Maybe the orchard next door was silent because Magnus's money troubles had finally come to a head. Feeling like the grim reaper, Dominic had recently hand delivered a letter to Magnus, his oldest and favorite client of the bank. The memory of their difficult conversation made him wince.

"I'm sorry. I'd do anything to stop this. I've argued and delayed as much as I could."

"I know. You gave me several extra years." The old man's mild expression had been philosophical, devoid of fear.

Dominic had held foreclosure at bay until the bank he had worked for failed. The new bank that had taken over—a corporate behemoth—had not been so understanding. "Damn.

I hate this business, but I have two kids and I need to keep my job."

"I understand. I'll sort things out."

Dominic didn't say what he was thinking, that Magnus was all out of options.

Magnus, as usual, wasn't thinking of himself. "I'm sorry about what happened, Dominic. To your family, I mean."

Dominic nodded. "I appreciate it."

"We're both due for a change of luck, *ja?*"

"I don't know what else to say."

"I understand. You're a young man, taking responsibility for your kids. None of this is your fault. Sometimes I think you're taking this harder than me." Magnus had wrapped a hand around the bowl of his ever-present burl pipe. He'd stopped smoking years ago but always kept the pipe in his shirt pocket. "Now. Did you take care of the will? You're still okay with being my executor?"

"Of course, if that's what you want."

"It's what I want."

Dominic nodded. He did his best to help. But sometimes his best wasn't enough.

He gave the leash a tug and headed toward the yard. Charlie could stay with him until he found a permanent home for the pup. His phone rang, and an unfamiliar number appeared on the screen.

"Dominic Rossi."

"It's Ernestina Navarro. I'm at Valley Medical."

Magnus's longtime housekeeper. "What's up?" asked Dominic.

"You heard about the emergency over at Bella Vista?"

"What emergency?"

"Old Magnus fell off a ladder."

Shit. "No." Suddenly his day was turned inside out.

FOUR

Tess's mother didn't return her call. This was no surprise. Shannon Delaney, on a work trip somewhere in the valley of the Dordogne and the Lot in France, was not the best at staying in touch. She never had been.

Before turning in for the night, Tess uploaded the pictures she'd taken of Miss Winther's Tiffany set and the other treasures she'd found at the old lady's house. Tomorrow an assistant would go over there to catalog everything and ready it for sale.

Tess tried not to think about the fact that she was going to bed alone again—always. She used to cherish her independence and freedom, but sometimes it felt more like loneliness. At least the scary heart rush had abated after she'd given the scones and cigarette to the panhandler.

She moved aside the clutter on her bed—yes, she lived amid clutter, as though the flotsam and jetsam of her life made the place feel less empty. Then she closed her eyes and listened to the clanging trolleys, sirens, the hissing air brakes of trucks, a distant train whistle. The noise and vibrancy of San Francisco was the soundtrack for Tess's life. Having followed her mother all over the globe, she'd grown to love the sounds of the city, and San Francisco was her favorite. If you were going to lie awake at night, unable to sleep, there might as well be something interesting to listen to.

The next day, she didn't even try calling her mother again, even though she wished she could tell someone—anyone— about her upcoming meeting with Mr. Dane Sheffield himself. Only Brooks, the office manager, knew about that. Her success at finding the Polish treasure was about to be rewarded. Everything she'd worked for, so long and so hard, was about to come into fruition. Sure, she could have used a pep talk from her mom, but she knew she could do just fine without it. She always had.

Rushing around the kitchen, she nuked a cup of water in the microwave for tea. Dunking a bag into the cup, she paused to study the pale green shamrock hand-painted on the cup. It was authentic Belleek, one of a few souvenirs of her childhood in Dublin.

Ah, Nana, she thought. *You'd be so excited for me today.*

Back when Nana was alive, Tess would have bubbled over like a pot, spilling the news about the treasures she'd found and her excitement about the sparkly, shiny possibility of a big career move. She and Nana had been thick as thieves, to hear Nana say it. When Tess was growing up, it had been Nana who raised her while Shannon Delaney traveled for work.

To be fair, Tess acknowledged that Shannon had tried to bring her daughter along on her travels. Tess knew this because one of her earliest memories was of flying with her mother. She was five years old and miserable with an earache, but by the time she reported this to her mom, they were airborne.

Her eardrum burst at thirty thousand feet, trickling blood and pus while she wailed for the next four and a half hours. It was then that Shannon had decided that trying to raise a child while constantly on the go was impossible.

Tess remembered a powerful feeling of relief upon being delivered back to the Dublin flat. Of course she'd missed her mom, but Nana had been the home port, in her colorful apartment and a magical shop she owned in Grafton Street, called Things Forgotten. The establishment was famous for antiques and collectibles, and as a gathering place for aficionados. While Shannon was on the road, Tess used to spend hours there, even as a tiny child, hiding amid the vintage washstands and armoires, or under Nana's massive proprietor's desk in the middle of the shop.

Nana had left the desk to Tess, an impractical but utterly beloved legacy. The piece had gone into storage until Tess finished college and settled in a place of her own. She'd attended Berkeley, where her mother had gone, and went to the ridiculous trouble of transporting it. Now the desk rose like a man-made atoll in the middle of the main room, gloriously ornate with carved flourishes.

Tess's earliest and fondest memories revolved around the massive piece with all its drawers and cubbies. She used to set up housekeeping for her dolls in the kneehole. She would swaddle them in blankets while listening to the murmur of Nana's voice as she talked with clients or on the phone. The game of make-believe never varied. Her dolls didn't go on adventures or travel the world in search of pirate treasure. Instead, they played a game Tess called "Family." The siblings squabbled, the moms and dads scolded them and put them to bed. In Tess's world, this sort of thing was high fantasy, something that couldn't possibly exist. She didn't have a family, not in the traditional sense. She never had.

At a young age, Tess had learned that it was not normal for a mother to come and go, in and out of her child's life. She'd heard her teachers and sometimes the mothers of her friends speculating about it, exclaiming over Shannon Delaney's work schedule and what a shame it was she couldn't stay home with her child.

Tess vividly remembered a day when her mother was packing for another trip. Tess could still picture the paisley lining of the suitcase, and the gray webbing of the compartment that held all her lotions and makeup. There was a little wind-up clock attached to a picture frame, which held Tess's school picture from second grade, her silly grin displaying a huge gap where her top front teeth had come out, both on the same day.

"Mommy, tell me about my dad."

"You never had a dad. The man who fathered you was not a dad. He was just…someone I once knew."

"Mirabelle says I'm a barstid."

"Mirabelle is a mouthy little brat," said Tess's mom. "And her mother is a mouthy big brat."

"Is it bad to be a barstid?"

"No. It's bad to be a brat. It's good to be who you are— Theresa Eileen Delaney, the first and only."

"Then why would she say something mean?"

"I don't really know."

"Is it because I don't have a father?"

"I don't know that, either."

"Sometimes when I see kids with their fathers, I want one in the worst way."

Mom hesitated, then said, "Fathers are overrated."

"What does that mean?"

"It means… My goodness, you ask a lot of questions."

Nana was the one constant in Tess's life. The two of them spent hours together in the shop. Whenever there was a lull in the day—and there was always a lull—she and her grand-mother would have tea together, often brewed in an heirloom Wedgwood or Belleek china pot, and perhaps served on a sil-ver tray. Nana loved old things and treated them with respect. However, she never kept them at arm's length.

Filled with the warmth of memories, Tess set down an imaginary tray. Perfectly replicating the lilt in Nana's voice, she said, "Put the music on, *a stór.* The quiet, slow music will make shoppers want to linger." That was Nana's pet name for Tess; it was Gaelic for "my treasure."

Maybe it was the music, or perhaps some other magic; Things Forgotten had a special atmosphere that drew people in and kept them coming back. Travel magazines, guidebooks and even the *New York Times* advised tourists and collectors alike to pay a visit. The unlikely little shop turned into a suc-cess.

Another gift of Nana's was her judgment. She had a shrewd head for business and nearly always made her margin. Yet every once in a while, she would let something go for a song, watching her profits walk out the door with a delighted new owner.

"Sometimes the true value of the piece is how much a per-son loves it." Tess quoted her grandmother aloud as she rum-maged in the desk, now thousands of miles and many years distant from the Dublin shop. She was looking for Nana's an-cient leather agenda to take to her meeting. Her planner and calendar were both on her phone now—her *life* was on her phone now, or so it seemed—but she still made notes in the agenda and transcribed them later.

A glance at the clock jolted her into action. She checked email and messages on her phone one more time; not a word from her mother. Typical. She shrugged it off; she didn't have time to talk, anyway. She slowed down while passing the polished burl framed picture of her grandmother, which sat atop the desk. "Wish me luck," she said, then dashed out the door, walking along as she sent a text message to Brooks, telling him she was on her way.

A half hour later, she arrived at the office, standing in front of a plate glass window, fixing her hair while trying not to act as if she had spent the past ten minutes in a taxi, yelling at the driver that her life depended on getting to this meeting on time.

It was the Irish in her. A flair for drama came naturally to Tess. Yet in a sense, her urgent need was no exaggeration. Finally, she was about to reach for her dream, and this meeting was a critical step in the process. She couldn't afford to be late or to be seen as a flake, or unreliable in any way.

The San Francisco fog had done a number on her hair, but the reflection looking back at her was acceptable, she supposed. Dark tights and a conservative skirt, cream-colored sweater under a gray jacket, charcoal-gray pumps. She wore a tasteful necklace and earrings. They were vintage 1920s Cartier, a gold, crystal and onyx set on loan from the firm.

She shook back her hair, squared her shoulders and strode toward the entrance to the glassy high-rise that housed Sheffield headquarters. Checking her watch, she saw that she was actually five minutes early, a huge bonus, since she couldn't remember the last time she'd eaten. Oh, yeah, the olives from last night's martini, the one that had preceded her elevator meltdown. Before heading inside, she stopped at a street cart to grab a coffee and a powdered donut, her favorite power breakfast. That way, she wouldn't have to show up at the meeting with Mr. Sheffield on an empty stomach.

She wanted it to go well. This was the biggest thing that had ever happened to her in her career, opening before her like a magic door. It *would* go well. She anticipated a move to New

York City, a significant raise and more of a role in the acquisitions process for the firm. The prospect of putting her student loans to rest and gaining complete independence gave her a fierce surge of accomplishment. Finally, after what felt like a very long slog, Tess felt as though she was truly on her way.

The only element missing was someone with whom to share her news—someone to grab her and give her a big hug, tell her "good job" and ask her how she wanted to celebrate. A nonissue, she told herself. The feeling of accomplishment alone was satisfying enough.

Clasping this thought close to her heart, she hurried into the building, juggling her briefcase with her breakfast-on-the-fly, and punched the elevator call button with her elbow. She shared the swift ride to the ninth floor with a young couple who kept squeezing each other's hands and regarding each other in a conversation without words. They reminded her of Lydia and Nathan last night, moving to an inner rhythm only they could feel. She imagined herself having a boyfriend, calling him, bursting with her news. Okay, she thought. Maybe the universe was trying to tell her something. Maybe she was ready for a boyfriend, a real one, not just a date for the night.

Not today, though. Today was all about her.

She left the elevator and walked swiftly to the Sheffield offices. She shared space with a diverse group of buyers, brokers and experts for the firm. A competitive atmosphere pervaded the San Francisco branch like an airborne virus, and Tess was not immune.

As she pushed backward through the door, the paper cup of coffee in one hand, her overloaded bag in the other, the powdered donut clamped between her teeth, she fantasized about her upcoming meeting with Dane Sheffield, already feeling a dizzying confidence, even though they'd never met. He had grown the firm so that it was on a par with Christie's and Sotheby's, and she was now a key player. The two of them would be kindred spirits, both dedicated to preserving precious things, each aware of the delicate balance between art and commerce.

"Someone is here to see you," Brooks announced from behind her, gesturing at a lone figure in the foyer.

Shoot, he was early.

Tess turned to look at her visitor. He stood backlit by a floor-to-ceiling window, his form outlined by the soft, foggy light from outside. His features were in shadow; she could only make out his silhouette—broad shoulders, a well-cut suit, imposing height, definitely over six feet.

He stepped into the light, and she caught her breath. He was that good-looking. Unfortunately, the startled gasp made her inhale the powdered sugar from the donut between her teeth, and an enormous sneeze erupted. The donut flew out of her mouth, dusting her clothes and the carpet at her feet with a sprinkling of white.

Both Brooks and Mr. Sheffield hurried to her aid, setting aside the hot coffee before it could do more damage, patting her on the back.

"She'll be all right," Brooks assured their visitor. "Unfortunately this is normal for Tess. She takes multitasking to the extreme, and as you can see, it's not working out so well for her."

"I'm fine," she assured them, sending a warning glare at Brooks.

With an excess of fussiness, Brooks covered the donut with a paper towel as if it were a dead mouse, carefully scooped it up and deposited it in the trash. She tried to act as composed as possible as she faced the stranger. "My apologies," she said with as much dignity as she could muster. "I'm Tess Delaney. How do you do, Mr. Sheffield?" He didn't look anything like his profile picture on the company website. Not even close.

"I'm Dominic. Dominic Rossi." He held out his hand. He had a slow smile, she noticed. Slow and devastating.

Tess had to regroup as she took in the man before her. "I was expecting someone else."

Brooks stepped in and wiped the remaining powdered sugar off her fingers before she shook the man's hand. "Mr. Sheffield just called," said Brooks. "He's running late and pushed the meeting back an hour."

"Nice to meet you, Mr. Rossi." Tess tried to hide her sinking disappointment that this amazing-looking person was not her employer.

"Call me Dominic, please." He had the kind of deep, sonorous voice that drew attention, even though he spoke in low tones. Tess could practically feel everyone within earshot tuning in to eavesdrop.

"All right, then," she said. "Dominic." Of course his name would be Dominic. It meant "gift from God." AKA a life-support system for an ego. Still, that didn't mean he wasn't fun to stare at. Dominic Rossi looked like a dream, the kind of dream no woman in her right mind would want to wake from.

She had always been susceptible to male beauty, ever since the age of ten, when her mother had taken her to see Michelangelo's David in Florence. She recalled staring at that huge stone behemoth, all lithe muscles and gorgeous symmetry, indifferent about his nudity, his member inspiring a dozen questions her mother brushed aside.

Now, with utmost reluctance, she folded her arms across her chest, walling herself off from the charms of Mr. Tall, Dark and Devastating. "So…how can I help you?"

"Shall I send out for more coffee?" asked Brooks. "Or maybe just disaster cleanup?"

"Very funny."

Oksana Androvna, an acquisitions expert, popped her head

above the walls of her cubicle. She spotted the visitor, then ducked back down. The handsome stranger had probably already set off a storm of workplace gossip. He didn't look like most Sheffield clients. "My office is through here," she said, heading down the hallway. She led the way, wondering if he was checking her out from behind, then mad at herself for wondering as she unlocked the door and turned on the lights. When she turned to face him, his gaze held hers, but she had the uncanny feeling that he *had* been checking her out. She wasn't offended. If she thought she could get away with it, she'd do the same to him.

As usual, her work area was a mass of clutter. It was organized clutter, to be sure, though she was the first to admit that this was not the same as neatness. "I'm a bit pressed for time this morning—"

"Sorry to arrive unannounced," he said, striding forward into the cramped confines of her office. "I'm not sure I have a good number for you."

"I never gave you my number," she said. *But I might have, if you'd asked me.*

He held out a business card. "I've been looking for you."

For no reason she could fathom, his words gave her a chill. In a swift beat of time, she tasted the intense sweetness of powdered sugar in the corners of her lips, felt the cool breath of the air conditioning through a ceiling vent, watched it ripple through some loose papers on her credenza.

"Miss Delaney?" He regarded her quizzically.

She studied the card—Dominic Rossi. Bay Bank Sonoma Trust. "You're a bill collector?"

He smiled slightly. "No."

She set aside the card and stepped back, considering him warily. He had the features and hair to match his physique and voice. The horn-rimmed glasses, rather than detracting from his looks, merely enhanced them, like a fine frame around a masterpiece. He stood just inside the door, seeming out of place in her space. "Yes, it's a wreck," she said, reading disapproval in the way he was looking at the various piles. "It drives Brooks crazy, but I have a system."

He found an empty spot on the floor and set down his briefcase. She placed her coffee cup atop a stack of art history books. He extracted a folded handkerchief from his pocket. "Er, you might want to…" He gestured at her lapel.

"What's the matter?"

"You're covered in powdered sugar."

She glanced down. The front of her blazer was sprinkled with the white stuff.

"Oh. Damn." She took the handkerchief—white, crisp, monogrammed—and brushed at the mess.

"Your face, too," he pointed out.

"My face?" she asked stupidly.

"You look like a cocaine addict gone wild," he told her.

"Lovely. I don't have a mirror."

He came around the desk to her. "May I?"

In spite of herself, she kind of wanted to say yes to this guy, no matter what he was asking. "Sure. Have at it."

Very gently, he touched a finger under her chin, tilting her face toward his as he dabbed at the corners of her mouth.

Up close, he was even better-looking than she'd originally thought. He smelled incredible and was perfectly groomed. The suit fit him gorgeously. It was probably a bespoke suit, made-to-measure. Because no normal man was built like this guy. Maybe she'd manifested him. Hadn't she just been thinking about how nice it would be to have a boyfriend?

Indulging—ever so briefly—in his touch, his very focused attention, she fantasized about what it would be like to have a boyfriend like this—attentive, patient, wildly attractive.

Though she had no idea who he was, she already knew he was going to make her wish she had better luck at keeping guys around. When he finished his ministrations, she hoped she wasn't blushing. But being a redhead, she couldn't stop herself.

"Better?" she asked.

He put the handkerchief back in his pocket. "I just thought you'd be more comfortable…"

"Not looking like a cocaine addict," she filled in for him. She forced herself to quit gaping.

For the first time, he cracked a smile. "Believe me, you're better off sticking with donuts."

"I'll keep that in mind." She did her best to ignore the pulse of attraction inspired by that smile. She flushed again, remembering her imminent meeting. "You'll have to excuse me, but I've got something on the schedule that can't wait."

"Just…hear me out." Somber again, he moved a stack of paraphernalia off a chair and took a seat. "That's all I ask."

"What can I do for you?"

He paused, a somber look haunting his whiskey-brown eyes. Oh, boy, she thought. He'd probably tracked her down for a valuation. People like this always seemed to find her. If he was like so many others, he wanted to know what he could get for his grandmother's rhinestone jewelry or Uncle Bubba's squirrel shooter. She often heard from people who came across junk while cleaning out some loved one's basement, and were convinced they had discovered El Dorado.

She shifted her weight, feeling a nudge of anxiety about the upcoming meeting. She was going to need all her focus, and Mr. Dominic Rossi was definitely not so good for her focus. "Listen, I might need to refer you to one of my associates in the firm. Like I said, I'm a bit pressed for time today—"

"This is about a family matter," he said.

She almost laughed at the irony of it. She didn't have a family. She had a mother who didn't return her calls. "What in the world would you know about my family?"

"The bank I work for is located in Archangel, in Sonoma County."

"Archangel." She tilted her head to one side. "Is that supposed to mean something to me?"

"Doesn't it?"

"I've been to Archangel, Russia. I've been to lots of places, traveling for work. But never to Archangel, California. What does it have to do with me?"

His expression didn't change, but she detected a flash of something in his eyes. "You have family there."

Her stomach twisted. "This is either a joke, or a mistake."

"I'm not joking, and it's not a mistake. I'm here on behalf of your grandfather, Magnus Johansen."

The name meant nothing to Tess. Her grandfather. She didn't have a grandfather in any standard sense of the word. There was one unknown man who had abandoned Nana, and another who had fathered Shannon Delaney's one-night stand. All her mother had ever told her about that night was that she'd had too much to drink and made a mistake while in graduate school at Berkeley. So the word *father* was a bit of a misnomer. The guy had never done anything for Tess except supply a single cell containing an X chromosome. Her mother wasn't even sure of his name. "Eric," Shannon had explained when Tess asked. "Or maybe it was Erik with a *k*. I never got his last name."

On her birth certificate, the space was filled in with a single word: "UNKNOWN."

Now here was this stranger, telling her things about herself she didn't know. She suppressed a shiver. "I've never heard of...what's the guy's name?"

"Magnus Johansen."

"And you say he's my grandfather." She felt strangely light-headed.

"I don't know him," she said. "I've never known him." The words held a world of pain and confusion. She wondered if this guy—this Dominic—could tell. She felt completely bewildered. To hide her feelings, she glared at him through narrowed eyes. "I think you should get to the point."

He studied her from behind the conservative banker's glasses. The way he looked at her made her heart skip a beat and made it harder to hide the unsettled panic that was starting to climb up her throat. "I'm very sorry to tell you that Magnus has had an accident. He's in the ICU at Sonoma Valley Regional Hospital."

The words passed through her like a chilly breeze. "Oh. I see. I'm…" She really had no idea what to say. "I'm sorry, too. I mean, he's your friend. What happened?"

"He fell off a ladder in his orchard, and he's in a coma."

Tess winced, flashing on a poor old man falling from a ladder. She laced her fingers together into a knot of tension, mingled with excitement. Her grandfather…her *family*. He had an orchard. She'd never really thought of anyone having an orchard, let alone someone she was related to. "I guess… I appreciate your coming to deliver the news in person," she said. She wondered how much, if anything, he knew about the reason she didn't know Magnus, or anyone on that side of the family. "I just don't get what this has to do with me. I assume he's got other family members who can deal with the situation."

She flashed on another conversation she'd had with her mother, long ago, when she'd been a bewildered and lonely little girl. "I want you to tell me about my father," she'd said, stubbornly crossing her arms.

"He's gone, sweetheart. I've told you before, he was in a car accident before you were born, and he was killed."

Tess winced. "Did it hurt?"

"I don't know."

"You sure don't know a lot, Mom."

"Thanks."

"Well, it's true. Were you sad when he died?"

"I... Of course. Everyone who knew him was sad."

"Who's everyone?"

"All his friends and family."

"But who? What were their names?"

"I only knew Erik for a short time. I really didn't know his friends and family." Her eyes shifted, and that was how Tess knew she was holding back.

She didn't even really know what her father looked like, or how his voice sounded, or the touch of his hand. She had only one thing to go by—an old photo print. The square Instamatic picture was kept in the bottom drawer of her mom's bureau. The colors were fading. In the background was a big bridge stretching like a spider web across the water. In the center of the photo stood a man. He wasn't smiling but he looked nice. He had crinkles fanning his eyes and hair that was light brown or dark blond, cut in a feathery old-fashioned style. "Very eighties," her mother had once explained.

"I still wish I had a dad," she said, thinking of her friends who had actual families—mom, dad, brothers and sisters. Sometimes she fantasized about a handsome Prince Charming, swooping in to marry her pretty mother and settling down with them in a nice house, painted pink.

Now she regarded Dominic Rossi, who had appeared as if out of a dream, telling her things that only raised more questions. He studied her with a stranger's eyes, yet she thought she recognized compassion. Or was it pity? Suddenly she found herself resenting his handsomeness, his patrician features, the calm intelligence in his eyes. He was…a *banker?* Probably some over-educated grad with a degree in finance from some fancy institution. Which was no reason to resent him, but she did so just the same.

"I've never had anything to do with Magnus Johansen," she said, deeply discomfited by this conversation. "And like I said, I've got a busy day ahead of me."

"Miss Delaney. Theresa—"

"Tess," she said. "No one calls me Theresa."

"Sorry. That's how you're named in the will."

Her jaw dropped. "What will? This is the first I've heard of any will. And why are you telling me this now? Did he die from the fall?"

"*No.* But…there's, uh, some discussion about continuing life support. Everyone's praying Magnus will recover, but… it doesn't look good for your grandfather. There are decisions that need to be made…." Dominic Rossi's voice sounded low and quiet with emotion.

The crazy heart rush started again. "It's sad to hear, and it sounds like you're…like you feel bad about it. But I have no idea what this has to do with me."

He studied her for a moment. "Whether he survives this or not, your grandfather intends to leave you half his estate."

It took a few seconds for the words to sink in. Despite her experience in provenance, she was fundamentally unfamiliar with the concepts of grandfathers and estates. "Let me get this straight. A grandfather I've never known wants to give me half of everything."

"That's correct."

"Not only do I not know the man, I also don't know what 'everything' means."

"He has property in Sonoma County. Bella Vista—that's

the name of the estate—is a hundred-acre working orchard, with house, grounds and outbuildings."

An estate. Her grandfather owned an *estate*. She'd never known anyone who owned an estate; that was something she saw on *Masterpiece Theatre,* not in real life.

"Bella Vista," she said. The name tasted like sugar on her tongue. "And it's…in Archangel? In Sonoma County?" Sonoma was where people went for Sunday drives or weekend escapes. It simply didn't seem like a place where people owned *estates.* Certainly not a hundred acres… "And why do I not get to find all this out until he falls off a ladder and goes into a coma?"

"I can't answer that."

"And you're telling me now because of… Oh, God." She couldn't say it. Couldn't get her head around the idea of being someone's next of kin. Finally she felt something, an unfamiliar surge—uncomfortable, yet impossible to deny. The thought crossed her mind that this…this possible legacy called Bella Vista might be a blessing in disguise. On the heels of that thought came a wave of guilt. She didn't know Magnus Johansen, but she didn't wish him ill just to get her hands on his money.

"Half of everything," she murmured. "A stranger is leaving me half of everything. It's like a storyline in those dreadful English children's novels I used to read as a kid, about an orphan saved at the last minute by a rich relative."

"Not familiar with them," he said.

"Trust me, they're dreadful. But just so you know, I'm not an orphan and I don't need saving."

An appealing glimmer flashed in his eyes. "Point taken."

"Who sent you to find me?" she asked. "And by the way, how *did* you find me?"

"Like I said, you're named in his will and…he's an old man

and it's not looking good for him. I found you the way every-body finds people these days—the internet. It wasn't a stretch. Good job on the Polish necklace, by the way."

"Rosary," she corrected him. "So what's your role? How are you involved in this situation?"

"Magnus redrafted his will recently, naming me executor."

She narrowed her eyes. "Why you?"

"He asked," Dominic said simply. "I've known Magnus since I was a kid. And I've been his neighbor and his banker for a number of years."

She felt an irrational stab of envy. How was it that this guy—this *banker*—got to know her grandfather, when she'd never even met the man?

Dominic's penetrating stare made her uncomfortable, as if he saw some part of her that she didn't like people to see—that needy girl, yearning for a family.

"Maybe he'll recover," Dominic said, reading her thoughts.

"Maybe? What's the prognosis? *Is* there a prognosis?"

"At the moment, it's uncertain. There's swelling of the brain and he's on a ventilator, but that could change. That's the hope, anyway."

Her stomach churned, the way it had the night before in the elevator. "I feel for you, and for everyone who cares for him. Really, I do. But I still don't see a role for me in all this."

"Once he recovers, and you get to know him—"

"Apparently getting to know me is not what he wants." She glanced away from his probing gaze.

"Magnus didn't just decide…" There was an edge in his voice. "I'm sure he has his reasons."

"Really? What kind of man refuses to acknowledge his own granddaughter except on a piece of paper?"

"I can't answer for Magnus."

She softened, felt her shoulders round. "It's terrible, what happened to him. I just wish I understood. Mr. Rossi, I really don't think there's anything to discuss." She was dying, *dying* to get in touch with her mother now. Shannon Delaney had some explaining to do. Such as why she'd never mentioned Magnus Johansen, or Archangel, or the legacy of an estate. A man she'd never known had included her in his will. She let the words sink in, trying to figure out how it made her feel. Her grandfather—her *grandfather*—was leaving her half of everything. As she shaped her mind around the idea, an obvious question occurred to her.

"What about the other half?" she asked.

"The other... Oh, you mean Magnus's estate."

"Yes."

"The other half will be left to your sister."

She nearly fell over in her chair. She couldn't speak for a moment, could only stare at her visitor, aghast. "Whoa," she said softly. "Whoa, whoa, whoa. Give me a minute here. I have a *sister?*"

"Yes," said Dominic. "Look, I know I've thrown a lot at you...."

"You think?" Tess struggled to assimilate the information, but she felt flooded by all the revelations. Her heart jolted into overdrive. It wasn't even ten o'clock in the morning, and she'd learned her estranged grandfather was in a coma he'd probably never come out of, *and* she had a...sister. The word—the concept—was completely foreign to her.

"What sister?" she managed to ask, although she couldn't hear her own voice over a rampant pounding in her ears. "Where is she? *Who* is this...oh, my God...this sister?"

"She's at Bella Vista, and she— Hey, are you okay?" he asked, again with that oddly penetrating look.

"Just peachy," she said. Her hands clamped the edge of the desk in a death grip. How could this be happening to her? In the middle of her perfectly normal life, this person had appeared, seemingly out of nowhere, to tell her about a legacy she didn't realize she had coming to her.

And a sister she'd never even known about.

Feeling trapped, Tess looked wildly around the office. Her pulse went crazy, hammering away at her chest with a vengeance. It was even worse than it had been the night before. Was she dying? Maybe she was dying. Inanimate objects started to blur and pulsate as though coming to life. Her throat constricted, and she felt her heart thudding against her breastbone. She made an involuntary sound, a gasp of distress and confusion.

"Miss Delaney… Tess?" asked Dominic.

"I…" Her throat felt swollen and clogged. Sweat broke out on her forehead, her upper lip. "Not feeling so hot," she managed to mutter.

"You look terrible, like you're going to pass out or something."

His voice sounded very far away, as if he was shouting down a long tube.

She pressed her hands against her chest. Her fingers felt as cold as ice. *Breathe,* Tess told herself, but her throat kept closing up.

"I need to…sit down," she managed to force out.

"Uh, you *are* sitting down."

She pressed her hands against the chair. *Dear God, what's happening to me?*

Dominic went to the doorway and stuck his head out into the hall. "Hey, we could use some help in here. I think she's getting sick."

Tess tried to protest. *I'm not sick.* Her voice was lost somewhere inside her, and besides, she couldn't swear the guy was wrong.

People gathered in the small space outside the office. Her blurred vision pulsed harder. A couple of faces pressed close.

Jude: "Jesus, Tess, you look like death on a cracker."

Oksana: "Maybe it's a heart attack. Tess! Can you hear me?"

Brooks: "Or a panic attack. Give her a paper bag to breathe into."

Jude: "I'm calling 911."

No, said Tess, but no sound came out.

"Where's the nearest emergency room?" asked Dominic. He took her wrist, and she felt his fingers, delicately feeling for her pulse. Of them all, the stranger was the only one who touched her. She trembled as though stepping into a freezer.

Emergency room? Was she having an emergency? No ER, she thought. That was where people went to have their chests cracked and ended up in the morgue with a tag tied to their big toe.

"Mercy Heights is just across Comstock," said Jude.

"Then that's where we need to go."

"Should I call—"

"No, that takes too long." Arms that felt as strong and solid as a forklift hoisted her up out of the chair. Dominic Rossi held her as if she weighed nothing.

"Grab her purse, will you?" he said. "And someone get the door."

Tess lay on a gurney covered with a crackly, disposable fabric. A thin hospital gown lay over her, and someone had given her a pair of bright yellow socks with nonskid dots on the soles. Little sticky things attached to wires led from her chest to a beeping monitor. More wires led to the tips of her fingers, attached by clear plastic clothespins. Flexible plastic tubing snaked behind her ears and blew chilly, strangely scented oxygen into her nostrils. Someone had left an aluminum chart lying across her thighs.

Bells and announcements went off. Hurried footsteps squeaked across polished floors. There were sounds of conversation, weeping, praying in at least three languages. Someone was moaning. Someone else was cursing fluently at the top of his lungs, and somewhere a patient—or inmate, perhaps—was barking like a dog.

A group of people in lab coats clustered around Tess. Mercy was a teaching hospital, and most of the coat wearers were young and appeared to be incredibly interested in her.

Tess felt limp and defeated, battered by the events of the past two hours. Dominic Rossi had brought her in, carrying her in his arms like a drowning victim. She'd been questioned, monitored, questioned some more, tested and scanned. They'd asked her if she'd ever considered or attempted suicide, who the president was and to describe her state of mind. The screening questions came at her in a barrage, melding together—Did she worry excessively? Had she experienced symptoms for six months or more? Was she unable to control her worry?

She felt numb, defeated, as she replied with dull affirmatives to far too many of the questions.

One of the med students, a pudgy, earnest guy no older than Tess, reported her case. He stood nervously at the end of the bed, reading notes from a rolling monitor station. "Miss Delaney is a twenty-nine-year-old female, height, sixty-seven inches, weight, one-hundred-nineteen pounds, with no previous history of health issues. She was brought in by..." He consulted the monitor. "A friend or coworker who became worried about her when she exhibited a variety of symptoms, including shortness of breath, elevated heart rate, disorientation, blurred vision...."

She felt like a different person, lying there, or maybe an inanimate item about to be put up for auction. Anyone within earshot could hear her story. The med student reported the replies to her "lifestyle choices" and results of the labs done in the ER. In flat tones, mercifully free of judgment, he told the attending physician that she was underweight and smoked. Her blood pressure and pulse were elevated. A chem panel revealed that she was not on drugs nor was she the victim of poison. The patient reported that she had experienced these symptoms before but never with this intensity.

When the student finished, the attending, an older man, stepped forward. "Your labs are in," he informed her.

"That's a relief," Tess said. Her voice was thin and strained, but at least she was beginning to sound like herself again. "I'm ready to get out of here."

"I'm sure you are. However, we do need to discuss the differential diagnosis—"

"The what?"

"Your condition."

"Condition? I have a condition? I do *not* have a condition. I have a meeting with—" Her heart sped up, and two of the monitors betrayed her.

A student adjusted her oxygen flow. The doctor wheeled a monitor into view. "I'll show you the results. There's nothing physically wrong with you." He went over her EKG and ultrasound, her blood tests and urinalysis. "However, your symptoms are real, and the good news is, very treatable. Have you ever heard of generalized anxiety disorder? Sometimes referred to as GAD."

"Anxiety disorder?" She hated the sound of that. "Disorder" applied to her housekeeping habits, not her health. "You mean, I had an anxiety attack?"

"You'll want to follow up with your primary care physician."

"I don't have a doctor," she said. "Doctors are for sick people."

"In that case, you'll want to find one to monitor your condition and help you treat the disorder with lifestyle changes."

"My lifestyle is fine," she said, and despite the extra oxygen, the monitor beeped faster. "I have no desire to change it."

"There are risks—particularly to your heart."

"My heart?" She swallowed, trying not to freak out again.

"Left untreated, your symptoms could result in heart damage due to cardiovascular stress. There are further tests for cardiovascular disease. Again, I would urge you to take this up with a physician."

"What are you?" she demanded. "Chopped liver?"

The man had an intractable poker face. "It could be situational. What's going on in your life?"

It was the first personal question he'd asked her. "Everything," she said. "I'm missing what's probably the most important meeting of my career. Some stranger showed up this morning with a crazy story about my... It doesn't matter. I just need to pull myself together and get out of here."

"You won't get far if you don't deal with this," he stated. "I have a list of referrals for you. And here's a pamphlet with some information on panic disorders. There are things you need to start doing right away in order to avoid lasting health effects...."

Wonderful, thought Tess. This was just too good to be true. In the space of a single day, she had found her grandfather, only to be told she was probably on the verge of losing him; she'd been informed that she had a sister she'd never met, and now this.

A Condition.

FIVE

In the bleak light of the emergency room, Tess put herself back together as best she could. A nurse came into the curtain area with some forms and more literature. His gaze took in her scattered belongings, the now-quiet monitors. She didn't bother trying to find a mirror; she knew without looking what she'd see—a wrung-out woman with donut powder on her clothes, bed-head and no makeup. Who wanted to see that?

"Is someone coming for you?" asked the nurse.

"What, for me?" Tess frowned. "Nope, don't think so." Jude had come along with that guy, with... Dominic. She hadn't seen either of them since she'd been wheeled into the curtain area next to a guy with matted hair, raving about the apocalypse.

"Maybe you could call someone," the nurse suggested.

"A taxi," she said. "That's all I need."

He regarded her for a second, then drew the curtain aside. "Good luck. Call if you need anything."

"Thanks." She felt slightly dazed, or maybe disoriented. In the waiting area, anxious people sat in molded plastic chairs or paced the tiled floor, clearly anxious for news of their loved ones. A quick scan confirmed that neither Jude nor Dominic had stuck around.

On the one hand, it was a relief to get out of this place. Yet on the other hand, she couldn't deny the fact that it was kind of depressing, having no one to bring her home from the ER.

Shouldering her heavy bag, she looked for the exit, feeling resolute. She didn't need anyone. She needed a cigarette in the worst way.

No more smoking. That was in bold type on the doctor's list.

The hell with him. She was going to find a convenience store. She was going to buy a pack of the nastiest cigarettes she could find and—

"Everything all right?" Dominic Rossi appeared before her. His coat was unbuttoned, his hair mussed, as though he'd run his hands through it repeatedly.

"What are you doing here?" she asked.

"Waiting for you."

"Why would you wait for me?"

He regarded her with complete incomprehension. "I brought you here. I'm not about to ditch you."

She was startled to hear this from a complete stranger. Even Jude had taken off when it was clear she wasn't knocking on heaven's door.

"Oh. Well, okay, then. I'm supposed to pick up something from the hospital pharmacy."

"It's this way." He gestured down a gleaming corridor. "I'll wait here."

"You don't—"

"But I will," he stated simply.

Surrender, Tess, she told herself. *For once in your life, let some-body help you.* "Be right back," she mumbled, and went to the pharmacy counter. A few minutes later, laden with more literature and pamphlets, she rejoined Dominic in the hospital lobby. It was hard to believe that only a short time ago, her heart was beating out of her chest. Seeing only concern in his eyes, she felt obligated to explain herself to him. "So it turns out I wasn't on the verge of dying. I don't know what came over me. Or rather, I suppose now I do. The doctor says I had a panic attack. I just thought it was an adrenaline rush. But it turns out it's some kind of…disorder. How embarrassing."

"That's nothing to be embarrassed about."

"I totally overreacted. I feel like a hypochondriac."

"Those symptoms looked pretty real to me."

"Yes, but—"

"Is beating up on yourself part of your therapy?"

"No, but—"

"Then go easy on yourself."

It was odd—and a little depressing—to find compassion from a virtual stranger. Odder still that she found his words comforting. "That's what the doctor said. He said a lot of things, like I'm supposed to learn what my triggers are, like what caused the symptoms, and try to avoid them."

"And this was triggered by…?"

"By you, in case you hadn't noticed. Therefore, you are to be avoided," she concluded. Yes, that felt right. Wildly attractive guys tended to cause trouble—in her experience, anyway. "It's not every day someone tells me the grandfather I've never known is in a coma, and on top of that, there's a sister I had no idea existed."

"Sorry. I thought you knew about Isabel."

Isabel. She tried to get her mind around the idea of this whole hidden family, people she might have known in her

life, if she'd been let in. Questions came in waves—how much
of this did her mother know? Did these people know about
Tess? "So I've just got the one sister?"

"That's right."

Isabel. What kind of name was that? The name of the favored child, raised in the sun-warmed luxury of a California
estate, basking in her family's adoration. Tess felt a quiver of
anxiety. Apparently she and the sister shared the same father.
Erik Johansen had been a busy dude before he died.

"And she knows about me."

"Yes. She's eager to meet you."

I'll just bet she is. "Are you the one who told her?"

He hesitated for a single beat of the heart. "The doctors advised Isabel to make sure Magnus's affairs were in order. She
found a copy of the will."

"So I'm guessing…she was surprised." Tess found a sign
for the exit and made a beeline for it. "I bet she didn't freak
out like I just did."

"Not that I know of."

"Then how did she react? What did she say?"

"She baked a pear and ginger tart," he said. "It was epic."

Tess could still barely get her mind around the notion that
she had a sister. A blood relative. She tried to imagine what
such a person might look like, sound like, yet no image would
form. All she could picture was a woman making a tart. "So
what is she, a compulsive baker?"

"She's an incredible cook."

"Is that what she does for a living?"

"The exit's over here," he said, and she wondered if he'd
deliberately ignored her question. He led her to an automatic
revolving door, and she crowded into the space with him,
breathing a sigh of relief as they escaped together.

"I feel better already," Tess said. "Not a fan of hospitals."

"When you need one, you need one."

There was something in his tone. She wondered what his experience with hospitals was. She was filled with questions about him but stopped herself from asking. "I don't intend to make a habit of falling apart for no reason. According to the people here, I'm supposed to find a physician and make life-style changes."

She patted her giant bag. "It's all in this brochure about my condition. Shoot. I hate having a condition." She started walking across the street.

"Where are you going?"

"To work. I've got a zillion things to do."

"I told your colleague...that guy..."

"Jude." *Jude the Disloyal.*

"I said he should let everyone know you wouldn't be back today."

She felt a flash of...something. Annoyance? Or was it relief?

"I *am* going back to the office. There's no way I can miss this meeting—"

"It's been canceled. Your assistant asked me to let you know."

"*What?* You canceled my meeting?"

"Wasn't me."

She pawed through her bag until she found a phone. Sure enough, there was a text from the office, informing her of the cancellation. Her heart flipped over. Had Mr. Sheffield canceled the meeting because she'd stood him up? Should she call Brooks and ask? No, there was probably enough gossip and speculation about her already.

"Now I need a coffee," she said, then eyed him defiantly. "And a cigarette."

"Just what the doctor ordered?"

She bridled. "You're probably one of those Mr. Healthier-Than-Thou types, aren't you?"

"Just your average non-smoker." He took her arm, steered her into a coffee shop. "Have a seat. I'll be right back."

She tried to resent him for looking after her, but he'd been nothing but kind to her. None of this was his fault. She sat at a small round corner table and took out the information packet from the doctor. What a day. A crazy, terrible day.

Dominic returned with a large, steaming mug, which she gratefully accepted. As the scent wafted to her, she frowned, wrinkling her nose.

"Herbal tea," he said.

"It smells like grass clippings."

She sniffed again, ventured a small sip. "Yikes, that's foul. I'd rather drink cleaning fluid."

"It's supposed to be good for the nerves." He showed her the menu description: lavender, chamomile, Saint-John's-wort, Valerian.

"Witch's brew," she said, and gave a shudder. "My nerves are fine."

He said nothing, but his silence spoke volumes. She found herself focusing on his hands—large and strong-looking, a big multifunction watch strapped to one wrist. Discomfited to feel yet another nudge of attraction, she added, "Anyway, I'm going to be fine. I have a whole program here." She showed him the information packet from the doctor. "Go ahead, take a look. After the ER, everybody in earshot knows all my secrets."

"Says here the effects of untreated anxiety can be harmful, not to mention unpleasant."

She shuddered, remembering the blinding sense of panic. "And people go to medical school for years to figure that out." She looked across the table, seeing compassion in his eyes. "Sorry. I doubt whining is helpful."

"After this morning, you're entitled to whine. A little."
He consulted the booklet she'd been given. "The good news
is, there's plenty you can do. Step One: breathing exercises."

"Okay, if there's one thing I could do without practicing,
it's breathing. Hell, I was born knowing how to do that."

"Breathing exercises are done lying down." He showed her
a series of diagrams.

"Otherwise known as sleeping."

"Meditation is recommended. I don't suppose you medi-
tate."

"How did you guess?"

He consulted the checklist again. "Yoga?"

"*Noga.*"

"Regular exercise of any kind?"

She scowled at him. "Running through airports. Power
shopping."

"'Cognitive behavioral therapy,'" he read from the list.

She chuckled. "Every day. Doesn't it show?"

"Sense of humor," he said. "That's not on the list, but it
can't hurt."

She inadvertently took a sip of her tea and nearly gagged.
"This stuff can't possibly be on the list."

"Here you go—foods to avoid." He turned the page toward her.

"Let me guess—refined sugars, alcohol, caffeine...."

"Good guess."

"Those are my major food groups." She waved her hand
dismissively. "I'm not going to do any of that stuff. It's just
not me."

"Look, I don't know you," he said. "But I'm going to take
a wild guess—if you do what the doctors say, it might help."

She heard an inner echo of the doctor's dire warning about
her blood pressure and stress on her heart. *You're too young to*

put yourself at risk. You need to take it easy.... Parking her elbows on the table, she regarded him through eyes narrowed in suspicion. "Why do I get the feeling you're experienced with doctors and hospitals?"

He shrugged. "Must be your uncanny insight. Here." He placed the information in front of her. "Start small. Pick one thing on the list and commit to it."

His baritone voice and whiskey-brown eyes drew her in, more persuasive by far than the geeky resident in the ER. *Dominic Rossi.* Who had a right to be that good-looking? It almost distracted her from the fact that he hadn't answered her question about doctors and hospitals.

"So much to choose from," she said with exaggerated drama, perusing the list. Diet, lifestyle, breathing, yoga, cardio... "Tell you what. You pick one." She pushed the notes back at him.

"You mean I get to pick something, and you'll do it?"

She folded her arms on the table and regarded him steadily. "I'm a woman of my word."

"Excellent. Quit smoking."

"I love smoking."

"You're a woman of your word. And excuse me for saying this, but you are way too beautiful to smoke."

His words had a ridiculous effect on her. "Wow. You are good."

When they left the coffee shop, he asked, "Shall I call you a cab?"

"No, thanks. I can walk from here. The walk'll do me good, right?" She still felt unsettled by the crazy day.

"I'll walk with you. Make sure you get home okay."

"It's not necessary. I know my way around. Besides, don't you have something to do? Like...banking?"

"I have backup."

She adjusted the strap of her handbag. "Suit yourself. You're not, like, an ax murderer or anything, right?"

"Not an ax murderer."

"Cool." They walked along through the rushing traffic, along Hyde Street, the shop windows flashing their reflection. The two of them looked like a couple, she caught herself thinking. He was in his thirties, she guessed. Tall and good-looking, he moved with a certain confidence that garnered glances from passing women and even a few guys.

"You all right?" Dominic asked.

"Fine."

"You were looking at me funny."

"I was just wondering what he's like," she said, her gaze skirting away. "Magnus Johansen, I mean."

"Kind," Dominic said immediately. "Steady. He takes care of people. Any of his friends and neighbors would tell you that."

"And how do you know him?"

"I barely remember a time when I didn't know him. My parents emigrated to the United States from Italy. They were seasonal workers when they first arrived in Archangel, and Magnus gave them a place to stay."

Migrant workers, she thought. His parents had been migrant workers. Suddenly she had to rearrange her image of Dominic Rossi as a spoiled, overprivileged finance major. "So Bella Vista is a working farm?"

"Orchards," he said. "Best apples in the county. I met Magnus when I was maybe seven or eight years old, when he caught me working at Bella Vista."

"What do you mean, he caught you?"

"He didn't want to be in violation of child labor laws. Anyway, to make a long story short, he took my sister and me under his wing. Helped us with everything from our parents' green cards to getting us into college."

"My grandfather sounds like a saint." She turned into her neighborhood of brickwork sidewalks lined with wrought iron fences and trees with their leaves just beginning to turn dry and crisp around the edges.

"I don't know about sainthood. When you come to see him—"

Her heart surged, a frightening reminder of the trauma that had landed her in the ER. "I'm not going. This has nothing to do with me."

"Sorry to argue, but it's got plenty to do with you."

"Am I expected to just drop everything and go haring off to Archangel to do what? There's nothing for me to do. And if there was, he's got another granddaughter. Did Isabel...? Does she live with her grandfather?"

"Yep. She grew up at Bella Vista. Magnus and Eva—his late wife—raised her."

"Then Magnus doesn't need me," Tess said, feeling a strange sense of hurt swirl through her like poisoned tendrils. "Seriously, this situation is awful, but I simply can't get involved."

"I understand. It's a lot to digest." He had the most amazing eyes. She felt an urge to keep talking to him, but she had no business doing that. "Here's my number." He handed her a card. "Call me if you change your mind."

"Her name is Isabel," Tess said to her mother's voice mail. "Did you know I had a sister? Not to mention a grandfather? And if you did, why the hell did you never bother to tell me? For Pete's sake, Mom, call me the minute you get this message. I don't care what time it is. Just call me."

Tess set the phone aside and looked around her apartment, filled with her old things, Nana's desk in the middle like a slumbering giant. Was it only this morning she had put herself together, racing into work to meet Mr. Sheffield? She felt as though she'd been away on a long trip.

Although the doctor's orders were for her to relax, she had paced up and down, worried and fretted. She'd searched Dominic on Google, as well as Isabel, Magnus, everyone he'd mentioned, to no avail, uncovering only frustrating bits and pieces about them, nothing helpful. There were things only her mother could answer. Her mother had never been good about answering hard questions.

The phone rang and she leaped for it, but the call was from Neelie. "I'm coming over," she said without preamble.

"But I don't need—"

"Too late. I'm here."

Tess heard the downstairs door buzz—Neelie knew the code—and footsteps on the stairs. Tess held the door open. "Hey, you."

Neelie brandished a large shopping bag from the local gourmet deli. "I've got chicken soup, and I'm not afraid to use it."

"Bless you. I was just about to nuke a frozen burrito."

Neelie clucked her tongue and busied herself in the kitchen. "Jude said you went to the ER. What the hell is that about?"

Thank you, Jude, thought Tess. "I'm fine."

"I knew you'd say that. But no healthy twenty-nine-year-old goes to the ER. Tell me everything."

Tess felt a small measure of relief, telling Neelie about her day. Neelie was her heart friend, someone who listened without judgment. She made all the appropriate oohs and aahs as Tess described the meeting with Dominic Rossi and the stunning news he'd delivered.

"Wait a minute, so this grandfather—this guy you've never heard of—is about to kick the bucket, and he's leaving you his estate in Sonoma County."

"Half his estate. Apparently I have a sister."

"Oh, my God. No wonder you collapsed and went to the hospital. How did you get there? Did some big hunky EMT rescue you?"

"You got the big and hunky part right. Dominic took me."

"The banker guy?" Neelie's eyes widened in bafflement. In their lexicon, "banker" was code for boring.

"He waited for me, too. I think he felt guilty for making my head explode."

"I certainly hope so." Neelie rummaged around in a cupboard and found a pair of big mugs for the soup. "What did the doctors say?"

"That my head is about to explode. Or, more accurately, my heart." Tess showed her the information from the ER.

"Oh, my gosh. I'm scared for you, Tess."

"I'm scared for me."

"Then you need to take care of yourself. You're all stressed out and this bomb that just got dropped on you… It's too much for anyone to process. First thing, you need some time off work."

"No way." Tess's reaction was swift, automatic. "I don't take time off work for anything."

"How do you suppose you got yourself into this situation, anyway, hmm?" Neelie led her to the kitchen bar, forced her to sit down. "Eat. Chicken soup. I hear it's good for the soul."

"I don't think the problem is with my soul."

"Whatever. Eat. You're too skinny. And as you know, skinny girls tend to piss off their friends." Neelie handed her a warm fresh bread roll from the deli bag.

Tess bit into the roll, redolent of herbs and butter. "I'm glad you're my friend," she said.

Neelie's fingers flew over the screen of her phone. "There," she said. "I just sent a text to Jude. Told him to let your office know you're taking some time—"

"What? Give me that." Tess grabbed for the phone.

Neelie held it out of reach. "Too late. Just eat the damn soup, Tess."

Resentfully, Tess sampled the soup. Delicious, but it tasted like defeat. "Today was supposed to be my big breakthrough at work. I had a meeting with Dane Sheffield himself. I'm pretty sure he was going to offer me a position most people only dream about—New York, right alongside the biggest players in the field. And I stood him up."

"You had a personal emergency. Tess, you get to have a life. I think what happened today is a sign that you *need* to have a life." Neelie paged through the recommendations from the ER. "So this is perfect. You need downtime. You could take some time, go to Archangel, figure out what this guy is talking about—a grandfather. A sister. In Archangel. I've been there, you know."

"Archangel?"

"It's in Sonoma County—the prettiest part, if you ask me. Boutique wineries everywhere, some of them world class. Ivar took me there—remember Ivar, the Norwegian hottie?"

"Two or three boyfriends ago."

"We stayed at a B and B. There's this amazing town square, fruit stands everywhere, scenery so gorgeous it doesn't even seem real. Wines you won't find anywhere else in the world. It was magic. It's the kind of place that makes you question why you live in the city."

"Because we have work here. Jobs and friends. Duh."

"Well, whether you like it or not, you have some personal matters to see to in Archangel. I know you, Tess. If you don't go, you're going to stress out about it, and that's exactly what you're supposed to be avoiding. You're going to lie awake at night wondering about this sister, and the poor old guy who fell off the ladder." She grabbed Dominic Rossi's card from the top of a stack of mail on the counter. "I'm calling him for you."

"Don't—"

"Eat."

"Bossy old thing," Tess muttered. But she ate.

The next day, Tess jumped out of bed, surprised by the time showing on the screen of her phone, but not in the least surprised that there was no message from her mother.

Leaping up, she rushed through brushing teeth and hair, pulling on dark wash jeans and a black cashmere turtleneck. Then she yanked open the closet and surveyed the cluttered press of clothing in her overstuffed closet. What did one take to the probable deathbed of a stranger, and to see a sister one had never met?

She flung a variety of items into an overnight bag, dropped her phone into the no-man's-land that was her purse, then added the charger, as well. This development—Archangel, Bella Vista, Magnus and Isabel—had left her completely scattered. She had no idea how to feel about all that had happened.

Figure out what the next step is, and then take it. Miss Winther's words drifted unbidden into Tess's mind.

"Okay, so the next step is—"

The buzzer went off.

"Answer the door," she muttered. Dammit, he was faster than she'd expected. Her apartment was in its usual state of disarray. She made no apology for that, though the arrival of Dominic Rossi made her self-conscious about her messy habits—piles of research clutter on the coffee table, sticky notes everywhere because she didn't trust her memory, last night's dishes she hadn't bothered to do, hand-washed lingerie draped over a lamp in the corner.

Too bad, she thought. She wasn't going to change her ways just to impress some banker.

However, the word *banker* did not compute when she opened the door and looked up at him. For some reason, he had the kind of face that drained her IQ down to two-digit territory.

"Um. I'm not ready," she said.

"I'll wait until you are," he replied easily. "I'm glad you called, Tess. How are you?"

"What? Oh, that. I'm okay. Really. You know, I never properly thanked you for helping out at the hospital, for being there."

"I wasn't expecting thanks. I'm glad you're all right." And he gave her that slow smile of his, brandishing it like a secret weapon. "Mind if I come in?"

"No, I just need a few minutes more." She felt a little self-conscious, watching him as he looked around her place. The apartment made perfect sense to her, but to a stranger, the old things probably seemed eccentric, or at the very least, sentimental.

"I like your place," he said, checking out a walnut radio console on the counter. "Is this a family heirloom?"

"Yes." She closed up her laptop and started rummaging around for its case. "Not my family, though. That radio— there's a message on the back."

He turned it and read, "'To Walter, a very brave boy, at Christmas. 1943.' Who was Walter?"

"I'm not sure. I just... I'm drawn to things that have a past. A story."

He picked up a deck prism, which she used as a paperweight.

"That's from the *Mary Dare,* wrecked at the mouth of the Columbia in 1876. The prisms were used to let light in below decks." She found the laptop case and put it with her overnight bag.

"And this?" He held up an elongated piece of carved ivory, with scrimshaw etchings on the surface.

"It's called a he's-at-home."

"Which is…?"

"A sex toy," she said, trying not to laugh as he quickly set the thing down. "On Nantucket Island, back in the days of whaling, the women used to get lonely when the men were gone for years at a time, hunting whales."

"No wonder whaling was outlawed."

"I need to grab a few more things," she said, ducking into the bedroom. Having a guy in her apartment had awakened her vanity, and she decided to add a few things to her bag. "Help yourself to something from the fridge," she called into the next room. At the same time, she thought, *Please do not look in the fridge.*

"Thanks," he said, and she heard the refrigerator door open. "Maybe I'll grab something to drink."

She cringed as he said, "You've got a stack of notebooks and papers in your fridge."

"Why, yes," she said casually, returning to the kitchen. "Yes, I do."

"Can I ask why?"

"Because there was no more room in the freezer." His puzzled expression made her want to laugh. "Those are my handwritten notes and papers. They're one-of-a-kind. I have no backup copy until I get them typed up."

"So you keep them in the refrigerator."

"If the place burns down, they'll be safe in there."

He nodded. "Good plan."

"And to answer the next obvious question, yes, I have a

fireproof safe. But I misplaced the combination and it's too small anyway."

"What is it that you do?"

"I'm a provenance expert. I authenticate things—art, jewelry, family heirlooms."

"Sounds…unusual. Interesting." He swung the refrigerator door wider and checked out the shelves. She had a supply of key lime yogurt, some boxed Chinese leftovers and a twelve pack of the only beverage she drank regularly—Red Bull. The energy drink was probably all kinds of bad for her, but it kept her from falling asleep on the job.

Dominic held a bottle up to the light. "Is this even legal?"

"Don't judge," she said, whipping a pair of purple lace panties off the lamp where she'd hung them to dry. She hoped he hadn't noticed.

"Nice panties," he said.

Okay, so he'd noticed.

"Again I say, don't judge."

"Never," he promised and twisted the cap off the soda bottle. He took a swig, and she could see him visibly trying not to gag. "You can tell a lot about a person by the place where she lives," he observed.

"Oh, really? What can you tell about me?"

"You like puzzles." He gestured at a stack of newspaper crosswords, anagrams and brain teasers, all of them obsessively completed.

"So sue me. What else?"

He perused a collection of yellowed documents and daguerreotypes. "You live in the past."

"No. I study the past for my work. I live in the here and now, which is perfectly fine for me. It's wonderful for me."

"Right. Got it."

She knew he didn't mean to seem critical when he said she

lived in the past, yet she felt criticized, as though she'd done something wrong. "I have a fascination for puzzles and old things. At least I'm not a hoarder. Please tell me you don't think I'm a hoarder."

"I don't think you're a hoarder. Your collection of old things is fascinating. I've never met a girl who had a he's-at-home."

"As far as you know," she said.

"As far as I know. Tell me about the desk," he said, gesturing at Nana's kneehole postmaster desk. It was by far the most dominant object in the place, almost architectural in its size and presence.

"I thought you were analyzing me," she said, trying to keep it light. She hoped they would both manage to keep things light between them, but it was hard. Because even though she barely knew this guy, she liked talking to him way too much. She liked the way he looked at her, the way he actually seemed to care.

"I am," he said. "Tell me about the desk."

He had to ask. It was the one thing in her apartment that was truly personal, truly *hers,* not some object with a history that had nothing to do with her. "My grandmother had a shop in Dublin. When I was a girl, I spent a lot of time with her there because my mother was always traveling for her work. Nana was a dealer in art and antiques."

"That's cool. You lived in Ireland?"

"Up until I came to the States for college."

"A redheaded Irish woman," he said.

"Don't ask me if I have a temper to match. Then I'd have to hurt you."

"Thanks for the warning. So your desk…"

"Was in Nana's shop. Antiques and ephemera, she used to tell people—called Things Forgotten. I can still picture her there, working at the desk. She was beautiful, my nana, and

Things Forgotten was my favorite place in the world. To a little kid, it seemed magical, like a world filled with treasures." Tess couldn't deny the feelings that came over her as she shared her private memories with this stranger, as if telling him about some nostalgic dream was going to help her finally make sense of her life.

Sometimes, in the middle of a tedious or frustrating transaction, or when she stood in an endless airport security line just knowing she was about to miss a connecting flight, Tess thought about Nana's shop. She imagined what it might be like to try a different path. Every once in a while, she wondered what it might be like to take a risk and open her own elegant antiques shop, one that had the same look and feel of the shop run by her grandmother, long ago. It was where the fondest memories of her childhood lay, hung with the ineffable scent of nostalgia—the dried bergamot and bayberry her grandmother kept in glass bowls around the place. She merely thought about it, though, because there was no way she would give up her hard-won role at Sheffield's.

"Do you get back to see her?" asked Dominic.

"She passed away when I was fifteen."

"Sorry to hear that. It's nice that you kept her desk."

"Is it? Sometimes I wonder if it's an albatross dragging me down."

"An anchor."

"I like that better." Turning away to hide a smile, she zipped up her bag. "Ready," she said. "I guess. I'm not really sure how to be ready for any of this."

He picked up her bag. She scanned the place one more time, then followed him outside.

She was surprised to see a taxi waiting on the street in front of the house. When he'd offered to take her to Archangel, she'd assumed he would be doing the driving.

"Isn't it, like, sixty miles to Archangel?" she asked.

"Seventy-eight. It's in the northern part of the county."

"Who's picking up the fare?"

He held the rear passenger door for her. "We're not taking a taxi all the way."

"Then—"

"I've got a faster way to travel."

Tess stood on a floating dock at Pier 39, regarding the twin-engine plane, bobbing at its moorings. Nearby, piles of glossy brown sea lions lazed on the floating docks, occasionally lifting their whiskered faces to the sun. San Francisco had its own ocean smell, redolent of marine life and urban bustle—diesel and frying food, fresh breezes and the catch of the day.

"If you're trying to impress me," she said, eyeing the small plane, "it's working."

He didn't say anything as he placed her suitcase in a wing compartment. Then he took off his suit coat and tucked it in, as well. She was not surprised to see a label from a well-known tailor. Yet, although the suit was well cared for, it was definitely not new.

He unlocked the cockpit and unfurled the mooring ropes. He had the shoulders and arms of a longshoreman, yet he moved with a peculiar athletic grace. She'd never known anyone remotely like him.

"Something wrong?" he asked her.

Caught staring, she ducked her head and tried to hold a blush at bay. "Archangel is inland, isn't it? So I was wondering where this plane will land."

He opened the door. "She's amphibious." Grasping Tess's hand, he helped her into a seat, then climbed up behind her.

Turning to him, she frowned. "Where's the pilot?"

"You're looking at him." He started flipping switches on the intricate array on the dashboard.

"You're a pilot?"

"Yeah. Want to see my license?"

"Not necessary. Or should I be more skeptical?"

"Seat belt," he said. "And put this headset on. It's going to get noisy in here." He got out and shoved off, expertly balancing on a pontoon as he stowed the mooring lines. In one fluid movement, he swung himself into the pilot's seat, put on his seat belt and headset and started the engine.

The twin propellers spun into translucent circles, pulling the small craft past the flotillas of sea lions and out into open water. Tess gasped as the takeoff stole her breath. For the next few minutes, she was glued to the window, admiring the view. San Francisco Bay was always a sight to behold, but from the air on a sunny day, it was pure magic. As the plane climbed through the sky, she looked over at Dominic, and the entire experience took on a surreal quality. She had flown all over the world, but this felt different, like a forbidden intimacy with a man she'd just met.

Once again, he caught her staring. He turned a dial on his headset. "Everything all right?"

His voice sounded distinct yet tinny in her ears.

"Under the circumstances," she said. "It's not every day I go flying with a strange man in a private airplane." *I could get used to it, though,* she thought.

"I'm not strange. I'm a banker," he said.

"You must be a really good one."

"Why do you say that?"

"I assume most bankers don't have their own private planes."

"This doesn't belong to me," he said. His expression changed just a little, but she didn't know him and couldn't read his face. There were things about this guy that didn't add up, and she found herself wanting to put him together like one of her most challenging puzzles.

He was uniquely distracting in a number of ways. He had brought her some extremely hard-to-digest news, yet he'd delivered it in person, and with compassion. He'd waited through her ordeal at the ER. Now Tess was about to find out about a whole part of herself that had been in the shadows until now. It was like cracking open a door and peeking through to an unknown world within. She'd yearned for family all her life, and it turned out they were here, all along, just a short distance away. The thought of all she'd missed made her heart ache. Her mother had a lot to answer for.

"Down there on your left," Dominic said as the city fell away behind them. "It's the Point Reyes lighthouse."

The slender tower of the light, perched on an outcropping of rock at the end of a precarious twist of steps, passed in a sweep of color. The plane seemed to skim along the craggy cliff tops while the ocean leaped and roared as it crashed against the rocks. They went northward along the craggy coastline, ragged fingers reaching out into the ocean. After a while, the plane banked and turned inland, over hills and ridges of farmland. The orchards, vineyards and dairies formed a crazy quilt of impossible shades of green and autumn colors, the sections stitched together by the silvery threads of rivers, flumes and canals, or the straight dark stretches of roads. The small towns of wine country sprang up, toylike, almost precious in their beauty, yet robust with commerce. She could see cars and utility vehicles on the roads, and farm equipment churning across the fields. Tess felt herself getting farther and farther from her life in the city.

They passed over the town of Sonoma itself—she'd never been there, but Dominic pointed it out—and after a while, descended into Archangel, a place she knew only by name.

The town looked very small, a cluster of buildings at the city center, surrounded by a colorful patchwork of vineyards, orchards, meadows and gardens.

The landing strip was located between two vineyards that swagged the hillsides. The plane touched down lightly, then buzzed along the tarmac, coming to a halt near a hangar of corrugated metal. A few other aircraft were tethered to the ground there.

Dominic switched off the radios and controls. "Welcome to Archangel."

"Thanks for the lift. It was…unexpected."

He got out and came around to help her down, his strength giving her a secret thrill. He had large hands and a firm grip, and he handled her as if she weighed nothing.

"This way," he said, slinging his suit coat over one shoulder and heading for the parking lot. Away from the landing strip and hangar, the air smelled sweet, and the atmosphere was aglow with autumn light. He opened the door of a conservative-looking SUV and she got in. The car was as neat as everything else about him. She'd never quite trusted pathologically neat people.

She rode along in silence, watching out the window. Neelie had always tried to get her to explore the wine regions of Sonoma County, but Tess never had time. She'd seen pictures, but nothing could have prepared her for the opulent splendor of the landscape here. The undulating terrain was cloaked in lush abundance, the vineyards like garlands of deep green and yellow, orchards and farms sprouting here and there, hillocks of dry golden grass crowned by beautiful sun-gilt houses, barns and silos. And overhead was the bluest sky she'd ever seen, as bright and hard as polished marble.

There was something about the landscape that caught at her emotions. It was both lush and intimidating, its beauty so abundant. Far from the bustle of the city, she was a complete stranger here, like Dorothy stepping out of her whirling house into the land of Oz. Farm stands overflowing with local produce marked the long driveways into farms with whimsical names—Almost Paradise, One Bad Apple, Toad Hollow. Boxes and bushels were displayed on long, weathered tables. Between the farms, brushy tangles of berries and towering old oak trees lined the roadway.

Tess felt a strange shifting inside her as the dark ribbon of the road wound down into the town of Archangel, marked by a sign where a bridge spanned a small waterway designated Angel Creek.

She told herself not to worry. Not to feel freaked out by the situation. She was used to unorthodox situations. In pursuing the provenance of an object, she had faced all sorts of people, from highly placed cultural ministers to art middlemen who were little more than gangsters, and she'd held her own. The prospect of meeting her half sister should not bother her.

But it did. She tried to remember the instructions the doctor had given her for breathing. Apparently she was an upper chest breather. This seemed to be a bad thing. She was supposed to inhale all the way down to her lower belly, until her stomach expanded, then exhale slowly, emptying her lungs. She took a breath, placing a hand on her stomach to see if it was puffing out.

"What are you doing?" asked Dominic, glancing over at her.

"Breathing."

"Glad to hear it."

"I'm doing the breathing technique they showed me in the ER."

"Anything I can do to help?"

"Don't make me talk. I need to breathe."

"Got it. But…is something upsetting you?"

"No. Of course not." *Just this whole crazy situation,* she thought. "I'll be all right." She practiced her breathing as they drove through the town. Archangel seemed quaint without being too self-conscious about it, with a subtle air of rustic elegance. The center of town had a pretty square surrounded by beds of white mums and Michaelmas daisies, a broad green lawn with iron benches, some sweeping eucalyptus trees, their sage-colored leaves fluttering on the breeze. In the very center was a fountain with a copper sculpture of a vine hung with grapes.

The buildings were well-kept, housing boutiques, cafés and restaurants with colorful awnings, a few tasting rooms, a couple of gourmet shops and an old-fashioned hardware store with wheelbarrows and flowerpots on the sidewalk outside. There were plenty of people out enjoying the gorgeous weather. An elderly couple strolled side by side, eating ice cream cones. A young mother with dreamy eyes pushed a stroller, and a group of rowdy boys jostled past, shoving each other, skirting around a good-looking family consisting of mom, dad, twin little boys and a dark-eyed teen girl.

Everyone looked normal and happy, enviably so. She wasn't naive enough to believe they *were* normal and happy. But in this setting, they resembled movie extras exemplifying the charms of small-town America.

Past the main part of town, they went by a bank, a low-profile midcentury building of blond brick. "Is that where you work?" she asked Dominic.

"Yes."

She waited, but he offered no more. They drove on, passing a grocery store and gas station, and a pair of churches on opposite sides of the road, as if squaring off at high noon.

Tall, slender trees stood in long rows that followed the contours of the terrain. A vineyard designated Maldonado

Estates went by; then at the next junction was a large rural
mailbox marked Johansen. At the roadside stood an old building with a sagging front porch and battered tin roof with a
crooked sign that read Bella Vista Produce. The place must
have been a farm stand at one time. It resembled a throwback
to other days, and she found herself picturing the place filled
with bunches of flowers and bounty from the farm, with cars
pulling off the road and people browsing the wares. Before
she could ask about it, Dominic turned down a gravel drive
marked Bella Vista Way. A lurch of anticipation knotted her
stomach. "Is this it?" she asked.

"Uh-huh."

They drove between rows of twisted, lichened oak trees,
beneath kettling hawks and a sky as blue as heaven itself. Orchards spread out on both sides of the drive. In the distance,
she could see a cluster of buildings gathered on a rise. Around
a bend in the drive, cars were parked in an open field, all kinds
of cars, from battered work trucks to electric and biodiesel-
powered vehicles to gleaming foreign imports.

"What's going on?" she asked.

"Your grandfather's friends and neighbors organized a healing ceremony for him. I think we're just in time to join in."

She pressed her feet against the floor mat as if putting on
the brakes. "Whoa, hang on a second. A healing ceremony?"

"It can't hurt, and who's to say all this energy won't help?
It's scheduled to start at four," he said, checking his watch.

"I thought he was in the hospital."

"He is. But everyone's here for his sake."

"Who *are* these people?"

"Neighbors and workers. Business associates. Magnus made
a lot of friends through the years." An unexpected catch
hitched his voice. "You'll see."

Tess bit her lip. Looked down at her outfit—the dark jeans

and sweater, heeled half boots. She had no idea if this was appropriate attire to wear to an event for the grandfather she'd never known. She set her jaw. "Do you realize how awkward this is for me?"

He braked gently, bringing the car to a halt. "Should I turn around?"

"Of course not. But you have to understand, this is weird for me. I don't belong here." She felt prickly, resentful. On the one hand, she was glad Magnus had such loyal friends and neighbors. On the other hand, what kind of person ignored his granddaughter all her life and then promised her half of everything after he was gone?

The air was sharp with the scent of lavender, wafting up from a broad field where the herb grew in row after row of blue-green clumps. A mariachi band was setting up in the shade of a California oak tree. Rows of folding chairs were set up, the configuration bisected by a turquoise carpet runner. At the front of the display were more flower arrangements than she had ever seen in one place, outside the *Marché aux Fleurs* in Paris. Danish and U.S. flags sprouted from some of the arrangements.

Dominic let her out near the seating area and went to park the car. Tess stood alone, watching people arrive. Some were somber, though a good many seemed more talkative and upbeat. People wore party clothes, the women in bright-colored dresses, the men in everything from crisp white shirts to plaid golf slacks. Several people gave Tess a nod of greeting. A gangly German shepherd dog trotted around, checking people out with a proprietary sniff.

The house itself was a rambling hacienda-style structure built of pale stone, with thick-trunked vines climbing the stuccoed walls. There was an open, colonnaded breezeway across the back. Through the open columns, she could see a center courtyard, planted with huge potted olive trees.

An aroma of baking bread wafted from a window flanked by rustic shutters and wrought iron bars. She edged toward the open back door. It was painted sky blue and propped open with an iron stopper in the shape of a cat.

She found herself on the threshold of a large, airy kitchen with terra-cotta tiled floors and tall windows open to a view of lavender fields and orchards. A log trestle table of scrubbed pine dominated the room. A bewildering array of utensils hung from the walls or were arranged upon the cobalt-blue counter tiles. Trays of food were arranged on catering carts.

At the far end of the room was a panel of wall ovens, clearly the source of the glorious smell. Tess could see someone there, a woman backlit by the sun shining through the windows. She wore her hair pulled back in haphazard fashion, a gauzy skirt and blouse and two thick oven mitts. Bending slightly, she opened one of the ovens like a door to a safe, and drew a big tray from the rack. Steam rose, intensifying the aroma.

Tess set down her bag. "Excuse me," she said. "I—"

The woman dropped the pan with a clatter onto the countertop. She swung to face Tess.

"Oh, my God," she said softly. "I didn't think you'd come."

PART FOUR

There's rosemary, that's for remembrance.
Pray you, love, remember.

—Shakespeare, *Hamlet*

••• • •••

GRAPE AND ROSEMARY FOCACCIA

....

The carnosic acid in rosemary shields brain cells from free radical damage. Therefore, consumption of the herb could play a role in preventing brain disorders.

Makes 8 servings

5 to 6 cups flour

1 tablespoon sugar

1 tablespoon instant yeast

1 teaspoon salt

2 cups warm water

½ cup extra-virgin olive oil

1½ cups green, red and/or black grapes

2 teaspoons chopped

fresh rosemary (1 teaspoon dried)

coarse salt

If using an electric stand mixer, combine 3 cups of the flour, and all of the sugar, yeast and salt in the bowl. Add the water, then mix well, using the paddle attachment. Then change to the dough hook and gradually add more of the flour, kneading well between each addition, until the dough is smooth, firm and no dough sticks to the side of the bowl. If not using a mixer, stir together 3 cups of flour, and all of the sugar, yeast and salt in a large mixing bowl, then add the water and mix together with a large wooden spoon. Turn the dough out onto a heavily floured board and knead while gradually incorporating more flour into the dough until it is smooth and elastic, about 10 minutes.

Place the dough in a lightly oiled bowl and cover with plastic wrap or a dry cloth. Let rest in a warm place until the dough has doubled, about 1 hour.

Preheat the oven to 425 degrees Fahrenheit.

Pour all but 2 tablespoons of the olive oil onto a 12-by-16 ½-inch baking sheet. Lift the dough from the bowl and gently stretch and press it to fit the pan. Drizzle the dough with the remaining olive oil and dimple the top of the bread with your fingertips. Press the grapes into the dough evenly all over the bread, leaving about 1 inch between grapes. Sprinkle the bread generously with the chopped rosemary and coarse salt.

Bake the focaccia until it is a nice crisp brown, about 30 minutes. Remove from the oven and cut with a pizza cutter into squares. Serve warm with cheese or butter.

(Source: Adapted from the California Grape Commission)

SIX

Tess stepped farther into the unfamiliar kitchen. Her senses were awash with sounds from outside—the breeze wafting through the boughs of the apple trees, the musicians tuning up, the murmur of conversation and rumble of engines. She inhaled the yeasty aroma from the oven, and blinked at the golden light streaming through the windows. Breathe, she told herself. *Breathe.*

The woman at the other end of the room stood unmoving, her posture a slender question mark, silhouetted against the light from the window. She had large dark eyes surrounded by thick lashes that appeared damp from crying. Her sable-brown hair was looped into a careless braid down her back, and she wore a gauzy skirt and blouse, an apron, a pair of oven mitts and espadrilles tied at the ankles.

The two of them stared at one another. The stranger shifted, stepping into a shaft of light through the open window. She

had the face of an old Hollywood movie star, with an aqui-
line nose and full lips. She wore little or no makeup; her olive-toned skin gave her an air of unstudied elegance, needing
no embellishment.

Tess finally found her voice. "You're Isabel, aren't you?"

The woman dropped her hands to her sides. "Theresa?"

"Tess." For a moment, she couldn't say anything else. Her
mouth went completely dry. *Isabel.*

"Come in," Isabel said. "Welcome to Bella Vista." She
shook off the oven mitts and reached out, clasping Tess in a
spontaneous hug.

Tess was not a hugger, particularly not with a stranger she'd
just met. Yet in the middle of the awkwardness, she nearly
melted with the sensation of being embraced. *I have a sister,*
she kept thinking. *A sister.*

Isabel felt soft and yielding; her blouse felt soft. Everything
about her seemed soft, and she smelled of dried flowers, rosemary, fresh-baked bread. This whole kitchen seemed alive
with a peculiar energy; in the old fixtures and furniture, Tess
sensed a place where cooking and eating had happened for decades, where people gathered to sample life's sweetest pleasures.

They stepped back, circling with a vague hint of wariness.
Isabel's gaze dropped. "I got flour all over you. I'm sorry."

Tess looked down at her sweater.

"I'm so sorry," Isabel said again. "I'm always doing that,
hugging people with my apron on. Here, I'll brush you off."
She grabbed a dish towel.

Tess took it from her. "I've got it." She gave her sweater a
few quick brushes. "No harm done," she said, handing back
the towel.

A strained silence drew out between them, invisible yet
palpable. She pictured Isabel as she had first seen her, alone
in the kitchen, moving with a peculiar grace and assurance

as she removed the last batch of bread from the oven. In that moment, she'd appeared to be completely in her element, a woman surrounded by the trappings of home. *How on earth could we be related?* Tess wondered, thinking about her own kitchen, a repository for work materials and take-out containers. Tess wanted to stare and stare at Isabel, to figure out what they had in common and how it was that they'd both been in the world all their lives without knowing each other.

Maybe Isabel had similar thoughts, because she said, "You look so much like the pictures of him. It's uncanny."

Him. Erik Johansen. Their common father.

"I've only ever seen one picture of him, so I don't really know what he looked like," Tess admitted.

"I can show you others later." Isabel stared unabashedly at Tess. "You're so...pretty. I mean, he wasn't pretty, but you still look like him. The two of us don't look anything alike, do we?"

Tess couldn't stop staring, either. "I suppose not."

"But we have a lot in common."

No, we don't, thought Tess.

"Can I get you anything?" Abruptly, Isabel seemed more animated, as if grateful to have a purpose. "I've got iced herbal tea or plain water, and I just took out the last of the focaccia bread. Salted rosemary."

"It smells fantastic, but no, thanks. Actually, I, um, could use the restroom."

"Sure. Of course. It's just down the hall there, under the stairs. There's a powder room."

Tess hurried down the hallway of the strange house, furnished in an oddly appealing combination of simple rusticity and old-world elegance. Passing a gallery of framed photos on the wall, she had an urge to study each one. Maybe later, she told herself. Assuming she was truly welcome here.

The powder room was spotless, with bowls of drying herbs, artisan soaps, embroidered towels. As she washed her hands with a bar of handmade soap that smelled of olive oil, Tess studied her face in the mirror. It was just her face. Pale skin and freckles, blue-green eyes, red hair. *You look like the pictures of him.*

She dried her hands and whipped out her phone, furious to see that her mother still hadn't returned her call. Zero bars of service.

Tess went back to the kitchen. Isabel was arranging cuts of the focaccia on a platter. "Is there no cell phone service here?"

"No. The closest service is over the hill. Sorry. I've got a landline."

"Thanks, I'll use it later."

Tess felt supremely uncomfortable, and a telltale tightness in her chest worsened matters. She wondered where Dominic Rossi had gone; he was the closest thing to a friend she had around here. "Listen," she said, "if it's weird that I'm here, we can always get together another time."

"No, it's good that you came. I was hoping you would get here in time for the gathering today."

A woman with white-streaked hair and hoop earrings, wearing a flowing wine-colored dress, hurried into the kitchen, the heels of her sandals clicking on the tiles. "There you are, Isabel. I knew I'd find you here." Turning to Tess, she held out her hand. "I'm Ernestina," she said. "Ernestina Navarro."

"Tess Delaney."

"Nice to meet you. Are you a friend of Magnus?"

"Not exactly. I'm…new…"

"He loves meeting new people." Ernestina turned back to Isabel. "Everything is about to start."

Isabel nodded. "I just came in to finish up the last of the bread." She untied her apron and set it aside.

"Of course." Ernestina's bold-featured face softened. "Are you going to be okay?"

Isabel offered a tremulous smile. "What's the alternative?"

Ernestina patted her arm. "You could have a meltdown."

"With all these guests to feed?" Isabel shook her head. Then she turned to Tess. "Ernestina lives with her husband, Oscar, and their son in the bungalow down the drive." She gestured at a lane bordered by apple trees, now crowded with guests.

"We've worked at Bella Vista for twenty years," Ernestina added. "How do you know him?"

Isabel turned to the older woman, paused, took a breath. "Tess is… She's my half sister."

The dark slash of Ernestina's brows arched upward. "I don't get it."

"That makes two of us," said Tess.

"We've got a lot to talk about," said Isabel. "You're staying, right?"

Tess didn't want to be here at all. She didn't want to stay. But Isabel's air of barely contained desperation moved her, and Tess herself couldn't deny a strong tug of curiosity about her sister, and the beautiful estate. "I, uh…yes, if that's all right. I mean, if there's room…."

"I've got nothing but room here. I love having guests."

The three of them left the kitchen together, stepping into the sun-flooded garden. Though the sound of the mariachis was unexpected, the music they played was curiously moving. Bright and brassy, the piece was in a minor key, its rhythm slow, punctuated with staccato blasts of the trumpet. The band members were dressed to the nines, covered in silver buttons and braided furnishings, their instruments polished like the crown jewels.

Tess looked around to see if she could spot Dominic, but in the crush of strangers, she didn't see him. A large framed portrait of Magnus was on display, depicting a distinguished man with a nimbus of white hair. He had a strong face and a handsome smile, and a twinkle in his eyes.

Chairs were arranged in concentric rings, each marked with a bouquet tied up with ribbons in the colors of the Danish flag—cherry red and white.

"Is there a particular place you'd like me to sit?" Tess asked Isabel.

Isabel nodded. "Next to me."

Tess had no idea what Isabel thought of the situation. She seemed nice enough, but why would she welcome Tess, a stranger, who now had a claim on half of the old man's legacy? Glancing over at Isabel, she could read only a deep sadness and worry in her expression. There was also something unsettled and mysterious about this stranger who was related to her by blood. Tess couldn't put her finger on it.

An elderly lady already sat in the inner circle, a string of well-worn rosary beads slipping through her fingers while her lips moved in silent prayer.

Isabel bent down and kissed her cheek. Then she gestured at Tess. "This is Theresa Delaney," she said. "She goes by Tess."

The old woman looked up at her. "It's good to finally meet you," she said. "Juanita Maldonado."

To finally *meet me?*

"My husband, Ramon," said Juanita. He sat next to her in a wheelchair, wearing a crisply pressed white shirt and trousers. "He and Magnus came through the war together."

Isabel gave the old lady's shawl-clad shoulder a squeeze. "How are you doing?"

"My feet hurt," said Juanita. "These shoes, they pinch."

"Then you should take them off."

"That's disrespectful."

"Not as disrespectful as having sore feet."

"This is true." Juanita leaned down and liberated her feet from the shoes, then discreetly tucked her sun-browned toes into the grass beneath her chair.

When Tess took a seat, Isabel leaned over and whispered, "Neighbors from way back. I'll fill you in later."

The mariachis concluded their piece. When they fell still, the voices of the crowd tapered off. It was a strange moment, that breath-held silence, which felt vaguely as if they were at a theater, waiting for the curtain to rise.

Looking around the gathering of strangers, Tess felt terribly alone. She focused on the shush of the breeze through the tree branches, and then the call of a bird, stark in the void of silence. A few coughs and sniffles came from the crowd.

Then, faintly at first, but gathering in volume, came the simple, clear sound of a ukulele. A young man in jeans and a T-shirt, his hair in a ponytail, walked from the left. In a clear, curiously wistful voice, he began to sing the Hawaiian version of "What a Wonderful World."

Tess could almost feel the emotion coming off Isabel in waves. Though tears streamed down her cheeks, there was something strong and noble in her manner. She was a pretty crier, Tess randomly noted. Tess herself looked a mess whenever she cried, her eyes and nose reddening like a drunk's. She made a point of not crying.

A priest arrived, a tall man who was so handsome that Tess couldn't focus on a single word he said. If not for the long white vestments, he might have stepped out of an ad in a glossy lifestyles magazine. She reminded herself of the gravity of the occasion, clearing her throat and sitting straighter in her chair.

Isabel leaned slightly toward her. "Don't worry, everyone has that reaction to Father Tom. It's ridiculous, how good-looking he is." She dabbed at her cheeks with a tissue. Tess forced herself to listen rather than stare.

"We come together today to ask for healing and mercy for our friend and neighbor, Magnus Johansen. So many of us owe much to this beloved man. He was a loving husband to his late wife, Eva, proud father of his late son, Erik, and beloved grandfather of Isabel Johansen and... Theresa..." He paused, checked his notes. "Delaney."

"I let him know at the last minute that you'd made it here," Isabel whispered.

Tess felt the scrutiny of a few dozen pairs of eyes. How much did these people know about her? Did they think she was a prodigal come home or a buzzard circling for the kill? She chafed under the attention.

"...but most of all," said the priest, "Magnus is the kind of man who knows how to be a friend to anyone in need. He does not confine his goodness to family alone...." Father Tom went on, extolling Magnus's virtues in a voice rich with emotion. He offered a tender portrait of a man who had lived a long and varied life, filled with abundance yet shadowed by tragedy. "We humbly ask for healing, but if it is time to let Magnus go," the priest concluded, "may we do so with grace and surrender."

Isabel gasped and crushed a wad of Kleenex to her face.

Jesus, thought Tess in exasperation. *Is this supposed to be helping?*

The priest must have caught her glare, because he quickly added, "However, if our good thoughts, our prayers and energy can bring him back to us, then let us pray for his speedy and complete recovery."

More songs and supplications followed, tributes from friends and neighbors, people who did business with Magnus, even the mayor of Archangel. Tess wasn't naive enough to believe she was getting a clear picture of the man; one's flaws tended not to be hashed over at an occasion like this. However, it was impossible not to be moved by stories of Magnus helping neighbors with their harvest, saving a toddler from choking, getting a tractor out of a ditch. Tess felt an ache in her chest, the grief of lost possibilities. How would her life have been different if she had known her grandfather? It was the not-knowing that filled her with regret.

The ceremony was not without its purely bizarre moments. At one point, a group of latent hippies in gypsy garb and bare feet performed an interpretive dance to "Age of Aquarius," their eyes closed and their hands reaching for the sky in a sequence of new-age craziness. Isabel leaned over and whispered that they were members of a food co-op that bought apples from Magnus. Tess had to suck in her cheeks to keep from bursting into inappropriate laughter.

Beside her, Isabel shuddered and quaked with sobs, each intake of breath a gasp of desperation. Then, glancing to the side, something clued Tess in. Isabel was inches from falling apart...with laughter.

Tess patted her sister on the arm, for the first time consciously thinking of her as a sister.

"I'm awful. I shouldn't be laughing," Isabel said in a broken voice.

"It's okay," Tess whispered. "Everyone will just think you're overcome."

"I hope you're right," Isabel whispered back. "They're really very sincere, but..."

Tess watched a woman in a tie-dyed shirt execute a move worthy of a flamenco dancer. "I know. I know."

Mercifully, the dancers finished, dropping to the ground like birds shot from the sky.

A man introduced as Lorenzo Maldonado stepped up, looking elegant yet a bit nervous. "That's gonna be a hard act to follow," he said, eliciting murmurs of laughter. He was handsome, with raven-black hair, narrow reading glasses perched on his nose. He indicated Juanita and her husband. "I'm here to speak for my grandfather, Ramon Maldonado, who can no longer speak for himself."

"He had a stroke," Isabel explained in a whisper.

"My grandfather was working on a ship in Denmark when the Nazis occupied the country. He met Magnus there, and they became lifelong friends. That friendship is the reason the Maldonados and the Johansens have been neighbors ever since. For those of you who don't know, Magnus saved Papacito's life, when they were both working against the Nazis as part of the Danish resistance. Papacito was caught sinking a German boat and was moments away from being executed. Magnus rescued him and they both escaped, though Magnus took a bullet in his leg. After the war, Papacito returned home to Archangel. Magnus followed with his new bride, Eva, and in gratitude, the Maldonados gifted the Johansens with Bella Vista, a small portion of their vast ancestral estate. I know I speak for the whole family when I pray for Magnus to recover from his accident."

That was some gift, thought Tess, looking around the rolling, golden hills. And once again, she felt a stab of regret. The Danish resistance was one of the most heroic aspects of World War II. She would have loved to hear of her grandfather's exploits.

The mariachis played a recessional. Father Tom and some of the guests spiced the air with herbs burning in censers. Everyone headed up a gravel path in a great ragged stream.

"We're going up the hill to pay tribute to Bubbie—my grandmother Eva," said Isabel. "*Our* grandmother. She died a while back."

Glancing around, Tess spotted Dominic Rossi, pushing Ramon Maldonado in his wheelchair. The day had warmed up, and Dominic had removed his jacket and rolled up his sleeves to reveal tanned and sinewy arms that looked out of place—but not unwelcome—on a guy who worked as a banker. The pain and worry in Dominic's face touched her unexpectedly, reminding her that Magnus meant something to him. As if he felt her gaze, he looked over and gave a nod of acknowledgment.

The procession passed fields of herbs and flowers dropping their petals and going to seed, and orchards of trees weighted with fruit, some of the harvest already in baskets on the ground and exuding an aroma of lush, heavy sweetness. A slight breeze tossed leaves and spent lavender blossoms and milkweed parachutes into the air, creating a small colorful storm. They came to a knoll overlooking the valley, which was threaded by a silvery stream.

There, a simple headstone marked the grave of Eva Salomon Johansen, "beloved wife and grandmother." Tess was intrigued to see a phrase in Hebrew characters. Her paternal grandmother had apparently been Jewish. Beside that was a marker for Erik Karl Johansen, inscribed, *Measure his life not by its length but by the depths of joy he brought us. He jumped into life and never touched bottom. We will never laugh the same again.*

Tess stood before the headstone, feeling an unexpected wave of loss, anger and abandonment that shook her to her core. *Hi, Dad,* she thought. *I wish I'd had a chance to know you.*

Someone took her hand and gave it a gentle squeeze. She was surprised to see Isabel standing there, her eyes filled with a haunting sadness, as if she'd read Tess's mind.

The mariachis played on, the mournful brassy notes from the trumpet like a cry to heaven.

More prayers were offered, and then a lone trumpet blared

out the poignant strains of "Amazing Grace." With each successive verse, the other instruments joined in, giving the melody a curiously appealing Latino vibe.

Then, in the midst of the sadness and despair, some of the young children started to dance. Tess couldn't see who started it, but she spied a group of little girls holding hands and skipping to the mariachis' rhythm. They giggled and tumbled down the hill of golden grass. Their clear laughter was infectious, and the band picked up the tempo with a lively tune. Soon, even some of the adults were dancing, clapping or tapping their feet to the rhythm. Within the span of minutes, a spontaneous dance party erupted. An overwhelming sense of community pervaded the gathering. It was all so foreign to Tess, who felt awkward, an outsider here. Why, oh, why had she told Isabel she'd stay?

She looked over at Isabel to see that her eyes were spilling over with tears again, streaming unchecked down her face. But she was smiling.

"Grandfather would love this," she said. "I wish he could be here."

Tess couldn't bring herself to back out of staying. Not now. Still, she did not know how to act around these people. They were like a big family, and Tess had no notion of that, large or small.

Later, in the central courtyard, mariachis set up and continued playing. In the middle of the patio, a fountain burbled, and some of the kids splashed in the water. Under a grape arbor, long buffet tables were set up, spread with a beautiful feast.

"Help yourself to some food," Isabel urged Tess. "I know this has been a long day for you."

"It can't compare to the day you've had. Come with me."

Isabel hesitated, then gave a nod. They each took a plate

and helped themselves to a feast that looked as if it had been prepared for a magazine layout. There was a salad sprinkled with fresh flowers—Isabel said they were baby pansies, nasturtium and angelica. The spread included plates of artisan cheeses and raw and grilled vegetables, big chafing dishes of fragrant casseroles, berries and apples with a variety of sauces, an array of local wines and water from Calistoga. The abundance was almost overwhelming to Tess.

"Your caterer did an incredible job," she said to Isabel. "Everything looks absolutely beautiful."

Isabel paused and frowned a little. "There's no caterer."

This startled Tess. The quality and presentation of the food, on hand-painted majolica ware atop the wrought iron tables, was light-years beyond the usual potluck fare. "Who did the food? I mean, I know you made the bread, but everything else… Did your friends and neighbors pitch in? God, I should have such friends and neighbors." Now that she thought about it, her friends only did takeout, and she didn't even know her neighbors' names.

"Isabel did the food," said Ernestina, who was filling her plate across the table from them.

"Really? I'm impressed by anyone who can cook anything that doesn't come from a mix. Which dish did you make?"

Isabel shrugged.

"All of it," Ernestina chimed in. "She's being modest. Nearly everything you see here came from Isabel's kitchen."

Tess sampled a spicy olive tapenade. "You've got to be kidding."

Isabel offered a fleeting smile.

"You're not kidding. Is that what you do for a living?" Tess asked. "You're a caterer, or a chef?"

"I stay busy enough around here."

It wasn't really an answer, but Tess dropped the subject.

She and Isabel had a lot of blanks to fill in, but not here and now. She caught sight of Dominic Rossi across the patio. In his banker's suit, he was one of the more conservative-looking guests. People seemed to know him; he chatted easily with anyone who happened by, yet she sensed that he was holding himself at a distance. She felt Isabel's gaze and flushed a little.

"He told me he's known your grandfather for a long time."

Isabel hesitated, then said, "Yes. For most of his life."

"I thought Lourdes and the kids might come," Ernestina remarked, "but I don't see them."

Tess nearly dropped her buffet plate. *Lourdes and the kids.* She set her jaw, realigning her thinking. So the incredibly hot banker-pilot-guy was married, with children. Of course he was. She should have realized that right away. Guys like him—handsome, stable, good-humored—got married. They had kids.

At the end of the buffet table, some of the guests clustered around Isabel, dispensing hugs and earnest conversation. Tess hung back, not wanting to intrude. She wondered what the people here thought of her, the long-lost relative. The by-blow of a careless man. Yet no one seemed shocked by her presence, and no one seemed to judge her.

Returning to the buffet, she helped herself to another piece of focaccia bread, the top glistening with a sheen of olive oil and sprinkled with big crystals of salt, fronds of rosemary and tiny curls of thinly sliced garlic. She tasted the bread and made a sound of pleasure that would have embarrassed her if anyone had heard.

"It's even better with this Cabernet." Dominic Rossi stood there with two full glasses of red wine.

Tess felt her face heat with a blush. Okay, so he'd heard.

"Let's have a seat over here," he said, gesturing at one of the café tables.

Sure, mister charming, married banker man, she thought. *Let's have a glass of wine together.* She wondered where his wife was. And against her better judgment, she wondered what the wife was like. *Lourdes.* Was she as mysterious and exotic as her name?

Taking her silence for assent, he handed her a glass and touched the rim of his to hers. "Welcome to Archangel."

"Thank you." She sipped the wine. It was beyond delicious. "What is this?"

"It's from Angel Creek winery."

"I've never heard of it."

"It's a small label." He pointed at a low spot in the distance, twined with the silvery stream she'd seen earlier. "Angel Creek is over there. The grapes are made from the vineyard on that slope and ridge."

"I don't think I've ever had a glass of wine in sight of the vineyard it came from." She took a sip of the Cabernet and another bite of the bread. It was as light as a cloud, the crust perfect, the wine smooth and flavorful. "This is heaven."

Most of the guests were eating and talking now; children chased each other around the central fountain, and the mariachis played on. People took turns greeting Isabel, offering hugs, some of them quietly consoling her. What a gift it was to have the kind of friends and neighbors who would gather in support in a crisis.

And what an alien concept for Tess—the idea of a permanent home, roots, history. Her neighbors were strangers who shared a common trash pickup day, and her friends... they were as busy as she was with work. If a disaster were to strike, she assumed they would rally around her—but only if she reached out for help, something she was completely unaccustomed to doing.

"I feel for Isabel," she said to Dominic, unsettled by a

strange, sharp yearning. "She must be so worried about her grandfather. Do you think I should try to visit him in the hospital? Magnus is allowed to have visitors, right?"

"Sure. I've been going every day."

"Is it awful? I mean, does he look...?"

"He's in bad shape, banged up from the fall, now hooked up to monitors and pumps. The docs can't predict when or even if he'll emerge from the coma, but they say it can't hurt to talk to him, hold his hand, that sort of thing. Would it be weird for you?"

"Um, *all* of this is weird for me."

There was kindness in his face; she sensed he genuinely wanted to help. So now he was hot *and* kind. And married. So what was he doing seeking her out, extending his sympathy? She pushed away her plate.

"You didn't eat much," he said.

"I'd rather drink." She finished her wine. "Good God, that's delicious."

He moved the plate in front of her again. "Don't let Isabel's cooking go to waste."

She sighed and picked at the grilled vegetables. She wasn't usually much for vegetables, but these were as delicious as they looked, perfectly seasoned with fresh herbs. "This could make me give up Cheetos," she said. "Scratch that. Nothing could make me give up Cheetos. They're like crack to me."

"For me, it's strawberry Newtons," he said. "How are you feeling, anyway?"

She bridled. "I'm fine. Don't I look fine?"

"Better than you did in the city."

"Thanks a lot. A piece of roadkill would look better than I did in the city," she said, trying a slice of herbed courgette. She fought against feeling drawn to this man. He had the sort of looks that infiltrated a woman's dreams—polished fashion on the outside, brawny underneath. The black-rimmed glasses merely added interest. Everything about him attracted her. Except, of course, the married part.

A boy and a girl dashed past, the boy ducking behind the leaf-clad frame of an arbor, then jumping out at the girl, who squealed with delight.

"Ernestina mentioned you have kids." Tess wanted to draw a clear boundary right away. He was too dangerously good-looking to do otherwise.

"I do. Trini and Antonio. They're with their mom today."

Something about the way he said "with their mom" tipped her off. "Oh. You and their mom aren't together?"

He shook his head. "We've been divorced for three years."

Now she felt slightly less guilty for lusting after him. But only slightly. This was not the time or the place to start a flirtation. Surely there was an unwritten social rule about hooking up with someone in the midst of a looming tragedy.

"I see," she said evenly. "It happens." *Lame, Tess.* "I mean, I'm sorry."

"Thanks."

She dropped the subject, even though a host of questions crowded into her head. What was the ex like? Why had they split up? Who in her right mind would split up with a guy like this?

None of your business, she told herself.

By the time everyone took their leave, full dark obscured the hollows of the surrounding hills, and indigo twilight twined between earth and sky. A line of glowing taillights from departing vehicles curved along the drive toward the main road.

In the kitchen, helpful neighbors or workers finished the last of the cleanup. Tess couldn't keep track of everyone. She observed a bewildering number of Navarro relatives who had been associated with the estate for years. Tess was fast developing a fascination with this place and people here. Despite her discomfort at being the outsider, she wanted to learn more.

After the cleanup, she and Isabel sat together in the courtyard, with a single votive candle burning on the table between them, and a rangy German shepherd named Charlie lying at Isabel's feet.

Tess felt completely enveloped by the deep and silent darkness and the scent of night jasmine and drying leaves on the breeze. Stars pricked the sky, the sweeping array overwhelming to Tess. The abundance of the night, unimpeded by city light, made her dizzy. The darkness added a sense of intimacy to the moment. It was *too* intimate. Too quiet. So quiet, she was at risk of hearing her own loneliness.

"I never see this," she said, tipping back her head. "The night sky, I mean. I spend all my time in cities, for the most part."

"What cities?" asked Isabel.

"I live in San Francisco."

"What do you do there?"

"I research and value things for a boutique auction house. We have offices in New York, Brussels and Berlin. Work takes me all over the place."

Isabel sighed. "I always thought I wanted to travel."

"You should, then. What's holding you back?"

There was a slight pause, maybe a heartbeat. "There's always something keeping me here. I was away at cooking school for a while. But I needed to come home when Bubbie got sick. After she was gone, I never went back. Turns out it wasn't for me. Without Bubbie, Grandfather was like a lost soul, so I couldn't leave him." She brushed an imaginary crumb from the tablecloth. "While he's in the hospital, I have no idea who I'm supposed to take care of."

"How about yourself?"

A smile flickered across her face and disappeared. "Actually, in his absence, I've got my hands full with the apple orchard. Grandfather isn't the most organized when it comes to running the business...."

Tess sensed more to the story. But Isabel didn't seem inclined to share.

From the kitchen, Ernestina called out a good-night. She and her husband, Oscar, made their way down the lane to their bungalow. Lighting the way with a lantern and silhouetted against the stars, they looked dignified and romantic, an older couple, almost identical in height.

Tess drummed her fingers on the table, craving a cigarette. Then she noticed Isabel watching her. "Sorry," she said. "I'm a reformed—*reforming*—smoker. A stupid habit, I know. Trying to get over it."

"I wish I could help you with that."

"You are, just by sitting there and looking all calm and healthy."

"I look calm and healthy?" Isabel offered a glimmering smile.

"Everybody around here does. It's freaky."

That elicited a brief laugh. Then Isabel's expression turned thoughtful. "So, what do you suppose happened?" she asked. "I mean, I can't say I'm sorry we found each other, but why do you think it took so long?"

"Good question. I've been trying to get hold of my mother to ask her just that," said Tess. "I assume you've done the same?"

"I never knew my mother. She died in childbirth."

"Oh." Tess hadn't been expecting that. "I'm really sorry. No wonder you're so close to your grandfather."

"He and Bubbie raised me."

"Here's what I don't get. How long has Magnus known about me, and why didn't he tell anyone?"

Isabel's gaze shifted to the votive candle on the table. "That's something to ask him after he gets better."

Assuming he does get better, thought Tess. "Would it be all right if I visited him in the hospital?"

"Absolutely," said Isabel. "You don't need my permission. I mean, I want you to. I thought maybe, I don't know, it might help him to get better, having you here. Just so you know, I have some questions for him, too." She looked exhausted, wrung out as she rose from the table, leaned forward and blew out the candle. "It's getting late. I'll show you to your room."

They went into the house together, Charlie at Isabel's heels. The kitchen was spotless, the sink and surfaces gleaming in the dim light. A hallway led to a big family room with a high cathedral ceiling crisscrossed by ancient-looking beams and a massive fireplace. In addition to the mission-style furnishings, there was an upright piano and a wall of bookcases. Tess could easily picture family gatherings here, candlelit holidays and parties. Yet she pictured it from a distance, as though studying a foreign culture.

"It's nice to have you here," Isabel said.

Tess couldn't take it anymore. She stopped at the bottom of the stairs. "Seriously? You can be honest with me, Isabel. We're strangers, and I wouldn't blame you one bit if you completely resented me."

"I don't resent you." She looked mystified. "And for the time being, I'm not going to think about what happens if he doesn't make it." Her expression was studiously earnest.

"No one would blame you for feeling that way, either. Least

of all, me." Tess felt drained and confused. "Let's talk again in the morning."

"All right. I meant what I said, though, when I said I'm glad you're here. This place feels much too big for just me." She led the way up the stairs. "Sorry, I don't mean to complain."

"That didn't sound like complaining to me. I could give you lessons in complaining." Tess looked up and down the hallway, orienting herself the way she did when checking into a hotel. Like the rest of the house, there was an old-fashioned feel to the upstairs, with its hall tables, the sconces on the walls.

"Charlie and I will give you the full tour tomorrow. He's new here, too." Isabel ruffled the dog's ears. "A gift from Dominic."

"He gave you a dog?"

"Charlie needed a home." She stepped into a room at the end of the hall and stood aside, motioning for Tess to go ahead. "Is this okay with you?"

Tess looked around the spotless room, with its high tester bed and huge armoire, tall windows, adjacent bathroom with lavender-scented soaps and lotions. "Are you kidding? This is lovely." This was the most comfortable, most peaceful place in the world. What she didn't say was that this room felt like a place where she could drown.

"Okay, then." Isabel stood uncertainly in the doorway.

"Okay."

"Let me know if you need anything."

"I will, thanks." Tess studied Isabel in the soft light from the table lamp, this stranger who was her sister. "I don't mean to stare," she said, but she continued staring.

"No problem. I keep catching myself doing the same thing. Sometimes when I look at you, I see Grandfather, but that might be my imagination."

"Hmm. That would be a first for me, being compared to an old man."

"I didn't mean—"

"I know, I know."

"You're really pretty, Tess."

No, she wasn't. Tess knew that. She wasn't vile, but she wasn't truly pretty, either. Men tended to think she was sexy, but that was different from pretty. "Thanks. I was thinking the same about you. Only I was thinking you're really not pretty, the way Sophia Loren or Isabella Rossellini aren't pretty. You're gorgeous. Like fashion magazine gorgeous."

Isabel's gaze dropped. "That's really nice of you to say."

Tess felt wildly out of place in this too-cozy, too-quiet, too-neat room. And Isabel—what in the world was she thinking? "Listen, I didn't come here because I expect anything. I mean, this is your world, not mine, and just because Magnus put me in his will doesn't mean I'm entitled to anything." Tess wanted to be very clear on this. "I'm here because...because this is all so new, and even though what happened to your grandfather is awful, it's kind of amazing to meet you."

Isabel edged toward the door, a bashful smile hovering on her lips. "Have a good night, Tess."

The linens were lightly scented with dried lavender, and a cool breeze drifted in through the window, but Tess felt discomfited by the pervasive quiet. She was accustomed to the night sounds of traffic and foghorns, streetcars, the occasional crescendo of a siren. Here, the peeping of a single cricket drove her nuts. She paced the room. She tried a piece of the nicotine gum Dominic Rossi had given her, wincing at the bitter taste, barely disguised by the cinnamon flavoring. Then she thought about Dominic some more, debating with herself about whom he more closely resembled, a movie idol or a star athlete. With glasses. And a well-cut suit.

And two kids and an ex-wife he seemed loath to talk about.

She decided to take a shower and was surprised to discover there was no shower, but a claw-footed tub. A bath, then. When was the last time she'd had a bath? Who had time?

What the heck, she thought, and turned on the tap. Spying some bubble bath, she poured in a little. More lavender, she observed, closing her eyes briefly as the scent wafted from the froth. While the tub filled, she hung her belongings in the armoire, wondering how long it would take to get this business sorted out.

As she sank down into the scented bubbles, she mulled over the conversation with Isabel. It was hard to get a read on her half sister, especially now, when Isabel was dealing with her grandfather's terrible accident. Isabel was clearly no fool. No doubt she had assumed she was the sole heir to this vast and beautiful property. Despite her protests, it could not have been a welcome surprise to discover that she would one day be sharing the legacy with a stranger.

Tess wondered why Isabel didn't seem more upset by that.

SEVEN

"We're broke," Isabel said the next morning. She set a platter of butter croissants in front of Tess. The two of them were seated on a flagstone patio adjacent to the kitchen, where an iron and tile table was set up, shaded by a broad umbrella.

Tess had woken up with her heart racing, her head aching, having tossed and turned most of the night. She'd done the breathing exercises the doctor had given her, but those only reminded her of Dominic Rossi, and the thought of him was hardly a calming one. And now this. She set down her coffee cup. "By 'we' you mean…"

"All of this." Isabel made a sweeping gesture to encompass the estate. "The commercial accounts and Grandfather's personal funds have run out."

"And this is something…you weren't aware of?" Tess searched this stranger's face but could detect no sign of deception. Which either meant Isabel was being straight with her, or Tess didn't know her well enough to detect deception. Tess did know herself, however. When Dominic had explained that she would one day inherit half of everything from a guy she'd never known, she already knew on some level that it was too good to be true. To escape the hurt of loss while at the same time being given an inheritance—that just didn't happen. This was something she had discovered in her line of work as well, recovering people's treasures. It was just as she'd initially thought—there was always a catch. Strangers didn't simply materialize out of nowhere, offering a fortune.

"He's always been really private about his accounts," Isabel explained, her voice subdued but completely guileless, "so I didn't find out until yesterday morning, when the bank called about some checks I'd written from Grandfather's account. I did more research last night when I couldn't sleep. His personal account and all the business accounts are virtually empty."

"I'm sorry to hear that," said Tess. "I've been broke before, and it's no fun."

"Have something to eat," said Isabel. "Please."

Tess bit into a croissant, which was still warm from the oven. "You made these?"

Isabel nodded. "I do love baking."

"It's so good, it tastes like something illegal."

Isabel laughed softly. "It's just a matter of training." Then her smile faded, and she pushed her plate away.

Tess tried to imagine what her sister was feeling, discovering that her beloved way of life was in peril. It was hard to reconcile the look of this place with the concept of being broke. The estate looked vast and prosperous—on the surface, at least. Bella Vista was stunningly lovely, the orchards well tended and clearly productive. If there was a place in the world that was closer to heaven, she wasn't aware of it. Bella

Vista—Beautiful View. A panorama view of the orchards, herb and flower fields radiated outward from the patio. The scents of ripe apples, lavender and roses rode the breeze, mingling with the mind-melting aroma of Isabel's fresh-baked croissants. But even with her mind melting over the glistening, flaky rolls, Tess couldn't dismiss the stark reality of what her sister had just told her.

Nor could she dismiss the fact that heaven was outside her comfort zone.

"What did you do when you were broke?" asked Isabel. "If you don't mind my asking, that is."

"I don't mind. I got busy working and dug my way out. Juggled a deck of credit cards. I even used those crazy blank checks they send you to pay bills."

"Didn't that put you even deeper in debt?"

"It's the American way. It was a Band-Aid, of course. The truth is, I'm loaded with student debt. I've got a good job that pays the bills, but just barely. Ultimately, I need to make a plan for the long term."

"This must be a real letdown for you," said Isabel, "to come into this situation...."

"I'm not exactly suffering here." Tess tried some of the jam. "This isn't better than *any* sex, but it's better than most."

Isabel flushed. "I just feel overwhelmed by everything."

"Judging by what I saw yesterday, you seem to have a huge network of friends," Tess observed. As the sun's warmth filled the morning, she noticed Oscar Navarro ambling along with his peculiar gait. Other people had appeared in the fields and orchards, getting down to the day's work. "I'm sure you'll get a lot of advice and support from them about your...situation." Although Tess was in no position to suggest it, she assumed Isabel had options. It wasn't just the beauty of the surroundings that made Bella Vista seem so special. It was the idea that this was a land that sustained people, the residents and workers and their families took care of the land and, in turn, were nourished by the orchards and gardens.

An overly romantic notion, she realized that. But this place had value, and if there was a cash flow problem, there had to be a way to fix it.

"What's that part of the building over there?" she asked Isabel, getting up from the table and crossing to the main courtyard, the one with the fountain in the center. The house formed three sides of a square around the stone-paved center, but she'd only seen one of the three wings.

"It's vacant," Isabel said. "At one time, there were quarters for workers and servants, room after room. And in the other wing there are mostly bedrooms and storage rooms. Bubbie once told me she and Grandfather wanted a big family, but they couldn't have kids."

"They had Erik," Tess pointed out.

"More kids, I guess she meant. For as long as I can remember, both wings have been empty, or just used to store odds and ends." Isabel rubbed her temples. "I'm sure Grandfather didn't mean to leave things like this. Even though he's old, he's always been in excellent health. But…accidents happen." She looked so fragile and exhausted by worry as she spoke.

Tess had an urge to reach out to her, but she had no comfort to offer. "Well," she said. "Broke is a relative term. Look at this place. You can take out a loan to help your cash flow, and find a way out of it. Dominic Rossi will help you with that. Isn't that what bankers are supposed to do?"

"One would think."

"So tell me about Dominic," Tess said, keeping her voice completely casual. "How did he end up being your grandfather's executor?"

Isabel sighed. There was a world of meaning in that sigh,

but Tess didn't know her well enough to make sense of it. "Ah, Dominic," she said. Her gaze shifted to the distant view, where the mist rose from the hills and softened the line of the horizon. "Grandfather has always been his mentor. He's always been so wonderful in that way. He used to say he'd been helped so much by others in his life. He wanted to do the same. I hope you get a chance to know him."

All he had to do was find me, thought Tess. And he hadn't. But Dominic Rossi had.

"So...the banker guy," she prompted, hoping she sounded merely interested, not obsessed.

"Dominic and Grandfather did business together, but they're more than business associates. I suppose that's why Grandfather designated him executor."

There was so much more Tess wanted to know, but she couldn't figure out how to ask. She wanted to know about Dominic's world, and why his marriage had fallen apart, and if he had a happy life these days. She wanted to know what his laughter sounded like, and what he looked like when he wasn't wearing a three-piece suit.

She wanted to know if he had a girlfriend. No, she didn't. Yes, she did. But she'd never admit it.

"A few months ago, Dominic's bank failed," Isabel said. "It was awful. It happened in a matter of hours. The building was surrounded by police, and federal agents seized all the re-cords. In a single day, a bigger bank came in and took over. A bloodless coup, I suppose. But after that, Grandfather seemed stressed out. He never talked about it. I could just tell." She sighed yet again. "After seeing the bank statements, I guess I understand why."

"I really would like to see him. Is it a long way to the hos-pital?"

"No, it's the county medical center, ten miles from here."

"Then we should go."

Isabel hurried to the side patio and started clearing the table. Tess followed her lead, reaching for a plate. Her hand brushed Isabel's. To Tess's surprise, Isabel's fingers were like icicles, and she was trembling violently.

"Are you all right?" she asked.

"I don't think I'm up to a hospital visit," Isabel said. "I might be coming down with something, so I'd better stay away. One of the biggest risks to Grandfather is infection. We've got to be really careful about that."

She didn't look as if she were coming down with anything, Tess observed, confused by Isabel's reluctance. Maybe it was just too hard for her to see her beloved grandfather in a coma. Tess wondered if there might be something more; this did seem like a family of secrets. "I'd still like to go," she said.

"Of course." She brightened a little. "I know exactly who'll go with you."

That evening, Tess borrowed Magnus's Volkswagen, which ran on biodiesel and was cluttered, a typical old man's car, as if he'd just left it moments before. Which of course, he had, never anticipating that trip to the orchard on the morning of his accident. The visors were stuffed with old receipts, a half-eaten Clark bar, the drink holder rattling with spare change and a tarnished St. Christopher medal. She drove along the winding byways that traversed the hills, crossing Angel Creek and taking a right at the mailbox marked *Rossi*. At the corner, she sat in the car for a minute, gathering her thoughts and trying to talk herself out of seeing him. He might think she was stalking him. She'd phoned him from the landline at Bella Vista, getting his voice mail. He hadn't called back, but Isabel had assured her it was fine. In Archangel, people dropped in on each other all the time.

That was certainly the case at Bella Vista. The day had sped by quickly, with people coming and going—neighbors and workers alike. Tess had also used the landline to phone the office, only to be told that there was business to be done, and she was holding up a number of transactions, not to mention the meeting with Mr. Sheffield. But this was important. For once in her life, she was willing to let business wait.

Tess had never been hesitant or apprehensive about guys, and she was not about to start now. Besides, this was not about seeing a guy. Isabel said he could take her to see her grandfather. Yes, she could go on her own, but it didn't seem right to simply show up, a stranger....

Taking a deep breath, she got out of the car. He lived in a vintage bungalow with a big fenced yard twined with climbing roses losing their petals. The place was surrounded by vineyards and orchards on all sides, and it didn't look like the kind of place where a man like Dominic would live, but she reminded herself that she barely knew him.

The front porch of the bungalow had a preternaturally neat shelf filled with soccer balls, and three bicycles arranged by size, the smallest one painted a sparkly pink, with streamers coming out of the handlebars. Dusty shoes were neatly lined up by the door, including some little Velcro sneakers featuring a cartoon character Tess didn't recognize, and bigger shoes with soccer spikes.

She racked her brain, trying to remember the kids' names. Trixie? Anthony? She inspected the pink two-wheeler and discovered a small fake license plate that read *Trini*.

That's right. Trini and... Antonio. Yes, that was it. Cute names.

An ominous flutter started in her chest, the now-too-familiar prelude to panic. Ignoring it, she stepped up to the door and rang the bell.

"I'll get it!" piped a girl's voice. "Maybe it's the pizza guy."

The door opened, and a little dark-haired girl peered up at Tess. "Oh."

Tess suppressed a smile at the disappointment in her little face. "Sorry. Not the pizza guy. I'm Tess. Are you expecting the pizza guy?"

"Yep. Dad said. But you can come in."

"You can't let a stranger in," said Antonio, who shared his sister's dark hair and big gorgeous eyes.

"She's not a stranger. She's Tess."

"Oh, the one Dad was talking about." The little boy grinned. "Yep, come on in."

"Thanks." He was talking about her? What had he said? She resisted asking as she stepped through the door. Unsurprisingly, Dominic Rossi's yard and home were as uncluttered as his car had been. How was it possible to have two kids and two dogs and a clean house? Maybe he really did have OCD. "What kind of pizza did you order?"

"I got to pick," Antonio said, guiding a soccer ball with expert moves of his feet. "I ordered pepperoni and melanzano." A lithe little shorthaired dog scampered around, trying to capture the ball.

Suddenly Tess felt like an intruder. Yes, she should have talked to Dominic first. "Sounds delicious," she said. "And you pronounced melanzano perfectly, by the way."

Trini crooked a finger, indicating that Tess should come closer. "He doesn't know melanzano is eggplant," she whispered. "If he did, he would think it's gross."

"We know lots of words in Italian," Antonio said, pausing to stick out his tongue at his sister. "Our dad speaks Italian because his parents come from Italy."

"Nonna and Papi," Trini explained. "They live in Petaluma."

"Well, it's very cool that you know some Italian," Tess said.

Technically, Tess didn't like children. They were noisy and in-attentive. Unpredictable and uncontrollable. These two were... okay, so far. They didn't seem too noisy at the moment, and they definitely were not inattentive.

Dominic spoke Italian, she thought. Of course he did. As if he needed one more thing to make him more appealing.

"Do you speak something?" Trini asked.

"I speak with an Irish brogue," Tess said in her thickest Dubliner accent, "on account of me grandmum was Irish."

Antonio stopped kicking the ball, and both kids stared at her as if she had spoken in Elvish.

"I understand you," Trini said, her voice a whisper of wonder.

"Then maybe you speak Irish, too, and you just didn't know."

"We don't speak Irish," Antonio said. "We understand it, though. We've watched *Darby O'Gill and the Little People,* over and over."

"So did I, when I was a little person myself. I watched it so many times, my mom called it *Darby Overkill and the Little People.*"

"Are you here to see our dad?" Trini asked.

"Yes, I am."

"He's in the shower. He got really dirty and sweaty work-ing in the yard."

The thought of Dominic, all dirty and sweaty in yard-work clothes, was impossibly sexy. "Oh...then maybe I'll come back another time." Tess started for the door.

"No, it's okay. He'll be really quick. He's always quick in the shower."

"It's a guy thing," said Antonio. "We're super quick."

"He sings 'Rubber Ducky,'" Trini said. "He'd be mad that I told you that."

The little dog gave up its tussle with the soccer ball and started sniffing around her feet. Technically, she didn't like dogs, either, but this one seemed as polite as the children, and its smooth, short hair felt like silk under her hand. "Tell me about your dog."

"That's Iggy," said Antonio. "He is an Italian greyhound."

"Which is why he's called Iggy," Trini explained. "After his initials—I.G."

"That's clever. I bet he can run fast."

"Like the wind," Antonio said.

"The wind at forty miles per hour," Trini said. "Our dad rescued him."

Of course he did, Tess thought. He was a handsome, Italian-speaking hunk with two adorable kids and a nice dog he just happened to have rescued. What was it Isabel had said? *He rescues people.* Dogs, too, apparently.

"From a puppy mill," Antonio said.

Trini went and opened a screen door to the backyard. In bounded another dog whose breeding was so uncertain, Tess wasn't even sure it was a dog.

"That's the Dude," Antonio explained. "Dad rescued him, too."

"Not from a puppy mill," Trini said.

Using the light, quick steps of an expert soccer player, Antonio rounded up the dogs and corralled them into a corner of the room. "Look, I'm the dog strangler," he said.

"What?" Tess lifted her eyebrows.

"Wrangler," Trini said. "He means dog wrangler."

"Yeah, that." Antonio regarded Iggy and the Dude with pride as they sat at attention.

"Is the pizza here?" Dominic asked, coming down the stairs. "I thought I heard— Oh. Hey, Tess."

He wasn't wearing a shirt. He wore only faded jeans that looked as though they'd been hastily pulled on after the shower. He had bare feet and damp hair curling into whorls, a chest and abs, shoulders and biceps that made her want to stare at him all day long, the way an art lover might stare at a masterpiece. Who knew so much male beauty could be concealed beneath that three-piece banker's suit? Suddenly she didn't give a hoot whether or not he had OCD. She almost didn't care whether or not he had a pulse.

She realized after a moment that it was her turn to speak. But her mouth had gone totally dry, and her normally high-functioning brain was filled with nothing but nonverbal lust.

"Uh…hey," she managed to get out, probably sounding like a sex-deprived cavewoman. "Um, I don't mean to intrude—"

"You're not intruding," he said. He must have felt the intensity of her stare, because he grabbed a gray hooded sweatshirt from the hall closet and took his sweet time pulling it on over his head.

Leave it off, she wanted to say, and probably would have if not for the presence of his two extremely attentive children.

The sound of a car door slamming sent both kids and dogs to the front door. "Pizza!" they yelled, as if they'd spotted Halley's Comet. "It's pizza time!"

The dogs barked in a frenzy.

"Money is on the hall table," Dominic said. "The tip is included."

While the kids swarmed the pizza guy, Tess edged away. "I can see this is a bad time. Sorry. I'll call you tomorrow," she said.

"No," he said. "What's on your mind, Tess?"

"That I'm an idiot for showing up without checking with you first."

He grinned. "Besides that."

"I wanted to visit Magnus in the hospital. Isabel said you went to see him most evenings, so I thought I'd ask to join you."

"I do go see him most evenings, but tonight I've got the kids."

"Which is why I'm an idiot for not checking with you."

"No problem," he said. "Stay for dinner. The pizza smells amazing."

"I don't mean to intrude."

"But we want you to," Trini said matter-of-factly, balancing a large pizza box on top of her head as she led a parade of her brother and two dogs into the dining room. "You're gonna love the melanzano. It doesn't even taste like you-know-what."

"I should go," Tess pointed out.

"We want you to stay," said Antonio, glaring at his sister as she elbowed him. "You can have a glass of wine, too. My dad makes it himself."

"I'll go grab a bottle." Dominic went out the back door.

Tess could tell they weren't going to take no for an answer. "Okay," she said. "I surrender."

Inwardly she braced herself for the wine tasting. In all her globe-trotting, she'd sampled some of the best wines, but her experience with homemade wine was limited. That didn't matter. If Dominic's wine gave her botulism, it would be no more than she deserved for having an inappropriate crush on him.

"Are you my dad's girlfriend?" asked Trini, grabbing a small stack of plates.

"What? *No.*"

"Didn't think so."

"Why not?"

"He's weird about us meeting his girlfriends."

"He doesn't want us getting attached," Antonio added.

"He's afraid we'll get our feelings hurt if the girlfriend doesn't stay," said Trini.

"They never stay," Antonio said.

"That's because he never has girlfriends, moron," Trini

said. "*Almost* never. And anyway, he and my mom are getting back together."

Oh, really? Tess made no comment. The girl spoke with casual confidence. Wishful thinking, or something more?

"They are not," Antonio said loudly.

"Are too, *moron*," Trini shot back. "Mom said."

"Dad," Antonio called out.

"Yeah, Bud?" Dominic came into the room with a bottle of wine and a pair of glasses.

"She called me a moron. Twice."

"Apologize for that, Trini-Meanie-Minie-Moe."

"Sorry I called you a moron," Trini said, then muttered under her breath, "moron."

"Hey," Dominic said.

"Melanzano!" Antonio flipped open the pizza box. "Can I start?"

"Go for it." Dominic poured them each a glass of milk and used a spatula to serve the pizza.

"Looks heavenly," Tess said.

"Mario is from Naples," Dominic said. "He built a replica of his family's wood fire pizza oven. You'll have to try it someday, before Isabel stuffs you full of health food."

He opened the wine with an expert twist of a corkscrew. The bottle had a plain-looking label that said *Rossi,* followed by some letters and numbers, and the year 2004. Oh, boy, she thought. Not only was he serving homemade wine, but it was bound to be spoiled. She would try to be polite.

He poured the wine into a lovely goblet—another surprise. Most single guys drew their wine from a box and poured it into recycled jelly jars. These were fine crystal, as delicate as soap bubbles.

"Was 2004 a good year?" she asked, eyeing the wine, a deep claret color in the glasses.

"One of the best."

"You're giving me a vintage wine?" He'd made the wine. This facet of Dominic intrigued her; creative people always did. Tess was in the business of finding things, not making them.

"It's not doing any good lying around in the bottle. Cheers." They touched the rims of their glasses together.

She brought the paper-thin rim of the glass to her lips and took a sip, letting a tiny amount pool in the cup of her tongue. Then she shut her eyes and swallowed, breathing in the after-glow of the wine's complex flavors and aromas.

"Well?" he asked.

Startled by pleasure, she opened her eyes. "I was bracing myself for rotgut."

"Rotgut? I'm wounded."

"I don't even have words for how good it is."

"It'll be even better after it breathes for a little while."

She turned the bottle toward her and read the other side of the label. "Angel Creek. This is what Isabel served last night. Wait a minute, you're a grower *and* a vintner?"

"It's a sideline."

"He's gonna get famous for his wines," Trini said importantly.

"What's rotgut?" Antonio asked.

"Just an expression," Tess said. "It means cheap wine that's not very good. It doesn't actually rot your gut."

"Not right away," Dominic said, expertly folding a piece of pizza over and savoring a large bite.

"How did you get so good at making wine?" she asked.

"He can't cook, but he can make wine." Antonio took a big bite of pizza.

"Hey," said Dominic.

"It's true, Dad. You *can't* cook."

"So sue me."

"Lots of people can't cook," Tess pointed out. "Very few can make delicious wine."

"It's his *passione*," Trini said with dramatic emphasis. "That's Italian for *passion*."

"And yet you became a banker," Tess remarked, savoring another sip. "Is that your passion, too?"

"That's my job."

"He's really good at it. He's got awards from the bank," Antonio said. "He's got a Navy Air Medal."

"That was from military service, moron," said Trini.

"Hey," Dominic said in a warning tone.

The pizza was incredible, just as the kids had promised. Paired with the wine, it was heaven. She felt an unexpected sense of comfort here, being with Dominic and his kids. It was…easy. Pleasant, in a way she'd never before experienced. "This is some wine," she told him.

"Thanks."

"You served in the navy," she prompted.

He reached over and refilled her glass. "That's right."

"How did you earn a medal?" she asked.

"His plane had a malfunction, and he had to do an emergency landing," Trini said. There was a tremor in her voice. "He almost got killed."

"I'm here now," he said, clearly not wanting to go into it. Tess didn't press for details, not in front of the kids. Although she'd grown up without a father, she remembered the feeling of worrying about a parent. Each time her mom took off and forgot to call, or got caught in a third-world country, Tess used to worry, standing at the window in Nana's Dublin flat, feeling her stomach twist into knots.

After dinner, the cleanup was minimal—definitely a side benefit of not cooking. As he loaded plates into the dishwasher, Dominic turned to Tess. "Are you up for ten minutes of soccer?"

"Eff, yeah!" Antonio said, punching the air.

"Easy, Bud," Dominic said.

"Sure," said Tess, following the three of them, along with the two dogs, out to the backyard. She was wearing ballet flats, hardly appropriate for soccer, but she knew she could last ten minutes. There was a goal set up at one end, aglow in the light from the porch. It wasn't a game but a free-for-all, including the dogs. Dominic's moves were executed with the smoothness of a professional. The kids were nearly as good, and Tess got into the competitive spirit of things, remembering how much she'd loved the game as a girl. When she drilled a goal home, the ball whizzing past Dominic, she danced a little jig of victory.

"Awesome," Trini declared. "Schooled you, Dad."

"Yeah," said Tess. "Schooled you."

The sweetness of victory didn't last, though. He grabbed her next shot out of midair, and kept her from making another goal. Mercifully, no one kept score. After a while, Dominic declared the game at an end. "Time to hit the showers," he said. "You're up past your bedtime, both of you."

"Aww," Antonio began.

"Hit the showers, and call me when you're ready for bed," Dominic said.

"Can Tess come and tell us good-night?" Antonio asked.

"If she wants." He turned to Tess, one eyebrow lifted above his horn-rims.

"I'd be honored." She didn't consider herself good with kids, but how hard could it be, telling them good-night?

Harder than she thought. They stomped up the stairs and took their time getting cleaned up and ready for bed. There was some kind of toothpaste war in the bathroom, followed by a rambunctious chase involving Iggy and the Dude. Finally they were in bed, and she was summoned.

They shared a room with bunk beds. The space was decorated with startlingly good taste, with sage-colored walls and modern bedding, plenty of cubbies for toys and books. "Your room is great," she told the kids.

"Bootsie was a room decorator," Trini explained. "It didn't work out for them, but she has mad skills."

"I can see that." Tess already knew she was going to give far too much thought to Bootsie, and even more to the idea that Trini believed her parents would reconcile.

The kids were finally snuggled in their bunk beds. Each was equipped with a reading lamp and an assortment of plush toys. Trini appeared to favor unicorns while Antonio went for jungle animals.

"We get to read for half an hour before lights out," Antonio said. He hugged a battered novel to his chest.

"Good night, you pair of rascals." Dominic gave each one a kiss on the forehead and tucked them in. Watching him, Tess felt her heart melt a little, moved by the simplicity of his affection and by the love that shone from his face.

"Good night, guys," she said softly. "Thanks for letting me see your room."

She and Dominic stepped outside. "No fighting, no biting," he said, leaving the door slightly ajar. "Say when."

"When!" yelled Antonio. "That's far enough."

Downstairs, he filled their glasses with the last of the wine. A faint air of exhaustion hung around him, though he was smiling. "So there you have it. Welcome to my life."

She looked around the living room, scanning the plain furniture, the nearly bare walls. The place was strangely devoid of personal objects.

"I'm not much for decorating," he said. "Bootsie and I

parted ways before she helped me with the rest of the house. My ex took all the knickknacks and tchotchkes."

She waited for him to say more, but he fell silent. Most people liked surrounding themselves with reminders of who they were—history, family, continuity.

"I'm sorry again about intruding," she said.

"You didn't. It's too bad we couldn't go see Magnus. Tell you what. I'll get you a schedule of visiting hours, and we'll work something out."

"I'd like that." She savored a bit more of the wine.

He was turning out to be a lot more interesting than he should be. She reminded herself that he was a stranger still. She wasn't supposed to think about how he'd looked with his shirt off, or how cute he was with his kids and dogs. She wasn't supposed to *like* him.

In spite of her misgivings, there was so much she wanted to know about this man, yet at the same time, she told herself she couldn't get involved. His "Welcome to my life" had been a stark reminder that they were worlds apart. She needed to conclude her business in Archangel and move on. Her job, her life in the city, was waiting for her. Yet she felt more and more pulled in, not just to her sister but to everyone at Bella Vista, and to this man with his lonely eyes and adorable kids.

"Thanks for the welcome," she said. "Honestly, I didn't come here looking to be entertained, but I have to say, the pizza was great, and this wine is amazing."

He held open the back door, inviting her out onto a railed porch. The stars were just coming out.

"Over here." He went down the porch steps and held open the back gate. Iggy raced after them, but the Dude stayed on the porch, sentinel-like, vigilant. "He refuses to leave the premises when the kids are home," Dominic explained.

"Did you train him to do that?"

"I didn't have to. He just started doing it. The vet says he's got Akita in him."

"Japanese guard dog."

"Yep. He's devoted to the kids."

"You have nice kids," she said.

"Thanks. I think so."

"I've spent too much time on airplanes with the sort of children who give all kids a bad name."

"You've been flying in the wrong birds, then."

"Yeah, about that. A navy pilot? Air medal? Sounds way more challenging than banking."

He hesitated. "Being a banker is the hardest thing I've ever done."

"You're kidding, right?"

"In the navy, I followed orders, I flew my missions. There was a plan for everything and it never varied."

"What kind of plane did you fly?"

"Jet, please. The EA-6B Prowler."

"Isn't that carrier-based?" She had dated a guy briefly who was in the navy, stationed on a San Francisco–based carrier. Eldon had been a walking encyclopedia of navy trivia, and after a few excruciating dates she had stopped seeing him.

"That's right."

"So landing a jet on an aircraft carrier is easier than banking?"

"Pretty much anything is easier than telling someone they don't get the home of their dreams, or that foreclosure proceedings are starting."

She winced, thinking of Isabel and what she'd discovered about Magnus's accounts. She wanted to talk to him more about it but didn't feel right without Isabel present. "Then why do you do it?"

"Stability for my family."

Iggy took off across the orchard, disappearing into the darkness.

"Is he going to be all right?" she asked.

"Yeah. I used to worry about coyotes, but Iggy's smart. And fast."

"What's that smell? It smells so good here."

"The orchard. This section is Magnus's favorite."

"That's Bella Vista land?"

"Yep. We share a property line." He led the way across the yard, which was bordered on one side by his vines and the other by a row of trees, heavy with apples. Reaching for a low branch, he picked a ripe one and handed it to her. "These are the Honeycrisps. Tastiest apples known to man."

She bit into the crisp flesh, and her mouth was flooded with fresh sweetness. "This might be the best apple I've ever tasted," she said. "It might be the best *anything* I've ever tasted." A cool wind swept through the rows of trees, causing the leaves to whisper. The moon rode high, brightening everything with a bluish glow. At moments like this, the city seemed so very far away, practically on a different planet.

"So tell me about the navy," she said. "Did you like it?"

"Loved it. But hated being away from the kids."

And your ex…? She wouldn't let herself ask. "Tell me about how you ended up with a medal. Trini said there was a malfunction…?"

He nodded. "They're too little to remember, and it's just as well. The incident happened during a Show of Force mission over some poppy fields where the bad guys like to hang out. Should have been routine, but there was a mishap during midair refueling. We had to make an emergency landing. We were on the ground and were ambushed."

He spoke matter-of-factly, and the danger and chaos were so hard to picture, here in this starlit field. But she imagined the terror must have been immense. If she knew him better, she would ask him about that. But she didn't know him; he was just giving her glimpses of his life, not letting her in. That was her impression, anyway. "What happened during the ambush?"

"We all survived. I got shot in the head. The kids don't know that part."

A chill slid over her skin. "Dominic…"

"I pulled through. Made an almost full recovery."

"Almost?" No wonder he'd seemed so familiar with hospitals. She studied him in the moonlight. He looked like a marble sculpture, the planes and angles of his face almost inhumanly perfect, yet the kindness and emotion in his eyes transformed him from a cold and unreachable statue into a man she could barely take her eyes from.

"I'm deaf in one ear," he said.

"That's terrible. I can't even begin to imagine what you went through."

"The worst part wasn't giving up a navy career, or losing my hearing. The worst part was knowing my kids had almost lost me. It was one of those wake-up calls life throws at you. Made me rethink everything. I came to the conclusion that I belong here, close to them."

"Stuck in a job you hate."

"I didn't say I hated it. I said it was hard. The schedule is predictable. I don't miss soccer games or scavenger hunts or dentist appointments or anything else they've got going on in their lives. That's huge. My marriage didn't survive the separations, but this is my chance to make sure my relationship with Trini and Antonio stays intact."

"You have lucky kids," Tess said. "My mom wasn't around much when I was growing up, and I missed her." She wondered, if her own father had survived, if he would have shown that kind of devotion.

Dominic caught her staring at him again, but for some reason, this didn't bother her, and she didn't look away.

"What?" he asked.

She watched his lips, and that made a flush rise to her cheeks. "You're a nice guy, Dominic. I like talking to you."

"You sound surprised."

"I am. A little."

"What, that I'm nice, or that you like talking to me? Miss Delaney, I think you need to get out more."

She laughed. "I stay really busy with work."

"If you're serious about following doctor's orders, you'll need to change that." He was standing so close to her, she caught the scent from his freshly showered body. He leaned toward her, and everything, breath and heartbeat, the wind through the trees, the clouds sailing across the moon—everything slowed down and the world narrowed to nothing but him.

Yes, she thought. Oh, yes. She wanted to touch him, wanted it in the worst way, with an intensity that startled her.

Snap out of it. She wasn't here for this. Taking a step back, she said, "I have to go."

"No, you don't," he said softly.

"You're right. I don't. But... I'm *going* to go."

He hesitated, and then he stepped back, too. "I'll take you to see Magnus tomorrow."

EIGHT

When he showed up at Bella Vista the next day, Dominic looked even better to Tess than he had the day before. She felt self-conscious about the moment that had passed between them the night before, and hoped he wouldn't bring it up. She also felt out of place in her jeans, half boots and black silk top. People around the estate wore work attire or casual clothes made of airy prints and hand-knit sweaters, sandals of braided hemp. Dominic seemed perfectly at ease as he greeted people on his way across the courtyard to the house. There was something about the way he carried himself—with confidence but no swagger—that captured her attention, made it hard to think about anything but him.

It was a silly crush. She didn't get crushes anymore, did she? Yet all the symptoms were there—the heat in her cheeks and the speeding up of her heart. Her fixation on his mouth and then his hands. The way she reacted, deep in her gut, to the timbre of his voice.

"How are you doing?" he asked Isabel. It was not a throw-away question; he really did seem to want to know, moving in close as though prepared to catch her if she fell.

Tess wondered how long these two had known each other.

Isabel glanced away, lowering her head as though embarrassed by the intensity of her grief. Dark tendrils of wavy hair coiled around the nape of her neck. "I keep having conversations with him in my head, questions I never got around to asking him. For some reason, we both acted as though we had all the time in the world."

Tess's heart gave a lurch. She used to feel the same way about Nana, when she was a girl. She never once imagined what life would be like without her. That was probably a good thing, though. Nana would never approve of being afraid of whatever was around the corner.

"Take it easy on yourself," she said to Isabel. "Are you sure you don't want to come with us to visit him?"

"Not today. But promise you'll call me if there's a change."

"Of course."

"You ready?" asked Dominic.

"Sure." As ready as she could ever be, under the circumstances. She followed him out to the driveway and got into his car. "I appreciate the ride."

"No problem."

Tess felt cautious around him, particularly after last night. She was so new here; she didn't know where the boundaries were. She was still the outsider, possibly the interloper. "Isabel should come, too," said Tess. "He's her grandfather. Her only remaining family."

"Only?"

"I don't count," Tess said. "We're strangers, don't you get

it? The one thing we have in common is a father who slept around." She checked her phone to see if her mother had tried to call or send a text. "What do I have to do to get a signal around here?"

"Paint yourself blue and slaughter a goat." He was so deadpan that she almost took him seriously.

"Very funny. I imagine I'll have better luck at the hospital. Getting a signal, I mean. In general, hospitals aren't such lucky places, are they?"

"When you need a hospital, it can seem like a pretty lucky place."

"I guess so. Mercy Heights was my first. When my grandmother passed away, she wasn't taken to a hospital at all. She died right in the middle of her shop."

"That's tough, Tess. What happened?"

"It was a blood clot that went straight to her brain. It was like being struck by lightning, or that's how it seemed to me at the time—just so sudden and arbitrary. At the funeral, her church friends kept saying what a blessing it was that she didn't suffer. I'm glad there wasn't any pain for her, but I've never been able to get my head around the idea that losing her was a blessing." She scowled down at the absent bars on her cell phone as a heavy jolt of remembered sadness hit her. "I was fifteen years old and I felt...as if the world changed color overnight."

"Must've been rough for you."

"Oh, it was." She almost never talked about Nana, but it felt good just now, with Dominic. "The worst moments were when, for a few seconds, I would forget she was gone. I'd rush out of school with some bit of news to tell her, and then it would hit me—she's not there anymore." She took in a deep, shuddering breath. "God, look at me. I'm a mess."

"I'm okay with messes."

His easy acceptance was both startling and gratifying. She was so used to people who shied away from emotion. "Are you—or were you—close to your grandparents?"

"Sure. Don't get to see them much, though. They're still in Italy," he said. "All four are still living."

"Now that's what I call a blessing."

"Agreed. Tell me more about your grandmother. You told me she had a shop...and you've kept her desk."

"Nana loved a sturdy cup of tea with sugar. She had a keen eye for quality and was a good businesswoman. And she was an incredibly patient, good person," she said, watching the scenery flow past in a stream of color, like walking through a gallery of Monet paintings. "I loved the shop in Dublin— the way it smelled, the way she changed the displays. When I was little, I had this idea that one day I'd create a place of my own, like Things Forgotten."

"Why haven't you?"

"Same reason you haven't become a full-time winemaker. Financing is a bitch. Besides, I've got a really good position with Sheffield House." As they passed through the town of Archangel, Tess was struck anew by its quaintness. Everything seemed to move so slowly here. Despite what the doctor had told her, she felt a flash of longing for the city—the coffee, the action, the hustle and bustle of deals being made.

Soon, she told herself. Once she did her duty and visited Magnus, she would be on her way. Sending a sideways glance at Dominic, she felt a flicker of regret. But she had no business getting to know this guy. He was here and she was there, and their paths weren't meant to cross.

"I liked hearing about your grandmother," he said easily, pulling into the parking lot.

"It was nice," she said before she could stop herself, "telling you about her." *Stop it,* she told herself. *Just stop.*

The automatic doors to the medical center swished open
with a mechanical sigh. The receptionist nodded with easy
familiarity at Dominic as he signed them in. Then he led her
down a hallway flanked by fire extinguishers, printed no-
tices and hand-washing stations. He'd told her that he visited
Magnus often; now she realized what a kindness that was.
She found herself wishing Magnus could somehow sense that.

There was a whiteboard beside the door designating Magnus a brain trauma patient. The attending physician was someone named G. Hattori. Tess stopped there, her palms suddenly
clammy.

"You want me to come in or wait outside?" asked Dominic.

"You do really well at hospitals," she remarked. "I mean
that as a compliment."

They both paused to use the hand sanitizer, then they
stepped into the room. Classical music drifted softly from a
radio on the windowsill. The TV was muted and set on the
Discovery Channel. The wheeled bed was angled toward the
window, which framed a view of a eucalyptus tree.

Tess approached the figure on the bed, her heart pounding.
He looked like...a stranger. Of course he did. A broken old
man, unmoving, hooked up to a network of tubes. His closed
eyelids were thin and bruised-looking. There was a healing
scab on his forehead, and his snow-white hair had recently
been combed. Ancient-looking scars marked his neck. He
didn't appear to be merely asleep. His arms lay stiffly at his
sides, and his legs were slightly bent as though frozen in place.

Tess stood still, a few feet from the bed. She honestly did
not know what she was feeling.

Troy, the nurse who had just come on duty, gave her the
details of the accident and subsequent coma. Tess also found
out that Isabel was her grandfather's designated representa-
tive. As such, she had yet to make a decision about the Do

Not Resuscitate order. Tess could sympathize. Who wanted to make *that* call?

Troy checked the screen of the laptop on its rolling cart. "There's been a change in the past twenty-four hours."

Tess's heart lurched. "Is that bad?"

"As a matter of fact, it's an improvement. The doctors want to take him off the ventilator."

Tess thought about the healing ceremony—the music, prayers and rituals. Could it be…? "So it's good, right?"

"He's out of immediate danger. We're focused on preventing infection and keeping him physically healthy. He gets a varied course of treatment, including physical therapy, sensory stimulation, and of course he's monitored constantly. There's brain activity, but so far no voluntary movement."

"And the prognosis…" *Please say he's going to make it.*

"We won't know the full extent of the neurological damage from his injuries until he emerges from the coma. Some patients fully or partially recover."

She looked from Troy to Dominic. "So, do we just…talk to him as if he can hear us?"

"Sure, go ahead." The nurse left them alone.

Edgy with anxiety, Tess felt a confusing mixture of hope, pity, anger and frustration. She touched his hand, studied the shape of his nails and the pattern of his veins through the thin papery skin. "I just found you," she said to Magnus. "I can't lose you now."

Shaken by an emotion she didn't understand, she felt the need to do something other than sit here. On a rolling table by the bed was a basket overflowing with cards and letters. "How about I read some cards," she said. "Hearing good thoughts from people can't hurt, right?"

The cards ranged from typical get-well wishes to silly jokes to handwritten notes. "You've got a lot of friends," she murmured. Someone had sent an eagle feather for courage, another contained a pouch of healing herbs. All expressed regard for Magnus. Near the bottom of the basket was a sentimental-looking card, handmade, adorned on the front with a sprig of dried lavender and a message that said Live This Day. The formal, spidery writing indicated the sender was elderly, carefully drawing the words "I'm sorry. Please get better." Tess stared at the signature. Something niggled at the back of her mind, then exploded into consciousness. "Annelise."

She recognized the message from the needlepoint on Miss Winther's kitchen wall. The card was from the woman with the lavaliere and the Tiffany set—Annelise Winther. What on earth was the woman doing, sending a card to Magnus Johansen?

Mystified, she searched her phone for the old lady's number and dialed. When Miss Winther picked up, Tess identified herself and said, "I'm sorry to bother you, but I'm in Archangel, up in Sonoma County. I came to visit a man named Magnus Johansen."

The silence was long and taut. "Is he all right?"

"He's... No. He's in a coma. Everyone is hoping for the best." She studied the pale, calm face, the wispy hair, the chest moving with the respirator. "I couldn't help but notice this card from you. So I assume you know him."

Another silence, this one shorter. "We're both survivors of the Nazi occupation of Denmark," said Miss Winther.

"I see. Do you know him well, then? I mean, were you acquainted in Denmark, or did you meet later?"

"I... No, I don't know him well." The woman sounded confused, or hesitant. "I never really did."

"But you know him." Tess felt confused, too. No way could this be a coincidence. "Miss Winther, I don't mean to pry—"

"Thank you. I appreciate that. I hope... Just, please. Give him my best."

PART FIVE

Plant a victory garden. Our food is fighting.
A garden will make your nations go further.
—National Garden Bureau poster, 1939–1945

··· • ···

BACKYARD GARDEN SALAD

In wartime, patriotic families cultivated "Victory Gardens" to promote self-sufficiency and help the war effort.

4 cups mixed greens

¼ cup fresh sprigs of dill

¼ cup fresh flat-leaf parsley leaves

4 large basil leaves, rolled up and thinly sliced crosswise

1 large lemon, halved

¼ cup fruity olive oil pinch of salt fresh ground black pepper to taste

1 cup toasted walnuts

¾ cup crumbled feta cheese

1 cup fresh edible flowers; choose from bachelor's buttons, borage, calendulas, carnations, herb flowers (basil, chives, rosemary, thyme), nasturtiums, violas, including pansies and Johnny-jump-ups, stock

Toss salad greens and herbs in a large bowl. Squeeze lemon juice (without the seeds) over the greens and season with olive oil, salt and pepper. Toss again. Add walnuts and feta and toss well. Divide salad and pansies among four serving plates and serve.

(Source: Adapted from California Bountiful)

NINE

Gyldne Prins Park, Copenhagen
1941

Annelise Winther stretched her feet all the way up to heaven. The wind rushed through her hair as she pumped her legs, pulled back on the chains of the swing and lifted her feet even higher. Against the blue sky, she almost couldn't tell how old and ill-fitting her scuffed brown shoes were. Mama said it was impossible to find new shoes in the city these days. She looked over at Mama on the swing next to her.

"Mama," said Annelise, "you're up in the sky like me!"

"I am," her mother said. "It's such a glorious day. Springtime is here at last. All the apple blossoms are out."

Mama looked so pretty on the swing, her face turned up to the sun. Her long yellow hair had escaped its pins, and now it floated like a banner on the breeze. So did the light pink dress she wore. Its sleeves fluttered like the wings of an angel.

Pink was Mama's favorite color because it matched her favorite piece of jewelry, a special necklace she almost always wore. The necklace had been a gift from Papa. He had brought it home from far-off St. Petersburg where he had been sent to do the King's Business. These days, Papa was gone a lot, working all hours at the hospital. Sometimes he came home very late at night when Annelise was supposed to be asleep, and his face was smudged with candle soot. When she asked how he got all sooty by working at the hospital's business office, he simply lifted her up into his arms and told her she asked too many questions. Then he tickled her until she screamed with laughter.

Mama turned to Annelise, and for no reason at all, the two of them smiled at one another. Annelise practically bubbled over with happiness. She smiled because she knew she had the prettiest, kindest mother in all of Copenhagen. In all the world.

"I'm touching heaven," she called out, leaning her head way back to view the world upside down. "Are you touching heaven, too?"

"Absolutely. We have to stop soon, though."

Annelise melted with disappointment. "Can't we stay just a little longer?" Then she bit her lip, trying to be a big girl and not complain. It was Mama's day off from volunteering at the hospital, and Annelise told herself to be grateful to have her for a whole day.

"You don't want to stop?" Mama asked. "Not even for a picnic lunch?"

"Hurrah! A picnic!" Annelise's disappointment popped like a rainbow-colored soap bubble. She dragged her feet to slow the swing, then jumped to the ground.

Mama had a way of making everything special, even an ordinary lunch. Due to something called Rationing, the bread was coarse and the cheese was made from curds, the way the farmers in the countryside served it.

"Your repast, Young Miss," Mama said, placing the bread and cheese on a cloth napkin in front of her with a flourish.

"Why, thank you, Madam." Annelise emulated her mother's formal tone, though she couldn't suppress a giggle.

"And we have ambrosia for dessert."

"Ambrosia!" Annelise had no idea what that was, but even the word tasted delicious in her mouth.

It turned out to be spiced apples sweetened with honey, which they shared from a jar. "I made it from the last of the fall apples," Mama said.

"Why were they the last?"

Mama's pretty face darkened, like a cloud drifting over the sun. "Now the soldiers take them all. They took the honey right from the hives, too."

Everything had changed since the German soldiers had come to Copenhagen, covering the city in a storm of leaflets dropped from their airplanes. To Annelise, it seemed they had always been here; she had even learned to understand their language. They were everywhere in their pressed shirts and shiny boots, all over the city, marching and bossing people about.

"Never mind that," Mama said suddenly. "Let's make sure this day is special."

"Why?" asked Annelise.

"Because every day should be special."

"Is that a new rule?" There were lots since the soldiers had come.

"Not a rule, but a reminder. We must live this day. We'll never get to live it again."

They basked in the sweet-scented breeze, and felt the sunshine warming their bare heads. Petals drifted from the gnarled apple and cherry trees, creating a pretty storm, like confetti.

They lay together in the grass, watching a beetle trundling through the blades, its clumsy movements reminiscent of the soldiers' giant transport trucks. Birdsong filled the air, horse buses clopped through the street, and somewhere along the city docks, a ship's whistle blew. When it was time to go home, they packed everything into the basket and walked together, their clasped hands swinging between them. Annelise loved these perfect days with her mother, when the air was warm and the tulips and daffodils were coming up.

At the end of their block, a canvas-sided truck was parked, blocking the roadway. "What are those soldiers doing?" Annelise asked.

"Hush." Mama's voice was sharp, and she gripped Annelise's hand very hard as she headed across the street, her heels thumping on the cut stone surface of the roadway. "It's nothing to do with us."

Annelise had to run to keep up. They were nearly home, approaching the black wrought iron gate in front of the house when two soldiers seemed to appear out of nowhere, blocking the walkway. "Frau Winther?" one of the soldiers said. "You must come with us now."

Mama dropped Annelise's hand and stepped in front of her. The sleeves of her dress fluttered, and she looked larger and somehow braver. Annelise was so proud of her pretty angel mother.

One of the men grabbed Mama, tearing the pretty spring dress. Annelise screamed and rushed forward. "Mama!" she yelled again and again. She kicked one of them in the shin, her scuffed shoe connecting with a shiny brown boot. A big hand swept downward and cuffed her on the ear, so hard that tears sprang to her eyes, and her ear stung and her head rang.

Mama tried to get away, but now two of them were holding her. They had hard eyes and fleshy lips twisted by meanness.

Annelise rushed forward again, but Mama shook her head very hard. "Annelise, get away. Run! Run and hide!"

"I want to stay with you," Annelise wailed.

The soldiers pulled her mother toward the truck with canvas sides.

"Get the girl, too," said one of the men.

"What for? She's harmless."

"Now, perhaps. But remember, nits make lice."

"Run!" Mama screamed again. "Annelise, do as you're told!"

A large, callused hand swiped out to snatch her. Annelise ducked to avoid it. And then she ran.

Boots drummed on the sidewalk. Sobbing, Annelise ran harder. There were more soldiers coming out of the house, swarming over the place and carrying things out.

Annelise kept going, though she couldn't see due to the tears in her eyes. She could hardly breathe past the sobs clogging her throat. Diving through a gap in a hedge and back into the park, she stumbled and fell, scraping her knees on the pathway and scuffing the heels of her hands into the gravel.

She picked herself up. More footsteps pounded on the pathway. She lurched forward, sped around the corner, ran some more. Help. She needed help. Wild fright muddled her thoughts.

"Help," she wheezed as she ran. "Please help."

A shadow fell over her. Strong hands gripped her arms. She fought with all she had, kicking and scratching, making sounds she didn't know she had inside her.

"Easy, easy, easy, little one," said a voice in Danish.

She stopped fighting long enough to look at her captor. He wore cheap civilian clothes, his reddish-blond hair like a halo around his head, sticking out from a flat cap of boiled wool. A thick red scar spread from his jaw down to his neck. He was really just a boy, with a bit of duck fuzz in place of a beard.

"You're the Winther girl?" the boy asked.

She didn't answer. He was a stranger. "Who are you?"

"A friend. Call me Magnus."

"They took my mama away. And they tried to catch me, but Mama told me to run for my life. Maybe my papa will come…" she said in a shaky voice.

"I'll take you somewhere safe."

She felt sick to her stomach, because in some small, horror-stricken corner of her mind, she understood that her father would not come. "The brownshirts took him, too."

The boy looked her over. Annelise read something in his silence. *I'm sorry.*

"You're going to have to stay quiet and trust me," he said. "It's scary, I know." He held out his hand.

She couldn't think. The day was still bright. A family of swans paddled by, three gray-fuzzed chicks behind a majestic white bird. Annelise didn't know what else to do, so she put her hand in the boy's and let him tow her along. This pale-haired, scar-faced stranger convinced her to come with him, even though she had no notion of what he might do to her. After seeing her beautiful angel mother dragged away by the brownshirts, she realized nothing worse could ever happen to her, today or ever. She told him about her grandmother up in Helsingør, and he said he'd take her there. Back when times were normal, Annelise and her parents took their motorcar or the local train or ferry up the coast to Grandma's. Magnus said it was safer to go by boat.

Before long, they came to the city docks. There, they faded into the shadows and waited. The boy kept hold of her hand. His skin was rough and scabby. After a while, he brought her down to an open dory, the kind Papa sometimes took her rowing in on Sunday afternoons.

"Put this on," said the boy, tossing her a canvas life vest. "Hurry, or—"

"Halt," barked a voice. "What do you think you're doing?" Two soldiers crowded in on them. Their uniforms were covered in badges and insignia, their belts shiny and bulging with holsters. Annelise cowered, remembering the men who had grabbed her mother.

"Taking my little sister boating this fine afternoon," the boy called Magnus declared. "Last I heard, there was no prohibition against taking a child boating." His tone was insolent but not quite defiant.

The taller soldier glared at them, first at the boy, then at Annelise. His eyes felt like daggers. Annelise fought the urge to run. She thought of her brave mother and stared right back.

"Off we go, then," said Magnus, grasping her under the armpits. In one powerful movement, he swung her up and over the gunwale of the boat. Just for a second, her feet were framed against the sky-blue background, as though stretching up to heaven.

PART SIX

··· • ···

TWEED KETTLE PIE

In wartime, nearly all foods were rationed. Families were encouraged to grow as much food as possible themselves, and to serve wild-caught fish at the height of freshness. Women believed creating nutritious meals was their munition of war.

2 pounds potatoes

salt

1/4 cup milk

4 tablespoons cream cheese

3 tablespoons unsalted butter

1/4 cup chives (minced fresh, or scallions)

6 tablespoons butter (divided)

4 tablespoons flour

2 cups milk

a few pinches salt

pinch ground nutmeg

pinch ground cloves

1/2 cup diced onion

2 cups mixed cooked vegetables: peas, carrots, cauliflower, whatever is in season

2 tablespoons chopped fresh parsley

4-8 ounces salmon filet, poached and flaked

1/2 cup grated cheddar cheese

Peel and dice the potatoes, and boil until tender. Combine with salt, ¼ cup milk, the cream cheese, 1 tablespoon butter and chives and mash or whip until smooth.

While potatoes are boiling, melt 4 tablespoons butter and combine with flour to make a roux. Slowly add the milk and stir on low until thickened. Season with salt, nutmeg and cloves.

Sauté the onion in the rest of the butter until soft. Add the rest of the vegetables, the parsley and salmon and combine well.

Pour the mixture into a wide baking dish and top with the white sauce. Spread the mashed potatoes over this and top with cheese. Bake at 350 degrees F until bubbly and brown on top. Let the casserole rest for about 15 minutes, and serve warm.

(Source: Traditional; of Scottish origin)

TEN

"Have you ever heard of a woman named Annelise Winther?" Tess asked Dominic as they left the hospital together.

"Doesn't ring a bell. Should it?"

"There was a card from her to Magnus in the room." She flushed a little. "It felt strange, sitting there with nothing to say, so I read the get-well cards aloud to him. One of them was from Miss Winther—a recent client of mine in San Francisco. It can't be a coincidence that they know each other."

"Maybe your sister can tell you more."

While she still had a signal, Tess phoned the office. Jude got on the line. "Where the hell are you?"

"I'm doing much better, thank you for asking," she said.

"Then why aren't you at work?"

"I had to… Something came up." She wasn't sure how much she wanted to share with him at this point. "A family matter."

He snorted. "Since when do you have a family?"

"Nice, Jude."

"I'm just saying. If you don't get back on the job, you won't have a job. Jesus, you went from a meeting with Dane Sheffield to playing Rebecca of Sunnybrook Farm."

"I never take time off," she protested. "A couple of days aren't going to matter. Brooks said Mr. Sheffield is going to reschedule our meeting. I'll come back to the city for that."

"You need to come back to the city for *good*. You know as well as I do, it's either-or. Assuming you see a future here. Look, I have to go. I'm getting another call...."

"Jude, hang on—"

"Get back on the job, Tess. I'm telling you this as a friend." He rang off before she could reply.

She glared at her phone, then stuffed it in her bag.

"Problems?" asked Dominic.

"My work. I've never gone AWOL before."

"You never had a trip to the emergency room before," he pointed out.

"This business...it's fast-paced. There are deadlines. Upcoming auctions. If things get away from me, it can screw everything up."

"I see. Didn't know antiquities was a life-or-death business."

"It is to some." She was quiet the rest of the way home. Back at Bella Vista, she thanked Dominic for the lift. "So I guess... I'll be heading back to the city," she said. "I mean, there's nothing more for me to do here, right?" Jude was right; she should get back on the job. Work was normal. She needed to feel normal.

"Up to you."

Tess couldn't figure out why she felt guilty about leaving. But honestly, she didn't know what she was supposed to do next. "Isabel is surrounded by friends," she said. "She really doesn't need me." She paused and looked at Dominic. "No comment?"

"I figure you're just thinking aloud."

"Well, since you seem to know everyone around here, I thought you might have an opinion."

"Everybody has an opinion. The smart ones keep it to themselves."

"Ha, ha." As they headed for the front entry, she inhaled the heavy sweetness of the apple harvest. Everything here seemed so abundant and ripe for renewal that she couldn't get her head around the idea that Magnus was flat broke.

"Oh, good, you're back," Isabel said, coming out to meet them at the door. She looked lovely but harried in a gauzy paisley skirt and peasant blouse. "How's Grandfather?"

"The nurse said they might be taking him off the ventilator," Tess reported.

Isabel's eyes brightened. "That's good, right? Please tell me it's good."

"It's a positive sign. Dr. Hattori said you can call him for more details."

"Speaking of details…" Isabel's gaze shifted nervously. "Dominic, do you have time to talk about finances?"

"I should go," Tess said, not wanting to intrude. "I need to pack up my things."

"What? Pack? You're not leaving." Isabel bit her lip.

"I don't belong here," said Tess. "I've left a dozen things up in the air in the city—"

"Please," said Isabel. "I know this is a strange situation, and it's all new to you, but I just… I would love it if you could stay."

Tess felt an itch of discomfort as she looked at Isabel. "Honestly, I'm a complete outsider here. I just don't see how I can help you."

"You're helping by being here." Isabel went to the window

and looked out. The peaceful scene seemed to mock the mood in the room. She turned back to Tess. "There's so much to sort out. And you're used to dealing with old records, right? I mean, in your job at the auction house?"

With every fiber of her being, Tess did not want to be involved in this. Regardless of her preference, she *was* involved, thanks to the whim of an old man. But it was the raw need and fear in Isabel's eyes that moved her. "You have to understand, I don't know anything about this situation."

"Then we'll work together." Isabel touched Tess's arm briefly. "Thanks."

Isabel fetched a tray of coffee and biscotti from the kitchen and led the way into a cluttered study. The room was dominated by a massive postmaster-style desk filled with drawers, cubbies and little nooks. It reminded Tess of a heavier, more masculine version of her nana's desk in Things Forgotten. "Grandfather built it himself," Isabel said with wistful pride. "He's made a hobby of creating carved boxes. Some of them have trick drawers and hidden compartments." There was no place to set the tray, so she put it down on a stack of files and papers.

An atmosphere of unfinished business hung in the air, mingling with the sweetish aroma of old pipe tobacco emanating from a rack of carved meerschaum pipes on the windowsill.

"The place is a mess, just as he left it," Isabel said. "It's as if he stepped out for a few minutes. I suppose, as far as he was concerned, that was what he did."

Tess scanned the bookcases, crammed with unsorted books on every conceivable topic—farming and flower arrangement, child rearing and religion. There was something oddly familiar to her about the disorganization and clutter. To Tess, this did not look like a mess, but like a work area. She felt at ease in this space.

"Do you know someone named Annelise Winther?" she asked Isabel. "There was a card from her in Magnus's room."

"Never heard of her," Isabel said. "Why do you ask?"

"She came from Denmark after the war. I met her in the city. Was there a group or network of survivors or immigrants? Maybe that's how they met?"

"Maybe. Grandfather didn't talk much about Denmark. Neither did Bubbie."

"She was Danish, too?"

"Yes."

There was a thick old-fashioned Bible, bound in leather with intricate iron hinges, on top of the desk. Tess lifted the cover and first few pages, revealing a record of births, deaths and marriages in what she presumed was Danish. The family tree dated back to the 1700s. She perked up with foolish hope. This was a record of her lineage—her family. But the records ended with the marriage of Magnus to Eva Salomon, dated 1954.

They sat around the desk and Isabel poured coffee and served the biscotti. By now it went without saying that she'd made them herself, and that they were delicious.

"So, is it true?" asked Isabel, leaning toward Dominic. "Are we as broke as I think we are? Or are there other accounts or funds…?"

Dominic nodded. "I'm sorry."

"Was Magnus aware of the situation?" Tess asked. She had a lot more questions, ones she couldn't voice just yet. Had Dominic known about the trouble when he'd come to get her? Of course he had. Then why hadn't he explained it to her? Did he think she'd refuse to come if she knew the estate was in distress?

"It's been an issue for a while," Dominic explained. "Magnus didn't want anyone to know."

"He was so stubborn that way," Isabel said. "He didn't want to worry anyone."

Dominic took a bound document from his briefcase and set it on the desk.

"Grandfather's will," she said. It was printed on legal-sized paper with pale blue backing.

She placed her hands in her lap as though loath to touch it. Tess turned to the signature page and stared at the name scrawled there in bold strokes. Magnus Christian Johansen. "Isn't this a little premature?" she asked, incensed. "Not to mention insensitive, bringing it up at a time like this?"

"It brought us together," Isabel quietly pointed out. "He rewrote it shortly before the accident, didn't he, Dominic?"

"Why then?" asked Tess.

"I don't know. Look, I don't like this any better than you do, but you both need to be informed," he said. "The two of you are named as his sole heirs, and everything falls to you in equal parts." Despite his words, the expression on Dominic Rossi's face indicated that things were not so simple.

"Isabel can get a line of credit," Tess suggested. "You could help her with that."

Dominic took off his glasses and rubbed the bridge of his nose. Lines of stress bracketed his mouth. "God knows, I wish I could. Isabel, I hate like hell that I'm having to tell you this."

"Tell me what?" She balled her hands at her sides.

His gaze flicked from Isabel to Tess and back again. Tess frowned, silently urging him to get on with it.

"Magnus took a loan against Bella Vista," Dominic said. "Three separate times, and the outstanding balances are now higher than his equity in the place."

The visions in Tess's head of a simple solution disappeared with an inaudible *poof*. She glanced over at Isabel, who had gone pale beneath her pretty olive-toned skin. She obviously didn't need help understanding what Dominic was saying.

"What's going to happen?" she asked.

A weighty pause pressed down on them. Through the open window, Tess could hear workers talking, the rumble of a truck motor and the grind of machinery.

"Dominic?" Isabel whispered.

He exhaled slowly, faced her head-on. "The property is going into foreclosure. Christ, Isabel, I hate this."

Isabel sank into a chair.

"Foreclosure? You mean your bank's going to take Bella Vista?" asked Tess.

He turned to her, his eyes joyless, his jaw hard with frustration.

"But aren't you…aren't…*you* the bank?"

"I work for the bank, yes."

Tess felt a blaze of anger. "Then can't you stop it?"

"Not this time," he told her quietly.

She wanted to strangle him for causing the stricken look on Isabel's face. "What do you mean, not this time?"

"I've managed to defer the proceedings for years," he said. "I'd still be doing that, except the bank changed hands. Regulations have changed, too. The new bank isn't local, and the underwriters won't grant any more extensions. There's a firm deadline."

"Does Grandfather even know about this?" asked Isabel.

"I told him right before the accident."

"Does your bank know they're foreclosing on a guy in a coma?" Tess demanded. "Does that matter at all? Isn't his accident some kind of mitigating circumstance to get the bank to back off?"

"Not under the current regulations. Now that the bank has changed hands, there are new rules in place."

"I don't get you, Dominic. You knew Magnus as well as anyone around here. You've got nothing but good things to say about him. And now you're foreclosing on his property."

"I hate it. If the bank had its way, it would have taken place long ago. I've used every postponement and suspension available."

He looked utterly frustrated, his jaw clenching and unclenching, hands gripping a stack of paperwork.

"So what's going to happen? How is this going to work?"

He explained the procedure that would be followed—the notice of sale, the appointment of a trustee to oversee the sale, the looming public auction. The whole time he was talking, Tess looked out the window at the harvest in full swing, feeling a sense of loss not for herself, but for Isabel. She pictured her sister having to remove herself from this place and make a new life elsewhere.

"That's grim," she said, tearing her gaze from the view. She paged through the document he handed her, the fine print and official language all but impenetrable. "Isabel? Are you getting this?" she asked, her heart aching for her sister.

"I had no idea things were this bad," Isabel said. "It's so sudden.... I guess I'm in shock."

"I'm sorry," Dominic said, taking her hand with a familiar touch. "I've pushed the deadline as far as I could."

"What will happen after the foreclosure? Will everyone at Bella Vista be evicted?" Tess demanded. "The Navarros, the workers, everyone?"

"You can stay as tenants paying rent, but that's a temporary solution. It might buy a little more time. There can be a settlement up to five days before the auction."

"But to make a settlement, we have to come up with cash." Tess shuffled the papers again. "Nobody has this kind of cash. Good lord, what was the old man thinking?"

Isabel winced and turned away. "He was looking out for everyone who depends on him."

Maybe it was a blessing, thought Tess, that she'd never had to depend on Magnus.

"He was waiting for the kind of year he had in 1997," said Dominic. "Everybody set records around here. We haven't seen a year like that since."

"So we're out of time, there won't be a bonanza year...tell us what to expect," Tess said.

"Oh, for Pete's sake, Tess, we all know the answer to that," Isabel said, getting up and pacing the room. "I'll have to vacate the premises. We all will. And then... Oh, God." She put her hands to her face.

"Listen." Tess stood. "You'll get through the mess. This is business. That's all it is."

"No," Isabel said, dropping her hands and rounding on her. "Maybe it is for you, but for me and Grandfather and people who have been here for years, it's our life."

"Then you'll find a new life," Tess said. "People do it every day—"

"That might be true for some people," snapped Isabel, "but not for me."

"You can't let this defeat you." Tess felt a headache coming on. She turned to Dominic. "What will it take to fix this situation? A miracle?"

"Yeah, a miracle. That would be good."

"Excuse me," said Isabel, picking up the tea tray and heading for the door. "I need to be by myself for a little bit."

Tess watched her go, feeling a deep welling of sympathy for her. Bella Vista was the only home Isabel had ever known, and she seemed singularly ill equipped to strike out on her own. She turned back to Dominic, rubbing her pounding temples. "Talk about kicking a person when she's down."

"I don't like any of this any more than you do." He studied her closely, his eyes reflecting concern. "Are you all right?"

She had the uncanny sensation that he could see her in ways most guys overlooked. Not to mention the fact that he'd already seen her in major meltdown mode. "Am I going to need a trip to the emergency room, do you mean? No. Do I feel like crap? Why, yes, yes, I do."

"Tell you what," he said. "Let's take a break."

They went outside together. The scent of ripe apples hung in the air. In the distance, Isabel melded with the peaceful scenery as she walked between the rows of trees in the orchard, the scented breeze lifting her skirt and twirling tendrils of her dark hair. Yellowing leaves danced on the breeze and wafted down to the dry grass. The day was aglow with the peculiar golden light of autumn. Isabel looked serene, but Tess knew that was a deception, played by the sun and the gorgeous landscape.

"Tell me about my sister," she said to Dominic.

His gaze shifted, just a little bit. There, she thought, reading the signal. Something about her question made him uncomfortable. "What do you want to know?"

"How about you start with what will happen to her after the foreclosure."

"That's up to Isabel."

"She seems…fragile."

"We're all fragile," he said, then hastily added, "Your sister will get through this. I think you'll find she has hidden strengths."

"I'm not surprised to hear it. She'll be needing that soon."

There was a sundial on a section of a patio exposed to the full sun. She paused to read a patina-blue copper plaque by the sundial: "What a joy life is when you have made a close working partnership with Nature, helping her to produce for the benefit of mankind new forms, colors, and perfumes in flowers which were never known before; fruits in form, size, and flavor never before seen on this globe."—Luther Burbank.

"It's the mission statement of Bella Vista," Dominic said. "Magnus and Eva had it cast in honor of their first harvest."

She studied the plaque in its bright setting and tried to picture the Johansens as a young couple, so full of hope for their future, fiercely believing the idealistic words. "It's nice. But not so helpful when it comes to scraping together cash for the bank."

"True."

She filled her lungs with fresh air and realized she hadn't thought about smoking a cigarette at all today. According to the package insert in the foul-tasting gum, it only took thirty-six hours for the physical dependence to go away. Thirty-six hours wasn't such a long time. If she'd known that, she might have tried quitting a long time ago.

"Where did all the money go?" she asked Dominic. "I mean, three mortgages? Is this operation just not sustainable?"

"It is," Dominic said. "Magnus is a good grower and not a terrible businessman. The trouble started years ago, when he got himself into a hole he couldn't dig out of. And then there were at least two more setbacks that I know about."

"What happened?" She imagined foolish extravagances, gambling problems, unwise investments, maybe scams. "Am I allowed to know, or am I prying?"

"I've never known a secret to do anything but damage," Dominic said.

His words startled her. "So how did he get into that downward spiral?"

"He took the first loan—a line of credit—when his wife got sick. Their insurance didn't cover the bills for her illness. Happens to people every day, unfortunately. In the case of his wife, he thought he was insured to the hilt, but the insurance company argued otherwise, and he had to pay for her treatment out of pocket."

"Why wouldn't they cover her illness?"

"They linked it to a pre-existing condition."

"What was the condition?"

He paused. "During World War II, Eva spent time in a concentration camp called Auschwitz. She must have been just a little girl."

Tess shuddered as a chill slipped through her. *Auschwitz*. It was a Nazi death camp where most of the captured Jews of Denmark had been taken.

Suddenly she had to realign her thinking about the stranger who had been her grandmother. "I noticed her grave marker had a Hebrew phrase on it, so I figured she was Jewish. But my God, a concentration camp?" Tess's heart ached. "What a nightmare."

"The insurance company claimed the fact that she'd been an inmate in a concentration camp created a pre-existing condition, which wasn't covered," said Dominic.

"What? You mean, being forced into starvation as a child is considered a pre-existing condition?"

"They said it was a precursor to the form of cancer that struck her six decades later."

"That's criminal. How can they get away with such a thing?"

"Magnus could have fought them, but that would have incurred legal fees and deadly delays, with no guarantee of the outcome. In the meantime, Eva needed treatment."

"That's horrible. I can't believe how horrible it is. Couldn't he have sued the insurance company after the fact?"

"People can sue anyone for anything. But again, you don't want to create a delay when someone's life is at stake."

The injustice made her chest ache. She knew taking on an insurance company was a David versus Goliath proposition, and that Goliath almost always won.

"The next two loans are for medical expenses, too," Dominic continued. "A worker had an accident on the job—a bad one. Magnus's liability was limited, but he wanted to take responsibility for Timon. He covered all his bills and ongoing care, as well."

"What happened to the guy?"

"Tim? He still lives at Bella Vista. He's the Navarros' youngest. He suffered a traumatic brain injury, and he's disabled. Magnus added a provision for him in his will, but under the circumstances, he won't be able to cover him."

She pictured the fallen, helpless man in his hospital bed. "So basically what we have is a saint who's about to lose everything he spent his life building."

"For what it's worth," Dominic said, "I'm sorry as hell about this."

"Just doing your job, right? It must be horrible for you, having a job that puts people out of their homes."

He didn't say anything. She knew her remark wasn't fair. He was in the business of making it possible for people to buy their homes, too.

"Why didn't you tell me about this mess before, when you came to find me in the city?" she asked.

"Would it have mattered?"

"No," she said quickly, "of course not."

"It seemed more decent to tell you and Isabel together. Again, I'm sorry."

She wanted to be mad at him, but instead, she just felt a wave of resignation. "Don't apologize to me. I haven't lost anything here. It's certainly nothing like the loss Isabel and her grandfather are facing. I have a perfectly fine life in San

Francisco—which, by the way, is where I'm headed this evening. I've gone twenty-nine years without knowing anything about my father's family, and I—"

"You're twenty-nine?"

She didn't understand the surprise on his face. Instant paranoia set in. Did she look older? Should she have gone to Lydia's Botox party last month? "Why do you seem so surprised?"

His gaze shifted away. "You look...younger than twenty-nine."

There was a hesitation in his voice—something else she didn't understand. At least he'd said the right thing—that she looked young. Maybe it was the freckles. "You're being weird about my age," she said. "Why are you being weird about my age?"

"I don't know what you mean," Dominic said.

"I do," Isabel said, walking toward them.

Tess turned in surprise. She hadn't heard Isabel approach and wondered how much of the conversation she'd overheard. Surrounded by the sunlit changing leaves of a grape arbor, Isabel resembled a dark fairy or a sprite. "He's being weird because I'm twenty-nine, too," she said.

Tess's head started to pound in sync with the sudden churning of her gut. If they were the same age, then that meant... Good lord, what kind of person had their father been?

If there was ever any question in Tess's mind about his integrity, she now knew the answer. But it only opened the door to more questions.

"Isabel, when is your birthday?" she asked quietly, her fists clenching. Which sister was older? Whose mother had been with Erik first; which woman had been betrayed?

"I was born on March 27. What about you?"

Tess nearly choked. When she finally found her voice, she said, "March 27, same as you."

No one spoke for several minutes. She could hear the breeze

through the arbor, bees bumbling in the lavender and milk-weed, and the distant, piercing cry of a hawk, the ticking of a wall clock.

"Are you okay?" asked Dominic.

The sick feeling that had sent her to the emergency room now washed over her in a wave, and without thinking, she took his hand. His fingers immediately tightened around hers, warm and reassuring. "Give me a second," she whispered, seeing the concern in his eyes. Then she turned to Isabel. "What the hell...? Did you know anything about this?"

"No."

"Did Magnus? Of course he did."

"I wasn't privy to the situation."

As her heart surged in uncomprehending panic, she looked down at their joined hands. Just that, the feel of that connection, eased the disorientation a little. She took a breath, then extricated her hand from his. "I... Sorry."

"No problem," he said quietly.

Tess had never considered herself a touchy person, yet all she wanted to do was touch him. In the awkward silence, she turned to Isabel. "You didn't know?" she asked.

"I had no idea." Isabel's voice wavered, and she looked as stunned as Tess felt. "I need to go bake something."

"I need to go shoot something," said Tess.

"I need to go back to the bank," Dominic told them.

"Actually," Tess said, "I'm going to give my mother one more chance to reply to my messages. After that I'll have to go find her and drag her here by the hair."

"We need to talk," Tess told her mother's too-familiar voice mail. Mystified and hurt, she paced back and forth in the great room, the house phone glued to her ear. "And if you don't get back to me by the end of the day, no matter where you are, then don't bother calling me again, ever." For good measure, she sent a text message and an email to the same effect. She knew now that her mother was hiding. From what? From having to reveal secrets she'd kept for thirty years?

Tess hung up, then checked in with the office. "I need more time," she told Jude.

"And I—we, everyone here—need you back at work. Or doesn't work matter to you anymore?"

"Work is everything to me. You know that. But there's... Something came up."

"You found a long-lost sister. I'm happy for you, really. But in the meantime, you've got a job to do. And last time I checked, you had an apartment, friends, a life in the city."

"We just figured out that we were born on the same day," said Tess.

"Come again?"

"Isabel and I. We have the same birthday. Same year."

"What, now you're saying you're twins?"

"No," she said in exasperation. "Same father, different mothers."

That silenced even Jude. She paced some more. A delicious aroma wafted from the kitchen. Isabel was in a baking frenzy.

"So for God's sake," she said, "I'm going to need to explore this situation a little deeper. If you were my friend, you'd come and help out. You should see this place, Jude. It's..." She stopped pacing to gaze out the window. "Just like Neelie said. Magic."

"You need to get your magic ass back here," he said.

"Have you always been such a tool, or am I only noticing it now?" she asked.

"Hey—"

"I'll check in with you later," she said, already forgetting him as she lowered the phone. Outside, Dominic's car rolled to a stop. Two kids and two dogs spilled out. Charlie, the shepherd mix, yelped with joy and raced to greet them.

Tess went outside, her spirits lifting at the sight of Dominic and his kids. "Hey, you guys," she said. "To what do we owe the pleasure?"

"Dad said Isabel was baking cookies," said Antonio.

"He said she was baking, moron," said Trini. "He didn't say what."

"Dad—"

"Trini." His voice alone was command enough.

"Sorry," she muttered.

"I have it on good authority that she is baking cookies."

"Yesss," said Antonio. "I knew it."

Isabel came out, carrying a platter. "I heard a rumor, too," she said, beaming. "I heard a rumor that there were two hungry kids on their way to the harvest fair. Ginger molasses, the soft kind. Help yourself."

The kids each wolfed down a cookie. It was all Tess could do not to follow suit, but she took a more dainty bite. "Isabel, you're killing me," she said.

"Yeah, Dad, you should learn to make cookies like this," said Trini. "I bet if you did, I'd end up getting straight A's in school."

"Then I'd better teach him," said Isabel.

"Not today," said Dominic. "Harvest fair, remember?"

"No," Tess said swiftly. "This is the first I've heard of it."

"It's the biggest celebration of the year in Archangel," said Isabel.

"And you're both coming," said Dominic.

"We probably shouldn't," said Tess. Harvest celebration? She went to happy hour, not harvest fairs. "We've got a lot going on here—"

"And you need a break from it," he said easily. "It'll do you a world of good. I entered you in the grape stomp."

Grape stomp. "This does not sound promising."

"You're going to love it."

"Whenever someone says that to me, nothing good ever follows," said Tess.

"I'm wounded," said Dominic, opening the back of the SUV for the dogs. "Grab a change of clothes, and let's go."

The change of clothes suggestion should have tipped her off. The town square had been transformed into an old-fashioned fairground, with striped pavilions set up, delicious smells everywhere, people milling around and kids and dogs racing everywhere.

"This town is so charming," Tess remarked as they headed down the promenade. "I'm surprised it's not overrun by tourists."

"We get our share. There's definitely a cadre of reclusive famous types who live here, hiding out from the paparazzi."

"Really? Like who? If you tell me, will you have to kill me?"

"Talk-show hosts, retired athletes, that type."

"Hmm. I think what you're not telling me is a lot more interesting than what you are."

"Most of them are in Sonoma or Healdsburg. Closer to the airport. People who come here tend to be the type who stick around for a while."

"I guess that rules me out," she said. She didn't know why she was so quick to tell him that. It seemed important to set that boundary.

"I'd never rule you out," he said quietly.

His words nearly stopped her in her tracks, but there was no time to pursue the matter. The kids insisted on taking all three dogs to the dog dash, a race to benefit the local P.A.W.S. shelter. Iggy won handily, causing the kids to nearly burst with pride. The Dude was given a ribbon for "most unusual," and Charlie for "funniest."

Dominic leaned down and spoke low into Tess's ear. "I think the point is that everyone is a winner."

When she went to claim Charlie's ribbon, the judge told her, "You have a beautiful family."

Startled, she turned back to see Dominic and the kids waving Isabel over to see the ribbons. "Oh," said Tess, "they're not..." Then she simply smiled and said, "Thanks."

They walked together from booth to booth, sampling wine and cider, jam and gourmet bites. Tess had to admit that Dominic was right—they did need a break from the troubles at Bella Vista. Isabel was more relaxed than she'd ever seen her, walking around and greeting friends, accepting well wishes for Magnus.

Tess was charmed by the sense of community she found here. Even though she was a stranger, she felt as if she belonged, thanks to the simple gesture of a friendly smile, the offer of a sample of food or taste of wine. At one point, her hand brushed Dominic's, and she flushed, wondering if he had any idea how attractive he was to her.

The grape stomp was the final event of the evening. Tess was designated the stomper, and Isabel the swabby. That was when she figured out why Dominic had advised her to wear cut-offs and bring a change of clothes.

"You're kidding," she said, regarding the stage, which featured a row of half barrels full of grapes.

"This is wine country," he said. "We don't kid about grapes. You're about to compete in the hope of being named America's greatest stomper."

"Really? Really?"

He grabbed her hand and led her up to the stage. "Come on, I'll be right next to you."

She eyed the mounded dark grapes in her barrel, then her

sister, who stood below to catch the juice from the spigot into a clear jug. "How come I have to stomp?" she demanded.

"You never stop moving," Dominic said. "You'll be a natural. Shoes off."

"Stompers, take your places," called the official. "The timer starts...now!"

Leaving all dignity behind, Tess jumped in. She immediately teetered on the mound of grapes and would have fallen, except that Dominic grabbed her by the arms and held her steady.

"It's harder than it looks," she admitted, holding on tight.

"In winemaking, everything is harder than it looks," he said.

She let go of him. "I've got this," she said, her drive to succeed kicking in.

The stomping frenzy was accompanied by loud cheers from the crowd. Tess found a kind of crazy pleasure in the sensation of the grapes under her bare feet, the cool juice spurting, turning her feet and ankles a deep, rich shade of burgundy. She was amazed at how liberating it was to simply immerse herself into the messy fun. She could hear Dominic next to her, laughing, encouraging his kids to take turns as swabby.

Showing an unexpectedly competitive side of herself, Isabel was an expert swabby, efficiently pulling the grape skins away from the screen and pushing juice toward the pipe. Tess sped up as the timer ran down, and the crowd counted out the final seconds until the bell rang.

Breathless and laughing, she stood in the delicious-smelling muck and cheered as Isabel hoisted her jug. However, when the official amounts were announced, the winners were Bob and Fay Krokower, who apparently had been in training for the event for weeks.

"We were close," Isabel said, spraying Tess's and Dominic's feet with a water hose. "But Bob's feet are huge, did you see? There's no competing with that."

★ ★ ★

Dominic brought them home just after dark. Tess felt grubby and sticky, but decidedly more cheerful than she had earlier in the day. "You were right about us needing to get out," she said to Dominic.

"Yes, thanks for that," said Isabel.

He said something in Italian. The sound of him speaking so fluently nearly undid Tess.

"Okay," she said, "translation, please?"

"Having a little fun never made a problem worse, right?" said Trini.

"You got it," he replied, turning up the long drive to Bella Vista. There was a big golden moon tonight, nearly full, lighting the orchards.

"I'll walk you to the door," said Dominic. He went around and let Charlie out of the back of the car.

"Good night, you two," said Tess. Trini and Antonio looked sweetly sleepy, slumped together in the backseat.

As she went up the walk, she felt Dominic's hand, very light on her waist. She sent him a questioning glance. Was his touch simply chivalry, or something else?

The long, sad process of sorting through the estate records had to start somewhere. Tess and Isabel elected to begin with Magnus's study the next morning, sifting through the souvenirs and relics of the life he'd lived since first coming to Bella Vista with his war bride. Although the foreclosure couldn't be stopped, barring a miracle or winning lottery ticket, there were key records that needed to be accounted for. More than that, there were questions that needed answers.

An air of unfinished business hung in the study, a huge, cluttered room with a big arched picture window and shelves as high as the ceiling. As they regarded the mounds of old records and papers, Isabel sighed in frustration. "It's hard to decide where to start. Getting his things in order is like finding a needle in a haystack. No, it's not," she corrected herself. "At least we know what a needle looks like. This is a disaster."

Tess looked around at the crammed shelves, the littered desk, the drawers stuffed with detritus. "Doesn't look so bad to me."

"It's completely disorganized. Look, he's shelved used checkbooks with back issues of the *Farmers' Almanac*. Who does that?"

"Just one used checkbook, see? He probably took some notes on the back of a check copy and— See?" Tess found a handwritten note on the back of a check: *Newtown Pippin.* "No idea what he meant by that, though."

"It's an apple variety," said Isabel. "We used to sell the entire crop of that variety to Martinelli's for cider."

Tess continued with the sorting. "Everything is so humble," she said. "Ordinary. A shaving mug and brush, a sewing kit, a cribbage board." Tess came across one of Magnus's special carved boxes. More than one person at the healing ceremony had spoken of his distinctive carving style and his affinity for puzzles. She was intrigued to see it for herself. The top depicted a stylized apple tree laden with fruit, the sides twined with sunflowers in bas-relief. The design was a combination of whimsy and abundance, with a subtle Nordic look. Nothing was symmetrical, but she felt a peculiar balance in the design of the piece.

She held it up, feeling the contents slide around. "Recognize this?"

"Definitely one of Grandfather's. He made so many of them."

"It's beautiful," said Tess, holding it out. "Very refined. Any clue how to open it?" The thing had no visible hinges or latches.

Isabel took the box and tipped it to and fro. "Grandfather loved his puzzle boxes. He made so many of them. He used to say they were for keeping family treasures." A wistful smile softened her face. "When I was little, I asked him why they were almost always empty. He said because I've grown too big to fit in a little box."

Tess could see the fresh wave of sadness breaking over her sister. To Isabel, this wasn't some puzzle or Nancy Drew mystery to be solved. Magnus was the biggest part of her life, and now he was likely dying, leaving her with nothing but memories.

Isabel shook the box Tess had found, her eyebrows lifting in surprise as she heard something rattling inside. "This one was a gift to Bubbie—our grandmother, Eva. I can tell because he always used a sunflower design in his gifts to her. He gave her a box each birthday, and she'd spend half the day trying to get it open."

Tess wondered if it was easy for Isabel to say "our" grandmother. "If he gave her a box for each birthday, I wonder why we're only seeing this one," she mused.

"He put most of Bubbie's things away after she died. Too many reminders of her made him sad. There's a cupboard in one of the closed wings.... I think he stuck them all away there." Isabel ran her fingers along the edges and joinery of the piece. Eventually she touched the center of a carved sunflower, and the lid cracked open.

"Very clever," Tess said. "What's inside? Please tell me it's the deed to Bella Vista, free and clear."

Isabel flashed her a rare smile and flipped open the box. It contained immigration papers, ticket stubs, items clipped from the paper—the sort of things people kept to remind them of a particular moment. "This is pretty," she said, removing an object from notebook paper with writing on it. "It's a little knickknack or ornament." She smoothed the paper on her knee. "Looks like a poem in Bubbie's handwriting." Taking a breath, she read, "'To the child I want who can never be/ please fill the empty cup of my heart/With the love I held in reserve just for you.'"

A shiver coursed through Tess. "What do you suppose that's about?"

"I don't quite understand," Isabel said. "I get that she was sad, though. She got that way sometimes. I know she lost her entire family in the war, and she always carried that sadness with her."

Tess picked up the knickknack. It was unexpectedly dense. Alabaster, she thought. The angel had golden wings, its halo a crown of leaves and its tiny hands holding a candle.

She peered through her loupe, inspecting each detail. She kept a poker face, but her gut clenched, the way it did when she came across something valuable. Her instincts vibrated like a tuning fork. "Do you know anything about this?" she asked Isabel.

"I've never seen it before."

"It's…unusual. Alabaster, with some amazing detail that's probably pure gold. This looks almost like a cameo in 3-D, doesn't it? The filigree pattern might be Polish or Russian."

"Pretty," said Isabel. "And Bubbie was never big on souvenirs. This must have meant something to her. I wonder where it came from."

"I'll do some research on it," said Tess. "I mean, if that's okay with you."

"Of course it's okay." Isabel was flipping through the photos. "You know what I think these are? Pictures for Bubbie's scrapbook collection. I remember, she gathered them all together years ago. She'd joined a scrapbooking club in town.

Women would get together and create these amazing books filled with family photos. The books were like works of art."

"So, did your grandmother ever create one?"

Isabel's eyes turned misty with affection. "She came home after the first meeting practically in tears. She was overwhelmed by the work it would take to put everything into some sort of order."

"That kind of project isn't for everybody," Tess said.

"Definitely not for Bubbie. She never went back to the scrapbooking club, although she felt sort of guilty about that. I remember she told me she could either spend her time working on a scrapbook about her life, or actually living her life. And she chose to live her life." Isabel picked up a print of a small, dark-haired woman in tennis clothes, grinning at the camera. She had bold features, and Tess found herself looking for a family resemblance. She couldn't find any, not in this picture.

"Seems like that was the right choice for her," Tess said, searching the face in the photograph.

"Absolutely," said Isabel. "About a year later, she was diagnosed with cancer."

"I'm sorry."

"Thanks. It's been years, and I still miss her every day. She was the only mom I knew."

Tess nodded at the box, suddenly consumed by curiosity about the strangers who had contributed half her DNA. "Do you mind if I take a look?"

"Go ahead," said Isabel. "This must be weird for you."

"It is. And kind of fascinating." She flipped over a photograph or two, checking the dates on the backs. "The pictures might be in chronological order."

"Maybe Bubbie did a little organizing, even though she never got going on that scrapbook."

The more recent shots were located toward the front of

the box. Tess paused to study a studio portrait of a smiling, ginger-haired baby, seated next to a sock monkey against a backdrop of fake fur.

"Our father was a beautiful baby," Isabel said softly. "Look at those green eyes."

A chill crept across Tess's spine. "This is not our father."

"What do you mean? It looks like all the other pictures of him."

"This is a color portrait," Tess said, her pulse accelerating. "Pictures didn't look like this in the sixties."

"You're right." Isabel frowned. "Then who…how?"

Almost reluctantly, Tess checked the back of the photo. One word was written there: *Theresa.* "How the hell did they get a picture of me?" she whispered.

"I have no idea," Isabel said. "Honestly, I don't."

Tess didn't know how to feel about this new development. The photo created more questions than answers, and it was the only one of her. The rest of the archive featured Isabel prominently, the star of the show. The snapshots told the story of a happy childhood in a storybook setting, nearly always in the middle of a party or celebration. If the photos were to be believed, the former Isabel was outgoing, constantly entertaining people, always on the go. Tess found this surprising, because the Isabel before her now, grieving and timid, seemed to have very little in common with the Isabel of the past.

"One day you'll have to tell me what it was like, growing up in one place," said Tess.

"And you'll have to tell me what it was like, traveling the world as you were growing up."

They regarded each other briefly, and Tess felt a twinge of emotion. A connection? Maybe not that, but a sense that went deeper than mere curiosity.

Tess went back to the photo archive. She noticed a change

in Isabel in the shots before she left for culinary school and after she came back home. The earlier pictures depicted a young girl just growing into her beauty, her expression on fire with excitement. The latter photos showed a more subdued, grown-up Isabel, her beauty muted or maybe even haunted. Tess wondered if the passage of time alone had changed her or if something had happened.

Losing her grandmother had undoubtedly been an enormous blow. Tess understood that; she still remembered the emptiness of life without Nana and the way she'd worn the grief like a hair shirt for months. However, eventually she'd shaken herself out of it, knowing Nana would scold her to kingdom come if she caught her moping.

"Look how young they were." Isabel showed Tess a black-and-white 8 x 10 shot of Magnus and Eva. The two of them posed in the flat bed of a farm truck between rows of apple trees, the boughs heavy with fruit. Between them, they held up a bushel filled with ripe apples. The label on the bushel read *Bella Vista Honeycrisps.*

"I think this was taken to commemorate their first harvest," said Isabel. "Bubbie was so young and pretty."

"It's a wonderful shot," said Tess. "They look genuinely happy."

Eva hardly resembled a farm wife. She was perfectly made up, and had every hair in place. She wore tailored slacks nipped in at the waist and a plaid shirt with the sleeves carefully rolled back. Tess studied her for a long time—her father's mother. She had deep-set eyes enhanced by thick lashes. The shape of her face, the arch of her brow, her smile—they added up to a very pretty woman, but Tess could see none of herself in Eva. For that matter, she couldn't see a resemblance to Isabel, either.

She tried to hold herself detached from Magnus and Eva, but there was something in knowing she was connected to them, that they'd lived in this world, moved through these rooms, cultivated the vast and colorful orchards and gardens. Their son had fathered her. She found herself yearning to know more about them, to know the sound of their voices and the smell of their hair, the feel of their hands, holding hers.

Her gaze was drawn to a shadow on the woman's arm. At first she thought it was a bruise. Then she frowned, looking closer. Finally she took out her magnifying glass, the high-powered, lighted one she always carried in her bag.

"What are you doing?" asked Isabel, who was sorting through more farm pictures.

"Trying to get a closer look. There's something on her arm."

Isabel hesitated. "It's a tattoo."

Auschwitz. Tess pictured a small, frightened girl being marked for life by her Nazi captors. With a shudder, she set aside the magnifier and stared at the smiling couple in the photograph. It was a miracle, she thought, that anyone could smile like that after such an ordeal.

"She never talked about it," Isabel went on. "I kind of wish she had, but I understand why she didn't."

Tess set the picture aside, her throat aching with grief. That was the trouble with learning the history of things and the secrets of another person. Sometimes you discovered hurt beyond imagining, and there was no way to make it better.

"Our father," said Isabel, laying a group of snapshots out on the table. Various phases of his life had been captured, from moon-faced newborn to strapping young man.

Tess bit her lip, drawn to the images of the stranger who had fathered them both, presumably within weeks or even days of each other. There was no denying he was a handsome boy, tall for his age in the class pictures, a high school jock and college fraternity brother.

"He looks so much like Grandfather," Isabel murmured. "And you. Do you see it?"

"I see a stranger," Tess said. She made herself study the shape of his nose and the tilt of his head when he smiled. "Okay, yes, it's weird, but there's something familiar about him."

"Let's keep these separate," Isabel said, placing them on a shelf.

Tess sorted through more photographs, most of them faded to soft grays and some even in sepia tones. There were stiffly posed formal portraits of long-gone strangers, shots of Magnus and his comrade in arms, Ramon Maldonado, both of them looking skinny and impossibly young, grinning from ear to ear on the deck of a ship of some sort. Near the bottom of the box they found some pictures of old Denmark. The Johansen family had lived in a genteel-looking area of old Copenhagen, and they'd had an apple farm out in the countryside in a place called Helsingør. As expected, pictures of the past were sparse. When Tess was doing research for work, the scarcity of evidence excited her, made her want to dig deeper. She felt that now, but with a heightened sense of urgency.

Lastly, she came to a translucent vellum envelope containing a hinged frame the size of a small book. Tess carefully opened it and laid it on the desk. "This might be the oldest of the lot."

Isabel peered over her shoulder. "I don't recall ever seeing that one."

The photo showed a boy of perhaps twelve, standing next to an older man by a Christmas tree lit with candles and hung with traditional wooden ornaments and sprigs of holly and woven paper hearts. The room was decorated with old-fashioned opulence. There was a fringed ottoman and in the background, a painting on the wall and a curio cabinet.

Tess studied the smiling face of the boy. It was the smile that shone on the faces of children everywhere at Christmastime—eyes sparkling with anticipation, lips ripe with secrets. Her gaze touched every detail of the photo. It was part training, part simple curiosity. As she scanned the background of the photograph, a frisson of awareness touched her spine. She made no sound, and her expression didn't change as she took out the magnifying glass again.

"What do you know about this picture?" she asked Isabel.

"Not a thing." Leaning in for a closer look, Isabel said, "The young boy looks like Grandfather. He had that smile all his life. So did… Erik. Our father. Yes, that's what he looked like as a boy, too."

"I wouldn't know," Tess murmured. Unlike Isabel, she hadn't been privy to any of this. "Who do you suppose the older guy is in this picture?"

"That, I couldn't tell you. Either his father or grandfather, I'd guess. He looks so formal and distinguished. And that room. I wonder if they decorated like that just for Christmas, or all the time."

Tess studied the photo even more closely, focusing on an item in the curio cabinet at the edge of the shot. She recognized some vases that looked like French crystal from the 1920s, alongside china figurines and other collectibles common to the era. But there was something else in the room's opulent clutter. Amid the figurines and glassware was a largish, garishly decorated egg on a footed stand. Most likely it was a common replica of a Fabergé egg.

But every instinct she possessed was urging her to find out exactly what she was looking at. Her gaze went to the tiny alabaster angel they'd found in Eva's box, then back to the egg in the photo.

"Tess?" Isabel peered at her. "Is something the matter?"

"Yes. Or, no. I mean, this piece in the photo might be…"

She stopped herself. Her idea was going to sound crazy, and, worse, it might get Isabel's hopes up for no reason.

"Go on."

"It might be worth checking out."

"Worth it...in what way?"

Tess ignored the question. "Do you mind if I take it out of the frame?" she asked Isabel.

"No, not at all."

"I'll be careful." She took a small flat-headed screwdriver from her bag. Catching Isabel's expression, she said, "I carry a lot of tools for work." She carefully pried back the little hinged fasteners from the back of the frame. Then she lifted out the back and set it aside. A thick piece of cardboard was next; it appeared to be from a cracker or cookie box in Danish. Slipped behind the yellowing print, between a sheet of vellum and the backing of the picture frame, she found a letter, handwritten in Cyrillic characters on linen stationery.

It was as if a cold finger suddenly touched the base of her spine. "Do you know anything about this?" she asked Isabel.

"No. I've never seen it before. The photo, or that...whatever that is."

"A letter. It's written in Russian. At least I think it's Russian. Would you happen to know any Russian speakers?"

"Not offhand," Isabel said.

"I do," said Tess. "My mother. Who refuses to return my calls."

"I'm sorry," said Isabel.

"Don't be. You'd think by now I'd be used to it."

Isabel indicated the letter. "What do you think it could mean?"

"I'll need to look into it. I think it might be significant." She decided to level with Isabel. "Okay, this is going to sound completely crazy, but this whole situation is crazy. That ornament on display could be a Fabergé egg."

"And a Fabergé egg is valuable," Isabel said.

Beyond your wildest dreams, thought Tess. "Assuming it's authentic. And assuming your grandfather is in possession of it."

Isabel looked around the piled shelves and crammed drawers. "That's a big assumption."

The back of the photograph had something written on it in fountain ink, the color fading to amber. "This is in Danish," said Tess. "You wouldn't happen to know any Danish, would you?"

"Actually…" Isabel frowned down at the words. *"Julen 1940, lige før Farfar blev taget af Gestapo."*

Hearing her sister reading the words with fluency reminded Tess that the two of them were still such strangers. Isabel had been raised by people Tess had never had a chance to meet.

The final word, however, was recognizable in any language: Gestapo…1940. Tess didn't understand the rest, yet the very blood in her veins felt chilly. She was swept by a sense of sadness and fear, regarding the happy boy—Magnus—and the older man, having no clue about the tragedy that was probably about to strike. She knew the Nazis had occupied Denmark during World War II, and that although the Danes had protested, they had officially submitted to the occupation. She wondered what had become of that happy household and all its little treasures.

She turned to Isabel, whose soft eyes were damp with tears. "A sense of loss is the worst feeling, isn't it?" asked Isabel. "It's so…futile to think about things we can never get back."

"Can you tell me what it means?" asked Tess.

Isabel nodded. "This says *Christmas 1940, just before Farfar—*that's Grandfather—*was taken by the Gestapo.*"

PART SEVEN

Proclamation! To the Danish Soldiers and the
People of Denmark!... [I]t is to be expected
that the... Danish people show good will and
not demonstrate any passive or active resistance against the German army. It would be
futile and it would be stopped by any means
necessary... The people are encouraged to con-
tinue their daily work and to ensure peace and
order! For the security of the country against
British assaults, control will accede to the German army and navy.

—Excerpt from a leaflet dropped from a
German aircraft bomber, 9 April 1940.
The text, in poorly translated Danish
and Norwegian, is believed to have been
written by Adolf Hitler.

··· ● ···

JULEKAKE

....

Julekake means Yule Cake or Christmas Cake. Every Scandinavian family has their favorite version, usually baked by Mor Mor (Grand-mother), who is always present, even if she's passed on. This cake should never be prepared alone. Stand beside someone you love as you cut the citron into chunks and blend it with the flour, cardamom, fruits, butter, eggs, yeast and sugar. The scent of cardamom will fill you with nostalgia as the aroma of baking fills the house.

Moist and tender, topped with gjetost (Scandinavian goat cheese) and a pat of butter, this is the holiday treat we wait all year for.

Turn on the oven for 10 minutes at 150 degrees F, then shut it off but keep the door closed. This is where you'll set the dough to rise.

Use a big wide mixing bowl to blend together:

5 cups white flour

1 tablespoon cardamom

2 cups candied fruit and citron

1 ½ cups raisins

In a pan, blend:

2 cups milk, scalded (can be done on the stove or in the microwave)

1 cup sugar, dissolved in the scalded milk

1 cup butter, melted in the scalded milk

Cool to lukewarm. Combine a little of the milk with:

1 packet active dry yeast

When dissolved, add it to the rest of the milk mixture. Then add everything to the flour mixture to make a soft dough. Add enough flour to create a pliable dough that doesn't stick to the sides of the bowl. Turn it out onto a lightly floured surface and knead further.

Place in a buttered bowl and turn it over once, so the oiled side is up. Place a dish towel over the top, and set the bowl in the warm oven for a half hour to 45 minutes. Punch down and knead again. This time, separate the dough into two loaves or rounds. Cover with a dish towel again, and let it rise once more for a half hour to 45 minutes.

Once risen, bake in a 400 degree oven for 30–40 minutes. Place a piece of foil over the tops after about 25 minutes if it gets too dark.

(Source: Adapted from *Christmas Customs Around the World* by Herbert H. Wernecke (1959))

ELEVEN

Copenhagen
1940

The camera flash left Magnus momentarily blinded, and a slight burn of sulfur lingered in the air. But he knew in the picture, he would be smiling from ear to ear, because magic was about to happen. It was the best time of year, a time of secrets and good things to eat and families gathering close—especially now.

Farfar squeezed his shoulder and gazed fondly down at Magnus. "There, it is official," his grandfather said. "Our Christmas portrait is done, so the festivities can begin."

"Assuming you didn't break the camera," said Uncle Sweet, working the crank on the side of the box. Uncle Sweet was not really Magnus's uncle at all. They just gave out that story for the sake of appearances. In reality, Sweet was Jewish, and the Johansens were hiding him and his daughter, Eva, in plain sight. Their real name was Salomon, and they were in big trouble, thanks to Sweet's wife.

The wife was extremely pretty and had huge breasts that made her look like a pinup girl so popular in American magazines. She liked fine wine and pretty things, and because he'd fallen on hard times, Sweet couldn't give her much. Last year when she had caught the eye of the German marshal at an Oktoberfest dance, she had gone waltzing off with the soldier and never looked back at the family she'd left behind—the husband destroyed by her betrayal, and the adorable, bewildered little girl. The betrayal of Sweet's wife was even more injurious, given the fact that she would embrace the very ones who wanted to eliminate her people from existence.

The Nazi death camps were rumors no more, but grim fact. The underground newspapers were full of eyewitness reports of people who had seen these places just over the border—Auschwitz, Neuengamme, Bergen-Belsen, Sachsenhausen—where prisoners were forced to work and starve in the freezing cold and were summarily executed for the smallest infractions. When Magnus thought of Eva, he could not get his mind around the Nazis' idea that her race of people were some kind of menace to humanity. All he saw was a little girl with nothing but goodness and hope in her heart, even in the face of the notion that her mother had abandoned the family and her father was a broken man.

"We can't all be as pretty as you," Papa said, coming into the room with a tray laden with mugs—hot malted cream with cardamom for Magnus and Eva, and apple cordial for the grown-ups.

"I'll partake later," said Uncle Sweet. "I'm going to take this down to the basement and develop the film to make some prints. They'll have to be my gift to you this year since the damn Nazis have made it impossible to have a proper holiday in Copenhagen anymore."

Magnus took a swallow of his malted cream and pretended he could taste real chocolate. The last time he had tasted chocolate was perhaps three years ago, but he had never forgotten the smooth flavor, as dark as night.

"Language, Sweet," said Magnus's mother, arriving with a plate full of homemade biscuits. She didn't scold him too harshly about his talk these days. Magnus suspected this was because Mama shared Uncle Sweet's opinion about the Nazis. Yet despite the shortages and rationing, she had managed to turn out the most delicious biscuits Magnus had ever tasted. They were redolent of butter, which Mrs. Gundersen up the hill traded for apples from the family orchard.

Uncle Sweet made a great show of fanning himself and swooning as he ate a biscuit. "Language," he said, "is nothing but a bunch of words, and there are no words to express how wonderful this cookie is. I swear, if you were not already married, I would have you locked in a workroom like Rumpelstiltskin's daughter, forced to bake for me all day." He stole another biscuit from the platter and headed for the basement, lighting his way with an oil lamp. No one ever asked where his photographic chemicals came from—no one wanted to hold the answer like a piece of stolen fruit.

Mama and Papa went to the settee. Their glasses clinked, and they snuggled together, and the sight of them made Magnus feel warm inside. No matter what the Nazis did as they overran the city, they could not steal the one thing that mattered most—the love shared by a family. Tonight they were celebrating Lille Juleaften—Little Christmas Eve—which turned December twenty-third into a special day. They'd given the house a final cleaning, and everything was ready for the next few days of feasting.

"Let's finish lighting the candles on the tree," said Farfar. "You're plenty old enough to handle that duty, eh?"

"I should say so." Magnus took a long wooden match and touched it to one of the candles. There were just a dozen this year because of the shortages. It didn't really matter, though. Thanks to the brown-shirted Nazis, Christmas had to be concealed from the world behind blackout curtains.

Although Magnus couldn't say so to his grandfather, he had plenty of experience with lighting fires lately. But the less said about that, the better.

Sweet's little daughter, Eva, came in, all dressed for bed. Fresh from her bath, Eva had that peculiar, scrubbed look that made everyone want to draw her close and protect her. When she saw the lighted tree, her eyes shone like twin stars, and she regarded Magnus as if he had personally invented the element of fire. Eva had never experienced Christmas before, but when Magnus had explained the concept, she was quick and eager to grasp it.

"It's beautiful," she breathed, her eyes shining with wonder. "Farfar, isn't it beautiful?"

"Not half as beautiful as you, my little flower." Farfar swept her up in one strong arm and held her so she could inspect the ornaments on the tree. He had embraced the role of foster grandfather to the little girl. "See this pinwheel here?" he asked. "It's made of celluloid and it belonged to my mother when she was your age."

"What makes it go round and round?"

"The heat from the candle is just below it," Magnus said importantly. "Heat creates energy, which makes it twirl around."

She nodded thoughtfully, as if she understood. "And this one?" she asked, pointing to a little carved ornament. "You made it all by yourself, didn't you, Magnus?"

"Indeed I did. Farfar let me use his tools." Magnus was

extremely good at carving things. He held the ornament so she could see it. "It's got a secret inside." He moved a hidden catch and the small box opened.

The little girl gasped with wonder. Inside the box was a tiny beeswax figure of a dog. "That's clever, Magnus. Isn't he clever, Farfar?"

"He certainly is."

Magnus shut the box and hung it back on the tree. "You'd never know it's hollow, right?"

She nodded enthusiastically.

"What do you want from the *nisse* this year?" asked Farfar. Earlier, he had regaled Magnus and Eva with stories of the mythical elf. "Remember, that in one magical night, the *nisse* can grant wishes to boys and girls. Maybe you'll wish for a baby doll, or a pair of skates?"

Eva turned somber. "My mama. That's all in the world I want."

Magnus could see Farfar's smile stiffen at the edges. They were all keeping a secret from Eva. She was too young to handle the truth.

"The *nisse* can't do that sort of magic," Farfar said.

"What good is he, then?" The little girl's chin trembled.

"That," said Farfar, "is a very good question. I must stay up late tomorrow night and ask him."

"Aren't you afraid?" Her eyes widened.

In spite of himself, Magnus shivered. The *nisse* was a friendly elf, but it would be strange to meet up with one.

But Eva was a child with a sunny spirit, full of hope. She seemed determined to be happy despite the fact that her mother had abandoned her and her father. When Magnus gave Eva the cup of warm malted cream, she accepted it with a smile that wrapped around his heart.

He looked around the room and felt awash with gratitude.

This was the fine essence of life, these moments when a family was together doing the simplest of things. His mother and father went over to the table to drink their cordial and write Christmas greetings to their friends. Farfar showed Eva more ornaments on the tree, embellishing the stories behind them. Uncle Sweet worked in the darkroom, whistling as he brought images to life on his special paper. The recipe for happiness was just so simple, Magnus thought. Yet something about it seemed incredibly fragile, as though it might be shattered at any moment.

"Have I ever told you about the story behind this?" Farfar asked, turning away from the Christmas tree. It was as if he wanted to distract the little girl from dwelling on false promises and wishes that couldn't possibly come true. He opened the curio cabinet against the wall and took out his proudest possession—a jeweled egg on an ornate stand.

Eva seemed happy to allow herself to be distracted. "It's very pretty."

"It's one of my favorite things. Let's have a look at it."

Magnus was drawn to the fire, where Farfar and Eva sat. The large, colorful egg was one of Magnus's favorite things, too, because it was so cleverly made. "It's got a secret," he said to Eva. "Can I show her, Farfar?"

"Of course. You know all its secrets."

Magnus found the cabochon ruby clasp and pushed it in, causing the egg to open.

Eva clapped her hands. "There's something inside!" She leaned forward to inspect. "It's an angel. A pretty girl angel."

Carved of alabaster and embellished with real gold, the figure resembled St. Lucia, with a crown of leaves and a candle held between her hands.

"That's right," said Farfar. "She even has a name—Maria.

The jeweler created this egg to commemorate her birth. The little girl's father gave it to me long ago as a token of gratitude."

"Farfar saved the girl's life," Magnus said, beaming with pride at his grandfather. "He's the best doctor there is."

"Was the girl sick?" Eva asked.

"Very sick," said Farfar. "But she was brave and determined to get better. Her parents were so grateful that they gave me the Angel egg and a letter, expressing their thanks."

"Her father was an important man," Magnus said. "A rich man."

"But he knew what all my patients discover, that all the riches in the world are worthless without one's health."

"Whatever happened to the little girl?" Eva touched her finger to the angel's, which was made of gold and abalone.

"She grew to be a lovely young lady, and she married a prince, and they moved to a far-off land where it was safe for them to live," said Farfar.

Eva twirled around the room, the angel cradled in her hand. "Does that mean she's a real actual princess now?"

"I suppose it does, at that," said Farfar. "Although she lives in exile."

"Where is exile?"

"It's not a place. Exile is when you don't get to live in your homeland anymore, because it's too dangerous."

"Like Daddy and me," said Eva, thus proving she probably understood more about the situation than they realized.

"Magnus, can you mind the fire?" his mother asked. "It's gotten cold in here."

He turned back the carpet runner by the Christmas tree to reveal the coal bin built into the floor. It was a clever innovation by him and his father. The coal was loaded into a drawer from the outside, and could be accessed from within, thus saving a trip out into the weather. Taking care with the scuttle, he added coal to the fire.

Just then a pounding rattled the door. "Gestapo," came a harsh voice. "Open up."

Magnus's father jumped up and hurried to the door. At the same time, his mother took Eva by the hand and headed upstairs, motioning for Magnus to follow. He didn't. Some impulse made him lower the jeweled egg into the coal bin before shutting the trapdoor and flipping the carpet back in place.

His heart hammered like a bird beating its wings against the bars of the cage, and he could scarcely catch his breath. He felt ill with fear, yet at the same time, the heated rush of blood through his veins made him feel exhilarated, every cell in his body pulsing with life. He composed himself as he went to stand beside his father and grandfather.

"Good evening," said Father. His face was as still and expressionless as a funeral mask. The German soldier stepped forward, filled with self-importance. He was shadowed from behind by two others. Something Magnus had noticed about the Germans was that they never went about on their own. They always traveled in groups. These three wore the winter uniforms of brown and buff-colored wool, hats flecked with snowflakes and tall boots polished so brightly that they reflected the candlelight from the Christmas tree. The leader of the three wore a long belted overcoat and black gloves. They all had holstered weapons, wearing them as casually as a watch on a fob.

"Which one of you is Dr. Johansen?" asked the leader.

"That would be me," Farfar said. "What do you want?"

"You will come with us," the soldier ordered.

"Not without an explanation." Farfar spoke mildly, yet there was a thread of defiance in his voice.

The German's clean-shaven jaw tightened visibly. "It is not a request, but an order. Your medical services are required."

"In what capacity?"

"Major Fuchs, the Hauptsturmführer, has taken ill. I will not waste precious time negotiating with you, explaining the situation. Get your coat and come with me."

"I have other patients and other duties to attend to," Farfar said. "If you would kindly give me the address, I will come around when—"

"You will do as you are told," the German insisted. "Now. Without delay. As a man of healing, you can do no less."

The other soldiers took a step closer. Magnus could see them scanning the room, their eyes lighting on the glasses of cordial on the desk, the dancing fire, the curio cabinet with its door left open. He couldn't tell what they were looking for. He tried to view it from their perspective. It looked like the home of an ordinary Danish family. He'd heard rumors, though, of the invaders helping themselves to people's artwork and jewelry, or taking it away to the local armory for safekeeping.

The Germans pretended their invasion was meant to safeguard the Danes. However, everyone knew the people of Copenhagen had been perfectly safe before that April morning when they'd woken up to the news that their country had been occupied.

Magnus studied the faces of the soldiers in their parlor. He wondered what was going on behind those darting, narrowed eyes. Did it feel awkward to them, coming into people's private homes, checking out their things?

"Pardon me," said Magnus's father, "but if the officer is so gravely ill, shouldn't he be taken to the hospital?"

"Dr. Johansen, you will come with us," said the Gestapo officer.

Farfar cleared his throat. "Let me get my kit and my coat," he said. "I will see what I can do."

Later, Magnus realized he should have recognized the signs that this was the last he would see of his grandfather. After he donned his good wool overcoat, Father helped him on with his muffler, slinging it around his neck and holding him close for a few seconds, whispering something and then kissing him. Farfar's eyes were bright behind his spectacles as he bent down and kissed Magnus, whispering, "You be as good and brave as I know you can be."

Then Farfar put on his hat with the earflaps, and his gloves, picked up his bag and followed the soldiers out into the night.

Magnus never gave up hoping to see his grandfather again. He later heard that the Hauptsturmführer recovered, declaring that he owed his survival to the brilliant Danish physician. However, unlike other grateful patients, he had given Dr. Johansen no reward, but instead pressed him into service to the German elite officers.

The Johansen family didn't have to wonder how the Germans had located a skilled doctor to cater to their needs. The Nazis intruded into everyone's lives, stripping away all their privacy, delving into their secrets. Magnus heard his parents speaking of it in low whispers, late into the night.

Though they could not arouse suspicion by appearing to flee, it was decided that Sweet would take Eva up to the family orchards to the north of the city, near a village called Helsingør, on the island of Zealand in the Øresund Strait. There was a small country house that was used in the summer, and some very basic cottages where the pickers stayed during the harvest.

After Farfar was taken and Uncle Sweet and Eva had fled, Christmas arrived, a subdued holiday with just Magnus and his parents. Friends came around in the afternoon and kind words were exchanged, but nothing was the same. Everyone in Copenhagen now understood that nothing would ever be the same.

Typically, the Christmas tree was left up until Epiphany, just after the new year. But the tree started dropping its needles on Christmas Day, and turned as dry as tinder. Magnus's mother announced that they would take it down before Epiphany this year. The end of Christmas was always a melancholy time, and far more so this year, without Farfar to remind everyone that the new year was here, bringing fresh opportunities each day.

Boxing Day was a miserable affair. It never even got light enough to extinguish the lamps. An icy rain hissed over the city, battering at the snow until the streets and sidewalks were covered in dirty pockmarks. Magnus's father went to the town council to file an objection that Farfar had been illegally pressed into service to the Nazis. Proper Danes did not take kindly to those they perceived as collaborators.

A few days later, Father came home wearing a scowl of frustrated fury, declaring that he had accomplished nothing. Over dinner that night, he and Magnus's mother barely spoke, though Mother said something Magnus would always remember—"It's as if they have sucked every bit of happiness out of the city."

"If we allow them to do that," said Magnus's father, "then they have already won."

She pushed aside her plate of eggs and rye bread. "Perhaps it has already happened. I don't even want to be here anymore. I wish we lived someplace else."

He patted her hand. "Where, then, my love? We're born and raised here. I grew up in this very house. Where else would we go?"

"America," Magnus piped up. "It's the place where everyone goes to make a new start."

"That's what some folks say." His father took a sip of mulled apple cider. "However, others say it's a haven for outlaws and criminals and misfits who can't make a go of life in their own homeland."

"The Nazis make me wish I could be an outlaw," Magnus declared. "In fact, maybe I'll become one." He thought about the fires he and his friends "accidentally" set around the German supply ships in port, when the soldiers weren't looking.

"You mustn't talk like that. One day, this will all be over, and we'll get our lives back." His mother sighed, then got up to clear the table. "I miss chocolate."

Father stood and kissed her cheek. "We all miss chocolate, love." He turned to Magnus. "Let's have a proper wood fire in the fireplace tonight, shall we? Not just coal in the stove."

"Yes," said Mother. "It'll brighten up the house as we take down the Christmas tree."

Magnus jumped up. "I'll bring in the wood."

"Bundle up, and don't forget to cover your ears."

He dressed for the weather, which had turned bitterly cold after the rains at Christmas. Now everything was silvered with a coating of ice, making it appear otherworldly, like a painting in a museum.

In the center of the garden was his mother's favorite piece—a tiered birdbath, which in the springtime played host to blackcaps and warblers. Since the Germans had arrived unannounced before Christmas, the birdbath served another purpose. Mother had hidden her good jewelry in the hollow section under the top tier. People in the city were taking precautions. The German marshal claimed his men were models of integrity. The Danes knew such grand pronouncements didn't stop the soldiers from having sticky fingers.

Ice had transformed the humble stone birdbath into a precious vessel; it resembled a pair of silver bowls one might find in a church.

The blackout curtain at the back door had been left up to give him some light for working. Through the glass he saw his mother crank up the Victrola; then he heard her favorite record start to play. Father swept her up into a dance hold, and they swayed together to the rhythm. In that moment they were a refuge for each other, holding the world at bay, if only for a short time. Magnus imagined they let themselves stop worrying about Farfar, and the shortages, and the soldiers who overran the city.

He turned to the wood shed and took up the maul, finding a refuge of his own in the violent labor of splitting a dry log into kindling.

Soon the cold gave way to the heat of exertion, and he welcomed the fire in his muscles. There was something immensely satisfying in breaking apart a thick log, wrenching it open to expose the clean-smelling heart of the wood.

From the corner of his eye, something in the house caught his attention. He paused in his work and looked up to see a different kind of movement through the glass of the door.

Soldiers.

The sweat generated by Magnus's labor suddenly turned as cold as the ice that coated the garden. His grip on the maul tightened convulsively as his stomach clenched in fear.

He saw three uniformed men moving menacingly toward his parents while the music played on. His first instinct was to protect, to rush inside with the sharp maul and split the Germans' heads open like fat blocks of wood.

Despite his rage and fear, he held the impulse in check. He was no match for three burly soldiers with their sidearms and bayonets.

It was terrible to watch. They were no better than thieves, rifling through drawers and cupboards while forcing Magnus's parents to stand against the wall, helpless and white-faced with terror.

He felt sick, his stomach churning, his heart pounding, his breath scraping in his chest. He shook like a palsied old man. He couldn't think. He had to think. If he rushed inside to be with his parents, they would trap him, as well.

If he went for help—there was no one to go to for help. The city police were powerless and under orders to obey the Germans. The thieves. Their harsh voices rumbled from the house. Magnus looked around wildly, wondering if he should sneak next door to the Hansens'.

No. That could expose another family to danger. He would not be responsible for that.

They were questioning his parents now, their voices sharp. Magnus was proud to hear his father's even tone. He didn't panic or plead. Magnus pressed himself into the shadows of the garden, hiding by the stacked wood. If the soldiers came outside, would they notice the tracks in the snow? Would they find the cache of valuables in the birdbath?

As the terror swirled through his head, the back door opened. The blinding glare of a handheld electric torch swept across the area. And somewhere inside himself, Magnus found a core of steel. He simply stopped breathing, so his frozen breath wouldn't give him away. He stopped trembling through sheer force of will and stayed as still as a statue.

The beam from the torch intruded like a nosy neighbor, pausing on the snow-clad apple trees, the acacia bushes, his mother's garden bench. Magnus continued to hold his breath, to hold himself motionless. The only sign that he was alive, and human, and just a scared kid was the one reaction he couldn't control, something that would haunt him with humiliation until the end of time—he pissed himself. He couldn't help it, didn't even know it was happening until it was too late, and by then he was powerless to stop.

A storm trooper came out to the edge of the back porch, his heavy boots thumping on the planks. The beam swung again, seeming to snag on the birdbath. Then it moved on, passing over Magnus's hiding place. He wondered if the German would see that someone had been splitting wood for a fire.

The soldier coughed, hawked up phlegm and spat loudly, then went back inside. Magnus let out his breath and scooped in lungfuls of fresh, cold air. A sound he couldn't identify came from inside, a clattering and scraping. He could no longer hear his parents' voices. Then everything went quiet, but a smell of burning filled the air.

He started to tremble again. He thought he might throw up but didn't let himself. He counted to ten, then concluded that the soldiers had left. Moving stealthily, he went to the door and peered inside. He could see no one, but the downstairs was filled with smoke.

Magnus broke out of his state of terror and burst inside, into the house, racing from room to room while calling for his parents. There was no answer, and they were nowhere to be found. They'd been wrenched away like Farfar.

The Christmas tree lay on its side, turned into a torch by the fallen candles, its treasures and ornaments scattered everywhere. He ripped off his overcoat and beat out the flames, coughing from the pine-scented fumes. A large hole had been burned in the carpet, and the floor itself was charred. The walls and ceilings were streaked with black, the family pictures that hung there obscured by soot.

Once assured that the fire was out, he made a more thorough search of the rooms, calling to his mother and father, all the while gulping with sobs of hopelessness. The house had been ransacked; he could see that the liquor cupboard and the pantry had been emptied by the greedy soldiers. Along with the reek of burning pitch, a feeling of violation hung in the air. This was no longer a home. It was not a safe haven. The German intruders had turned it into a place of peril.

They had taken more than just liquor and valuables; they'd taken the things that made the house a home—the sense of family, of love, of security. What they probably did not realize was that they had left something behind—a very scared, very angry boy.

TWELVE

Tess slept poorly, trying to ignore the soft and secretive sounds of nighttime in the countryside. In between bouts of wakefulness, she catnapped, her rest plagued by dreams of Magnus. She missed the city. The silence and fresh air of the deep countryside were overrated, in her estimation. She didn't find the sounds of birds and crickets restful at all, but repetitive and distracting. The noise of the city, with its clanging and screeching trolleys, its sirens and ships' horns, made a better soundtrack for her life.

Magnus was no longer a stranger to her, no longer just a name on a piece of paper or an academic problem, like an object whose provenance she was charged with uncovering. He was a person with a haunted history, someone whose childhood had been ripped apart in ways she could only imagine. He had clearly suffered great losses, yet then he'd survived and built a future for himself. He was a man whose life had mattered.

She thought briefly of her own life and how it mattered—or not. Yes, she had a career she was passionate about. Yes, she was going to move to the next level in the firm once she concluded things here at Bella Vista. That had been her goal all along, hadn't it?

The idea caused a flurry of nerves in her stomach. Family and friends—not work—were the things that made a life matter. Being here, being pulled deeper and deeper into the heart of this place, she feared work had taken precedence over everything else, and now she felt...unbalanced. Her friends in the city were great, but were they the heart-mates of a lifetime? Just asking herself the question made her uncomfortable, so she pushed the troubling notion aside.

It was still dark when she abandoned sleep altogether and went to her laptop. She'd taken a series of high-resolution pictures of the old photo and document. Using her photo enhancement program, she went to work, her excitement building as she brought each detail into focus.

All too soon, the sounds of night gave way to the sunny chirps and whistles of songbirds at daybreak. She abandoned any attempt at further sleep and got dressed for the day, pulling on a good pair of jeans and a striped top. That was another thing—she was running out of clothes to wear as her visit to Bella Vista lengthened.

The smells of Isabel's kitchen elevated her mood somewhat. There was something incredibly uplifting about getting up in the morning to a perfect cup of coffee and a freshly baked treat from the oven. The kitchen was the heart of the house at any time of day, but mornings in particular were grounded in the sunny space, open to the patio. The start of the day was a small celebration of sorts, with people coming through the kitchen for their coffee and to have a chat, lingering before heading out for the day. So far, none of the residents or workers knew about the financial state of Bella Vista. They gathered as usual while *Morning Edition* drifted from the radio and Charlie the dog trotted from person to person, looking for handouts.

It was a sharp contrast to the mornings Tess was used to. In the city, she would tear out of her cluttered apartment, stopping off for fast-food coffee and a donut as she raced to the office.

Yes, she missed the city. But she had to admit, Isabel's coffee and freshly toasted and buttered *tartines* softened the blow. She spied a knot of people down by one of the sheds, gathered around a cider press. Phone in hand, she went down to join them. She had not yet surrendered the hope of getting a decent signal. Ernestina's husband and two other workers, dressed in their coveralls and John Deere caps, worked the press, filling the air with the crisp scent of fresh cider.

At the center of it all was Isabel, as ethereal as a princess in a fairytale. This was her world, and the people who lived and worked here were her family. Although Tess was just getting to know her sister, she understood that being forced to leave Bella Vista would practically kill Isabel. And what would become of the Navarros, getting on in years, caring for their disabled son?

Finding their grandparents' photo archive had given Tess a glimmer of hope that perhaps there was a way out of this. Magnus had clearly come from a family of means; perhaps the treasures were valuable enough to stave off the bank. But with the foreclosure looming over them like the blade of an ax, she worried that they would run out of time before they uncovered the mystery behind Magnus's treasures.

She sipped cider, tasting heaven and easing her worries, if

only for the moment. "Why do people drink anything else when they can have this?" she asked Isabel.

"Don't let the wine growers hear you say that."

Isabel opened the door and led the way inside. Hearing a voice, Tess had a sense of impending tension; some part of her knew what was about to happen.

"Hello," Isabel called. "Ernestina, is someone here?"

The tension subsided into a dull sense of ambivalence. Tess could feel Dominic's hand fall away behind her.

She stood unmoving as a slender, auburn-haired woman hurried down the hallway to throw her arms around Tess.

"Oh, baby," she said, "are you all right? I came as fast as I could."

"Hi, Mom," said Tess, feeling a terrible combination of fury and relief. "I guess you got my messages." For a moment, she hung on, taking in her mother's scent of designer perfume from the duty-free shop, which she always used to freshen up after a long flight. No matter how old she got, no matter how much time they'd spent apart, Tess always sought security in her mother's embrace. Never mind that it was an illusion, particularly in light of what she'd learned since coming to Bella Vista.

She stepped aside, turning to face Dominic and Isabel. "This is Shannon Delaney, my mother. Mom, this is Dominic Rossi and Isabel Johansen. I guess you've met Ernestina."

"She was kind enough to receive me."

Ernestina excused herself and left through the kitchen door.

Shannon gave Isabel's hand a squeeze, then let go. "You're Francesca's daughter."

Whoa, thought Tess. How would her mother know that? When had Shannon seen Isabel's mother? Had they known each other?

"I am." Isabel studied Shannon, wide-eyed.

"My God, you look just like her. Is she here?" asked Shannon.

Isabel frowned. "My mother passed away a long time ago."

"Oh, no. What happened?"

"She died in childbirth."

She died on our birthday, thought Tess.

Shannon put a hand to her mouth. "I'm sorry. I didn't realize. And I'm sorry about Magnus. Tess told me he had a terrible accident."

"I didn't tell you," Tess said before she could stop herself. "I sent you an email, because you didn't return my calls. Or my texts. Or my follow-up emails."

Dominic cleared his throat. "Looks like you have some catching up to do, and I need to get home," he said. "It was a pleasure to meet you." He turned to Tess. "Will you be all right?"

"Yes, sure, fine," she said. "Really." God, was it that obvious that her mother made her crazy?

"Boyfriend?" Shannon asked, watching him go.

"No," Tess and Isabel answered at once. They both sounded overly eager to clarify this.

"He's, um, a family friend," Isabel explained. "Please, let's go to the kitchen. I'll get you something to eat."

"As you can imagine," Tess said bluntly, "we have some questions for you."

"Tess—"

"I don't even know where to start. Maybe with this one. Maybe you could tell us how the hell the two of us came to be born on the same day."

"What?"

"We have the same birthday, Isabel and I. Don't you find that totally bizarre?"

"I didn't know. My God." Shannon's mouth hardened and her posture stiffened as she followed Isabel into the kitchen. "Unfortunately, the two people who know the answer to that are no longer with us."

Isabel had always enjoyed a house full of people. *Feed your friends, and their mouths will be too full to gossip,* Bubbie used to say. *Feed your enemies, and they'll become your friends.* Throughout Isabel's childhood, the Johansen household had been full of people coming over, sitting down for a glass of wine or a slice of pie, staying up late, talking and laughing. Bubbie and Grandfather had been determined that she should never feel like an orphan.

Except that, despite their efforts, sometimes she had. It wasn't their fault, she reflected as she placed wedges of quiche on plates. There was just something inside her—an urge, a yearning—that made her long to be someone's daughter, not the granddaughter. She never said so, though, not aloud. Yet somehow, they heard her. Somehow, they knew.

Perhaps, in the aftermath of Bubbie's final illness and passing, that was why Isabel had become so bound to Bella Vista. Now she couldn't imagine being anywhere else. Her heart resided here, her soul. She still loved having people over, creating beautiful food, watching the passing of the seasons. Even now, with all the trouble afoot and secrets being revealed like the layers of a peeled onion, she found the rhythm of the kitchen soothing.

She ground a dusting of nutmeg onto the quiche, then brought a tray to the long pine table. There, Tess was speaking intently and in low tones to her mother, but she fell silent when Isabel appeared.

Isabel thought about the mysteries of the mother–daughter

relationship. She'd idealized it in her head, but clearly things were not always smooth.

"Don't let me interrupt," she began, setting down the tray. "Like Dominic said, you've got some catching up to do."

"*We've* got catching up to do," Tess said. "Sit down. Please." Isabel liked the "we." It made her feel less alone.

"This is the first real food I've had since the patisserie trolley at the Bordeaux airport," Shannon said. She took a bite, and an expression of rapture came over her face. "They'll probably close the borders of France to me for saying this, but I've never had a better quiche lorraine."

Tess's mother possessed a combination of Irish charm and whimsy and American directness. According to Tess, these traits had served her well in her profession and maybe in her social life. As a mother, perhaps not so much, judging by what Tess had said. With her auburn hair and English tea rose complexion, Shannon didn't really look like anyone's mother.

"Here's a puzzle for you," Tess said, showing Shannon the baby picture they'd found in Grandfather's study. "How did Magnus end up with a photo of me?"

Shannon turned pale. "Call it impulse," she said softly. "Sentimentality, I don't know." She gazed down at the image, her eyes misting. "You were so very beautiful, and I was so proud of you. I wanted Erik's parents to have something, even if they didn't know who you were. It's such a lovely shot. I'm glad they kept it."

"You didn't include a letter? You didn't tell them who you were? Who I was?" Tess sounded incredulous.

"I was afraid," Shannon said. "I didn't know Francesca was gone, and I didn't want them to think I wanted anything from them."

"Well, at some point Magnus figured out who I was and changed his will."

"I had nothing to do with that," said Shannon. "I swear. I'm so sorry, Tess. But I'm glad I'm finally here." She helped herself to another wedge of quiche.

"Isabel's an amazing cook," Tess said, though she was merely picking at her salad.

"Thanks," said Isabel. "I always thought I'd do it professionally one day." She hurriedly sampled her quiche, wishing she hadn't said anything. There were bound to be follow-up questions to that.

"Did you go to culinary school?" asked Shannon.

"I attended the Culinary Institute of America in Napa," said Isabel. "For a while."

"I believe your mother was a talented cook. She personally prepared nearly all the food at Erik's funeral reception."

"How did you know my mother?" asked Isabel, desperate for every last crumb of information.

"That," said Shannon, her eyes glazing with jet lag and memories, "is complicated."

"And why the hell have you been lying about my father all these years?" Tess demanded.

"That," her mother said, "is even more complicated."

THIRTEEN

Berkeley, California
1984

In the middle of a lengthy lecture on Russian literature—
taught in Russian—Shannon Delaney bolted for the ladies'
room. Unfortunately for her, Wheeler Hall was a gigantic
building with hallways a mile long, and she didn't quite make it.

She puked all over the floor of the historic, marble-halled
building.

Long ago, she'd ceased being grossed out by her own puking. Every day, something had made her throw up. Although
the pregnancy books she'd read (and she had read them all)
said that morning sickness generally lasted through the first
three or four months of gestation, Shannon's "morning" lasted
all day. The nausea had been with her like a plague throughout her pregnancy.

As if being alone, pregnant and broke wasn't hard enough, this baby, this tiny hiding stranger, seemed determined to make her life as difficult as possible. Shivering and damp with sweat, she hurried to the restroom to tidy up. Afterward, she went to the janitor's closet between the restrooms and used her key to open the door. Yes, she had a key. Because not only was she alone, pregnant and puking, she earned extra money doing janitorial work on campus. It was the only way she could figure out to stay in school. She was just half a year away from getting her master's degree and she refused to give up, even if it meant scrubbing the toilets of California's most famous university.

The wheels of the mop bucket creaked as she pushed it toward the mess. Letting out a shuddering sigh, she got to work. Simple bending was an ordeal now that she was as big as a house. Everything these days was an ordeal—making ends meet, studying at night without falling asleep in her chair, explaining her predicament to her professors and fellow students. Nothing, however, compared to the task looming ahead.

She had to tell her mother. She'd been putting it off, but one of these days, Mom would visit from Dublin, and then, the jig would be up. Shannon was confident her mother wouldn't judge her. God knew, having a baby out of wedlock was something of a tradition among Delaney women. But she'd be disappointed, for sure. And worried. Shannon hated worrying her mom.

She thought back to when she'd first met Erik Johansen last year, introduced by a TA named Zia Camarada, with whom she'd become friends. He'd swept into her life like a whirlwind, driving a red convertible Karmann Ghia and filling her days with adventure and her nights with more love and tenderness than she'd ever felt from a man before. With his striking Nordic looks and passion for life, he'd been like a force of nature. She fell for him fast and hard, so hard that when he said his wife had recently left him, she'd simply believed him.

Dizzy with love, she assumed the feeling would last forever. Erik was a California boy with nothing to his name except a liberal arts degree, the heir apparent to a huge apple farm in Sonoma, ably managed by his doting parents. He and Shannon had spent endless lazy mornings in bed together, in her little garret on the north side, fantasizing about their future. Under the cheap canopy of India print cloths she'd draped from the ceiling to hide the bare lightbulbs, they'd talked for hours about the life that awaited them. They would travel the world; she would pursue her dream of bringing precious works of art to museums and private collectors. Everything was golden.

Then one day he'd arrived, his usually brash air subdued. "I love you," he'd said, and words had never hurt Shannon so much. They hurt, because some deeply intuitive part of her sensed what was coming next: "I have to break it off."

It was a story as old as time. The wife who had left him was back—and she was pregnant. Erik owed it to Francesca to repair the marriage and take care of her and their child. A few weeks afterward, Shannon herself was a ball of misery, nauseous and alone, shocked to find herself pregnant, too—but determined not to tell him that she was as foolish as his wife.

Then Shannon did something stupid, something all the rule books cautioned against. She became obsessed with Francesca. Though it could only make the hurt worse, she simply had to see this woman, whose very existence had killed Shannon's dreams. She went crazy one day and borrowed her friend's VW and drove all the way to the tiny town of Archangel.

She didn't have a plan. At the edge of the Bella Vista apple orchard was an old-fashioned building—a fruit stand. It was whitewashed and featured a front porch edged with carpenter

Gothic trim, and it looked as inviting as lunch with a friend. But looks, she knew with painful certainty, often lied. There, she encountered a petite older woman with an accent, and the beautiful Francesca. It had to be Francesca. And she was beautifully pregnant.

"Can we help you?" Francesca's voice sounded like liquid silk.

"Just…looking."

"When is your baby due?" asked the dark-haired woman.

"March."

"Mine, too." Francesca smiled, smoothing her hand down over the graceful curve of her stomach.

They were both due in March. Erik had gone from one woman's arms to the other's. Numb with shock, Shannon fled. There was nothing but heartache for her here.

And that had been the last of it. She was on her own.

As she was mopping up a dull green hallway floor, a buzzer signaled the end of the class sessions, and students came pouring out of the classrooms. Undergrads. They all looked young and slender and carefree, barely affording her a glance as they headed out into the sunshine of the quad. As the last of them departed, she saw a man silhouetted at the entryway—and she froze.

It was Erik. She recognized his broad shoulders and manly stance, even though she couldn't see his face. Her first instinct was to dive into the janitor's closet to hide, but she could tell from the sudden stiffening of his posture that he'd spotted her.

"All right, then," she said, leaning on the mop as he approached her. In spite of herself, she had a wild thought: *He's come for me. He came to his senses and realized he can't live without me and here he is.*

He stared at her. She could feel his astonishment as his gaze traced the ungainly curves of her silhouette. She was not one of those glowing, graceful pregnant women. She was ridiculous, in loose thrift-store clothes, her face splotchy, her hair done up in a careless twist. "How did you find me?" she asked.

"I got your schedule out of the graduate registrar's office."

Charmed it out of them, she thought. He had a talent for that. "We agreed not to see each other anymore," she reminded him.

He ignored that. "Why didn't you tell me?" he asked. He kept his hands pressed firmly to his sides.

She tried to blot out the memories of those hands, and how tenderly they'd stroked her, cupped her face to tilt her mouth upward for a kiss. "We broke up," she said. "How did you find out?"

"Your friend Zia. She thought I deserved to know. And she's right. This…it changes everything."

"Does it?" She waited for him to say that the pregnancy was proof of their love. It was Fate telling them they should be together after all.

He said none of those things. His face was taut with earnestness and frustration as he said, "I can't be in your life the way you deserve, but I'll take care of you. I will. You and the baby. You'll never want for a thing."

I'm already wanting, she thought, instantly skeptical. He was completely dependent on his family. Even if he had the means to support her, she didn't for a moment think his wife would approve. Somewhere inside herself, Shannon found a reservoir of icy steel. "Just go," she told him. "Zia should have kept her mouth shut. This is totally messed up, and it'll never be sorted out. We need to cut our losses and move on."

"Absolutely not," he said. "I won't abandon you."

You already have.

"I need some air," she said, and walked outside together to a place they'd once considered their "spot." It was a pretty little wooden footbridge on campus near a log cabin known as Senior Hall, and it was their spot because they'd shared their first kiss there, after a Def Leppard concert at the Greek Theatre the night they'd met. They had both been high on pot and Southern Comfort, and the electricity between them had been irresistible.

She'd been too stupid to ask him if he was married. He'd later confessed that he had been, but that his wife had left him. He hadn't divorced her, though. She should have asked. For someone in one of the most selective grad programs on the planet, she should have been smarter.

Eric touched her shoulder, and she flinched away. He clenched his hands on the bridge railing. "I swear, I'll make things right for you, as right as I can."

"Given the fact that you already have a baby on the way with your wife." The nausea rose up through her again. "How are you going to make things right, Erik? How? You made your choice—to stay with your wife. I don't need anything from you, not a damn thing." *Except your heart,* she thought with a twist of pain. *And you won't give me that.*

"I'll take care of you financially," he said, his eyes begging her.

Shannon knew it wouldn't make the pain go away, but it would certainly help with her student loan payments, medical bills, babysitting.... "You don't have any money of your own."

"I'll get it. Trust me, Shannon. You have to trust me."

"What are you going to do, rob a bank?"

"I'll come up with a plan."

"The plan is, we go our separate ways."

He bridled, turning fierce and commanding. "I have rights."

She narrowed her eyes, reacting to the threat. "Don't you dare."

"I don't want to make trouble. I just need to give you what I can so I'll know you're taken care of."

"I don't need you, Erik."

"You need money," he said. "Quit thinking about your pride and think about your child. Our child."

She was one gulp away from puking again. "I won't take anything that has strings attached."

"Agreed. If you want, I'll sign a paper, I'll do anything...."

He would pay any price, she realized, to be free of her. To put her and her child conveniently aside. *Fine,* she thought, hardening her breaking heart. *Let him pay.*

FOURTEEN

"Why didn't you ever tell me any of this?" Tess asked her mother. "How could you keep it from me?"

Shannon sighed, looking from Tess to Isabel, and then down at her empty plate. The quiche had been followed by an apple and thyme turnover with cups of tea. "I just didn't see the point of telling you. By the time you were old enough to understand, everything was so deep in the past—a past no one could change."

"But it was part of me," Tess said. "Part of my history. Don't you think I was entitled to know?" All her life, the man who had fathered her had been a mystery. Her mother had let her believe she knew nothing of him, of his family or his past. "You told me you never knew my father's last name, that he was a one-night stand."

"It was the only way I knew to protect you," her mother shot back. "He was charming, handsome and careless with other people. I found out about the carelessness far too late. And then, once he was gone, there was no reason to pursue the issue. I can't regret knowing him, though, because he gave me you."

Oh, her mother was good, Tess conceded. A master manipulator. "All right," she said. "That was Erik. But why would you keep me from knowing my grandparents? Or my sister?"

"First of all, our life was elsewhere, thousands of miles away in Dublin. Jobs were hard to come by in those days so we had to live with your nana. And secondly, look around you. Look at this place. It's paradise. The American Eden."

"So horrifying," said Tess. "No wonder you protected me from it."

"I protected you from yearning for it. Can't you understand? I knew I could never give you a life that could compete with a place like this. If I'd brought you here, I would have given you a glimpse of paradise, saying oh, isn't it wonderful at Bella Vista? But guess what? You can never have it. You would have always been the outsider, the one born to the rogue's mistress."

"Now I get it," Tess said. "This was never about me. It's always been about you."

Isabel was watching the two of them like a spectator at a tennis match. Tess turned to her. "Sorry. Mom and I tend to push each other's buttons. Although keeping me in the dark about half my DNA takes button-pushing to a whole new level."

"Bubbie and I used to go at it, too," Isabel admitted. "I called my grandmother Bubbie," she told Shannon. "Her real name was Eva. Did you know her, too?"

"No, as I said, I was the outsider. I came to Bella Vista thinking... Honestly, I don't remember what. That's when I realized it would be best to keep my distance. Bringing Tess into the picture would have been messy and caused a lot of hurt. I'm so sorry. Sorry for your loss, and…" She turned to Tess. "For everything." Then she stifled a yawn. "Jet lag. It never gets easier."

Isabel got up. "I'm going to make sure your room is ready."

"I don't want to impose," Shannon said.

"Please," said Isabel. "I'd love for you to stay as long as you like. There's lots of room."

"Thank you, then. I've been traveling so much for work, it would be nice to take a breather."

"Diplomatic, gorgeous, cooks like an angel," Tess said after Isabel went upstairs. "But she's too nice to dislike."

Shannon gave her a weary smile. "I'm glad the two of you found each other."

"No thanks to you. Mom, what were you thinking?"

"That we'd never be having this conversation. Which was incredibly stupid of me. I realize that now."

Tess stifled a sigh and picked up one of her mother's bags. "I'll show you upstairs."

"This is perfect," Shannon said, running her hand along the chintz-covered bed in the cozy room Isabel had prepared. Turning, she gave Tess a lingering hug. "I'm so sorry about… everything."

A hundred accusations built up inside Tess, but she pressed them down into a little compact ball. "I'll be all right," she said. "I always am."

Shannon's smile softened with relief. "It's what we do, we Delaney women, isn't it? We find a way to be all right."

Isabel turned down the featherbed. "Do you give lessons? Because I could use some."

Shannon patted her arm. "I'll show you everything I know."

The next morning, Tess found Shannon on the kitchen patio, surveying the view. In one direction, Dominic's Angel

Creek vineyards festooned the hillsides, the leaves a bright sunny yellow. In the other direction was a much bigger, commercial operation—Maldonado estates. Closer in, the orchards of Bella Vista looked denuded after the harvest, the trees neatly pruned for winter, the lavender trimmed to low mounds. The kitchen garden was still thriving with herbs and fall vegetables, each row marked with sprays of crimson-and-gold mums, and the last roses of the season.

"It's wonderful here," Shannon said.

"Yes." Tess swallowed a lump of bitterness. "Listen, I need your help."

Shannon turned, eyebrows raised. "You never asked me for help before. You've always been so independent."

"By necessity," Tess told her.

"We're too much alike, we two."

"Speak for yourself. I've always needed you, Mom."

"Then you should have told me."

Tess gave a short laugh. "I didn't want to bother you. But look, I need some answers, not just about everything you've been hiding from me."

"Tess—"

"I know, you had your reasons." She just felt weary of the argument. "There's something more immediate."

Isabel came out and joined them, looking worried. Tess wondered how much she'd overheard. As succinctly as she could, she and Isabel described the troubles with Bella Vista and the imminent foreclosure. Then Tess showed her mother the photos and documents she and Isabel had found. "And then there's this. It's something you really can help with. How's your Russian?"

"Sharp as ever, I suppose." Shannon studied Tess's enhanced scans of the photo, letter and ancient receipt. "Well. This is intriguing, to say the least."

"I hope that means it's good news," Isabel said softly.

The three of them gathered around the table. Shannon read the words aloud. Hearing her mother speak fluently in Russian reminded Tess of her mother's depth of expertise and experience. In spite of everything, she respected her mother's knowledge.

"Well?" she asked.

"This letter is a note of gratitude," Shannon explained, "giving an art treasure called 'The Angel' to Christian Johansen, free and clear."

Tess was stunned. She made her mother go over and over the letter.

"I don't get it," Isabel said.

"This sort of document, assuming it can be authenticated, is a provenance expert's dream," Tess said. "A direct personal gift is a swift route to proving ownership of an object." The strange and ancient letter convinced her that the impossible just might be true. "What do you think?" she asked her mother.

"It's too crazy to contemplate, but I believe you're right. That's a Fabergé. If you can figure out what became of it, everything could change."

Tess was surprised by her mother's enthusiasm. Usually they respected each other as colleagues but tended to go their separate ways, focused on their own projects. Now the three of them put their heads together and discussed their next move.

"You need to ask the bank for more time," Shannon said. "This is definitely worth looking into."

"True," Isabel said softly. "But I doubt Dominic will be able to give us another extension."

"You owe it to yourself—to Magnus—to try," Shannon said.

"If this treasure exists, and it's as valuable as Tess thinks, then why didn't Grandfather use it long ago?" Isabel asked.

"That's one of the first things we'll ask him when he wakes up," Tess said.

FIFTEEN

Each day on his way to work, Dominic drove past the air-park where people kept their private jets and airplanes. Sometimes he dreamed about flying, soaring on his memories of the speed and power of flight. The aircraft here were a far cry from the high-tech Prowlers he used to pilot in the navy, but even the little Cessnas and Otters at the airpark caught at him. A couple of clients sometimes let him use their birds for the price of fuel. Just the sensation of leaving the earth, even for a little while, reminded him of who he used to be and the dreams he used to dream.

That had been a different life, and it had happened to a different person. And then, in an instant, everything had imploded—the house of cards that had been his navy career had come crashing down, both literally and figuratively, taking his marriage as collateral damage.

He didn't miss that life, though, and had no regrets about

relegating it to the past, closing it like a novel he'd finished and left behind in an airport lounge. His rebuilt life was designed to keep him close to his kids. Close, and out of harm's way.

So if he felt a twinge when he pulled into the bank parking lot each day, and stepped through the doors of his glass-walled office, he had only to remember how much his son and daughter needed him to be this person, this rock of stability and predictability.

He missed the flying, though. Man, did he like flying a plane.

Taking out his phone, he scowled at the latest text message from his ex-wife. It had been sitting on his phone screen like a dormant virus, waiting for a response. Can you stay for dinner when you pick up the kids tonight?

This was her latest thing. Apparently Lourdes had dumped yet another boyfriend and was back to trying to reconcile with Dominic. She did this periodically. For the sake of the kids, he handled the situation with as much compassion as he could muster, knowing his ex-wife's attention would wander away soon enough. He just wished she would stop planting seeds of false hope in the children, particularly Trini. They were already scarred by the divorce, and Lourdes's manipulation simply reopened old wounds.

He sent her a simple No, thanks and scrolled through his agenda for the day. Underwriters and regulators didn't amount to a lot of excitement, but he reminded himself that mortgage lending had its upside. A guy could do worse than help people buy their homes. Some days, when he enabled a hardworking couple to qualify for their first mortgage, when he saw the look on their faces as they signed the papers, he felt like a latter-day George Bailey in *It's a Wonderful Life,* dispensing dreams to deserving people.

Other days, he thought, as the Bella Vista white SUV

swung into the space beside him, he felt like Mr. Potter from the same movie, crushing hopes like a bug under a boot heel.

Tess Delaney got out of the car with her characteristic ball-of-energy movements—thumb skimming over her phone screen, the other hand jamming a sheaf of papers into her oversize handbag. To Dominic, it seemed the woman was never still. Which was probably a good thing for him, because if she slowed down for about two seconds, she might figure out that he couldn't take his eyes off her.

Her appeal went deeper than looks, though her long red hair and that pale, expressive face were enough to stop any guy in his tracks. There was something else about her. There were things about her that he couldn't stop thinking about. Lots of things.

Don't go there, he told himself. *That way lies madness.* He'd been the walking dead after his divorce. He'd tried to connect with other women since, and God knew, women had tried to connect with him. Nothing ever came of it, though.

He did want to be in love again—but on his terms, with someone who made sense in his life, not with someone like Tess Delaney. She was an unlikely candidate, anyway, given that he was in charge of foreclosure proceedings on her grandfather's place, and she was pursuing some supercharged career in the city. But damn.

She woke him up in ways he hadn't anticipated. It was no surprise that she turned him on, not with those looks and that attitude. The surprise was that she lit him up, made his heart remember what it was like to love someone.

He wasn't about to try explaining that to her, though. She wasn't ready to hear it. Yet he found himself intrigued by that busy restless energy and the way it concealed a side of her that was soulful and soft, something he'd only glimpsed a time or two. He'd seen that side of her when she'd visited Magnus.

She'd seemed as if she was in another realm for a moment. Not this moment, though. Right now, she looked as if she'd eaten roofing nails for breakfast.

"I don't have an appointment," she said, barely looking at him as she headed for the door. "So you're going to have to make time for me right away."

Maybe the appeal was in her personal charm, he thought, holding open the door for her. Yeah, right. "Good morning to you, too," he said.

She paused for half a second. "I think it might be. Maybe."

"Tea?" he offered. "There's a selection of herbal—"

"Coffee," she insisted. "Black, with sugar. *Refined* sugar, or is that against the law in this town?"

His assistant, Azar, gave a nod and headed to the staff room. Dominic gestured toward his office. "Have a seat."

She glanced around. "Wow, how do you get any work done in this space?"

His workspace was as neat as hers was messy. He liked to think he wasn't freaky about it. Just practical. Life was too short to spend his time trying to find stuff.

"Believe me, work is all I do in this space." There had been a time when work had consumed his life, with no boundaries between duty and personal hours. These days he was strict about keeping bankers' hours. The rest of his time was taken up by kids and grapes.

"It makes it easier to find what you're looking for. Plus, when you work in a glass office where the whole world can see you, it's best not to look like a slob."

"Better to look OCD?"

"Ha, ha."

"There is not a single personal item in this space. Hey, maybe you're sick in the head, like me."

"My personal stuff doesn't belong at work."

"Seriously, not even a photo of your kids?"

"I know what they look like." There was more to it than that. He had strong reasons not to put his daughter and son on display, but he would not go into it with Tess. He hit the power button on his computer. "Now, besides admitting to my undiagnosed mental illness, what can I do for you?"

Her expression lit up, and for a second, the breath left him. That inner fire of passion, burning so close to the surface, completely entranced him.

"I've found something," she said. "Isabel and I—we've found something. It could turn this whole situation around."

Dominic tried not to allow his inner skeptic to kick in. He didn't point out that he'd been trying to turn the Bella Vista situation around for years, literally. "I'm all ears," he said.

Tess studied him. There was a world of knowledge in the look she gave him. He wasn't fooling her for a second. "Right," she said; then her gaze shifted to the ceiling. "This bank is filled with cameras."

"It's a *bank.*"

"Can we go outside? Maybe take a walk?"

He glanced at the clock. He usually spent his first hour at the office dealing with email and reports, research and market studies. Tess Delaney was a lot more interesting than email and reports.

"Let's go," he said and held the door for her.

The bank was situated at one end of the town's main street, which bore the overly auspicious name of The Grand Promenade. It was a boulevard with a park in the center, shaded by plane trees and lined with benches for whiling the day away. The rich smells of autumn spiced the air—drying leaves and flowers going to seed, wood smoke from someone's chimney.

"What do you know about Magnus's past?" she asked him suddenly.

"Why do you ask?"

"Humor me. I might be onto something."

"What you heard at the gathering at Bella Vista just about sums it up. Magnus isn't the kind of guy to dwell on the past. And he seems more focused on putting things behind him rather than putting up a struggle. The health insurance dispute's a perfect example. He focused on his wife's treatment, and after she was gone, he didn't have any fight left in him."

"I don't get it at all," said Tess. "Why not fight back when his entire life's work is at stake?"

"That kind of struggle can wear a guy down." Dominic had developed an intimate understanding of this as he'd dragged himself through his divorce. Lourdes was a lawyer who knew everyone in the local legal community, and she'd brought up every possible dispute. He'd reached a point where he wanted it to be over rather than fairly settled. Letting himself dwell on the inequitable settlement would only keep him shackled to the past, to the failed marriage and to mistakes he couldn't change. Such things could eat you alive from the inside out if you let them. Ultimately, you had to let go.

They reached the town plaza, where the center strip of the boulevard widened into the big sculpture park in the middle of town. There were a few people around at this hour, but for the most part, the park was deserted.

She gestured at a concrete table in the shade. Some impulse of chivalry made him stand aside, placing his hand lightly on her waist as she took a seat. The casual touch startled the hell out of him. That subtle feminine curve, the light flowery scent of her hair, reminded him of just how agonizingly long it had been since he'd been close to a woman.

"Are you all right?" asked Tess.

"Fine. Why?"

"You look like you're in pain."

He cleared his throat. "So, what is it you don't want the bank cameras to record?"

She leaned toward him, and the breeze played with her hair. "There's news. We found something." Her eyes caught the light through the canopy of leaves overhead. He watched the glint of shifting sunlight in her red-gold locks. There was nothing sexier than red hair on a woman, he thought. He was fascinated by her energy, the passion that lit her face as she opened a folder on the table in front of him—copies of an old photograph, a yellowed letter in a foreign language and a diagram showing what appeared to be a family tree. Excitement transformed her from a harried, impatient woman into someone he found more captivating than ever. Not to mention the way her sweater fit. It was hard not to just sit there and stare at her...assets.

"Hey," she said, "I need you to pay attention."

"I am," he protested.

"To what I'm showing you, not to my boobs."

"I wasn't—" He stopped himself. He was a lousy liar. *Guilty as charged.*

Her eyes narrowed, and she straightened her top. "I mean it."

"Sorry. I'm listening," he assured her. And this time, he wasn't kidding. If she had a solution to the dilemma, he sure as hell wanted to hear it.

"Does—did—Magnus have a safe deposit box at the bank?"

"No. Not at my bank, anyway. Are you looking for something in particular?"

"Treasure," she said simply, as if it were the most common thing in the world. In her world, maybe it was. "That's what I want to show you. This old photo is from 1940, taken in Copenhagen. It's a shot of Magnus and his grandfather, Christian Johansen. Isabel and I found it in a box of old photos and memorabilia."

He studied the smiling boy in the picture, then looked up at Tess. "The family resemblance is pretty incredible. He looks like he could be your brother, and the grandfather is a twin of Magnus in his later years."

"Really?" For a moment, unguarded pleasure lit her eyes, and a blush stained her cheeks. Dominic was kind of crazy about the way she blushed so much. He liked that it made her seem a little vulnerable. Or open, maybe.

"I'm happy for you, Tess," Dominic said. "Finding a treasure is all in a day's work for you. It's not every day you find yourself a family."

At that, she bridled, narrowing her eyes and folding her arms in a self-protective gesture.

Oops, thought Dominic. *Way to put your foot in it.*

"That's not what I need you to focus on," she said. "It's this." She pointed to an object in the photograph, then took out a digital enlargement showing it bigger. "I enhanced the image so we could see more detail."

"Looks like some kind of knickknack or figurine." If anyone besides Tess were showing it to him, he would dismiss what she was saying. But Tess was in the business of finding treasure. "Judging by the expression on your face, I'm thinking it's something more than that," he added. Thinking about Magnus and Eva, about Isabel, and all that had happened, he wanted it to be. "Please tell me this is like one of those rare baseball cards and it's going to save the day."

"I don't deal with baseball cards. That's my colleague Jude's department." She tapped her hand on the enhanced photo. "This is more like a *deck* of rare baseball cards. A million decks."

"Now you're talking."

She took another document from her seemingly bottomless handbag. "It's a Fabergé egg," she said. "You've heard of them, right?"

"Sure. Tell me more."

"The House of Fabergé was founded by Gustav Fabergé in Russia in the 1800s. He married a Danish woman, and their son Carl's work caught the attention of the Tsar, who commissioned an Easter egg from him each year to present as a gift to the Empress, or to commemorate an event—like marriages, coronations, births, that sort of thing. The artist had complete creative freedom. The only stipulation was that the egg contain a surprise inside." She took out a small figurine. "So far, we have this."

He studied the small angel. "This is the surprise?"

"I believe so, yes. The eggs were made of solid gold and precious stones. This is alabaster. We found it among Magnus's things." She showed him some printouts of more recent photos of insanely elaborate eggs. They looked like clocks, like Cinderella's coach, like the Kremlin itself. They looked like stuff old ladies ordered from the back of *Parade Magazine*.

"I have to admit, I'm not an aficionado."

"The originals are rare and worth a fortune," Tess said. "The rarest of all are the Imperial Eggs, created for the Romanovs—the Russian Imperial family. Only fifty-four were ever produced, and of those, only forty-two have survived. After the 1917 revolution, a lot of the treasures were confiscated and stored in the Hermitage. Some of them went missing from there. An undiscovered Imperial Egg is like the Holy Grail to collectors."

"What do you mean, undiscovered? Were they stolen or hidden?"

"During the Bolshevik Revolution of 1917, most of the Imperial Eggs were confiscated and moved to the Kremlin Armory to be cataloged and stored. By the time Joseph Stalin began selling them in 1927, some had disappeared from the inventory. Others were sold to private collectors, who usually insisted upon anonymity. In all, eight of the Imperial Eggs are currently considered lost."

She regarded him with those fiery eyes and smiled briefly. "Sorry. I get wonky about this stuff."

"Go on. I'm intrigued."

"If this is what I think it is, it's known as the Angel." She indicated the figurine, small and smooth and exquisite as he held it in his hand. "It was designed to commemorate the birth of a daughter of Nikolai and Maria Romanov. Since she was their only child, born when her mother was forty, the assumption is that her birth was considered something of a miracle."

"No kidding." Every birth was a miracle, thought Dominic. He still remembered the incredible feeling of holding a newborn in his arms, studying the tiny limbs and features. He'd wanted more than two kids, but Lourdes, perhaps with a prescience he didn't possess, had her tubes tied after Trini. "So how did it end up with Magnus and his grandfather?"

She handed him another piece of paper, this one a color copy of what appeared to be a receipt of some sort. "This letter—it's in Russian—explains it. Magnus's grandfather was a physician. Nikolai was living in exile in Copenhagen, and his daughter was ill. According to this letter, Dr. Johansen saved her life, and Nikolai gave him the egg as a token of gratitude, and because he lacked the cash to pay him. I need for you to understand what this means. Ninety percent of my job involves tracing the provenance of an object. In this case, I have the clear chain of ownership right in front of me. This almost never happens. There are no ambiguities in its lineage. None. Curators would kill for this kind of provenance. It's perfect. You almost never get such a concise letter and a receipt, so obviously Nikolai knew what he was doing. He gave Dr. Johansen proof that the egg wasn't stolen or transferred illegally.

A find like this…it could be exactly what's needed to bail out Magnus and Isabel."

He noticed she didn't include herself in the bailout plan.

"So what's the value of this egg?" He couldn't imagine how a knickknack could cover Magnus's debts.

"At this point I can only estimate. Just for a point of reference, in 2007, a Fabergé egg once owned by the Rothschilds sold for £8.9 million. There was another, called the Winter Egg, which sold for $9.6 million. And these two eggs hadn't been missing for ninety years. The publicity alone for finding one of the lost Imperial Eggs would elevate the final price to… an impressive level. To say the least. The record amount paid for an egg—and it wasn't even an Imperial Egg—was $17.7 million, by a Russian collector named Ivanov."

He stared at her. "You're kidding. You're not kidding."

"It's my job to know these things."

"That's crazy."

"To most people, yes. But based on a piece's uniqueness and rarity, the value can go off the charts. This particular piece has something more. It's been lost for generations. A new discovery can amp up the excitement that builds around an item. There was a lost van Gogh that resurfaced in Amsterdam last year that went for a hundred million."

"You're throwing a lot of numbers around," Dominic pointed out. "Best guess."

She eyed him with something like admiration. "Twenty million. Just remember, this isn't an exact science."

He said nothing but felt an inner leap of hope. He couldn't show this to her, though. Not yet.

His silence must have made her nervous. She placed a hand on his arm. "It's not a lie. I'm not saying this to get you to put a stop to the foreclosure."

He liked the feel of her hand resting on his arm. He liked

her. She was a prickly, impatient woman, still a relative stranger, but there was something about her that completely challenged and intrigued him.

As if sensing his thoughts, she took her hand away.

"Why wouldn't Magnus have told me about this?" Dominic asked.

A shadow flickered across her face. "Maybe he didn't understand its value."

Sensing the deeper meaning of her remark, he wished he knew of a way to comfort her. There were some things, he reminded himself, that hurt more than financial distress.

"How soon can you come up with the money?" he asked. "Because, believe me, that's the first thing I'm going to be asked."

"Okay, yes. That." She clasped her hands around one knee and drew it up to her chest. "It might take some time. That's why I came to you. Because we need more time."

Great, he thought, remembering how hard he'd already pushed, going on years now, to protect Magnus from the proceedings. With the new bank in place, being put off was no longer an option.

"How long?" he asked again.

"I can't give you an exact date. But look, this is worth taking our time with. It's real, it's a fortune, and it could change everything."

"Excellent," Dominic said.

"There's only one issue," she added.

"What's that?"

"It's kind of major. See, this piece—the egg—is missing. No one knows where it is."

PART EIGHT

There is nothing like a plate or a bowl of hot soup, its wisp of aromatic steam making the nostrils quiver with anticipation, to dispel the depressing effects of a grueling day...rain or snow in the streets, or bad news in the papers.

—Louis P. De Gouy, *The Soup Book* (1949)

··· • ···

MULLIGATAWNY SOUP

Mulligatawny is a comforting curried soup of Indian origin; the name is a corruption of the Tamil phrase "Milagu thanni," which means "pepper water."

1 whole boneless chicken breast, cut into bite-size pieces

salt and pepper

4 tablespoons butter

diced fruits and vegetables, including a whole onion, a whole apple, a stick of celery, a carrot, a tomato and a bell pepper

1 clove of garlic, minced

¼ cup flour

1 tablespoon curry powder

1 teaspoon garam masala

4 cups chicken stock

1 cup cream or plain yogurt

cayenne pepper to taste

Season diced chicken with salt and pepper. Warm 2 tablespoons butter over medium-high heat in a wide, deep pot. Add chicken and sauté until golden; remove the chicken and keep warm. Add the rest of the butter to the pot and reduce heat to medium. Add diced vegetables and garlic and sauté until the mixture starts to brown. Sprinkle in flour and curry powder.

Add the chicken stock and stir to combine, then simmer

until vegetables and apple are soft. Puree in batches or with an immersion blender; the soup doesn't need to be perfectly smooth. Add the cream or yogurt and the chicken, and warm through. Season with salt and cayenne. Soup may be thickened with rice and topped with unsweetened coconut.

(Source: Adapted from *The Encyclopedia of Creative Cooking*)

SIXTEEN

Copenhagen
1941

"Have you ever worked with dynamite before, boy?" the Teacher asked Magnus. Mysterious and vaguely dangerous, the man known only as the Teacher led the ragtag band of saboteurs. He had a grizzled beard, thick black-rimmed spectacles and scarred hands, and he worked for the Resistance. He ran a gang of schoolboys known as the Lost Boys, a group of unruly orphans like the ones in that English adventure novel *Peter Pan*. Only this was no tropical island called Neverland; it was the heart of Denmark's capital city. And these days, it was more dangerous than a swamp filled with alligators.

No one in the organization knew much about anyone else,

so that if someone got caught he wouldn't have any information to hand over to the enemy.

Magnus had been one of the Lost Boys ever since German soldiers had blown his world apart, one night not long after Christmas.

"No, sir," he said. "I've never even held a stick of dynamite." Though eager to take on the challenge, he knew better than to lie to a fellow like the Teacher.

"Here you go." The Teacher had tossed him one.

Magnus had caught it gingerly, half expecting it to blow up in his face.

The Teacher chuckled. "Don't worry, it can't do anything without fire."

The thing looked and felt pretty innocuous, actually. It was shorter and fatter than a candlestick, and not colored red like it was in the comic books or the new Technicolor cartoons that still ran at the cinema every Saturday afternoon. Magnus had no money for such things anymore, but sometimes he and Kiki—another boy who worked for the Resistance—sneaked into the theater through an unlocked window.

"I'm listening," he said to the Teacher.

"Good, because we can't have any mistakes." The Teacher made him go over the plan until he could practically recite the steps backward.

In the game of cat and mouse the Underground played with the German soldiers, Magnus's weakness—the fact that he was a skinny, pale boy—became his greatest strength. He looked exactly like the kid he used to be—an ordinary schoolboy in his winter woolens, ice-skating on Byendam, a traditional winter recreational area in the center of town. The difference between the boy he once was and the orphan he'd become was that now, his bulky winter overcoat was lined with sticks of dynamite, spools of fuse cord and a big box of kitchen matches.

His target was an arsenal a short distance up the frozen stream that fed the lake. The building hadn't always been an arsenal, of course. It was simply an old pump house made of cut stone. The Germans used it for storing ordnance because its thick walls and the lack of windows protected the contents from the weather, and from intruders—so they thought.

But the Teacher liked it as a target. Those same thick walls could contain the blasts they intended to set off, thereby minimizing the damage done by the explosions.

On the appointed day, Magnus went to Byendam, stopping in the skating house to put on his skates. He left his rucksack with his shabby winter boots under a bench and glided onto the ice amid the others for a turn around the lake. Skating in seemingly aimless circles, he mulled over the plan.

Despite the bone-drilling cold of the winter day, he felt hot and sweaty with nerves. It was a strange feeling—fear mixed with rage. These soldiers had come uninvited to Denmark, bringing their threats and their war machine and doing whatever they pleased. The Teacher advised Magnus and the other boys to channel their fear and anger into determination. Magnus vowed to do whatever it took to disrupt the Germans' mission.

Feeling the heaviness of the concealed dynamite, he felt reckless and wild. He didn't care about himself. He didn't care what happened to him. He had already lost everything in the world that mattered. If something went wrong and he was wiped out in the explosion, no one would miss him. They might notice his empty place in the school room and quietly put his things away, but with his parents and Farfar gone, there would be no one to mourn him.

Magnus had heard the expression "living by one's wits."

He might have read it in a book somewhere. But he'd never really understood what it meant until he had to do it. In the aftermath of his family's disappearance and the near destruction of his home by the German soldiers, he was completely on his own. He didn't know whom to trust or how to protect himself.

In all the ways that mattered, he had died the night they'd taken his parents away. He was still breathing, his heart was still beating in his chest, but he was dead because his life had been taken from him. In his place, another boy was reborn. In the middle of that terrible winter, right when everything had been destroyed while he cowered in the backyard, he had discovered within himself an inner fire of determination. He was going to survive. More than that, he was going to fight back.

That night, which seemed so long ago, he had gathered what he could from the ruined house. The soldiers took all the items of value they'd been able to get their hands on, but they had overlooked a few important items. Mother's good jewelry, for one thing, had stayed safely hidden away in the hollow pedestal of the stone birdbath in the garden. Papa's coin collection resided in the false back of a drawer Magnus had once carved.

And then there was Farfar's egg. Magnus had always considered it a silly ornament, the orb of gold and jewels with the carved gold and alabaster angel inside, but he knew it was valuable because of the letter from the very rich man from Russia.

With a feeling of terror and sadness pressing on his chest, he had pushed away the smoldering skeleton of the Christmas tree and folded back the ruined carpet. He'd retrieved the egg, along with the special letter from the Russian man, and two family photographs that were important to him.

No, three. There was a recent "family portrait" featuring Magnus, his parents and Farfar, along with Uncle Sweet and Eva. Magnus didn't understand the Germans' special hatred for Jewish people. They were just people, after all. As he thought about it, Magnus realized he had never understood hatred at all...until that night. Since then, he had learned what it felt like, a furnace inside him that burned so hot he knew he would never freeze to death, not so long as there were Germans to fight.

The ice in his bones strengthened him as the Klokkespil chimed the hour of four. It was the signal he'd been told to expect. Twilight came early in the winter, and it would be dark soon. He became hyperaware of his surroundings, as if experiencing heightened sensations. He could hear the hiss of his skate blades over the surface of the ice, and the subtle, almost undetectable sound of the water flowing beneath. He could hear the burble of laughter from the schoolchildren circling the pond. Many of the children were his age, yet he felt older than rock itself, artificially aged by grief and fear and anger.

In addition to taking his home and his family from him, the soldiers had stolen the remainder of his childhood. He could never be a boy again, could never let loose with carefree laughter, never spin around on the ice until he fell down dizzy, just for the sheer silliness of it. In place of the youngster he'd once been was an angry, cynical young man made dangerous by the fact that he had nothing more to lose. In destroying an innocent boy, the Germans had unwittingly created their own worst enemy.

A few other boys arrived with some hockey sticks and a puck, and Magnus joined in. To the casual observer, he was just some kid ice-skating with his friends—though they were fake friends, fellows he barely knew.

Slapping a puck back and forth between them, the boys reconnoitered the ordnance shed. It was not heavily guarded because it was supposed to be not only impenetrable but a secret.

The Germans were too cocky to fear what the Danes were capable of. The thick heavy doors, banded by iron, faced the street, and the stone block walls surrounded the rest.

The only other way in was a drainage pipe the size of a big tree trunk from the base of the building extending out to the frozen river that fed the pond. That was where Magnus's small stature came in. The boys clustered near the drainage pipe, fighting for the puck, shouting and laughing.

A pair of soldiers walked to the snow-crested riverbank. "Shoo," they said. "Go on with you now. Go back to the pond."

The boys fell silent, then took up their sticks and puck and headed for the main part of the lake. The soldiers went back to their pacing in front of the building. Within minutes, they were drawn to the heat emanating from a vendor's cart on the street nearby. It had been set up by an enterprising Danish woman selling nuts roasted in honey. The irresistible aroma was surpassed only by the taste of the warm hazelnuts.

No one had told Magnus the woman worked for the Resistance. He just knew.

As the soldiers went to warm themselves around the roasting cart and to sample the hazelnuts, a couple of the boys gave Magnus a boost so he could crawl into the pipe. It was a tight squeeze, but he was able to fit through the big iron tube. Inching his way through the pipe seemed to take forever. It was frightening, that tight, lifeless space, but he persevered, knowing he had to crawl only a short distance. In the complete darkness, he couldn't see a thing, but eventually he felt his way to an iron grate.

His hands shook as he pushed at the corroded metal, eventually lifting the grate. Even through his mittens, the cold iron bit at his hands, and his fingers stiffened like icicles. Trying to hold steady, he shoved the bundled sticks of dynamite through to the floor of the building. Then, with the wiry fuse in hand, he backed down the pipe. The space felt impossibly cramped, its rough surface scraping at his jacket and trousers. He moved as fast as he could, wondering how long the guards would linger at the woman's cart. He needed them to stay away long enough for him to light the fuse and escape unnoticed. The other boys would create a distraction; he had to believe that.

Moving backward and blind, he had no idea who might see his skates emerge from the opening of the pipe, or what could be waiting for him. But here was the trouble for the Germans—Magnus didn't care. If they arrested him, if they threw him in prison or shipped him to one of their death camps, so be it.

The Teacher had spoken to him about this, told him he needed to find a purpose. A reason to live. He hadn't found that yet, but at least he knew what he would die for.

After what seemed like an eternity, he pulled himself free and dropped down onto the ice, sweating despite the cold. He looked around, his legs trembling, skates slipping on the slick surface. There was no one in sight. It was nearly full dark now. Most of the skaters had left the lake, hurrying home before the curfew horns sounded. Only the other boys remained, creating a phony ruckus in the middle of the lake to distract the guards.

This was the critical moment. He used his teeth to pluck off one mitten, and pulled out the box of red-headed matches. His hands were steady as he struck a match.

The first match flared, then flamed out as a cold wind swept through. He hunched over and tried again. The second and third attempts failed. He started to feel nervous, perhaps like the Little Match Girl in a story he always despised by Hans Christian Andersen. Suppose all the matches failed?

He tried again, using his body to shield the flame from the

wind. He held the bright flame to the fuse, but this, too, went out. More matches, more attempts. Finally, when he was nearly out of matches, the cord caught and sizzled, flaring up. He shielded the light with his body, praying it wouldn't be seen. A terrible heat licked at his neck. His muffler had been set aflame. He jumped back and yanked off the burning fabric, dropping the scarf to the ground. The pain was terrific, but he didn't make a sound other than a sharp hiss. The fuse burned steadily, the sulfurous spark disappearing into the drain pipe.

Magnus stuffed away the matches and put his mitten back on. Then he skated away into the darkness, moving as fast as he dared. Across the lake, the other boys dispersed, melting into the twilight. Magnus knew he had only seconds to find safety. His shoulder slammed into a low-hanging branch on the opposite bank of the river. He scrambled up the steep, snowy incline, ripping his skates off and then running to the skating house in his sock feet. In the shelter of the skating house, he stopped, sank down on a bench. His quick panting breath made frozen clouds in the night air. Peering through the darkness, he focused on the distant shadowy bulk of the building across the river.

Nothing happened. His heart sank. After all that, the attempt had failed.

The city was eerily quiet now that curfew was being observed. Magnus felt a cold chill of disappointment. *Nothing.* After all the planning, all the risk, the operation had been a waste of time. Slowly he shouldered his rucksack and leaned down to pull on the worn-out gum boots he'd had on the night of the fire.

He turned away. The trudge to shelter would be a long one.

Then he heard…something. A deep, dull rumble of thunder, more of a feeling in his gut than an actual sound. He froze, holding himself perfectly motionless, watching. The building still lay in darkness. Then another rumble came from some-where, and he saw a flash under the eaves of the clay-tiled roof.

The flash expanded into a crashing orange cloud, and the building's tile roof blew straight up into the air. The noise was so loud, his eardrums hurt. The brilliant explosion sucked the very air from his lungs. Debris flew everywhere. There was a sound like close thunder, rocks raining down, brick and stone and tile crashing through the river ice.

It was beautiful to see, prettier than the fireworks let off on the Prince's birthday, more magical than any celebration. The air raid sirens began to shriek.

The noise covered the sound of Magnus's laughter. He flung out his arms and laughed for the first time since the soldiers had stolen his life away. He laughed until the tears streamed from his eyes.

"Yes," he shouted, though he did not know what he was saying yes to. "Yes, yes, yes."

Magnus had done what the Teacher had advised him to do. He had found his purpose.

After Magnus blew up the ordnance shed, the Underground gave him more and more things to do. His confidence grew as he made the most of his small stature, sneaking through im-possibly close spaces to commit whatever mayhem was thought to be most disruptive to the occupying force. Trains were de-railed, supply barges sunk, warehouses torched.

He wondered why finding his purpose did not diminish his anger and grief. Like the livid burn marks on his neck from the ordnance incident, the feelings became a part of him, never to fade. Still, sabotage was something to do, he supposed.

The Teacher said it wasn't enough to find a purpose. A man also needed a reason to live. The Teacher didn't explain how to find this, however.

In general Magnus was kept in the dark about operations, merely given a task like a school assignment, which he was expected to carry out without question.

One spring day the Teacher asked him to come to their customary meeting spot, a simple wood frame house atop an embankment on the east side of the city. Magnus thought it might be the man's home, an unlovely place that lacked running water and was cluttered with camping supplies. Blankets were piled on the sagging corner bed, and bottles lined the windowsills and kitchen bench. There were books everywhere, in stacks and atop the rickety table, books on every possible subject in Danish, German and English. Magnus imagined that in another life, in better circumstances, the Teacher was a man of learning.

"You have shown how good you are at destroying things," he said now. "Let's see if you are equally good at rescuing." The reek of Akvavit emanated hotly from his breath as the words slurred together.

"I like the sound of that," Magnus said.

"The organization has sprung a leak," the Teacher explained.

"They're onto us, you mean."

"Yes. But we're onto them, too. They're going to make an arrest today. The target is a couple who've been with the Resistance from its inception, Mr. and Mrs. Winther. Their home is on Gyldne Prins Park."

It was a gentrified area of town, not far from where Magnus's family had once lived.

"Mr. Winther works at Bispebjerg Hospital," the Teacher continued. "His wife is a volunteer there. The hospital does a lot of charity work."

Now Magnus understood. "Charity work" was code for underground work. Magnus was not supposed to know this, but in fact the hospital's ambulance system and morgue were involved. A patient would be pronounced dead and sent to the morgue for processing. There, the "deceased" would leap up and don street clothes, and quickly disappear. Records furnished to the Germans listed him as having died of a contagious disease, like tuberculosis, something to scare people away from looking too closely at the closed corpse bag. It went without saying that a number of these "fatalities" were Jews and wanted men. Others were spirited away in ambulances to the fishing villages of Zealand to be ferried to Sweden.

"They have one child, a daughter, Annelise."

The words chilled his blood. He remembered that little Eva, whom he hadn't seen in more than three years, used to play with the Winther girl. In a flash, he relived the night his parents had been taken. Only, unlike Magnus, she might not escape. She might be swept up into the Germans' net and taken God-knew-where.

"She's very young, perhaps ten years of age." The Teacher took a drink from his chipped stoneware mug. "God damn. This is wearying. Perhaps—"

The Teacher's telephone rang, startling them both. It was like a big black beetle, crouched on a cluttered desk, emitting a shrill alarm. He scrambled to answer it. "Yes?" He coughed. "Today? But I thought... Never mind. I'll see to it."

He slammed down the phone. "It's today. The arrest is to take place today, in broad daylight. Fucking Nazis. Let's go, boy." He muttered the street address. "Do you know it?"

"Yes, sir." It seemed forever ago, but Magnus used to play in the park near there. Perhaps he'd even seen the Winther family out walking in the sunshine or hurrying home from an engagement.

"We've got to make haste." The Teacher grabbed a battered saddlebag that fit on the back of his motorbike. Then he ripped open the front door.

There was a popping sound, like that of a rock thrown on a bonfire. The moment Magnus heard it, he *knew*.

The Teacher didn't stagger dramatically like a guy in the movies. He was slammed back as though smacked by a giant hand. A red dot marked his forehead. The back of his skull disintegrated. Pieces of bloody matter spattered everywhere.

Magnus could feel the wet heat of blood on his face. He didn't think. He didn't look at the mess. Since losing his family, he had turned himself into a survivor, and he acted on instinct now, like a scared wild animal. He raced out the back door and half ran, half tumbled down the bank behind the house and ran along a bargemen's path by the creek. He paused by the creek only long enough to scrub the blood from his face with the brackish water. He tried to rid his mind of the image of the Teacher, his head blown to kingdom come. There was blood on his clothes, too, and he did his best to rub it out, praying it wouldn't attract attention.

His mind started working again after he'd run perhaps a kilometer. He thought about what the Teacher had said about Dr. and Mrs. Winther. The Teacher was dead now, but he would have wanted Magnus to save them.

There was no time to grieve. Magnus had no idea who the Teacher was, anyway. Just a man who loved books and hated the Nazis.

Magnus started running again. He knew where the Winther family lived. Maybe he would get there in time to warn them. Pain bit into his side as he pushed himself faster and faster. He took a shortcut across Gyldne Prins Park. In the distance he could see children and their mothers playing on the swings. A pretty lady and a yellow-haired little girl got off the swings and left the park through the wrought iron gates, crossing the boulevard while holding hands. They stopped to speak to a man. A pedestrian. Perhaps he was part of the Underground.

A contingent of brownshirts marched down the street, and the pedestrian hurried away. There were canvas-covered trucks parked in the roadway. A uniformed man approached the woman in the pink fluttery dress, and a second later, she was surrounded. Even from a distance, Magnus could see the tension and terror in the woman's posture. To be accosted in one's own neighborhood added to the shock and violation; Magnus knew this. The little girl clung to her mother with a desperation Magnus felt in his gut. That same desperation had gripped him the night Farfar had been taken and, later, his own parents.

The urge to rush into the situation was as powerful now as it had been that night, but just like that night, he resisted. An even stronger instinct ruled—self-preservation. He would be of no use at all to Mrs. Winther if he exposed himself without a plan.

He was trying to decide on a plan when the little girl did something surprising. She wrenched herself away from the knot of soldiers, and she ran. One of the brownshirts took a halfhearted swipe at her, but she darted away with the quickness of one familiar with the neighborhood.

Magnus felt a fierce surge of protectiveness. There was something about the little girl, all alone, running for her life, that made him strong with both fury and determination.

He kept himself out of sight and skirted the edge of the park, walking quickly but trying to be discreet. One thing he'd discovered early on was that running merely drew attention to a person.

The girl rounded a corner, and he feared he might lose track of her. He spied a bike leaning against a fence, and he stole it without a blink of guilt, not even breaking stride as he hopped on and rode away. After that, it was a matter of moments before he caught up with the panicked girl.

The breathless sobs that emanated from her wrenched his heart, because, despite her terror and grief, she never stopped running. Survival was a powerful driving force, stronger than hatred and love combined. With each breath, she voiced her fear: "Help. Please, help. Please."

He called out to her to stop, saying he was there to help, but she either didn't hear him or was ignoring him in her panic. In one flowing motion, Magnus ditched the bike and made a grab for her. She fought like a feral cat, exuding a fierce strength that was out of proportion with her size. She scratched and kicked and bit until he was forced to squeeze her in a tight embrace while saying into her ear, "Easy, easy, little one," trying to sound soothing, the way Farfar used to soothe the nervous patient.

The fight went out of her with the suddenness of a balloon losing air. She felt oddly fragile in his arms, her sturdy strength melting into surrender.

"You're the Winther girl," he said. "Annelise, right?"

She pulled back and stared at him with haunted eyes. He saw her studying the ugly burn scars and the spray of drying blood on his clothes. They were the color of his mother's best china. *I'm sorry,* he conveyed silently. *I'm sorry for what you're about to go through.*

"You'll have to trust me," he said. "It's scary, I know. I'm here to help you."

"My momma…" Her chin trembled.

"She wanted you to be safe," he told her, guessing now but knowing that was a parent's main concern. As he spoke, he took the girl's damp hand and started walking. He didn't hurry. They looked like a brother and sister, out for a stroll. Completely innocent.

The girl was quiet, so he added, "Your mother urged you to run away from the brownshirts, didn't she?"

The child said nothing, so he took her silence as assent. "My parents wanted the same for me. They said if soldiers ever came around, I should run away as fast and as far as I can. And that's what I did."

The girl squeezed his hand. The tiny gesture nearly undid him. What kind of crazy world did they live in, where parents had to teach their children means of escape rather than their multiplication tables or the books of the New Testament?

"Do you have friends or relatives you can visit?" he asked. Some families had pre-devised elaborate escape plans and contingency arrangements.

"My Mor Mor has a cottage, up by the seaside."

"Where?" he asked.

"It's called Helsingør."

Magnus kept walking. "I know the place. I'll take you there. Don't be afraid."

She nodded. "I'm not."

"There are people who care about your family and want to help. I'm one of them. Do you like boating, Annelise?"

"Oh, yes. Papa likes to take me out in the wherry when the weather is fine."

Magnus had never helped with an escape before. He might even be wrong about his plan. Perhaps the four-kilometer paddle to safety was a myth circulating through the Resistance to give them hope; he couldn't be sure. For the girl's sake, he had to try to make the crossing.

He'd heard of a special operation, deeply secret, tasked with ferrying Resistance workers on the run out of Denmark, across the Strait of Øresund to Sweden…and safety. Thus far, the Germans had left the Jews of Denmark alone, but rumors swirled that they might one day be rounded up and shipped off to the work camps.

The escape route could be a myth; he would soon find out. The rescue effort operated clandestinely from the seaside town of Helsingør, made famous as "Elsinore" by the English bard Shakespeare. From there, the shores of Sweden could be seen on a clear day.

At the dock, he spotted a pair of soldiers loitering around. They challenged him, of course. They clearly had nothing better to do.

"Can't a fellow take his sister boating on a fine afternoon?" he asked with just a bit of cheekiness. "Or is that now prohibited?"

"Watch your tongue, boy," one of the soldiers said. "Move along, and don't make trouble."

Just you wait, thought Magnus, leading the Winther girl along by the hand. Without even a twinge of conscience, he selected a nicely polished wherry moored among the other boats. He picked it because it looked sturdy and also because it had canvas lifejackets stowed in the bow and a single gaffrig sail for catching the wind.

"Put this on," he said, silently willing the girl to refrain from crying or acting scared. He needed the soldiers to believe they were going boating, nothing more.

She complied in silence, buckling on the canvas vest. Either she understood, or perhaps shock had set in. On some level, she probably realized she might never see her parents again.

Taking hold of her under her arms, he swung her high up over the gunwale of the boat, saying, "In you go." Her feet in their scuffed brown shoes looked very small against the vast blue sky.

He untied the wherry and shoved away from the dock. Then he started to row at a leisurely pace. His plan was not well formed in his mind. Helsingør was too far away to reach, at least forty kilometers to the north. His immediate goal was to get to Saltholm, a flat island inhabited mainly by geese and wild swans. From there, they might be able to reach Sweden if there was a decent wind and they could duck the patrol boats.

He faced the little Winther girl and was startled by her expression. Behind the terror and grief was something else— gratitude and relief. Thinking about the covered trucks and hordes of soldiers who had surrounded her house, Magnus realized what he had done. He had saved a life.

He thought about what the Teacher had told him about finding a purpose and a reason for living. In embracing the Resistance and disrupting the German war machine, he had found a purpose. Now, regarding the helpless little girl in the boat, he had discovered the other part of it. He had discovered something to live for.

SEVENTEEN

"Isabel is in denial," Tess said to her mother that evening. The two of them were on the patio, setting the long rustic table for dinner. Through the arched doorway to the kitchen they could see Isabel at the stove, adding hot broth and white wine to a wide copper pan of risotto. Ernestina was slicing tomatoes on a tray next to slices of fresh bread.

"I never knew denial could be so delicious," Shannon murmured.

Tess poured water from a big stoneware pitcher. "I tried to tell her the meeting at the bank hadn't gone well, but she didn't want to hear it."

"Didn't you say the bank had left the door open for delaying the foreclosure?"

Tess pressed her back teeth together in frustration. She'd been so excited, so certain the possibility of a priceless treasure would turn everything around. But that hadn't been the case. "Sure, but that's probably putting off the inevitable. According to Dominic, he's been holding the proceeding at bay for years, like the kid with his finger in the dike."

"And you believe him?" Shannon asked.

In Shannon's experience men were not to be trusted. This fact always made Tess a little sad, because it made for a lonely life, but that was Shannon's choice. She was beautiful in a way Tess would never be, and maybe this contributed to Shannon's issues with men. When Tess was growing up, men would come into Shannon's life, and some of them were wonderful and did everything they could in order to stay. They would bring presents for Tess, or they'd play her favorite games or take her on outings. Sometimes she would pause for a moment, and a funny emotion would wash over her: *This is what it feels like to have a father.*

Inevitably, he would stop coming around. When Tess would ask, Shannon usually gave the vaguest of replies. "We wanted different things" was her favorite, and Tess heard it so frequently, she eventually stopped asking.

"I do," she told her mother now. "I do believe Dominic."

"Believe what about him?" Isabel asked, bringing out a big salad with edible flowers tossed in.

"Isn't it true that Dominic held off Magnus's creditors until the bank failed and was taken over?"

"I wouldn't know," Isabel admitted. "Grandfather never talked about it. It wouldn't surprise me, though. Dominic rescues people. It's something I've observed through the years. He always seems to be bailing someone out in one way or other. He probably doesn't even know he's doing it. He once tried to rescue me, but it didn't work out."

"What did you need rescuing from?"

She offered a half smile. "Myself."

"If you're saying I need rescuing," Tess said, "you're wrong. And if he thinks I need to be saved, he's wrong, too."

"Well, he definitely was on a rescue mission when he married Lourdes."

Lourdes. Even the name of his ex sounded exotic, slightly mysterious. Tess's imagination went into overdrive as she tried to picture the woman, named after a town where daily miracles occurred. "Was she in some kind of trouble?"

Isabel ducked her head. "I shouldn't have said anything."

"Come on, Isabel. You can't bring up the guy's ex-wife without filling me in. Was there a big drama?"

"Not really. She was just…really stressed out by law school—"

"She's a lawyer?"

Isabel nodded. "They married when Dominic was in the navy. It was a formal military ceremony, followed by a reception at the Maldonado estate. I made a carrot cake with raisins and Tortuga rum."

She set down the salad and expertly gave it a toss, her movements smooth and assured. She misinterpreted Tess's stare. "You don't like the salad?"

Edible flowers, Tess reflected. "How did I go from subsisting on Red Bull and microwave burritos to having edible flowers in my salad?"

Isabel visibly winced. "That was your diet?"

"Nearly every day."

"I've never actually tasted Red Bull. Or microwave burritos, for that matter."

"I think the point is, you don't taste it. You just bolt it down and go on with your day."

Shannon spread her arms, palms up. "Don't look at me. I didn't teach her that."

No, thought Tess, *you didn't.* The vehemence of her own thoughts both startled and dismayed her. "And how can you be so neat about tossing a salad?" she asked, softening the moment with a laugh. "Whenever I try that, things get tossed on the floor."

"It's the size of the bowl," Isabel pointed out. "It needs to be more than twice the size of the salad. And you toss with a light touch, so things don't get bruised. Here, give it a try."

Tess gamely stepped up and took the large wooden spoon and fork.

"Gentle but steady," Isabel coached her.

"Got it," Tess said, and discovered her sister was right. "Size does matter," she added. "But now I'm wondering how we went from talking about financial ruin to tossing organic flowers."

Isabel shrugged. "It's a gift."

Over dinner, Tess told them in detail about the meeting with Dominic. "I didn't expect him to believe my crazy story," she said. "It's weird that he did. Unfortunately, we didn't hand him the main thing he needs in order to extend the deadline."

"The Fabergé egg," Shannon said.

"It's such a long shot to think we can track it down in time to put off the foreclosure."

Tess felt so torn between the urge to stay at Bella Vista and the need to get back to her own life. Each time she tried to escape, something happened to make her stay. She wondered why she didn't just turn her back on the whole situation.

The Navarros came to dinner, along with a couple of workers. Oblivious of the tenuous state of affairs, people were laughing, talking, relaxing, enjoying Isabel's delicious food. The energy was something she'd never felt before. They were acting like a family, and there was something terribly seductive about that. Even though she was still a stranger here, she felt included in a way that had always eluded her...until now. *There,* she thought. *That's why I can't walk away.*

"How do you know it's a long shot?" Isabel asked, passing a

platter of grilled squash and squash blossoms stuffed with qui-
noa and herbs. "Maybe you gave him exactly what he needs."

Tess thought about Dominic and what he needed, and the
seductive spell intensified.

She went upstairs to her room, but she couldn't seem to
relax. She paced back and forth, feeling an unpleasant frisson
of anxiety. Her *disorder*. She hated having a disorder.

She was supposed to see a physician and make major lifestyle changes. Instead, she'd lost herself in the situation at Bella
Vista. She went to the window, open to the autumn sky, and
watched the sun go down, leaving behind a glorious smear
of color. *Breathe,* she reminded herself. *Breathe in, breathe out.*
The air smelled of ripe apples and dry grass and flowers, a
soothing combination.

Yet she didn't find it soothing. Her mind churned, and she
debated with herself about staying here or going back to her
life. She couldn't stand the idea of leaving without knowing
what would happen here. In work and life both, she was all
about uncovering the facts. She was determined to find out
what Dominic was doing with the information she'd given
him. She wasn't going to be able to calm herself down until
she found out.

On impulse, she grabbed her phone, then remembered the
lack of a signal. She could always use the landline. On the
other hand, she could simply go to see him in person. Wasn't
that what people did around here? She tried to resist, but the
idea of seeing him again, away from the bank, away from everyone, was too tempting. Calling herself a smitten fool, she
went downstairs.

"I'm going out," she said, keeping her tone matter-of-fact
as she passed through the sitting room. Isabel and her mother
were there together, sorting through more of Magnus's papers.

"Give Dominic my regards," said Isabel.

★ ★ ★

By the time she found her way to Dominic's house, the sun had already set. The shimmering pink and orange glow lingered in the sky, throwing long shadows across the road as she parked. There was a moon, rising early in the evening. Riding above the gentle curves of the hills, it was huge, its orange glow firing the horizon's edge.

His dogs announced her arrival, the big one sounding like a rabid hyena as he bounded out into the yard. If she hadn't already met him, she would have shrunk from the gate. "Down, Dude," she said. "Easy, boy."

He smacked his lips, jaws flapping.

Dominic came out, looking relaxed in faded jeans—the top button undone, she was forced to note—and a UC Davis T-shirt. "Hey," he said.

"Is this a bad time?"

"Nope. Just me and the pups tonight. How about a glass of wine on the back porch?"

"Perfect." Maybe too perfect. She felt herself liking him more and more. It was like a hunger that wouldn't abate.

The house was as freakishly neat as it was on her last visit, though quieter without the children. "I was wondering if you got an answer yet from the bank."

"You're not going to like it," he said, pouring two glasses of wine.

Her heart sank. "They weren't impressed."

"By the idea of a priceless family treasure, yes. But they're dealing with a board of overseers and the SEC. They can't declare something an asset until it's found and valued." He led the way to the back porch and handed her a glass of wine.

She took a quick sip. "Delicious. Thank you. Did you tell them I intend to find it?"

"Sure. I told them I'd help you, even."

This piqued her interest. "Really?"

"That didn't change their minds, either." He studied her for a moment. She liked the way he watched her—with appreciation but also respect. "There is something," he said quietly.

She perked up. "I'm listening."

"I did some research and came across an archaic banking rule that's still in force. It provides for an automatic continuance for people claiming unrecovered or foreign assets. It was meant for liquid assets, but the regulation doesn't spell that out, so it's possible to claim the egg is an unrecovered asset."

"That's some catch," she said.

"Took me all day to find it. I already filed for an extension based on that rule. No idea if it will fly with the underwriters, though. And I meant what I said. If there's anything I can do to help, let me know."

"Now I'm seriously impressed." She studied him thoughtfully, trying to read deep into the whiskey-brown eyes behind his glasses. "Do you work this hard for all your clients?"

"I have a personal interest in helping Magnus."

"Yeah? What else is in that will?"

"I'm not letting him leave me a thing, but—" He cut himself off abruptly.

"Go on. What were you going to say?" She watched his mouth, finding herself intrigued by his lips.

He stood against the porch railing and held her gaze. "I once made a promise to Magnus, a long time ago. I promised I'd look out for his family, the same way he looked out for mine when I was a kid."

He was such a Dudley Do-Right. He was too good to be true.

"Unfortunately," he went on, "my good intentions are not enough. I don't know if I can stop this."

"I'm sure he'd understand," she said, even though she wasn't sure at all. They sipped their wine in silence for a few min-

utes, listening to the rustle of the breeze through the vineyards. She moved toward him, drawn by the warmth of the
wine on her tongue, by the quiet evening, by the glimmer
in his eyes. The most important part of this conversation had
nothing to do with words.

They shared a long look. Then his hands descended to her
shoulders, holding her firmly in place as he bent closer, his
scent and his warmth enveloping her. A piercing need took
her by surprise. She had always considered herself good at kissing, in the technical sense. It was something she had studied
closely since the age of fifteen, when she kissed her first boy in
the back of her nana's shop. Since then, there had been kisses
with boys and men of all shapes and sizes, all over the world.

But she'd never been kissed like this. From the first tender,
searching touch of his mouth against hers, something new and
unexpected started happening. She felt an irresistible pull toward
him, and an intense sensation bloomed in her chest. His lips felt
firm and cool, turning warm and deliciously moist as the pressure deepened. Closing her eyes, she lost herself in his kiss, letting
it take her to a place where she stopped thinking and worrying.

It took all her self-control to stifle a protest when he lifted
his mouth from hers and stood gazing down at her.

With the lightest of touches, he skimmed the pad of his
thumb across her lower lip. "It's probably all kinds of wrong,"
he continued, "but I've been wanting to do that since the first
time I saw you."

"In my wreck of an office."

"You were covered in powdered sugar."

"You must've thought I was crazy. And then a couple of
hours later you found out you were correct."

"*Are* you crazy?"

"Completely," she said, and clutched the front of his shirt
and kissed him again.

EIGHTEEN

Tess, Isabel and Shannon spent hours and hours sorting through decades of things at Bella Vista, piecing together the journey of a man who had been too busy living his life to keep decent records. What had happened with Dominic last night was a secret Tess kept close to her chest, uncertain about what to do with it. Yet at the same time, she had an urge to tell Isabel. Maybe she would, later.

"Okay," Isabel said, her shoulders tense with frustration, "did he have to save every *Farmers' Almanac* from the beginning of time?"

"He probably wasn't saving them," Shannon pointed out. "Just didn't bother to throw them out."

Isabel straightened up and went to the window of the study. She placed her hands on the small of her back, absently massaging herself. The window framed a view that looked like a postcard. "I just don't understand how someone could be so disorganized." Her voice sounded exhausted, broken.

Isabel was still intensely worried about losing a man who had been everything to her. Tess would never forget the terrible emotional agony of losing her grandmother. It was like stepping into a strange new reality, one filled with a fear and pain that took her over, darkening the entire world with a cold heavy shadow that would never, ever lift.

She glanced over at her mother, who was browsing through a stack of reports. Shannon had been traveling when it happened. She'd raced back to Dublin, as inconsolable as Tess. They'd held each other, and it had felt like a new closeness, as if they were two shipwreck survivors, clinging to a raft. In time, though, they'd drifted apart again, with Shannon caught up in work while Tess finished high school. America had beckoned, and she'd opted for college at Berkeley.

"Actually," Tess said, wanting to coax Isabel away from her worries, "he isn't disorganized. Judging by the stuff around here, there's a method to his madness."

Isabel turned to face her. "I don't know what you mean."

"Here, I'll give you an example." She turned her attention to a shelf piled with old tractor calendars. She knew with a quick flip-through that he hadn't saved them because of the nice photographs. "He probably kept these on purpose, because of the notations on various dates. He intended one day to sit down and copy the notes he'd made about plantings, payroll, birthdays and such."

Isabel frowned at her. "That's ridiculous."

"Or it makes perfect sense," said Tess. "Maybe this stuff is organized in a way only he can understand. I do that at work. Drives my assistant crazy, but there's a method to my madness. We just need to figure out if your grandfather had a method." She felt a strange, friable kinship with Magnus in that moment.

Isabel looked drained as she surveyed the boxes and papers.

Tess felt another pulse of sympathy. Clearly, they needed a break. "How about we take a walk?" she said.

Isabel nodded. "I'd like that."

"You two go ahead," Shannon said. "I'm going to finish organizing this chest of drawers." She shook her head. "How many pocket knives does one person need?"

Tess led the way outside. The weather was beautiful as usual, the afternoon awash in golden sunlight and blue skies, with an autumn-scented breeze blowing across the hills. Tess tried to focus on her breathing, and for once, it wasn't such a chore. She felt things inside her changing and shifting. The rhythm of life at Bella Vista pulsed through her, and having a project made her feel a part of things. She had somehow figured out that if she didn't check her messages every five minutes, the world didn't actually come to an end.

"I'm still getting used to the weather here," she said.

"So you miss the damp and fog of the Bay Area?" Isabel asked with a little laugh.

"Not as much as I thought I would."

Isabel sent her a slightly bashful glance. "I'm glad you're here, Tess."

Tess couldn't figure out whether or not *she* was glad to be here. It was all so…weird, being charged with sorting out a situation that had been dropped into her reluctant lap. Even weirder, she found herself unable to stop thinking about a man who was completely wrong for her. She couldn't stop reliving the feeling of being in his arms, the night filled with so much promise. She wondered if he thought about it, too, or if he'd simply relegated it to a lapse in judgment. Which, in all likelihood, had been the case.

They strolled in silence for a bit, following a path of chipped gravel that wove between sections of the orchard and wound down to a vast field of lavender. Although it was late in the season, some of the herbs were still in bloom, attracting a host of indolent bees.

"I was planning to start some beehives," she said. "I'd still like to, but it makes no sense to plan anything since it looks like we're going to lose this place."

Tess wasn't sure what to say to that—"Congratulations on coming out of your denial" didn't seem appropriate. It was hard to imagine Isabel finding a life beyond Bella Vista.

"Do you ever get stung?" Tess asked, flinching from a slow-moving bee.

"Almost never," Isabel said. "I used to be afraid of them when I was little, but Grandfather always told me they're just minding their own business. And he was right. You're not likely to get stung if you leave them alone."

"That rule applies to people, too," Tess observed.

"Yikes, that's cynical."

"I suppose so. Sorry. I don't mean to be." Then, before she could stop herself, she blurted out, "I kissed Dominic."

Isabel stopped walking. "On purpose?"

"Of course it was on purpose. I mean, I didn't plan it, and he didn't, either, but it happened. And it was…nice." Better than nice, she remembered, looking away to hide the flush in her cheeks.

"You could do worse." Isabel walked on at a slow, thoughtful pace. A fleeting shadow darkened her face. "Don't feel bad for kissing him."

"I'm not sure how I feel about kissing him."

"Maybe you need to do it some more. See where it goes."

"Or not," Tess said, too quickly.

"Why not?"

"Because there's no point in getting tangled up with a guy

like Dominic. No matter how nice it is to kiss him, it would be crazy to start something."

"What's wrong with starting something?"

"Our lives would never mesh. God. How did my head go from thinking about a simple kiss to thinking about our lives meshing?"

"Maybe it wasn't your head. Maybe it was your heart."

"Seriously? Where do you come up with this stuff?"

"I'm just saying, keep an open mind. He's a good man. I've known him forever and…" She hesitated, looked away. "He's a good man."

"How long is forever?" In spite of herself, Tess wanted to know everything about him—what he'd looked like as a kid. What he used to dream about. What his life was like as a navy pilot. Why he was so devoted to Magnus.

"Since we were kids," Isabel said. "Grade school. His sister was in my grade, and Dom was a few years older. They didn't speak a word of English at first. But Dominic spoke the universal language of soccer. That got him the respect of the whole school. His sister, Gina, was just as good. The two of them were amazing to watch."

Tess could imagine this too easily. Dominic moved with the grace of a gifted athlete; she'd seen that when he was playing with his kids. "So Dominic said his parents worked for Magnus."

"They did. I don't recall that part; I suppose I was too young. The family had some trouble; his father was injured and his mother got sick. Grandfather helped them out. Dominic was desperate to go to college. That's why he went into the navy."

Tess didn't want to like the guy. She didn't want to think of him as an adorable immigrant boy, proving himself on the soccer field. Or a kid from a poor family, wanting an education. It was simpler to think of him as the greedy banker de-termined to evict everyone from Bella Vista. However, the more she learned, the more she was intrigued by him. "What about his marriage? He said the stress of separation was too much when he went to sea."

"Is that all he said?"

"He didn't exactly say she cheated on him, but somehow I get the idea that she might have."

Isabel said nothing.

"Stomp your foot once if I'm right, twice if I'm wrong."

"You don't need for me to do that."

Tess's eyebrows shot up. "Whoa."

"Hazards of living in a small town."

"You'd think being in a fishbowl would make people be-have better," said Tess. It was far too easy to build up a head of righteous steam on his behalf. The guy was off serving his country, and his wife couldn't wait for him? Tess could only imagine what that betrayal must have felt like to him. "His kids are cute," she said.

"Very cute," said Isabel.

"The little girl made a point of saying her parents are get-ting back together."

"I'm not surprised. Lourdes has no filters, not even around the kids. Trini might have overheard something."

Tess wanted to know more, and yet she didn't. The more she learned about Dominic Rossi, the better she liked him. She didn't want to like him, because she couldn't imagine any-thing but heartache resulting from it. She had plans. A life in the city. A burning dream he could never be part of, because he was irrevocably tied to Archangel. Pursuing their attrac-tion just seemed reckless.

Isabel bent down and plucked two stalks of lavender. She

handed one to Tess and tucked the other behind her ear. "Have you ever had your heart broken?" she asked.

Good lord, was the woman a mind reader?

"By a guy?" asked Tess. "Not since high school. Declan O'Leary asked me to a dance, and I was pretty sure we'd get married and have babies and live happily ever after. Instead, when I refused to put out, he started a rumor about me that I was a slut. I thought the world was coming to an end. For three whole days. And then I snapped out of it." Despite the fact that more than a decade had passed, she still felt dark echoes of the terrible, dizzying hurt of betrayal, all from putting her trust in someone who didn't deserve it.

Clearing her throat, she changed the subject. "So, back to Magnus. I'm probably committing career suicide by spending so much time away from work, but I'm not giving up on figuring out what happened to the egg. This is such a huge place. Where on earth would he put something for safekeeping?" She stopped walking, placed her hand on Isabel's arm. "Wait a minute. I can't believe I haven't asked. Is there a safe?"

Isabel grabbed her hand and pulled her toward a small cluster of buildings. "The superintendent's office."

A few minutes later, they stood with Jake Camden, the produce foreman. Tess remembered him from the healing ceremony. Built like a trainee for the Mr. Universe pageant, tattooed in places she wasn't supposed to stare at, he filled the small cluttered office with his sheer bulk.

"We'd like to have a look in Grandfather's safe," Isabel said.

"You're not the only one," replied Jake.

Tess's head snapped up. "What's that supposed to mean?"

"Lots of folks would like to get into Magnus's safe," he said simply.

"Like who?"

"Magnus, for one. Three days before the accident, he tried

opening it." Jake led the way into a space that was part barn, part office. The safe was covered with a saddle blanket and littered with papers, a battered-looking Mac, a selection of sports drinks and odds and ends.

"What do you mean, he tried?" Tess asked.

"He could never remember the combination, and no one else had it."

"Then why wouldn't he have brought in a locksmith, or someone who could open it?"

Isabel said, "I wish I knew. I didn't realize there was anything in it. He never used this thing except for a piece of furniture."

"As far as we know." Tess tapped her foot. "We've got to find a way to open it."

NINETEEN

"I need a safecracker," said Tess, standing in the doorway of Dominic's office.

Startled by her sudden appearance, he glanced up from the spreadsheet displayed on his monitor, which he'd been pretending to study for the past half hour. He'd been pretending because ever since Tess Delaney had appeared in his life, his concentration for other things was blown.

And now here she was again, the fantasy made flesh. And she wanted... "Sorry," he said, shaking free of the thought, "you need what?"

"A safecracker. You know, someone who can get into an old-fashioned safe without a combination."

"I know what a safecracker is," he said.

"I need one. Isabel showed me an old safe in Magnus's business office. Nobody knows what's in it, and we can't get it open."

She made him smile. He couldn't help himself. "And I can?"

"Can you?"

"Actually, yes."

"Let's go, then."

A part of him balked, knowing the cautious thing to do would be to keep his distance. But when it came to a woman like Tess, he wasn't that rational.

He found himself reaching for his suit coat. "It's almost closing time anyway."

He followed her to Bella Vista, noting that she drove Isabel's car the way she did everything else—too fast, and with brash confidence.

"You always seem to be in a hurry," he said, arriving a full minute after her and finding her waiting in front of the foreman's office. Her arms were folded, and her foot looked as if it was trying not to tap.

"That's because I usually *am* in a hurry," she said.

"There are some things that should go slowly."

She tossed her head. "Such as?"

"Your sister's cooking."

"Fine, you're right. There's no way to rush her salted focaccia bread or her romesco sauce. I don't cook, though."

"Kissing," he said.

Color flooded her cheeks. "I beg your pardon."

"Another example of something that should go slowly." Dominic looked at her steadily, his gaze lingering on her lips. Since he'd kissed her, he couldn't get the taste of her out of his head. The fact was, until he'd kissed her, he thought he was done with that kind of heart-thumping, crazy feeling of lust. Tess set his body clock back a good fifteen years.

"And sex," he added, enjoying the flustered expression on her face. "Goes along with kissing. Slow is better."

She folded her arms across her chest. "This is such a bad idea."

"Opening the safe?"

"Flirting with each other," she said.

"I don't know about that. I'm kind of enjoying it. What's wrong with a little flirting?"

"It's distracting. It leads to more kissing, which in turn can lead to sex, and—"

"I'm not seeing any downside here."

"Then you've obviously smoked too many of those special flowers that grow in the hills."

"Hey, how did you know about that?"

She sniffed. "Lucky guess." She turned decisively away and went into the building. "Here you go, man of steel. Take a crack at it. Get it? A crack."

"You're hilarious. I'm dying here." He peeled off his coat and removed his cufflinks. They were stainless steel ones with the Harley-Davidson logo. The kids had picked them out last Father's Day. Who knew Harley-Davidson made cufflinks?

He rolled back his sleeves and hunkered down next to the safe. It had a four-stop combination lock, plus a key lock. He was familiar with both. "I don't suppose there's a key around here anywhere."

"No. We looked and looked."

"You and Isabel?"

"And Jake Camden, the foreman. Do you know him?"

I've known him since I found out he was banging my wife, thought Dominic. "Yeah. Not surprised he wasn't any help." Dominic flipped open his briefcase and took out a pick set, inserting a slender rod into the keyhole.

"Don't tell me you learned this at banking school," said Tess.

"Nope." He tried a different rod.

"And who taught you to crack a safe?"

"It was my cousin Joey Pistone. Yeah, his name's Pistone, and yeah, we have a nickname for him."

"So is he a mobster, or a mafioso?" She paused. "Oh, my God, he is."

Dominic said nothing. It couldn't be said that Joey Pistone was the black sheep of the family, because he was like a lot of Rossi cousins—charming, shady, well connected to a web of small-time crooks and criminals. He had his uses, though. There was no lock he couldn't pick, no safe he couldn't crack. He'd shown Dominic his techniques many years ago.

"Let's see if we can figure out the combination," he said, shifting his attention to the dial. The old combination lock definitely had some loose tumblers, unlike the new digital ones that were more secure. Dominic got quiet and felt his way around the dial. It was not unlike flying blind. The process was all about a light touch and feel of the instruments, and letting sensation tap into something deep and intuitive. Like making love to a woman for the first time.

He kind of wished he hadn't let his mind go there, not with Tess leaning over his shoulder, close enough to touch. Her hair smelled like flowers, and he could still remember how her skin felt, and the sweet texture of her mouth....

Focus, he told himself. He was good with numbers and patterns. Grabbing a pencil and a scrap of paper, he made a grid and quickly scribbled out some possibilities. Then he tried each one in turn. He could see the tension in her face.

"I'm not liking this," he said. "Even if I figure out this lock, there's still the key thing. Do you care if the safe gets damaged?" He took out a chisel.

"I don't. I doubt Isabel would, either. She says she's never known the safe to be used as anything other than a piece of furniture."

"Excellent. You should have said so earlier." With the chisel and a hammer borrowed from a drawer, he worked away at the shaft cover between the combination lock and the key lock. Within a few minutes, the catch gave way. He turned and grinned at Tess.

"Well?" Her eyes lit up.

"We have a winner." He drew back the door.

"You did it." Tess threw back her head and let out a lusty laugh. "Genius."

"That's me, a genius."

She shone a desk lamp into the safe, illuminating the thick walls of enameled steel and an odd assortment of objects. "What's this?" She picked up a plastic Ziploc bag and held it at arm's length. Inside was a bluish, powdery square.

"A moldy cheese sandwich?" Dominic asked.

Tess burst out laughing. "My God, is the old man nuts?"

Leaning forward, Dominic pulled everything out of the safe and set the seemingly random collection on a desk.

Tess stepped back and regarded the contents of the safe. "I don't see anything remotely like a Fabergé egg. Looks like more papers and photos to sort through. We'd better go tell Isabel."

Dominic found an empty cardboard feed box and loaded everything into it, tossing the spoiled sandwich into the trash. Outside, Charlie the shepherd trotted over and gave them a sniff, then went back to stalking a bird in the meadow grass. Evening was coming on, the warmth of the day still lingering in the air, shadows lying long on the ground.

"I can get this," Tess said. "I mean, if you have to get back to your kids—"

"They're with their mother."

"Then Isabel will insist that you stay for dinner."

"Isabel will not have to twist my arm. Let's see, canned ravioli and a microbrew? Or Isabel's home cooking?" Their footsteps crunched on the gravel pathway as they headed for the house. "Where do people hide their treasures?" he asked Tess. "You're the expert."

"You'd think I would know," she said. "But what I've discovered is that there is no end to the human imagination or to a person's ingenuity. I've found treasures in every conceivable location, from the bottom of a two-hundred-foot dry well to the inside of a rolling pin. Sometimes the most clever thing to do is to hide an object in plain sight. I had a client in New York who kept his Stradivarius violin on a plastic stand with a beat-up guitar and a souvenir ukulele from Maui. His place was robbed twice, and both times, the thieves overlooked the violin."

"So sometimes the most valuable thing in a room doesn't look like much."

"True."

"Do you think an untrained eye would recognize a Fabergé egg?"

"A lot of them look like knickknacks, something you'd order from an infomercial on late-night TV."

"Did Magnus understand its value?"

"I wouldn't know. But the fact that he kept his proof of ownership tells me he probably had a clue."

"Then why didn't he offer it as collateral when he knew Bella Vista was in trouble? I don't get it.

"Maybe the thing is lost for good and all he has is a piece of paper saying it had once been given to his grandfather."

"You think I'm on some crazy egg hunt to get you to stall the foreclosure."

"Not so. You know what you're doing. And for someone who uses a refrigerator as a fireproof safe, you seem to understand your granddad just fine."

Tess stopped walking. She clutched at his sleeve. There was a sparkle in her eyes that blew him away. "We need to look in the freezer."

Tess felt a surge of hope as she strode into Isabel's kitchen. "Dominic is here," she announced. "Can he stay for dinner?"

310

SUSAN WIGGS

Isabel set aside whatever delicious thing she'd been preparing, something with fresh basil and roasted peppers. "Sure."

"Thanks," said Dominic. "You'll be rescuing me from a
bad night with Chef Boyardee."

"Don't be hating on Chef Boyardee," Tess said in a warning voice. "He and I are on intimate terms."

"Did you find anything in Grandfather's safe?" asked Isabel.

Tess gestured at the box Dominic was carrying. "More papers to sort through. But I have an idea." She made a beeline
for the industrial-sized side-by-side fridge and swung open
the freezer door. A blast of cold struck her as she surveyed the
contents. The shelves were arranged with painstaking neatness, a collection of tempered glass containers, rolled parcels,
the occasional packaged item. Unlike Tess's freezer in the city,
there was no sign of one-of-a-kind papers alongside ice-furred
microwave meals.

"Can I help you find something?" Isabel asked.

Tess could tell she didn't like anyone rummaging around on
her turf. "It occurred to me that Magnus might have stashed
something in here."

Isabel tucked a stray dark lock behind her ear. "Like what?"

"I don't know. Something he wanted to keep safe."

"You won't find anything like that. It's a working freezer.
I can recite the entire contents from memory."

"Of course you can. You probably lie awake at night taking stock."

Isabel laughed. "Sometimes," she admitted, unapologetic.

Tess picked up a white wrapped parcel. A pound of grass-
fed Kobe beef. "You're sure he didn't stick something in here
for safekeeping?"

"Sorry, no." Scowling, she glanced at Dominic.

"She had a hunch. She keeps things in her freezer."

"How do you know what my daughter keeps in her freezer?" asked Shannon, coming into the kitchen.

"I've been to Tess's place in the city."

"And you looked in her freezer."

"She keeps things in there for safekeeping."

Tess's mother swung to face her. "He's been to your place. Was that before or after you kissed him?"

"Mom." Her face heated. "Isabel, why'd you have to go and tell my mother?"

"I didn't know it was a secret."

"It's not. But…oh, for Pete's sake, Mom. He came to the city to tell me about Magnus, which was more than you did."

Shannon paled. "I had my reasons."

Dominic cleared his throat and folded his arms. "You've been talking about me."

"Don't look so smug." Tess was grateful he was here to change the subject, even if the subject was her attraction to him. "I talk about my bromeliad plant and my bathtub mold, but that doesn't mean they're important."

He put his hand to his chest. "I'm wounded."

"I didn't mean… Oh, for God's sake."

"There's another freezer," Isabel said suddenly.

"What do you mean?"

"In the basement storage area. We have another one, an old trunk freezer. It's almost never used these days, but as far as I know, it's still working."

The freezer was located in a daylight basement. Isabel led the way past drying racks for apples and herbs. The big freezer was pockmarked with rust spots of age and decorated with an assortment of souvenir magnets—Big Sur, Malibu, Yosemite, the Grand Canyon. Tess imagined Isabel visiting these places with her grandparents, and felt a sting of envy. It wasn't that Tess had been deprived of travel when she was growing up.

On the contrary, Shannon had taken her traipsing all over the world. Yet as exotic as that sounded, there was a key element missing—the feeling of family, the delight of discovering something together. Tess's travels with her mother included endless periods of waiting while Shannon conducted meetings and negotiations. Tess's memories were filled with a changing array of airports, train stations and hotels. There had been no chance to set down roots and make friends. Tess still remembered the spike of yearning she often felt when she saw school kids linking arms and chatting away, ignoring the lonely girl watching from the periphery.

It would have been nice to know she had a sister.

The freezer was not a neat archive like the one in Isabel's kitchen. It was a jumble of things, some labeled, some not.

"Grandfather took a lot of payments for things in trade," Isabel explained. "People he dealt with were cash poor, but they had produce and livestock. He once got an entire side of beef in exchange for one of his used trucks."

"Please tell me there's not a side of beef in here," Tess said.

"Not anymore," Isabel assured her. "It's mostly berries." Leaning over the freezer together, they methodically removed the parcels and placed them on a nearby table. Tess's fingers went numb from the cold. She was about to declare her hunch had been wrong when she came across a box wrapped in oilcloth and tied with string. It was the string that gave it away—old-fashioned twine.

"Let's check this out," she said. Best not to act too excited, setting herself up for disappointment.

She cut the string and unfolded the oilcloth, then opened a musty-smelling cardboard shoebox that had once contained a pair of ladies' "Patsy" flats, size seven.

Holding her breath, she lifted the lid. Then she looked

across the table at Isabel. "These are not the droids we're looking for.'"

"Star Wars," Isabel said. "My favorite movie."

"Really? It's mine, too." Tess liked finding points of commonality with Isabel. At the moment, however, it failed to take the sting out of the disappointment. "No egg," she said simply.

"So what is all that stuff?" asked Dominic.

"More pictures of Erik," Tess said.

Her eyes met Isabel's. Neither of them had a relationship with her father, yet both were deeply curious about the man who had fathered them, then died before they were born.

"Why would he keep photographs in a freezer?"

"This looks like a collection of old passports and ID papers," Dominic said. "Really old."

"I bet Grandfather used these during the war years." Isabel laid them out. Rows of somber, stiff-faced strangers stared up from the yellowing travel documents.

"These are travel papers," said Shannon. "My lord, look at them all."

"I'm sure they were used to help people get to America during the war," said Isabel. "I wonder why he kept them."

"In the freezer," Dominic added.

"You said he could never remember the combination of the safe," Tess reminded him. As she studied the old passports and IDs, something niggled at her. She picked up a card in Danish with a fading photograph and an official-looking embossed stamp. "My God."

"What?" all three of them asked in unison.

"Annelise Winther. The one I was asking you about earlier. There's a card from her in Magnus's hospital room." Tess stared at the girl in the photo. She was a small girl, blond and wholesome-looking, remarkably pretty.

"What do you make of this?" Isabel was paging through a folder. "These are Bubbie's medical records."

Tess looked over her shoulder. "They go back to… Look at that. Back to the 1960s."

Shannon took the folder and paged through the forms while Tess, Dominic and Isabel sorted through other materials. After a few minutes Tess noticed her mother had fallen uncharacteristically silent.

"What's up?" she asked her.

"Eva had a hysterectomy." Shannon's cheeks paled.

"I never knew that," said Isabel.

"Look at the date. It was before you were born."

"I suppose that's why I didn't know," Isabel said.

"Look again," Shannon said. "It was before *Erik* was born."

There was a long, frozen moment as they all digested this. They checked and rechecked the date. The color fell from Isabel's cheeks. "It has to be a mistake."

"Every single record and form in this file shows the same date in 1960," Shannon said. "It's not a mistake. And Erik wasn't born until 1962."

"If Eva wasn't his mother, who was?" Tess asked.

"I can't imagine," Isabel said.

She held her arms wrapped around herself, looking as if she wanted to throw up. Tess glanced at Dominic, who offered a shrug of bafflement; clearly he didn't know anything about the situation. "Who fathered Erik?" Shannon asked. "Was he adopted?"

"He couldn't have been," Isabel said. "He looked just like Grandfather—we've all seen the pictures, right?"

"Or are we just seeing what we want to see?" asked Tess.

"No, they're the image of each other," Shannon said.

"Isabel, did your grandfather…? Could there have been another woman?"

"No," said Isabel vehemently.

"Maybe they used a surrogate," Tess suggested. "Did they do things like that back then?"

"Unlikely," Shannon said.

"Good lord. If those records are correct… How could he keep something like this from me?" Isabel gave a shudder.

Tess touched her arm, an awkward pat. "I'm sorry." *It sucks, finding out secrets about the people you love.* She might have said it aloud if her mother weren't present.

"If Grandfather would get better, we could dig to the bottom of things and forget about all the other trouble," Isabel said.

Tess caught Dominic's eye, and she sensed they shared the same thoughts. Isabel was still in denial about the foreclosure.

"I should go," Dominic said. "I've got some hungry dogs to feed."

"I'll walk you out." She kept her distance as they went out into the star-pierced night. "Can she really be that naive?"

"Isabel? Sure. It's what works for her."

"She needs to plan, Dominic. Her troubles are not going to magically melt away, even if Magnus gets better."

"True. What about you, Tess? Do you have a plan?"

He was offering her a chance to discuss…them. As in, the two of them. But that would require her to acknowledge that there *was* such a thing as the two of them.

There wasn't, she told herself. There was…some kissing. A yearning inside her. But there was fear and uncertainty, too, a hard protective shell around her. She was better off alone; this was something she'd always believed. That way, she couldn't get hurt. "My plan is to help Isabel as much as I'm able. And then I need to get back to my own life—my job, the city, my friends."

When Tess returned to the house, she found Shannon and Isabel going through more of the papers they'd found. "Check this out," said Shannon. "It's a customs declaration form. Dated 1946."

"Is the egg listed?" Isabel brightened.

Shannon handed over the faded paper. "Just ordinary things, and precious little of that. A set of butter knives. Christmas ornaments. Four books of negligible value…no treasures that I can see. But then…" She fell quiet. Tess leaned over her shoulder and spied a folder marked *Erik*.

The cache contained a collection of mementos—school photos, baseball cards, a baseball program autographed by Bob Knepper, some scribbled notes and a college transcript from UC Berkeley. There were some papers bound together with a rubber band that disintegrated at first touch, along with some snapshots.

Who are you? Tess silently asked. She studied his eyes, his face, seeing echoes of her own. As she gazed at his image, some other feeling pushed through the sadness. Familiarity. Looking at her father was like gazing at a wildly distorted mirror. Yes, he was a stranger, but some elements were weirdly similar. They both had dimples. Their eyes and noses were shaped the same, and they had the same hairline.

Did you know Eva wasn't your biological mother? she wondered. *Or was that another secret, stashed deep inside Magnus?*

Shannon's face went white as a sheet, and her hand trembled as she touched the old mementos, taking out an old, creased document from Western Union.

"Mom, are you okay?" asked Tess.

Shannon regarded her with wide eyes, misted by tears and memories. "Erik had it," she said.

"What do you mean?" Tess asked. She felt a prickly sensation tiptoe over her.

"Erik had the egg."

TWENTY

"Don't hang up." Erik Johansen's voice pleaded through the phone line.

Shannon Delaney slammed down the phone, her heart racing. What did he mean, don't hang up? What did he think she was going to do? Sit there and listen to him? He'd already screwed up her life quite enough, thank you very much. After their latest meeting, when he'd discovered she was pregnant with his child, she had come to understand that he would never be a part of her world, or a part of the baby's, either. To imagine otherwise was to make herself crazy.

She glared at the now-silent phone and felt like ripping it out of the wall but thought better of it. First, her landlord wouldn't appreciate the destruction, and second, she might be needing the phone in the next few weeks as her due date approached.

"We're on our own now, kiddo," she told the baby, studying the huge mound of her belly. Today, Little Delaney was draped in a thrift-shop maternity dress in a fairly vile mustard color. The fabric was soft and comfortable over Shannon's itchy skin. These days, being comfortable was all that mattered to her. Months ago, she'd had no idea about swollen ankles, having to pee every twenty minutes, thrashing around in bed as she tried to find a position to sleep.... The doctor at the free Planned Parenthood clinic had given her books and pamphlets to read, but they only served to depress Shannon. The literature showed a devoted male in the idealized pictures, rubbing the pregnant woman's back and feeding her ice chips during the birthing process. Seeing a "normal" couple only made her feel more alone.

"Erik says he wants to take care of us," she told the baby. "That's why I keep hanging up on him. If I let him stay in our lives, there'll be strings attached. Believe me, I know. I was tempted at first, when he said he'd find a way to pay all my expenses. How nice would it be to have money for student loans and hospital bills? I can't do it, though. Taking his money would mean sharing you. My friend Blackie, in law school, warned me about something called paternal rights."

The phone started ringing, but she ignored it. A pain tweaked at her lower back, and she stood up and rubbed the spot. Then she brought the palms of her hands over her belly, feeling the itchy tightness of her skin. In the past couple of weeks, the baby had grown enormous, no longer kicked or fluttered. There wasn't room. The movements now felt like a twisting and turning sensation, as if the child couldn't wait to stretch himself out.

"Paternal rights," Shannon said again. "As if ejaculating

gives a guy a right to be a dad. It's not like it cost him anything to provide his DNA."

She'd taken to talking to the little stranger as if the baby
could understand her. "I shouldn't have gotten my hopes up
with Erik. He said his wife had left him. It never occurred to
me that it could be a temporary situation."

For a grad student often described by professors as "brilliant," Shannon felt like an idiot. A walking cliché. The wife
was back. She was pregnant, too, or maybe she'd already given
birth. So for Erik, there was no other option but to stay with
her. *Francesca*. She was as beautiful as her name. Did she have
any inkling of Shannon's existence, or had Erik covered up
his extracurricular activities? Maybe Francesca, Erik and their
child were like those families in the pregnancy books, the
three of them bonded into a single unit, like the chambers
of the heart?

"We'll be a team, just the two of us," she told the baby, her
voice breaking. Damn hormones. She was a weeping mess
these days. "You and me against the world."

The life Shannon had imagined for herself, traveling the
globe, doing her work in the world of art, had shifted irrevocably the day she'd realized she was having a baby.

Getting rid of it had crossed her mind. Of course it had.
For a girl in her position, there were safe and legal ways to
handle it. But her conscience, prodded by her Irish Catholic
upbringing, had intervened, a Celtic voice whispering in her
ear. Even more powerfully, the notion of having a baby of
her own had taken hold of her. People would come and go,
in and out of her life, but a son or daughter would always be
there for her. Yes, her life had shifted, but she still had her
dreams and goals. She would just have to go after them with
a little stranger by her side.

She still hadn't broken the news to her mom in Dublin.

She'd decided to tell her in person after graduation. Her mom would be shocked and no doubt disappointed, but the baby would trump everything. Babies had a way of doing that.

The phone stopped and started a few more times. Shannon continued to ignore it, instead getting down to work on a paper that was due the next day. With sheer determination, she put Erik from her mind, typing with a fury on her secondhand IBM Selectric about object conservation and preservation techniques.

A few hours later, Erik came roaring back in the form of a flimsy canary-yellow piece of paper with tract-feeder margins. A telegram. She'd never received a telegram before. The boxy print on the form spelled out his intent—sort of. There was a string of numbers at the top along with the date, and a bold statement below: Meet me tomorrow 4:00 Trianon Fine Art & Antiquities. Important.

She knew the gallery. The proprietor, Michel Christiansen, had given several guest lectures to MFA students. He had impeccable taste and was incredibly well connected in the world of art and antiquities. It was not unusual to find a Constable original in his gallery, a three-hundred-year-old Wedgwood plate or a piece of estate jewelry that had belonged to Consuelo Vanderbilt.

What in the world was Erik thinking?

Shannon told herself not to go. She wouldn't go, wouldn't give him the chance to break her heart again. What could he possibly do or say to make this situation better?

Yet her heart, though battered by him in the past, was a traitor. She spent a restless night, unable to escape the memories of how magical everything had been when she'd first met Erik. He'd seemed like something out of a dream, handsome and assured, tall enough to turn heads when he entered a room and exuding a kind of charm that didn't seem at all forced. And when he touched her, kissed her...

She groaned with frustration and loneliness. He was the worst kind of liar, the kind who took hearts as hostages and broke them with impunity. She knew this, but in spite of everything, she couldn't stop thinking about that moment long ago, when he'd looked her in the eye and said he'd fallen in love with her.

None of that mattered. She couldn't let it matter. And yet... and yet... Her imagination took flight. She couldn't help herself. She pictured him at the elegant Trianon gallery, selecting the perfect antique ring. In her mind's eye, she saw him go down on one knee, proffering an Edwardian or art deco engagement ring that had once belonged to an heiress, declaring that he couldn't possibly live without her, that he'd left his wife and wanted to be with Shannon forever. They would be a family, the kind of family she used to fantasize about as a girl in Ireland. Instead of being shunned as the village bastard, Shannon's child would be the nucleus of a beautiful new family.

Shannon didn't have a car. In these times, when gas was over a dollar a gallon, who could afford a car? She took the trolley and walked the rest of the way down the hill to the shop, which was near the Embarcadero. It was a beautiful day in the city, one of those days when you knew springtime was more than an empty promise. The sunshine broke free of the dreary shackles of winter, glaring on the damp sidewalks and shop windows.

It was wrong, going to see Erik like this. Only yesterday, she had steeled herself to his persistence, declaring herself done with him and ready to face the future on her own. Yet something—the telegram or the intrigue, her own fickle

emotions or maybe hormones—had filled her heart with romantic expectations, and she couldn't help herself. Maybe she
just wanted to see him to tell him it was over. Maybe she'd
simply listen to whatever it was he had to tell her. She knew
that no matter what happened, she would always remember
the smell of the air this day—the after-rain smell of sunshine
on sidewalks, a fresh breeze from the bay.

What she never expected was that he wouldn't show, not
after his persistence in calling and finally sending her a damn
telegram.

She loitered up and down the block. Her ankles started to
swell, so she looked for a place to sit down. There was an open-
air café across the street from the gallery. She sat drinking a
coffee the way they did in the old country, making the deep
cindery flavor last even as the dark sweet liquid turned lukewarm. People came and went from the gallery, nearly all of
them empty-handed. One couple emerged hugging and snuggling, clutching a bright shopping bag between them, and the
sight of them gave Shannon a pang. Lately, happy couples had
that effect on her, reminding her that she was all alone and
making her wish someone would look at her that way, with
tenderness and caring, as if she were the center of the world.

The romantic outcome she'd fantasized about all night
looked less and less likely. A waiter came and took away her
cup and refilled her water glass. She thanked him quietly but
kept staring at the shop across the way. Just how deep did she
want to take the humiliation?

The irony of the thought brought a brief and bitter smile
to her lips. Here she was, nearly broke, unmarried and pregnant, and she was worried about being *humiliated*.

She waited longer than she should have. He said he would
be there at four o'clock. The hour came and went, the sunlight
of early spring broken by the tall trees all around the bridge.

He'd changed his mind. Or chickened out. Or failed to procure the wad of money he'd promised her. Shannon told herself it didn't matter. She mentally gathered up the pieces of her heart and melded them together into a cold ball of ice.

I'm done with you, Erik, she silently told him. *I'm done with you.*

She paid for her coffee and left a tip, and headed over to the shop. A small brass bell over the door chimed gently as she entered. The gallery smelled of old things and furniture polish, reminding her of Mom's place in Dublin. Shannon let herself enjoy a beautifully framed and illuminated Old Masters painting and a line drawing by Picasso. At the back of the shop were the glass display cases rigged with alarms to safeguard the treasures within—vintage cameos and medallions, and a cache of wedding and engagement rings.

She found herself wondering about the owners of the rings. Were they long gone, and had they given up their rings when they died? She wondered, if she put on one of those rings, would she be filled with the love and hope of the original owner? It was a fanciful thought, she knew. A ring was just an object. The things it symbolized—love, commitment, devotion—were far more transitory than the precious metals and stones.

"May I help you?" asked Mr. Christiansen.

She could feel his gaze assessing her. She'd dressed with care today, though she'd told herself not to put in any extra effort for the sake of Erik. She had only one decent outfit that covered her ungainly figure. It was a loose Liz Claiborne jumper over a cap sleeve white T-shirt, and a pair of flat espadrilles. Her swollen ankles spoiled the effect, but she didn't look totally ghastly.

"I'm Shannon Delaney," she said. "A grad student in Berkeley's MFA and museum studies program. I saw your lecture about avant-garde Russian art last year."

That warmed him up a little. "Welcome. Are you looking for something in particular? I hope it's not a job. I'm over-staffed already."

"Nothing like that." What was she going to ask, after all? *Have you seen the father of my child? He begged me to meet him here but he stood me up.* "I was supposed to meet…a friend here today, but I guess he's running late. Erik Johansen?"

"Ah. We had an appointment."

And…? She was desperate to hear more. "I thought maybe he'd called you about being delayed."

"Sorry. No." He pressed his lips into a seam of discretion.

"Well," she said. "If he does happen to show up, maybe you can let him know I was here."

"Of course, Miss…"

"Delaney," she reminded him. "Shannon Delaney. I'm in the phone book and the student directory."

He didn't quite look at her very pregnant belly, but she sensed him thinking about it, maybe putting things together in his mind. At the same time, her heart was coming apart, again, maybe this time sustaining permanent damage.

"I'll be sure to do that," Mr. Christiansen promised.

When she stepped aboard the bus to the city, the passengers parted to give her plenty of space, as if what she had was contagious. She took a seat vacated by some guy, offering a vague smile of gratitude. Clinging to a pole, she gazed dully at the passing scenery—flickers of Telegraph Hill between the shoulder-to-shoulder shops and office buildings.

The bus ride made her nauseous. Indecision made her nauseous. Everything made her nauseous. She lurched off the bus and stood on the west side of campus, wondering where the sun had gone. Low clouds pressed a chill down on her. She was in an agony of curiosity about what Erik's real intent had been today. If it had been to send her on a wild-goose chase, he had succeeded.

Since she'd already humiliated herself at the Trianon shop, she figured she might as well go for broke. She couldn't call Erik at his home number—what if his wife answered? She could easily picture his wife, dewy-eyed and pampered as she gracefully gestated the legitimate child. The favored child. One thing that should have been a red flag when Shannon and Erik were going out was that he hadn't introduced her to any of his friends. Every time she'd asked about this, he used to kiss her and say, with a sincerity she too easily bought, "I want you all to myself."

She knew the name of his best friend—Carlos Maldonado. They were neighbors in the town of Archangel where they'd grown up. Erik had described their exploits as kids, climbing the apple trees of Bella Vista, stealing jugs of wine from the Maldonado winery vats. Carlos always looked older than his age and had no problem sneaking into racetracks for betting. He was addicted to betting on horses, Erik had once explained. It caused the family no end of trouble.

And that was the extent of what Shannon knew of the people who knew Erik. What a loser she was, getting knocked up by a relative stranger.

The campus library had a collection of all the phone books in the state. She perused the shelves in the reference section, finding a fat California Bell tome marked *Greater Sonoma County* with a list of communities—Kenwood, Santa Rosa, Healdsburg… Archangel.

Her fingers felt clumsy and chilly as she flipped through the thin pages. And there it was: Maldonado, C. Hacienda Drive in Archangel.

She rushed to a pay phone before losing her nerve, and dialed the number she'd scribbled on the back of an envelope.

"Hello?" A woman's voice.

"Yes, hi. My name is Sh... Sharon Smith." *Great, Shannon,* she thought. Could the name have sounded any more contrived? "I was hoping to speak to Carlos Maldonado."

"Carlos? He— Lourdes, stop that. Leave the dog alone— Sorry. My daughter's being a pest. What was it you wanted?"

"I was wondering if I could speak to Carlos."

"Look, if you're from the collection agency, I can tell you right now, we—"

"No." Shannon had the feeling of wading into murky water. "Nothing like that. I, um, I found something that might belong to him." *Oh, way to lie,* she thought.

"I'm sorry, what— Lourdes, what did Mommy say?"

"Sounds like this is a bad time," Shannon said, regretting the impulse to call.

"When you've got two little kids, there's no such thing as a good time for a phone call. But anyway, Carlos isn't back yet. He went to the city."

"With someone named Erik Johansen?"

"Who is this?" the woman asked sharply.

Shannon hung up quickly and stepped out of the phone booth.

Had Erik come to the city with Carlos? What did that mean? And where the heck were they?

Shannon decided to treat herself to Chinese takeout for dinner that night. The doctor at Planned Parenthood had told her to avoid salty foods and stuff with MSG. Shannon was usually pretty good about that, but today she felt like breaking the rules. Just the thought of Moo Goo Gai Pan made her salivate. Min Cho's, her favorite place, had a TV in the bar, always set to the local news. While waiting for her cardboard pail of Moo Goo Gai Pan, she stared dully at the screen, un-moved by reports of mayhem and murder.

The TV news anchor droned on about a horrific fatality accident this morning on the Redwood Highway. There were worse things, Shannon reminded herself, than being stood up by some guy. She took her dinner home and sat at the kitchen table, savoring the sautéed chicken and veggies while perus-ing the latest *Smithsonian Magazine*. Sonic Youth's "(She's in a) Bad Mood" streamed from the radio, its ugly melody a good match for the lyrics.

She'd eaten half her dinner when the highway patrolmen showed up at her door. She stood there, staring at the two officers in confusion while the words they spoke took her world apart. Mr. Christiansen of the Trianon gallery had said she might have some information for them. They were in-vestigating an accident on the Redwood Highway. Evidence at the scene had led them to the Trianon, and the proprietor had given them her name.

"What happened to Erik?" she asked, swaying against the door frame.

The older of the two officers eyed her pregnant belly. "We're sorry, ma'am," he said.

The officer looked a bit like Steve McQueen, Shannon thought, just a second before she upchucked her Moo Goo Gai Pan all over the floor.

TWENTY-ONE

Tess pictured her mother, young, alone and pregnant, getting the news from the highway patrol. "I'm sorry," she said quietly, her throat thickening and her eyes burning. She looked over at Isabel. To her surprise, Isabel was dry-eyed. It must have been hard to hear, a story about her father sneaking away from her mother to meet with his pregnant mistress.

"So what was his plan? Did he intend to sell the egg to the gallery and give you the money?" asked Tess. "If he did, that would mean he was incredibly naive, or he didn't understand the true value of the egg."

"I think so. I mean, I *want* to think he was trying to help me. We can only speculate."

"What about the friend?" asked Tess. "Carlos Maldonado, the guy you made the phone call to."

"He died, too. A drowning." Isabel quickly found a link online to the archive of the *Archangel Trumpet,* the town's weekly newspaper. Older articles had been scanned and presented as images showing newsprint that was yellowed and brittle with age. There were two photos of equal size displayed on the page. Erik Johansen and Carlos Maldonado. The headline boldly proclaimed: "Double Tragedy Strikes Local Families."

"My lord," Isabel said softly. "Look at the date. Carlos Maldonado died right after our father, and four days before you and I were born."

The juxtaposition of their birth date and a horrible dual tragedy gave Tess a chill. Staring at the picture of the man who had fathered her, Tess felt an overwhelming sense of loss. *I wish I'd known you,* she thought. *I wish you could have known me.* Maybe he'd made some lousy choices, maybe he'd screwed up Shannon's life, but judging by all she'd learned of him, he'd made his parents happy. People around Bella Vista had loved him.

And then there was Carlos Maldonado, about whom she knew virtually nothing.

"So his friend died, too," Tess said. "Was it some huge, tragic coincidence, or were they related?"

Isabel read the paper's explanation of the connection:

"'The day after Erik Johansen's fatal accident, tragedy struck again, this time at the Maldonado family. Carlos, who had been best friends with Erik since boyhood, drowned in an irrigation pond on the family property. The county coroner's office ruled it an accident. He leaves behind his parents, Ramon and Juanita Maldonado, his grandmother Flora Maldonado, his wife, Beatrice Maldonado, and his daughter, three-year-old Lourdes.'"

She stared at the list of names. "Lourdes? As in Dominic's ex-wife, Lourdes?"

Isabel nodded. "The same."

"Okay, that blows my mind."

"Here's my mother's obituary," said Isabel, scrolling to a page dated four days later.

Francesca Johansen—Isabel's mother, Erik's wife. It might well be Isabel herself, smiling up from the page. They had the same deep-set, soulful eyes, thick, wavy dark hair, generous lips and patrician noses. The three of them looked at it for a long time, each lost in her own private thoughts.

"I was in Berkeley," Shannon said softly. "Just back from Erik's funeral."

"Whoa. You went to his funeral?"

"I… I wasn't thinking clearly. I was in shock, and I… It was something I needed to do. I didn't know anyone, just introduced myself as a friend of Erik's. I expressed my condolences and went away. Could be Magnus knew more about me than I realized. Perhaps Erik had said something."

Isabel shut the laptop. "What a mess he made."

Shannon placed her hand on Isabel's arm. "He wasn't a terrible person. None of us was. He was young, younger than you two are now. He made a stupid mistake. With me, and with Francesca. His legacy is something amazing, though. Look at the two of you. *You* are the legacy. You're both in the world because Erik did what he did, so there can be no regrets."

In the morning, Tess found Shannon in front of the main house, standing on the stoop with her suitcase. Battered and worn in spots, it was the same one she'd used for years.

"You always leave," said Tess, trying to stifle a too-familiar sinking feeling.

"I have a job. I have responsibilities."

"You have a *daughter*."

"I have an incredible daughter." Shannon stuffed her hands into the pockets of her tunic-length jacket. "And about Dominic Rossi—I'm hardly the one to give advice in this department, but I just want to say, if it turns out you really like this guy, then let yourself like him, Tess. I wasn't the best role model for making a relationship work, but you can do better."

Tess felt a flood of warmth in her cheeks. "Romantic advice from you," she murmured. "That's a new one."

"I mean it, Tess. I've been watching the two of you together. I never…let myself be vulnerable. You have the chance. I wish…" She shook her head. "I have to go. Really."

Tess took a deep breath. For once, she was going to speak her mind with her mother. "I get it. But before you go… I've never said this before, but sometimes I need you, Mom. You. Not your expertise at your job, or your excuses. You. When I was little, I used to think there was something wrong with me, that you were never around."

Shannon smiled wistfully. "Now you know better. There's not a thing wrong with you. It's me. I know it's not very helpful, but I'm sorry. I'm sorry I kept things from you, and sorry you had to find out this way. I know it's no excuse, but I truly did think it would be better if you didn't know."

"I just don't understand how you could think that."

"It can be worse—knowing. My father was never married to my mother."

"So you've told me. But at least you knew who he was."

"I'm glad you think so. But growing up in a small Catholic town in Ireland, it was impossible to avoid the gossip." She winced as though the pain was still fresh. "I never told you this, but my father had a wife and several kids."

Tess frowned, digesting this new information. "Wait a second, what?"

"He was married when my mother took up with him. And, yes, I'm sure my mother realized how wrong and foolish she was being. He made all the promises a man makes to his mistress—he was going to leave his wife, and my mother, she simply needed to be patient while he negotiated his freedom, divorce being a tricky business in Ireland at the time… and like the worst of clichés, she fell for it."

Tess stared in disbelief, trying to rearrange her thinking about the grandmother she'd known. "Nana? She was always so levelheaded."

"Not when it came to my father. I spent my early years in Ballymun, outside of Dublin, and back in those days, the shame was horrible. I had to go to the same school, the same church as my father's 'legitimate' family. It was torture."

Tess could too-easily picture her mother in the close-knit clannish community of Ballymun, being jeered at and shunned. Prior to this, all Shannon had ever said of her early years was that at the age of thirteen, she'd moved with her mother to Dublin. Nana had founded Things Forgotten. It had never occurred to Tess that they'd been fleeing a terrible shame.

"I'm sorry you suffered," she quietly told her mother. "But that doesn't mean I would have."

"Maybe, maybe not. I didn't want to take that chance. I never wanted you to feel the way I did in Ballymun, so that's why we moved around so much, why I was always leaving. Tess, can you forgive me?"

"You were trying to protect me." She felt frustrated, though. Her career was all about unearthing the past, yet now she was discovering whole gaps in what she knew about her own history, more than she'd ever suspected.

Just then, Isabel came out through the foyer. "Oscar said you're leaving."

Shannon nodded. "He's giving me a ride to the Santa Rosa airport."

"I see. Well, it was very nice meeting you. Promise you'll come back."

"Of course. I wish I'd been of more help." Shannon gave Isabel a brief hug. Then she turned to Tess and hugged her, too. "I raised a smart daughter. You're going to figure this out, one way or another."

Tess studied the shadows haunting Isabel's eyes. A sleepless night was etched there, in those dark half-moons.

"You okay?" asked Tess.

Isabel nodded, pulled her shawl around her. Despite the bright morning sunshine, the days were getting shorter, chillier. "Yes," she said. "You?"

"I've had a lot of practice at telling my mother goodbye. I just wanted to make sure you're not, I don't know, upset by the things she told us."

"What happened, happened. And like she said, we're in the world because it happened."

Tess suspected they were both feeling weighed down and emotionally exhausted by the drama and tragedy of what had happened in the past, not just to their father, but to both their mothers.

Tess had quickly grown to care about this woman; they'd gone from being strangers to sisters, bonded by their worries about Magnus and his estate. Isabel's need to hold on to Bella Vista was a tangible force; it was clear even when Isabel was engaged in the simplest of things, like sweeping off the stoop or walking down to the crating warehouse.

Isabel turned toward the house. "I feel the need to bake something. How about you?"

Tess gave a little laugh. "Never been tempted, thanks."

"You probably think it's silly, all the time I spend in the kitchen."

"Not at all," Tess said swiftly. "I'm envious, in fact. The way you take care of people here is remarkable to me. I love how you cater to their most basic needs in such a beautiful way. It's your gift, Isabel."

"Thanks." Her smile was fleeting, a little bashful.

Tess thought about her mother, and how disconnected she was, and a shiver passed over her. *Please don't let me be that way,* she thought.

"I need to do some thinking, make some calls," she said. "I'll see if the Trianon gallery is still in business. And we should talk to the Maldonados. Do you think they'd be open to that?"

"Possibly. I can give them a call, invite them over."

"I feel like going to see Magnus," said Tess. "It's kind of strange, but sitting there with him…it helps me think."

By now, the people in the reception area knew Tess, greeting her with pleasant nods as she made her way to the elevator. Ironically, the maternity floor was one below the ICU. When the elevator stopped there, she caught a glimpse through the nursery window of little bundles, wrapped like special gifts, in their clear bassinets. Today, an exhausted-looking but smiling Latino man got into the elevator with her. He held a toddler by one hand and in the other was an empty baby carrier. Though he said nothing, Tess could feel his pride and excitement at the prospect of bringing home a new baby. The little kid with him bounced up and down on the balls of her feet and whispered something in Spanish to her dad.

What a magical time in the life of a family, thought Tess, and she felt a surprising twinge of something that might be envy. Or yearning. With Dominic, she was feeling things for the first time, and it was risky and exhilarating and impossible to resist. She felt so torn between the life she thought she wanted and the life she'd glimpsed here. It was so unlikely but at the same time so seductive.

The elevator stopped and she smiled at the man and the little girl as they got out. Then the doors swished shut, and she was whisked to a different world, one where worry and desperation hung in the air, mingling with the smell of disinfectant. Stripped of all privacy, the mostly elderly patients lay in their mechanical beds, surrounded by monitors, drip bags, oxygen tanks.

Don't let it end here, she thought.

She stepped into Magnus's suite. His vitals were noted on the whiteboard, and the lights had been dimmed, the blinds of the single window shut against the day. She took a seat on a rolling stool by the bed.

"Hey, Magnus," she said, having taken to speaking with him as if he could hear her. "I could really use some help here. I feel as if Isabel and I have collected a bunch of puzzle pieces, but we're having trouble putting everything together."

The sigh and hiss of a pump was the only reply. Since he'd been taken off the ventilator, he looked more human but frail and vulnerable, as if he could slip away at any moment. She studied his face, the pale skin lined, the white hair tousled. She fancied she could see the face of the boy in the old photos, and the proud young husband, the grieving father, the indulgent grandfather. The man who'd had a child out of wedlock.

She wondered what his voice would sound like…and if she'd ever get to hear the sound of his laughter.

Lately when Tess came to see him, her impulse to obsessively check her messages wasn't quite so strong. The hospital was one of the few places where she got a good signal, yet sometimes she was content to just sit here, to listen to the rhythm of his pumps and monitors and think about everything—or nothing at all.

"I'm losing my edge, out here in the country," she confessed. "I should really go back to the city and get on with my life." She placed her hand on his. The wrist was encircled with bar-coded hospital bracelets. His skin was warm and papery-dry. "Something's keeping me here, though," she continued. "Actually, a lot of things are." She squeezed his hand. "And you're one of them."

She looked up the Trianon gallery and discovered that it was still in business, and that Mr. Christiansen was still in charge. When she called, she was told he was gone for the day.

"I'd better get going," she told Magnus. "I'm getting too emotional, hanging out with you. Just...please get better, Magnus. We'd love to have answers from you, but it's more important just to know you're here." The moment she spoke the words, she felt a wave of emotion that left her breathless. This man was a stranger, but he was so important to her.

When she returned to Bella Vista, she discovered Isabel in her manic-baking mode. The kitchen was filled with the aromas of butter, vanilla and cinnamon. She'd created Danishes and rugelach and crispy twisty things that promised to glue themselves promptly to Tess's hips.

"How's Grandfather?" Isabel asked, dusting flour from her hands.

"The same."

"Was his color good?"

"I guess."

"What do you mean, you guess? Did he look pale, or—"

"He looked like a guy in a coma, okay? I mean, it's not okay, but..." Tess snapped, suddenly irritated with Isabel. "Listen, if you want to see how he's doing, then *go see him.*"

"You're right, I need to do that. I'll go later, take some ginger molasses cookies to the staff."

Tess felt a mixture of exasperation and admiration. "Man does not live by cookies alone, Isabel. I'm not like you. I can't make myself believe that a well-cooked meal is going to fix what's wrong with me."

"Don't patronize me," Isabel muttered. "Please. I never got to have some big life in the city—"

"You never 'got' to?" Tess wanted to tear her hair out. "Right, you were forced to suffer here at Bella Vista, in the bosom of a family that adored you."

She flinched.

"Have a cookie, Tess."

"No, thank you."

"They're good for what ails you." She held out a perfectly baked cookie on a spatula. "A peace offering."

"I don't need a peace offering," Tess stated. "And what makes you think anything's ailing me?"

Isabel's eyes turned dark. "You won't let anyone get close to you, Tess. Not your mother, not me, not even Dominic, and he's crazy about you."

"Baloney." Yet her heart skipped a beat at the notion.

"You travel the world, running from…what? From yourself?"

Tess's cheeks were still hot with fury when she left the house. She had to get out, had to go…somewhere. Away. Away from Isabel and her grief and desperation, and from the fact that when Tess looked into her sister's eyes, it was like looking in a mirror. This was something she'd never had to deal with before, and she wasn't sure she liked it, the fact that she was inextricably tied to someone who was nothing like her… yet at the same time, everything like her.

Like Isabel, Tess was scared, too. She was scared of living a lonely life. Both sisters feared the things they couldn't control; the unknown made each of them nervous. But unlike Isabel, Tess was not going to give up on herself, hiding from reality.

Nor did she want to be the person her mother had become, traveling through life alone the way her mother did, never forming a deep bond with anyone. Maybe that was what filled her with crazy daydreams of Dominic. Something was coming over her, something real and powerful, like some kind of madness, or like a dream.

Walking, Tess decided as she struck out for the far edge of the property, was underrated. There was something in the rhythm and movement of a purposeful stride that loosened the clench of anxiety in her stomach. In the city she walked to get from point A to point B. Here at Bella Vista, she didn't have a destination in mind. She just needed to move. Wearing a bulky sweater she'd found in the hall closet, she crossed the fields on foot.

The weather was uncharacteristically foul, the sky heavy with brooding clouds whose bellies bulged with unshed rain. A wind like the siroccos of Italy swept down through the valley. The return stack orchard heaters, propelled by slowly rotating wind machines, breathed warmth into the chilly air of late autumn. She felt the crackle of dry grass and fallen leaves underfoot.

The steep hills of San Francisco had always challenged her lung capacity, but lately, out here in the fresh air, she felt as if she could walk forever.

Unfortunately, the weather didn't care what her purpose was or how far she felt like walking. As she wended her way down through the orchard, the rain-swollen clouds crowded the sky, obliterating the light. Within minutes, the occasional droplets thickened to a steady downpour. Twin veins of lightning split the horizon, quickly followed by a roar of thunder.

Great, she thought, feeling an icy trickle of rain down her back. Her heavy sweater fast became a dead weight on her body, heeled boots slipped through thick mud. A gust of wind shivered through the trees, adding drama to the downpour.

She headed for the nearest shelter—Eva's old fruit store at the roadside. With its wooden gingerbread construction and railed wraparound porch, it was a welcome refuge from the storm.

The building wasn't locked, so she let herself in through the creaky door in the back, recoiling from a thick swag of cobwebs. "Lovely," she muttered. "This is all just so lovely."

The rain sounded like machine-gun fire on the tin roof of the building. Shivering with cold, she peered through the shadows. The space was vast, much bigger than it looked from the outside, with sloping display tables, rustic shelves and fixtures on the walls. She spotted a potbellied woodstove and some hurricane lamps, a long counter with a big cash register of tarnished brass. Despite the dust, the vintage wrought iron fixtures and hand-lettered signs exuded an unassuming charm. Beneath the cobwebs and heavy air of neglect, the shop seemed suspended in time, as if it were under an enchantment. Large picture windows, one of them scored by a diagonal crack, framed a view of the sagging front porch and the road. Maybe she could flag down a car. Except that on this dreary afternoon, no one seemed to be around. The light was fading fast.

She decided to wait it out here in the abandoned building. If Isabel got worried, so be it. Teeth chattering, Tess peeled off the sweater, which now reeked of wet wool. Maybe the electricity worked, if she could just find a switch. She took out her cell phone to use as a flashlight. Getting a signal at Bella Vista was impossible, but the flashlight app offered a bluish beam, just enough to spot a field mouse skittering across the floor.

With a squawk of surprise, Tess jumped up onto a stool by the counter. Ugh. *Rodents.*

Then she noticed something on the screen of her phone—

one bar of service. Maybe she could make a call, get someone to come rescue her.

Her finger hovered over the number to the main house, but she hesitated. Fresh off a quarrel with Isabel, she didn't want to have to beg for help. Instead, she dialed Dominic. Of course she did. There was no pretending she didn't want to see the guy.

A gleam of headlights swung through the storm. It was nearly dark now, and Tess's fingers were numb. When Dominic came into the shop on a swirl of wet wind, she flashed on Heathcliff from *Wuthering Heights* and started to shiver again.

"Nice day," he said, looking around the place.

"I thought so," she replied. "Thanks for coming. The mice and I kept hoping the rain would slack off, but it's not letting up. Yes, there are mice, which is why I haven't gotten off this stool."

He found an old box of kitchen matches and lit one of the hurricane lamps. It exuded a plume of oily smoke, and its yellowish flame bathed the place in a golden glow. "You're soaked," he said.

"And freezing. And miserable." But so happy to see him, she couldn't help smiling.

He lit a couple more lamps. "Your lips are blue."

"I told you I was freezing."

"Jesus, Tess." He took off his jacket and slung it around her shoulders. She welcomed the enveloping warmth of his body heat.

"I appreciate this. Did I pull you away from something important?"

"The bank at quitting time. No problem," he said.

She deflated just a little. She'd fantasized—momentarily—that *she* was important, the kind of important that made a guy drop everything and dash away to find her. She wasn't sure she'd ever been that important to someone. It was a terrible thing to want to be, but she couldn't help herself.

"So how'd you get caught in the rain?" he asked.

"I had to get away," she confessed.

"What's the matter?" He grabbed her hands and rubbed her cold fingers. "Besides the obvious, I mean."

"It's hard, having a sister."

"I've told my sister so, many times."

Having a sister was wonderful…but hard. It was different from having a friend. Friends tended to come and go, but once she'd discovered she had a sister, someone who shared her father, her DNA, possibly a whole hidden history, she couldn't *not* have her.

"Is Isabel okay?" Dominic studied her.

"Everyone asks that about Isabel. Maybe if we all quit tiptoeing around her, she'd stop being afraid of her own shadow."

"What happened?"

"I went to see Magnus and when I got back, I snapped at her and now I feel terrible."

"Sounds like a pretty normal exchange between siblings."

"Does it? I wouldn't know. I really want us to get along."

"Everybody gets along with Isabel."

"It's just… I'm starting to care about her so much."

"What's wrong with caring about someone?"

"I'm not saying there's anything wrong with it, but it's not easy. I don't like seeing her hurt, or scared, and I can't fix it for her."

"A word to the wise," he said. "Nobody can fix another person. But everybody tries."

"Ouch," said Tess. "I assume this means you tried fixing someone."

"You're starting to know me pretty well."

"Yeah?"

"Don't look so smug. It's not a stretch. I'm a guy, remember?"

"Like I could forget that."

He grinned. "Grab your stuff and I'll give you a ride."

"All right."

"Unless you want to hang out here."

She was surprised. An opening? "To tell you the truth, I'm curious about this place now. I wouldn't mind exploring. What do you know about it?"

"I haven't been in here in years," he said. "I liked coming here as a kid. There was always something to eat, always something interesting to look at, like a puzzle of bent nails or one of Magnus's boxes, things made of beeswax from the local hives."

"Isabel said her grandmother used to be in charge of the shop." Gratefully she buried her nose in the fleecy lining of his jacket. *I'm such a goner,* she thought, lost in the scent of him.

"During the harvest season, it was a busy place. Eva sold produce from the orchards, local honey, baked goods, freshly pressed cider.... Man, I'll never forget her cider and homemade donuts. As I recall, you've got a thing for donuts."

"Ha, ha. Isabel must've inherited her talent in the kitchen from Eva. Why didn't the place stay open?"

"It was Eva's baby. She organized it into a co-op for growers and artists. After she got sick, no one else was around to take it on."

"That's a shame," Tess said, looking around at the empty shelves and display tables. She shivered and drew the jacket tighter around her.

"I'll make a fire," he said, helping himself to wood from a bin by the stove.

"That's too much trouble," she said, feeling silly for wanting to linger here with the rain battering the roof.

"What, you don't want a fire?"

"Of course I want a fire," she blurted.

"Then sit tight and let me make one. I like making fires." He whistled as he laid old paper and kindling in the stove and opened the flue. Within a few minutes, the place was alight, and warming up quickly.

"My grandmother had a shop," she said, looking around, filled with nostalgia.

"You kept her desk," he said. "You used to play around it when you were a kid."

"I'm impressed that you remember me telling you that."

"I remember everything you told me. You'd be surprised how much I think about you, Tess."

"Really?" She wondered if it was even half as much as she thought about him. The wind whipped past, banging the battered sign outside against the eaves. "It's strange to think Eva had a shop, as well. One of my earliest recollections was of watching the hand-painted sign swaying in the wind against a stormy sky, kind of like today."

She could still picture it perfectly in her mind's eye. *Things Forgotten* was written in gold leaf script on black. Underneath, in smaller lettering, it said "B. Delaney, Proprietor." The memories were powerful, imprinted on Tess's heart, and she felt a wave of sentiment as she thought of that girl long ago, dashing in from the weather to a hot cup of tea.

"Two shop-keeping grandmothers," Dominic said. "It's in your blood."

Looking around the derelict building, she pictured the shop, revitalized. At present, the space was a great hollow box, waiting to be filled from the wood-planked floor up to the hammered tin ceiling. She was quiet, listening to the fire and the rain on the roof, imagining the shop she would have. "Nana had exquisite taste," she told Dominic. "Her clients came from all over."

"And your grandfather?"

"Nana never married," Tess said, thinking about what her mother had shared about the shame and hurt of growing up the mistress's daughter. "She had bad luck with men."

"What about you?" he asked. "Do you have better luck?"

Her standard answer was that she did just fine without a guy in the picture. Instead, she said, "That depends."

TWENTY-TWO

Dominic took her to his place, which was exactly what she wanted, even though she knew it would complicate things. Maybe, she thought, she could handle a few more complications. He gave her a WWF robe to wear while her clothes tumbled in the dryer. The bulky sweater was hung on the porch to drip dry.

Combing her fingers through her hair, she indicated the robe. "WWF? That's very…badass of you."

He laughed. "Right. Here, try this." He went to the counter and poured her a glass of wine.

She savored the deep, complex flavors. "Amazing," she said. "I'm sure there are all kinds of terms for this—peppery, floral, with notes of red crayon and Tootsie Roll, right?"

"Very funny. I'll stick with *amazing*." He grinned at her. "Drink up. I have some others for you to try, if you want. The kids are with their mom."

"'The kids are with their mom,'" she repeated. "That's got to be some kind of code."

He nodded. "It's a direct invitation."

She could see it in his eyes, behind those ridiculously sexy horn-rimmed glasses. "I'd love to try some others," she said.

He lined up several glasses. "This is a flight of my last four vintages, oldest to youngest. I can get incredibly geeky about it and give you all kinds of information, or I can just let you sit back and taste."

"I don't mind a little geekiness," she said. "I like it when people talk about something they're passionate about."

"Okay, so this one is... You're looking at me funny," he said.

"I'm not laughing." She finished the final glass of wine. "You're like two different people, Mr. Rossi, the banker, and another guy entirely when you're talking about your wine."

"It's a bit more interesting than amortization schedules and conversion clauses."

"And *you're* more interesting when you're doing something you love."

"There are a lot of things I love doing."

The look in his eyes was unmistakable. Her breath caught. "Yeah?"

"Yeah."

She actually had butterflies in her stomach. Butterflies. She'd never had that sensation with a guy before. Everything about him was different, unexpected. Impossible to resist. Like magnets, they leaned in toward each other until she could feel the gentle heat of his breath, until she could almost taste his kiss.

The dryer beeped, startling them apart.

Dominic gave her a slight smile. "To be continued," he said, and fetched her clothes. She changed in the bathroom, feeling flushed and, to her shock, a little shy. Normally she wasn't shy at all with guys.

Dominic went upstairs, and when he returned, he looked much more relaxed in faded jeans, a well-worn T-shirt, tennis shoes.

"Put this on," he said, handing her a fleece jacket. Unexpectedly, he took her hand. Iggy and the Dude trotted to the door, clearly reading his intent.

In the wake of the storm, sunset lay in a pink-and-amber swath over the rolling landscape, the trees in the orchard casting elongated shadows on the hillside. To the other side of the slope were Dominic's vineyards. The vines were heavy with fruit, the dense bunches of grapes nearly black in the deepening light.

They held hands like a couple of teenagers. It felt ridiculously good to hold hands with this man. His touch was both safe and sexy at once. He walked with her through the vineyards, pointing out the different grape varieties, planting dates, grafting techniques. And always, like a song playing in the background, was the sense that they were moving together toward something, and she was scared and eager all at once.

"Taste this," he said, plucking a darkly colored grape. "It's one I developed on my own. I call it Regina. Means 'reigning queen.'"

He held the grape gently to her mouth. The soft flesh of the fruit wore the fresh chill of evening. She bit into it, letting the juice fill her mouth. It had a mysterious flavor, not like the sort of grapes found on a cheese platter but something more exotic and sensual. The taste was earthy and barely sweet at all.

"Well," she said, wondering if he could see the warmth in her cheeks. "I'm pretty ignorant about grapes, but it tastes like something that could turn into a delicious wine."

Grinning, he tossed a grape into the air and caught it in his

mouth. "You have no idea." He fit seamlessly into his surroundings, as if he'd never done anything but cultivate grapes.

She stepped back, gazing up at him. He reached out with
his thumb and caught a drop of juice that lingered on her
lower lip.

It was all she could do not to groan aloud. She stepped
back, trying to get a grip on herself. "Why don't you do it,
then? Why not be a winemaker, doing something you love?"

"As a profession, it's about as stable as betting on horses."

"You need something steady for the sake of your kids."

"Exactly. But this—" He encompassed the vineyards with
a sweep of his arm. "I do it the way some people make art or
play a sport. Just trying to do well at it makes me... It's hard
to explain. It makes me a better person, maybe, better than I
would be without it."

He was showing her his dream, the same way she'd shown
her dream to him in the abandoned shop. Dreams changed a
person, and there was a little danger in that, because having
a powerful dream made you vulnerable to failure and disappointment.

"Listen to you," she said quietly, "going all romantic on
me."

He slipped his arms around her waist, pulling her snugly
against him. "I'm finding it easy to do when you're around."

"Yeah?" Her heart sped up. "I bet you say that to all the
girls."

"You lose. You're the only one I've ever said that to." He
was smiling as he slowly and gently lowered his mouth to hers.

She knew instantly that their previous kiss had not been a
fluke. It really had been that good, because this one affected
her the same way—it made the world disappear. His evoca-
tive touch made her feel as soft and ripe as one of his designer
grapes, and her hands moved searchingly over him, up his

arms and along his shoulders, fingers tangling in his hair. She pressed herself against him, fiercely needing the closeness, and a small sound moved in her throat, a nonverbal signal of yearning. She wanted the kiss to go on forever, but at the same time, she craved so much more than a kiss.

After a long time, he pulled back. "Well," he said.

She detected a world of meaning in that single syllable. "My thoughts exactly."

It was nearly dark now. Flames from the distant orchard heaters cast an eerie, intriguing glow over the rows of trees on the Bella Vista side.

"Let's go back to the house." Keeping hold of her hand, he started walking. "I'll give you a taste of the 2006 Regina."

"Okay, you said that on purpose."

"I like the way it sounds." He stared down at her for what felt like a long time. She grew self-conscious under his gaze. "I want you to stay tonight," he added.

A hundred questions crowded into her mind, sprouting like weeds. His statement could mean all kinds of things. Did he want to start a relationship with her, or just get laid? Did he see some kind of future for them together? Was there any possible way to construe this as a good idea?

She knew the risks. She understood perfectly the hazards to her heart.

But all she said was, "Yes."

They barely made it back to the house. She found his impatience incredibly sexy; the feeling that he wanted her so much was like an aphrodisiac. Just inside the back door, he pressed her against the wall and started kissing her again until she forgot the whole world. Her skirt rode up, his jeans rode down and she wrapped her legs around his body as he lifted her against him. How quickly she was lost, forgetting everything except a crazy overwhelming need to be close to him. It was over all too quickly, leaving her breathless, her forehead leaning against his, both of them dazed and practically hyperventilating.

In a fog, she slid down his body as if it were a tree trunk.

He let out a long, shaky sigh and pulled up his jeans, leaving the top button undone. "I've been wanting to do that since the first time I met you."

And I've been wanting it. She didn't say so. The admission made her feel too vulnerable.

"Mission accomplished," she said softly, straightening her skirt.

The dogs clicked into the kitchen, offered them a diffident look and moved on.

"Not hardly," Dominic replied, bending to trace a path of kisses down her neck. "We're only getting started."

After rearranging his jeans, he grabbed a bottle of wine and two goblets in one hand and led her into the living room. "I hope you don't have other plans for tonight," he said.

"Um…no, why?"

"I want to take my time with you."

A shiver of anticipation coursed through her. "That sounds… God, Dominic, what are we doing?"

He flashed a cryptic smile. "Everything."

Then he went and made a small fire in the grate, just enough to ward off the twilight chill. They sat together on the sofa, and she felt mesmerized by the gentle bright flames, and the color of the wine and the crazy anticipation flowing through her.

"To your dream," she said, touching the rim of her glass to his. The wine was as delicious as he'd promised. The flavor was deep and slightly mysterious, and it went straight to her head.

He stared at her for a long time. Though sitting close together on the sofa, they weren't touching...yet. She was still buzzing from the encounter in the kitchen.

After a while, he poured them each more wine, and they clinked glasses again. "Here's to...something new," he said.

Her heart stumbled. "This might not be such a good idea."

He kissed her, his mouth flavored by the wine. "Are you kidding? This is the best idea I've had in a long time. Maybe ever."

"I've never been anyone's best idea before," she admitted.

"Then you're not hanging out with the right people."

She flashed briefly on her friends in the city, ready to say something in their defense. Her friends cared about her. They did all kinds of things together—going out, staying in, shopping and gossiping, celebrating life's victories and commiserating when someone fell down. However, none of them ever put her first. They weren't there for her, not for the important things.

"And you're the right people," she said, unable to keep from smiling.

He answered by setting their glasses aside and kissing her again, deeply and with lingering intent while his hands mapped the contours of her body. He moved slowly, as though savoring her. She didn't think a guy had ever savored her before.

A little inner voice crept up, warning her not to start something with this man. She brushed aside her misgivings. She was on fire, and all hesitation burned up in the face of her yearning. If what had happened in the kitchen was any indication, the two of them were extremely compatible in at least one key area.

"All right," she said. "I'm in."

He laughed softly. "You're not anteing up for a card game here. It's not a game at all. I don't play games."

Something in his tone made her hold still and catch her breath. "Neither do I."

He led her to the bedroom, where he yanked off his sweatshirt one-handed over his head and let it drop. Her breath caught at the sight of his bare chest and enviably fit abs.

"What are these scars?" she asked, leaning forward to kiss a sickle-shaped ridge near his collarbone. "From the accident when you were in the navy?"

He nodded, and she felt a pulse of grief, hating the image of him wounded, suffering. "Oh, Dominic..."

"They're just scars," he said. "I don't hurt anymore." Then he undressed her slowly, taking the time to kiss and explore every part of her. In contrast to the clash of lust in the kitchen, this was a slow, exquisite torment, each moment leaving her more and more on fire.

Her last coherent thought before she completely drowned in sensation was that he was going to be either her best time ever...or her biggest mistake.

TWENTY-THREE

Dominic woke early the next day, with his arms curved around a warm, redheaded woman.

He had a powerful urge to stay right where he was, to kiss and tease her awake and take her again while she was half-asleep and sweetly compliant. Just the thought was almost enough to override his common sense. *Focus,* he told himself. He had a ton of things to do, starting with turning off the winery pumps. He'd never forgotten them before. But last night had been all Tess, all the time. He'd forgotten everything.

Last night had blown his mind. The two of them, so new to each other, should have been awkward and uncertain together, but instead, some unspoken familiarity created a rhythm, as though they were dancing to silent music. It was the kind of night he'd probably fantasize about for a long time, the one his mind would go back to again and again, the night by which all others would be measured. He couldn't analyze why. Maybe he didn't want to analyze why. She was adventurous and tender in bed, surrendering to him while at the same time inspiring him to give more of himself than he could ever remember doing. It didn't bug him to be vulnerable with her, and he didn't know why that was, either. She was not the domestic sort, enamored of small-town life in sleepy Archangel. She had every intention of picking up for the city as soon as her business here was concluded. He ought to be bracing himself for that. Instead, he found himself thinking, what if....

She stirred a little in her sleep, giving him a chance to extricate himself from the bed without waking her. But then she clung to him, and he couldn't keep from wanting her again. Without saying a word, before she even opened her eyes, he lifted himself to cover her, and it was as brief and intense as an electric storm, leaving him shuddering, his mind blank. The sleepy smile on her lips afterward was like the rising sun to him.

"Go back to sleep," he whispered, filled with a crazy happiness as he kissed her temple. Yes, happiness, something he hadn't felt in every cell of his body since before the divorce. He didn't even know he was allowed to feel this way again. "I need to shut off the pumps. Didn't mean to leave them on all night."

Her response was a wordless sigh of contentment. She stretched, drawing the covers over her bare shoulder, and went back to sleep, a smile still curving her lips. Then she chuckled. "I love it when you talk dirty to me."

Dominic winced with regret as he slipped from the bed. He was dying to stay longer with her, but he had to get his day started. There was never enough time to get everything done—the kids, his job, his winemaking. He loved being a dad. He even loved being a single dad, but it made for an insanely busy schedule. Lourdes would be bringing the kids back to him at dinnertime, and they were his for the next week. He couldn't wait to see them, but he had a lot to get done today.

And all he wanted was to spend a lazy day in bed with Tess, making love to her over and over again, pausing only to do something ridiculous, like maybe taking a bath together or peeling grapes and feeding them to her. However, duty called.

He dressed quickly, took one last look at her in his bed, which inspired a fresh wave of desire. He was jolted back to reality by a sound from his phone, indicating a work email. Without even looking, he could guess what it was about. The regulators, who never seemed to sleep, were breathing down his neck, contesting the extension he'd requested based on the unrecovered assets contingency. He wondered if he was a fool, putting his job—his children's livelihood—on the line, for the sake of a friend.

Without looking at his email queue, he decided to head out, the dogs trotting along with him. Dogs were so easy. They didn't judge, ever. They approved of everything.

It was no simple matter, taking up with a woman. Particularly with a woman like Tess Delaney. The simple solution would be to declare last night a lapse in judgment and back off.

"Who am I kidding?" he said to the dogs as he headed to the shed. "I'm in this."

Iggy and the Dude swirled happily around him.

"It's true," he assured the dogs. "I'm all in." He swung open the doors to the shed, inhaling the musk of grapes. "My life is about to get very complicated."

Tess stretched luxuriously, unraveling herself from a strange and sensual dream. She was in the apple orchard, watching buds turn to blossoms and then fruit as if through time-lapse photography, and all the while, Dominic was holding her close, kissing the side of her neck, tasting her skin with his warm tongue.

She moaned softly and shifted, reaching out to gather him closer, but found only rumpled sheets and pillows…and there was Iggy, licking away at her neck and shoulder. "Oh, come on," she said, pushing him away. "Really? Really?"

Though she had nothing against dogs, it was Dominic she wanted. Last night had been pure magic. He had the kind of hands that knew just how to touch her, just where, just when, as if he could hear the rhythm inside her. His touch left her with a warm sensation flowing all through her body, making her greedy for more. She sat up and looked around, waiting for the customary churning anxiety to hit, but for once, the unpleasant feelings stayed away.

"Remarkable," she muttered to the little dog. "If I'd known a night with Dominic would be a cure-all, I would have jumped his bones a long time ago."

Iggy's ears pricked up, and he skittered away, his nails clicking on the hall floor and then the stairs.

She levered herself out of bed and reached for her skirt. Then, spying a blue denim work shirt, she grabbed that and slipped it on. The garment was soft and faded with wear, and his scent hid in the fibers, enveloping her like a phantom embrace. She headed into the bathroom, which was as neat as the rest of his house, and helped herself to his toothbrush. After last night, the barriers between them had dropped; she was sure he wouldn't mind.

Then she headed downstairs to forage for food. Isabel's kitchen had spoiled her for ordinary breakfast fare, but she figured she would find at least a cup of yogurt or maybe a bagel. Like everything else in the house, the kitchen was spotless, even after the orgy of wine and sex that had begun only hours before. Did the guy have cleanup fairies that swept in when no one was looking?

The pantry yielded a shockingly unimaginative but perfectly organized assortment of prepared foods. Bad prepared foods, like canned spaghetti and ramen noodles. How could this man create such exquisite wine, yet have no yearning for fine food?

He was a mystery. Perhaps that was why she found him so intriguing.

She discovered a box of Pop-Tarts, a foodlike substance. Tearing open the wrapper with her teeth, she took a bite. Despite its cardboard texture, the gummy filling tasted vaguely of fruit. It wasn't half-bad. Chewing thoughtfully, she wandered around the kitchen, checking out the world of a man who was quickly becoming far too important to her.

His life appeared to be governed by his kids and his job. There was a calendar page on the fridge with highlighting on the weeks he had Trini and Antonio with him. In his neat banker's script, he had written down the times for soccer matches, tutoring, work meetings.

And the item at the month's end caught her eye: *Bella Vista matter.*

The Pop-Tart curdled in her stomach. She was an idiot, falling for a guy who, voluntarily or not, was about to wreak financial havoc on her sister. Suddenly Tess felt very protective of Isabel and sheepish about their quarrel the day before. Yet at the same time, something was happening between Tess and Dominic, something powerful and unexpected.

She'd always considered herself good with men. She could handle them. She was capable of availing herself of their charms without risking her heart. This—whatever it was with Dominic—felt risky, though, and when it came to her emotions, she was risk-averse.

Yet the only thing that felt more risky was to walk away now. Her gut kept telling her not to blow this.

Her head and her heart were at war.

Head: His entire life is here in this tiny burg.

Heart: Hello, he's an ace pilot. He can be anywhere in an hour.

Head: Every other week belongs to his kids, one hundred percent.

Heart: They're adorable. We could be a family.

Head: You don't even like kids.

Heart: That's just in general. I like *his* kids.

Head: He's the enemy. He's foreclosing on Bella Vista.

Heart: He doesn't want to. It's the last thing in the world he wants to do. We're lucky he's in charge, because he's giving us every break he can find.

Head: This can't work. You're going to end up getting hurt.

Heart: If last night was any indication, being hurt by him feels like heaven.

She heard the tread of footsteps at the back door, and her heart won the battle. Wearing his work shirt and nothing else made her feel both vulnerable and wildly sexy. "I wanted you to wake me up and have your way with me again," she called to him. "Get in here and do it now."

"Sorry," said an annoyed, female voice, "but that's not the way I roll."

The half-eaten Pop-Tart dropped to the floor, scattering crumbs at Tess's feet. She stood frozen with mortification as a woman walked into the kitchen. She was dressed as though she'd stepped from the pages of the Sundance catalog in a flowy skirt, hand-knit sweater and ballet flats, a hemp bag in one hand, a cartoon character backpack in the other.

"Obviously," she said, "you weren't expecting me."

Tess wanted to wilt into the ground like the Wicked Witch

of the West after a slosh of water. But she cloaked herself in dignity, praying the cloak was not as skimpy as the work shirt.

"I'm Tess," she said. "And no, I wasn't expecting you."

The woman subjected her to a frosty glare that looked out of place on her overtly pretty face. "Lourdes Maldonado," she said.

Dominic's ex-wife was nothing like the slit-eyed viper Tess had pictured. She looked...pleasant. Pretty. Like a very well put-together soccer mom rather than a two-timing nightmare who cheated on her husband while he was off serving his country. *Bad things sometimes come in nice packages,* Tess reminded herself.

"I'll just come right out and say it," Lourdes informed her. "I intend to reconcile with Dominic—did he tell you that?"

Tess managed to keep her jaw from dropping. "Frankly, he doesn't talk to me about you."

Lourdes appeared to be unfazed. "He and I both know it's best for our family."

"This is probably something you should talk to him about."

"Just so you know, Dominic and I, we're not over. We never were. Not by a long shot. You're just a distraction."

Tess sensed a strange vehemence behind the words. "I'm not discussing this with you."

"There are children involved. Fragile, hurting children. I'm telling you to step aside."

Wow. This woman was some piece of work. "You don't want to start ordering me around," Tess said quietly, feeling the hairs on the back of her neck stand up.

"That isn't the point, is it? What I should really say is that it makes no sense at all for you to get involved with Dominic. You're only here for a short time, so there's no point. It'll only confuse my children more."

Tess had engaged in a similar debate with herself. She

couldn't deny it. "How do you know anything about my plans or intentions?" she demanded.

"Small-town life. Get used to it. Or not. Where's Dominic?" asked Lourdes.

"Right behind you," he said. "Are the kids all right?"

Lourdes's demeanor changed entirely as she turned to face Dominic. She visibly softened, moistening her lips. "It's Trini. She forgot her lucky spelling-test shirt."

Dominic's face was as unreadable as a marble statue. "You could have—"

"Called, I know," she finished for him, "but I don't have my phone with me, and I wanted to catch you before work. I think we should go over the latest progress report. You do have time for our daughter's school report?"

"Excuse me," said Tess. "I need to get going." She slipped past the glorious Lourdes, heading for the stairs. The sensual warmth that had enveloped her a few minutes before had frozen to a sheen of ice. She dressed hurriedly, keeping her gaze away from the rumpled bed and her thoughts away from what they'd done there last night. When she got downstairs, Dominic was alone.

"Hey," he said. "Sorry about that."

"Don't apologize. You have an ex-wife and kids. Nothing to be sorry about."

"She—Lourdes—has a problem with boundaries."

God, why did he have to look so good to her? Even now, she wanted to fall into his arms. "She wasn't what I expected," Tess said.

"What did you expect?"

"I'm not sure. Someone…harsher. She seems nice and…organized, I guess. Except the bit about forgetting her phone. She told me—and believe me, I understand this—she wants a chance to reconcile with you."

"Look, if there was any chance of that, don't you think we would have made it happen before now?"

"I honestly don't know. But, Dominic, I don't intend to compete with the mother of your children."

"You're not—"

"I'm not anything like her."

"Maybe that's what I like about you."

"You loved her once."

"I did. I loved her a lot, the best way I knew how. It ended, though, and I moved forward. Why would I go backward, looking for the same kind of person?"

"Because that's the way it works. You—"

"Don't tell me how it works. I'm interested in *you,* Tess. I want *you.*"

The tone of his voice gave her chills. He spoke with absolute conviction, and she realized his certainty made her nervous. "I need to go."

"Not yet." He gently caught hold of her wrist. "Tess—"

"Really, I should go." She took her hand back despite the fact that with every cell in her body, she wanted to hang on. She wanted to stay.

He took her face between his hands and gave her a long, slow kiss that reminded her of how good they had been together last night.

Although she yearned to melt into his embrace, she felt a powerful inner resistance. Falling for him was too easy. Falling in general was easy. It was the landing you had to watch out for.

TWENTY-FOUR

"So now you're having sleepovers with strange women?" Lourdes said to Dominic. She had returned after work with the kids to drop them off with him. As always, his house was filled with warmth now that Trini and Antonio were here. However, Lourdes's presence was a chilly shadow as she stood on the front drive, talking to him across the fence.

He pressed his teeth into his tongue, hard, to keep from rising to the bait. Lourdes had had her share of sleepovers, too. The difference was, she hadn't waited until after the divorce.

He turned to make sure the kids were out of earshot. They were in the backyard, having a game of fetch with the dogs. "There's something I wanted to ask you," he said.

She gave him a hopeful look that made him feel lousy. He quickly asked, "What do you remember about your father?"

Her look turned to anger and confusion. "My father? He's

been dead for years, you know that. I was tiny when he died. Why would you wonder about that now?"

"Just trying to help out Magnus and Isabel with some things."

"By picking my brain about a guy I have virtually no memory of?" Her eyes narrowed in suspicion. "You've always had a soft spot for Isabel," she said, her tone accusing. "And now for her sister, as well. Although I guess you're not so soft when it comes to her."

"Hey, sorry I asked." Was he ever. He should have known she'd be in a rotten mood when she dropped off the kids.

She massaged the side of her neck with her hand. "I remember he had a big laugh, and he liked to drive fast. Sometimes he'd come home with an armload of presents for me." She frowned, shut her eyes briefly. "He and my mother fought. They yelled a lot. But we were always so happy at Christmastime. I guess that's probably why it's my favorite time of the year."

There was a Maldonado family tradition of putting up the tree and decorating it with special ornaments that had belonged to Carlos; each had a certain meaning. When he and Lourdes were married, they made a big deal of it with the kids. After the divorce, Lourdes had taken all the sentimental keepsakes with her, and he was happy enough to let them go. He did miss the feeling of family from those times, the warmth and closeness, the magic sparkling in the children's eyes. But unlike Lourdes, he knew better than to believe it could be rebuilt, not after all the damage that had been done.

"Anyway," she said, "the holidays are coming up. How about you come decorate the tree with us?"

"Thanks, I'll let you know." He knew it would be painful and awkward. He would try too hard, she would drink too much, and the kids were old enough now to notice. "Do you have time to talk about Trini?" He held open the gate.

She hesitated, and he could see her mentally measuring the time it would take. That was the thing about having been married to someone. You knew what they were thinking. Lourdes was yearning for her nightly bottle of wine, something that had become more important to her than anything, even fixing her marriage.

"All right," she said, following him to the front porch. They took a seat there. "Her teacher says she's struggling in school, having trouble concentrating."

"This isn't news to me," he reminded her. "I took her for a checkup, we had her tested by the school diagnostician, and I've been helping her with her schoolwork. Did the teacher say there was no improvement?"

"She keeps forgetting things, and she doesn't pay attention in class. Dom, she's troubled because we're not together."

This was his ex-wife's weapon of choice. She used the kids to manipulate him. "Trini is troubled because we're not doing a good enough job making this work for her."

"How can it work when all she wants is to be a family? God knows, I hated growing up without a father. I feel like a monster, passing that along to my kids."

"We tried, Lourdes," said Dominic. "I gave it everything I had for the sake of the kids."

"Then let's try again. Don't you think our kids are worth it?"

"They're worth everything," he said. "We've always agreed on that. They deserve the best life we can give them. I can't do that with you. I can't go back and fix something that wasn't right in the first place."

"Dom—"

"We don't have to be together to help them be happy and feel loved. We just have to work at it. Tell you what. Let's go back to that counselor we used in the divorce. She was really good with the kids. She'll give us some fresh strategies."

"You want to go into counseling?" Her eyes lit with a hope he wished he didn't see.

"For the kids. Yeah, I'm willing." He was frustrated. There was a part of him—no small part—that wanted to love this woman again. She was the mother of his children. Staying together as a family had an appeal that reached the deepest part of him. Yet he couldn't manufacture an emotion that simply was not there. What they'd once had was gone, as empty as the wine bottles she used to try to hide from him. In the early days, crafting the perfect wine had been a shared love, but when she became an alcoholic, all that had changed. Now, his passion was his ex-wife's poison.

"We can't keep having this conversation," he concluded. "The four of us will never be the family we once thought we'd be."

Trini appeared around the corner from the backyard, her face pale and chin trembling as she glared from one to the other. "You promised," she hurled at them both. "You said you'd fix things and we'd be a family again."

"Sweetheart, we didn't make you any such promise," Dominic said. It was so hard to make the kids understand. There was no way to explain what had really happened, that Lourdes couldn't handle the loneliness of separation while he was away, that she'd turned to other men and to drinking. It wasn't fair to saddle the kids with that. "We *are* a family, but your mom and I can't live together anymore."

"Why not? That's what moms and dads do. Mom *said*."

He regarded his daughter, his heart feeling ripped in half. She'd been so little when they'd divorced. She didn't remember the chilly, strained silences, the heavy fog of discontent that had hung over them all.

"I tried, baby," Lourdes said, standing up and giving Trini a hug. Lourdes was antsy now; Dominic could practically see her craving. "But I have to go now, okay?"

Trini stood stiffly, watching Lourdes get in her car and take off. Then she turned accusing eyes on Dominic. "I just want to be a real family again."

"We are a real family."

"I hate the way we are."

"Ouch."

"Well, I do." She kicked at a tuft of grass. "What's for dinner?"

"I don't know. What do you feel like? Want me to fix you something?"

"No, *thanks*."

"Okay, how about you fix me something," he suggested.

Just for a moment, a flash of interest lit her eyes but was quickly shuttered. "I only know how to fix toast."

"Cool, then let's make toast."

Her chin trembled, and the look in her eyes tore at his heart. "Trini," he said. "It's going to be all right. Swear to God it will. Maybe not right now or tomorrow, but it will." He gathered her into his arms, feeling a wave of emotion. When she was a baby, he used to hold her and gaze down in wonder into her precious face. She'd seemed so fragile and vulnerable to him, all he'd wanted was to protect her. Now she felt fragile in a different way, and he simply didn't know how to make things better for her.

Charlie had taken to sleeping in Tess's room. She didn't know why. She'd never had a dog and never considered herself a dog person, but that didn't seem to matter to the gangly German shepherd. She had no objection to his company, however. Some mornings were rough; she'd wake up with her heart racing in a generalized panic, and the sight of the big dog, curled up on the braided rug beside the bed, had a calming effect on her. He generally loved his sleep, but this morning, he awakened her with a tentative *woof* and trotted to the door.

"What?" she mumbled, blinking at the clock. "It's six-thirty in the morning."

He woofed again, so she got up, shrugged into a hoodie and tennis shoes and followed him down the stairs. He headed straight for the kitchen, nails clicking on the tiles, leading her straight to a pair of intruders.

"Hey," she said. "What are you two doing here?"

Trini and Antonio Rossi stood inside the back door. "It wasn't locked," said Antonio.

"Isabel never locks," Trini added.

"That doesn't answer my question. Does your dad know you're here?"

"He doesn't mind," Trini said.

"We're hungry," said Antonio.

"There's no food at your dad's house?" Tess helped herself to a glass of water and regarded them skeptically. They were so darn cute. But more than that, just the sight of them, the sound of their voices, even at the crack of dawn, lifted her heart. She let the dog out the back, into the chilly fog of early winter. The landscape was muted by mist in the windless air, the empty trees skeletal against the dun-colored grass.

"The food's better here," Antonio said.

"The food here is better than anywhere," Tess pointed out.

"What a nice thing to say." Wide awake and dressed for the day, Isabel breezed into the kitchen. "Hello, you two. You're up early."

"They're hungry," said Tess.

"My favorite kind of kids," said Isabel. "Hungry ones."

"What do you like for breakfast?" Tess asked them.

"Everything," said Trini. "Just not Dad's shredded wheat." She wrinkled her nose.

"We can do better than shredded wheat." With smooth efficiency, Isabel put a kettle on for tea, then handed each kid an apron. She tossed one to Tess. "Do you mind pitching in?"

Within a few minutes, the biscuit-making had begun. "This is the first thing my grandmother taught me to bake," Isabel explained, "because it's the simplest. But don't be fooled. A lot of things can go wrong with biscuits, and they could turn out like hockey pucks."

"Yeah, I hate when that happens," said Tess.

"I take it you've never made biscuits from scratch." Isabel demonstrated her techniques, letting them in on her trade secrets, such as sifting the flour from a height of at least a foot and grating the cold butter into the bowl. Within a few minutes, the kids were dusted with flour and giggling, and Tess forgot that mornings were supposed to be hard. Her heart was opening up, almost of its own accord. Bella Vista had woven a spell on her, and she no longer even tried to resist.

"Can you show me how it's done?" she asked Isabel, following a crazy impulse.

"What, baking biscuits?"

"Not just baking. Fixing a meal." *All right,* she told herself. *Say it aloud.* "I want to cook like a grown-up, not like I'm stuck in college."

"Say no more." Isabel took a pastry cloth from a hook on the back of the pantry door.

Tess joined in the lesson, surprised at how enjoyable it was to roll out the dough and place the dusty biscuits on an old, weathered pan.

She slid a sheet of biscuits into the oven and stood back, watching as Isabel coached the kids through cutting up apples, slicing grapes and celery and chopping walnuts for a fruit salad. Isabel had some kind of dressing to toss it in, made with honey and cardamom. It was nice, observing her sister's gentle guidance.

"You're good with kids," she said. An olive branch, extended to bridge the gap after their quarrel.

A smile glimmered on Isabel's face. "I'm good in the kitchen."

"It's more than that. You're a good teacher."

"Yeah? Thanks."

And that was all it took to get over their quarrel, Tess realized. A look, a kind word. She was getting to like having a sister.

"Cooking's fun," said Trini. "Baking, too. We bake with our mom at Christmastime."

Tess vibrated to attention like a struck tuning fork. She pictured the beauteous Lourdes, sweetly presiding over the holiday traditions.

"I bet that's fun," said Isabel.

"Not as much fun as presents," said Antonio.

"And decorating the tree. Every year, we put up the tree in honor of our grandpa who died," Trini said, her expression softening.

"You mean your grandpa Carlos?" Isabel said.

"He died a long time ago. It's sad for our mom. She has a box of special ornaments that used to belong to her dad. Keepsakes, she calls them." Trini used her finger to draw a *K* in the flour on the countertop. "Dad doesn't have any keepsakes."

Tess's heart went out to the little girl, to both kids. "That sounds like a nice tradition," she said.

"This year in school we made 3-D snowflakes," said Antonio. "I wish it would snow. My favorite ornament is a mouse on a sled."

"Mine's a big gold one that opens up," said Trini. "Sometimes Mom puts candy in it, and we're supposed to think the treats are from Santa."

Tess smiled. She was very comfortable with Dominic's kids. "When I was your age, I had Christmas at my grandmother's house in Dublin. My favorite ornament was a little bell made of white Belleek china. It had shamrocks on it."

"This one's all gold with swirls."

Tess felt the smallest nudge, but she tamped it down. "Swirls, you mean like a color?"

"Yep. It's really pretty."

The phone rang, jangling into the morning. Isabel went to answer it. Trini ducked her head, but not before Tess read the guilt in her eyes.

"That's your dad, isn't it?" she asked the girl.

Trini nodded, gave the fruit salad a stir.

"You didn't tell him you were coming here, did you?"

Without looking up, Trini shook her head.

"He'll be here in a few minutes," said Isabel, putting the phone back in its cradle.

"Are we in trouble?" asked Antonio.

"That's up to your dad," said Tess. "I'm guessing it's not okay to take off at the crack of dawn without permission. Just a wild guess." She hurried upstairs to get dressed, running a comb through her hair and brushing her teeth with a vengeance. Dominic arrived, looking tousled and put-out in a V-neck sweater and jeans, his glasses slightly askew, which Tess found wildly attractive.

He gave her a brief, smoldering look, but quickly turned his attention to the kids. "Not cool," he told them both. "Not cool at all. What the h— What were you thinking?"

"It was Trini's idea," Antonio protested.

The timer rang, and Trini rushed to the oven. "The biscuits are ready!"

"Let's all sit down to breakfast and talk about it," said Tess.

"We have a rule," Trini said. "No arguing at the breakfast table."

"I wasn't suggesting an argument." She helped Isabel lay the table with warm biscuits, butter and jam, bowls of fruit salad and a pot of tea. There was something about the rhythm of the morning that felt right, despite the fact that it was horrendously early, and Dominic was ticked off at his kids. It made Tess feel as if she had a family. That was the part that felt right.

The kids dug right in. "Best breakfast ever," Antonio said. "But it was still Trini's idea."

"If you didn't like breakfast at home, you should have spoken up," Dominic said. He slathered a biscuit with butter and sampled it. "You're right. It is the best breakfast ever."

"The kids made the biscuits," Tess said. "They did a good job."

"Fine," said Trini, "I'm speaking up now. Breakfast is better here. So is lunch and dinner."

"You can't have breakfast, lunch and dinner here," said Dominic.

"No offense, Dad, but the food's way better here," Antonio said.

"I never did learn to cook," Dominic confessed to Isabel and Tess. "Went straight from home to the navy."

"Mom doesn't cook, either," Trini mumbled.

Tess saw Dominic stiffen. "You're a smart guy," she said quickly. "You make the best wine I've ever tasted. Fixing food's got to be easier than that. How about you let Isabel teach you, same way she taught the kids this morning? Could you do that, Isabel?"

"Definitely." Isabel served more fruit to the kids.

"I'm eating celery, Dad," said Antonio. "See?"

"I thought you didn't like celery."

"I thought so, too."

"It's all in the execution," Tess said. She'd found this morning's cooking lesson ridiculously charming. It made her feel closer to Dominic's kids, filling her heart with a kind of warmth she hadn't felt before. Isabel's kitchen was a magical place in that way, she was discovering.

"Who knew?" asked Dominic.

"We can have another tonight, then." Isabel pushed back from the table. "You can come over after work."

"Yeah, Dad." Trini jumped up and helped clear the table. "It'll be fun."

He shot a look at Tess. "I have you to thank for this."

"You're welcome."

"And you're not going to get out of helping."

"I already had a turn cooking with Isabel," said Tess.

"Ah, but cooking is like any other fine art," Isabel reminded her. "There's always something new to learn."

PART NINE

···　•　···

RUSTIC TOMATO SAUCE
WITHOUT
ANY BITTERNESS

....

*People go to too much trouble to chop things fine. It's also not necessary
to oil the pan for fresh tomatoes. Let the food keep its own character.*

6 pounds beefsteak or heirloom tomatoes

4 star anise pods

1 vanilla pod

sea salt & cracked black pepper to season

white sugar—a pinch, if needed

2 sprigs of fresh thyme

1–2 bay leaves

Infusion:
fresh garlic
one bunch fresh basil
extra virgin olive oil

Heat a heavy gauge pan. Place a heavy cast iron pan to heat
up on the rangetop. Wash the tomatoes and cut into rough
halves or quarters. Place into the hot pan and season with salt,
pepper and a touch of sugar. Add the anise and vanilla. As
the tomatoes start to cook, press them gently with a masher
to release their juice. Reduce the heat to a simmer and slowly
cook to a thickened paste. This should take 1–2 hours. The

slow evaporation of moisture will produce a deep flavor without any bitterness.

Meanwhile, prepare the infusion. Warm the olive oil in a pan. Crack the garlic with the flat of a knife and add along with the basil. Combine with the warm tomatoes and finish with a good amount of oil. Serve over pasta or bread, with a grating of cheese on top.

TWENTY-FIVE

Tess spent the day exploring the many rooms of Bella Vista. In her profession, the act of seeking something often yielded information she didn't know she needed—a repair stub, a letter, a receipt from a pawn shop. That was her hope, anyway. The two upper stories were a maze of bedrooms and linen closets, none of them used in what appeared to be decades. She found herself wondering about the families that used to live here, inhabit these rooms. What had become of them? What other secrets did they hold?

"I try to dust every few weeks," said Ernestina, parting the drapes of one of the rooms to reveal tiny particles drifting in the sunshine. "It gets away from me, though."

For the most part, the rooms were orderly, crammed with vintage furnishings, shelves of books and collectibles. Tess noticed a rare Limbert turtle-top table with curved ends, a Gustav Stickley bookcase and an impressive collection of

Rookwood pottery vases worth thousands of dollars. The liquidation sale, once the foreclosure went through, was going to be remarkable, she thought, her heart sinking.

"Which room was Erik's?" she asked Ernestina.

The housekeeper started down the hall. "On the far end, here. I'll show you. There's not much to see," she cautioned.

Tess wasn't sure what she'd feel, seeing the room where her father had grown up. It was spare, a twin bed with a plaid coverlet of boiled wool, a desk and bureau. Everything was perfectly neat, as though frozen in time for a teenaged boy. There was a Berkeley Bears pennant and a Pink Floyd poster on the wall, and a few framed photos of Erik as a boy. But she saw nothing telling, nothing that would fill in the blanks of the missing egg. And certainly nothing that would fill in the blanks Tess had carried around inside herself forever. She felt absolutely no connection to this long-gone person.

There was a collection of postcards on a tack-board. She picked it up and studied the images—Las Vegas in all its kitschy 1980s glory, Big Sur, the Santa Monica Pier, the horse racetrack at Santa Anita Park.

"Those are from Carlos Maldonado," said Ernestina. "He and Erik were best friends."

"Would it be all right if I read them?"

"Of course. He was your father. I've heard it said that the dead keep no secrets."

"That's not been my experience," murmured Tess. "What was he like?"

Her eyes misted. "He was bright and charming. He made everyone laugh. He was not perfect—who is? He was young and reckless and made mistakes. But everyone loved him."

Including his wife and mistress, thought Tess.

In a desk drawer amid old papers and dried-up markers, she found a small framed needlepoint phrase: Live This Day.

She took a quick, cautious breath. "Do you remember when Erik was born?"

Ernestina smoothed her hand down the coverlet on the bed. "Eva had female troubles. She and Magnus went to the city to see a specialist, and she spent months there. Erik was tiny when they brought him home, but he grew fast. Before long, everyone forgot how he'd started out."

That evening, as Isabel prepared for another cooking lesson, she seemed to blossom, a woman totally in her element. Tess wondered if her sister lay awake at night, worrying that she would soon have to leave this place and find herself adrift in a world she found deeply threatening.

"Can I ask you something?" She felt tentative, bringing up the subject with Isabel.

"Sure."

"Um, suppose the foreclosure goes through, Isabel. Suppose you have to vacate Bella Vista."

Isabel took out a clean apron, her face impassive. "I can't think like that."

"Listen, I'm really sorry to be the one to bring it up, but we should figure out a Plan B for you."

"I know you mean well, Tess, but it's not..." Her voice trailed off.

"Not what?"

"It's not time. Not yet, anyway."

"Time's running out. Much as we both hate the idea, there will probably come a day when we have to vacate the premises."

"But not today." Isabel tied on the apron with a firm tug.

"Right. Not today." Denial, she reflected, had its uses.

"Fine, then." Isabel turned to the fridge and took out a sack of tomatoes.

"Fine. No matter what happens," Tess said to her sister, "no matter how this turns out, you're going to be fine. Anyone who can cook like you has a bright future."

Isabel offered a wan smile. "It's so hard to get my head around the idea of a different life. You've inspired me, though, the way you've adapted to being here. I don't know what I would have done without you."

"I haven't adapted," Tess admitted. "I've spent practically every day here wondering when I can get back to my life in the city, my job and friends. I'm sorry, Isabel, but as nice as it is here, I just don't belong."

"That's not the impression I get when I see you and Dominic together."

They shared a look, and Tess felt a wave of emotion. How quickly she'd found an affinity with Isabel, a woman so unlike her, they might have been from different species. Only a short time ago they had been strangers. Now she couldn't imagine not knowing Isabel, her guileless and fragile sister. They shared a birthday, they shared their father's DNA, but the bond now ran deeper than that; it ran as deep as blood and secrets.

"We're going to be all right," she said to Isabel. "One way or other, we'll be okay."

It was never a good idea to argue with denial. Or with magical thinking.

The process of cooking seemed to anchor Isabel, and she exuded contentment as she went about her business with a smooth competence Tess had never felt in a kitchen. She tried to act as if this were any other evening, but the prospect of Dominic coming over with his kids had filled her with a kind of breath-held anticipation she'd never felt before. She had done her makeup and dressed with special care in faded jeans and a dove-gray turtleneck, a pair of freshwater pearl earrings she'd found in one of the upstairs dressing rooms, her hair looped back in a ponytail. She studied her image in a small mirror on the wall. The line of tension between her eyebrows had eased; just letting in the feelings she was having for Dominic seemed to cause something inside her to unfurl.

"Nice," said Isabel, checking her out.

"Am I too transparent?"

"Not at all. He's into you, no matter how you're dressed."

"You read my mind," Tess admitted.

"That's what sisters do, right?"

"I met his wife," Tess blurted out. "His ex, that is."

Isabel busied herself arranging herbs and tomatoes on a big olivewood cutting board. "And?"

"She came barging into his house while I was over there, as if the place still belonged to her."

"Sounds like Lourdes," Isabel murmured.

"He said she has a problem with boundaries. She's not what I expected. Actually, I don't know what I expected. I figured she'd be pretty, and she is. Down-to-earth, too. Nice, even. Not to me, of course."

"I'm sorry."

"It's understandable. She's a lawyer, right?"

"A good one. She's a partner in a local practice."

"She told me flat out she wants to get back together with Dominic."

Isabel paused in setting up the cutting board. "She's never made a secret of it."

"What's up with that?"

"I don't know. Maybe being single isn't all she thought it would be. She's had a few boyfriends, and none of them have worked out. Could be she didn't realize what she had with Dominic until it was over. Does it worry you?"

"Hell, yeah, it worries me. I hardly know anything about

him. For all I know, there are still feelings buried inside him—"

"You can't think like that, Tess. If he says he's moved on, he's moved on."

"But they have a family. A past. History…"

"We all do. You can't rewind life or undo things."

"How'd you get so smart?"

Isabel smiled. "I take after my big sister." She was referring to the gap of a few hours, after Tess had been born but before Isabel had made her appearance. "Grandfather says—"

"We're here," sang Trini, coming in through the back door. "We're ready for more cooking." Charlie trotted into the room and barked a greeting, and Antonio started tussling with him on the floor. Dominic arrived last, straight from work with his dress shirt unbuttoned at the throat and his sleeves rolled back, a grin lighting his face. He always looked so happy around his kids. No wonder Lourdes wanted him back, thought Tess. Look what she'd lost.

"First, the hand-washing," Isabel announced. "Doesn't matter how delicious the food is if it's contaminated." Everyone took turns at the sink, and Isabel handed out the aprons.

"Allow me," Dominic said to Tess, stepping behind her. He tied it on with a peculiar intimacy she hoped was lost on the kids. It was far too soon to involve them in the equation.

Isabel started with a simple pasta sauce, created with the last of the heirloom tomatoes from the fall garden. "The key is to taste," she said. "You have to taste the tomatoes to determine how much sweetness to add." She passed everyone a wedge of tomato, which they dutifully ate.

"It's good," said Antonio.

"Does it taste sweet to you, or tart?"

"It tastes like a tomato."

"Sweet," said Dominic. "Definitely sweet."

"Now, here's where a lot of people go wrong. They heat the olive oil in a big pot and dump everything in. You don't want to do that. Tomatoes are juicy enough to stew without the oil—that comes later. You don't even have to cut up the tomatoes. Just slice them in half and put them in this big shallow pan without oil. We're going to keep the heat low. No good meal ever came from hurrying."

Antonio was fascinated by Isabel's razor-sharp knives from Japan. He made *kia* sounds like a karate expert as he sliced the tomatoes and added them to the pan. There were some unexpected ingredients, things Tess would never dream of putting in tomato sauce—whole star anise, a vanilla bean split down the middle, a sprinkling of sugar, a sprig of thyme and bay leaves from the herb garden.

"You want the tomatoes to be *concassé*." Isabel gave the word a French pronunciation. "Now, some people think that means you have to peel and seed them, but that's totally unnecessary. They'll be *concassé* if you gently stew them in their own juices." She used a wooden spoon to demonstrate the technique of pressing the fruit against the side of the pan. "Give it a try," she said to Dominic.

"Yeah, Dad. Give it a try." Antonio seemed amused, watching his father cook.

Dominic used the spoon, the way Isabel showed him. "Is this *concassé*?"

"Not yet. Take your time. The slow evaporation of the juice will produce a nice deep color without any bitterness."

The sound of Isabel's voice and the gentle rhythm of the meal in progress had a soothing effect on Tess. Maybe there was something to what Isabel had said, that the art of creating in the kitchen was good for the soul. Regardless of anything else that was happening here, Tess conceded that she was learning to take her time. Lately, she didn't automatically jump to check her messages or her email the moment she woke up anymore, or immediately start making a plan. She was starting to see that there was nothing wrong with sometimes letting the day unfold according to its own rhythm.

"Now we'll make an infusion," said Isabel.

"Have you ever heard of an infusion?" Tess asked Trini.

"It's just what it sounds like," Isabel explained. "You warm the oil, and it becomes redolent of all the flavors you put into it—the garlic and herbs and spices. After the tomatoes have been stewing for an hour or so, we mix in the infusion."

"It's like science time," said Antonio, peering over his father's shoulder as Dominic stirred the pot.

"Only tastier." Dominic gave him a sample of the sauce.

Antonio nodded and gave it two thumbs up.

"Your turn," Dominic said, offering a spoonful to Tess.

"Délicieux," said Tess, kissing the tips of her fingers.

"What does that mean?" asked Antonio.

"Delicious, numbskull," said Trini. "It's practically the same word."

"Why do you kiss your fingers?" asked Antonio, ignoring his sister.

"It's an expression of accomplishment," Tess explained. "Like, ta-da. I've seen it in movies. And cartoons."

"It was the signature gesture of Hugo Bernard," Isabel explained. "He was one of the premier food critics of France. His approval meant everything to the chefs of Paris."

"I'm seeing a lot to approve of here," said Tess. She caught Dominic's eye and they shared a smile. She loved seeing him in this mode, relaxed and having fun with his kids. The more she watched him, the more she unfurled inside, letting go of tension, making room in her heart for something different, something more. Maybe this was what her mother had been trying to tell her about the day she left. It was a quiet awakening, invisible, even, but she could feel it, a change coming over her, as inevitable as the advancing of the season. At moments like this, she felt as if she was emerging from a long, heavy sleep filled with unremembered dreams, and waking up to find there was nothing left to dream about.

I don't want this to end. The intensity of the notion took her by surprise. The changes in Tess's life were happening swiftly and inevitably, and something told her not to question them. Yet an inevitable reality check told her that her time in Archangel would soon be done, whether she wanted it to or not. Despite the loophole Dominic had found, it provided only a temporary hold on the proceedings. The bank was going to foreclose. Tess would go back to the city. Isabel would be forced to leave Bella Vista. And Dominic…

Maybe one day she would step back and try to sort it all out, but until then—

The phone rang, and she checked the caller ID: Trianon Galleries. Her heart sped up, though she kept a poker face as she said, "I've got this," and answered the phone. "Tess Delaney."

"It's Michel Christiansen, returning your call, Miss Delaney."

"Thanks for getting back to me."

"We've done some happy business with Sheffield, though I don't believe you and I have met. How can I be of service to you?"

Shaken, she moved into the living room, leaving the happy sounds of the kitchen behind. "This is a long shot," she said. "Goes all the way back to 1984. I understand you were affiliated with the gallery back then."

"Indeed I was. It's a family business."

"Then…can I ask you…there was an incident in March

of that year. Do you have any recollection at all about a man named Erik Johansen?"

"Thirty years ago? Doubtful..."

"He had an appointment with you," she said, not wanting to give him too much information.

"In that case, it would be on the company agenda. We hand-wrote everything in those days."

"Have you kept the agendas?"

"Organized by year," he said. "However, the actual agendas were pulped long ago."

Her heart sank. "So you wouldn't have a record..."

"Everything was scanned and digitized. Hang on."

She couldn't breathe. Her heart felt as if it were lodged in her throat.

After a few moments, he said quietly, "Yes, I've found the appointment. March 1984."

"I don't believe he ever made it to your establishment," she said.

"That's correct," he said after a moment. "We never met face-to-face. It was most unfortunate. Mr. Johansen had a terrible accident that day."

"Yes, I... I know that part of it. He was my father."

"Miss Delaney, I'm terribly sorry."

"Thank you. I never met him. I was born after the accident. Did he give you any information on the item?"

"He did. He said he had an item from the House of Fabergé, a family heirloom."

She nearly hyperventilated. "That's all he said?"

"I believe so. I thought it could be worth a look."

You have no idea, she thought. "Thank you. I was hoping... I mean, I was wondering if you had any other recollection of that day."

"In fact, I do. I made a notation… Hold for a moment, please. My business diary is in a different file folder."

Hearing the click of a keyboard, Tess felt the beginnings of a panic attack as she held the phone pressed to her ear, listening to empty air.

"I keep everything in date order," said Mr. Christiansen. "My notes are right here. March 23, 1984." His voice trailed off; then he added, "I had a call later that day from a gentleman named Carlos Maldonado."

Tess's grip tightened on the phone. "He was a friend of Erik's."

A pause. "Perhaps."

She stopped breathing. A casual listener might not have noticed the pause, but Tess was trained to detect every nuance when she was working on a provenance project. People paused before an answer when there was more to the story. One thing she'd learned in her line of work was that very few friendships were able to withstand the temptation of financial gain.

"And did Carlos Maldonado say what it was about?"

"He intended to complete Mr. Johansen's transaction."

Tess felt a ball of ice forming in her stomach.

"Of course I told him I never deal in objects lacking a clear provenance," Mr. Christiansen continued. "I never heard from him again."

And there it was. Her father had intended to support her mother. Maybe that wasn't the same as having a father, but now for the first time, she knew for certain that he had once cared about her.

Had he cared so much it had gotten him killed?

TWENTY-SIX

The shadow of the bank's deadline loomed like a gathering storm. The strain was wearing on Isabel; Tess could hear her pacing the floors at night. Still, they never gave up the search. So far, every avenue had led to a dead end, yet Tess couldn't stop herself from believing the puzzle could be solved. She was hanging on by a thread to her job in the city but this was too important to abandon.

Thanksgiving Day at Bella Vista dawned damp and gloomy, an inauspicious start to the festivities. Tess wandered into the kitchen while it was still dark and staggered toward the carafe of coffee and steamed milk Isabel always set out.

"You've been up for hours," she said to Isabel.

Isabel was working on the turkey with single-minded focus, slipping fresh sage leaves and butter under the skin and monitoring a delicious-smelling broth on the rangetop. "Since five," she admitted.

"What can I do?"

"Drink your coffee. If you want, you could set the table—I've made a seating chart."

"You're kidding."

"It's a good-sized crowd this year. We've got Father Tom coming. The Navarros, of course; Ernestina's making her famous tamales. Dominic and his kids, and his sister, Gina. You're going to love Gina."

Tess studied the penciled chart. "My mother?"

"I invited her."

"And she said yes? Okay, I'm finally ready to admit it. Your food *does* have magic powers." She couldn't remember the last time she'd spent Thanksgiving with her mother. It was one of those family-oriented holidays that made people without families feel like crap. In the past, she'd sneaked away to Vegas, or to Vancouver, where it was just another day. One year, she'd joined a crew from the firm serving dinner at the Tenderloin Sheltering Arms. But never had she spent the holiday like this—with friends and family.

She sipped her coffee and went into the dining room. There was already a fire crackling cheerfully in the fireplace, the flames illuminating the morning frost on the windows. The big rustic table of hewn pine and hammered iron dominated the room. Ernestina said it was original to the house, more than a hundred years old. Tess tried to imagine the family gatherings the table had seen. Where had Erik sat? Did he have a favorite food? Had his wife, Francesca, brought traditions of her own into the family? On the last Thanksgiving of his life, had Erik thought of Shannon while feasting with his wife and family?

And now Shannon, the sole survivor of that generation, was going to take her place at Bella Vista's table at last. Tess couldn't imagine what Isabel had said to entice her back to Archangel.

According to the penciled seating chart, Tess would be between Dominic and Shannon. Isabel had seated Father Tom at the head of the table, with herself at his right hand. Interesting. There was a place setting for Magnus, she noticed, at the other end of the table. She set it with care, as if he might come walking in at any moment.

"I can finish that for you," Ernestina said, bustling into the room with a centerpiece of stargazer lilies and dried milkweed, a trio of slender candles in the middle. "You go help in the kitchen."

"That's like asking me to help Rembrandt paint," Tess objected.

"She's very gifted, isn't she?" Ernestina fussed over the centerpiece.

"I wonder why she never pursued it as a career."

"Maybe she will, one day." Ernestina paused. "Maybe she'll have to." Tess's expression must have betrayed her, because Ernestina added, "I know about the foreclosure. I know Bella Vista will have to be sold."

Tess nodded, her chest tight with regrets. "There's enough for wages through the end of the year, but after that…"

"After that we'll need a miracle."

"Right."

"Go help your sister."

Tess returned to the kitchen. She paused in the doorway, watching Isabel arranging the turkey in a roasting pan. She worked with unconscious grace, and whatever she was thinking made her luminous, her eyes soft, her mouth turned into a tiny smile. Or maybe she wasn't thinking at all. When Isabel cooked, she did it with love.

"Ernestina made the prettiest centerpiece," said Tess.

"She has a knack. She makes candles from local beeswax, too."

"We should take a Thanksgiving dinner to Magnus in the

hospital," Tess said. "I mean, I know he can't eat it, but... maybe it's silly..."

"It's a lovely thought. I say we do it." Isabel motioned her over to the sideboard. "You're going to make the dressing."

"Oh, no. No way. You're not saddling me with that. Dressing polarizes people. I am not going to be responsible for making the dressing everyone will remember as the worst in Thanksgiving history."

"It's going to be delicious. Get another cup of coffee, and then I'll show you."

They worked side by side, and Tess found it unexpectedly relaxing, all the chopping and mixing, chatting with her sister while she worked. Eventually, the talk drifted to speculation about their father. What had happened? What was Carlos Maldonado's part in the drama? It was still a puzzle, the solution dangling just out of reach.

The day lightened, though the weather stayed damp and gloomy, the sky a dramatic iron-gray. The kitchen windows steamed up from the cooking, and the smells that filled the air nearly made Tess swoon.

At midmorning, Charlie clamored at the back door, and it swished open. In walked Dominic on a swirl of cold wind, the kids right behind him. He carried a wooden wine crate, and the kids had bunches of amber-colored mums.

The dizzying heart rush was by now a familiar sensation to Tess. She no longer even bothered to pretend she wasn't crazy about him.

"Hey, you," he said, coming up behind her and nuzzling her cheek.

"You're indecently early," she accused, practically melting against him. "We're still in our bathrobes." She felt the children watching them. "Hi, guys," she said.

"Don't worry, we know Dad likes you," Antonio said.

"He does, does he?"

"He like *likes* you," the little boy added.

Tess grinned. "Good to know."

"Can we watch the Thanksgiving Day parade?" asked Trini.

"Sure," said Isabel, washing her hands. "I'll put the TV on in the family room."

The kids followed her out of the kitchen. Tess nestled her cheek against Dominic's shoulder, inhaling his scent. Then she turned in his arms, took his face between her hands and lifted up on tiptoe to kiss him.

"This feels like my lucky day," he said. "What's that for?"

She laughed. "Because I *like* you."

He skimmed his knuckles along her jawline. "The feeling's mutual."

Rising up on tiptoe, she whispered, "I love you, Dominic Rossi. I never want to leave you."

"Sorry, what? That's my bad ear."

"I..." Tess was appalled at herself. Had she really just said that? She was just so caught up in this tumult of emotion, she no longer trusted herself. She was afraid to say it again, afraid he might not welcome her declaration, afraid she might be fooling herself about this man. She gave him another kiss. "Tell you what. I'm going to take the kids some hot chocolate and watch the parade with them."

"I heard that," said Isabel, returning to the kitchen. "You still have to finish making the dressing."

"I will, I promise," Tess said. "After hot chocolate, okay?"

A few minutes later, she was hunkered down with Trini and Antonio, keeping a tally of the floats. "What's the coolest one so far?" she asked.

"Godzilla, for sure," said Antonio.

"Tintin's my favorite," said Trini. "I'm collecting all the books."

"I like the giant wedge of cheese myself," said Tess. "How's the hot chocolate?"

"Good." Antonio swirled his spoon in his mug. "Can I have another marshmallow?"

"In the kitchen."

"So do you *really* like my dad?" Trini asked after he'd gone.

"Yes," Tess said, unequivocally. It felt ridiculously good to say it. But...love? Did she? Could she?

"I can tell you like him. I can tell by the way you sometimes stare at his mouth."

"You're very observant."

"Are you in love with him?"

Yes. "I might be, one of these days."

"That's nuts. Either you love somebody or you don't."

"It's not always so simple. You have to like someone first, and sometimes it grows and turns into love."

"How does *that* happen?"

"It's...mysterious. You just like someone more and more, and eventually you realize you love him."

"My dad, you mean."

She didn't say anything for a few seconds. Good lord, had she really just told Dominic's child she was falling in love with him?

"How long does it take?"

"It's different for different people. Love takes time."

"I loved Iggy as soon as Dad brought him home. I didn't know him, and then he walked through the door, and *wham*— I loved him."

"Sometimes it works that way, too," Tess said. "I bet when you were born, your dad took one look at you, and he felt the *wham*."

"I don't get why love stops."

"That's a hard one. Sometimes it's just a mystery. It doesn't always stop, though."

"She's right," Dominic said quietly from the doorway.

"No fair eavesdropping," Tess said, her cheeks burning even hotter. "We're having girl talk."

"I speak girl," he said.

"Barely," Trini muttered.

"Hey." He took her mug and set it aside, then scooped her onto his lap.

Watching them, Tess finally put a name to the crazy ride of emotions that had taken her over. She was in love.

With Dominic Rossi.

But more than that, she loved his children, and his life in Archangel. She had come to savor the languid pace of the small town, the orchards and vineyards, the neighborly charm of farm stands and homemade goods, shared meals and living close to nature.

The life she thought she wanted had silently, stealthily fallen away as her heart opened up to something brand-new. Everything she used to think was important had changed. She was in love for the first time. It felt exhilarating and risky, like jumping off a cliff and discovering she could fly.

"You look different," said her mother, adding vodka to the shaker of spiced cranberry cocktails. She wasn't much of a cook, but she knew her bar drinks, and this was her contribution to the feast.

"I don't know what you mean," said Tess. "I suppose I've gained weight, with all of the incredible food here." Suddenly self-conscious, she smoothed a hand down the front of her sweater.

"Taste." Her mother strained a drink into a crystal highball glass. "Tell me if it needs anything."

"Delicious," she said.

A shout went up from the adjacent family room, where everyone was watching the football game. "Go, go, go, go, *score!*" It turned out Father Tom, the Navarros and Dominic had some bets going, and the action was ramping up. The priest, once a quarterback for Gonzaga, was utterly cutthroat about winning.

"More cinnamon?" asked Shannon.

"No, I think the cinnamon stick in the glass is just right."

"It's not that you've gained weight," Shannon mused. "It's something else...."

"I needed a break from work. Jude claims I'm committing career suicide, though."

"Are you?" her mother asked sharply.

Tess was actually able to laugh at that. "I'm good at what I do. If Sheffield lets me go, I'll find something else. Something better." The very thought of losing a job she loved used to send her in a panic. Now she felt a new kind of confidence. The foolish kind, probably.

Shannon put the finishing touches on the cranberry cocktails and handed one to Tess. "Not to toot my own horn, but these are going to do justice to Isabel's appetizers. Cheers."

"Cheers, Mom." Tess took a small sip of her drink. "I'm glad you came back," she added.

"You're going to be even gladder when I tell you what I found out about Carlos Maldonado."

"What?"

"You didn't think I was simply going to walk away from you when you needed me, did you?" Shannon looked at her for a moment, then sighed. "You did think that. Tess, I went away because I wanted to help you. I didn't make any promises, because I wasn't sure I was going to find any information you don't already have. One of my researchers used to be a forensics archivist for the state patrol, and he supplied some details of Erik's accident. Oh, and I visited Beatrice, his widow."

Tess was stunned. "What did you find out?"

"That there's still hope of finding the egg. Carlos Maldonado was not the hero his father was. According to his widow, he had a bad gambling problem. He needed money, and he needed it fast."

"The egg," said Tess, her grip tightening on her glass. "He must have realized its value. It didn't keep him from drowning, though, almost immediately after Erik—my father—was killed."

"My friend in the highway department doesn't think the drowning was an accident. It's classified as a cold case—unsolved. But Beatrice gave me an interesting tip. She drove away from the Maldonado estate with nothing but the clothes on her back, her little girl and a trunk full of odds and ends." Shannon polished off her drink and poured another. "Now you've got problems. You're going to have to pay a visit to Dominic's ex."

TWENTY-SEVEN

"I have a dilemma," Tess said to Lourdes Maldonado. "I wonder if you'd be willing to discuss it with me."

Without speaking, Lourdes held open the door to her house. It was a small place in town with a fenced yard littered with kids' toys. Inside, there was a vaguely musty smell nearly masked by the scent of a bayberry candle and freshly cut pine. The entryway was cluttered with shoes, coats and unopened mail. A couple of laundry baskets crowded the hallway.

Lourdes looked exhausted, even though it was early evening. "You've got a lot of nerve, coming here. I told you, I've been trying to put us back together—"

"Like I said before, that's between you and Dominic—"

"There can't be anything between me and Dominic so long as you're around."

"Look, this has nothing to do with my personal situation. I'm trying to help my sister. That's why I'm here."

"You're not making any sense."

Tess took a deep breath to compose herself. She hadn't told either Dominic or Isabel about the theory she and her mother had come up with at Thanksgiving. She needed to check it out on her own first. Shannon had tracked down Carlos Maldonado's widow in Placerville. A far cry from the heartbroken young mother Tess had imagined, Beatrice Maldonado—now Beatrice Perkins—did not harbor cherished memories of her first husband. He'd been a drinker and gambler, and he ran with a rough crowd. After the drowning, Beatrice had left Archangel and made a new life for herself. Carlos had died in debt and intestate; she'd ended up with a financial mess, and a small collection of keepsakes and personal items, which she'd subsequently passed on to her daughter, Lourdes.

"I've been trying to help her find something that was lost. It's a Johansen family heirloom, something that's really important to her and her grandfather."

"I have no idea what you're talking about or why you'd come to me with this."

"I'd love to explain it to you, if you have some time."

Lourdes expelled a dramatic sigh. "Come on in. I have nothing against Isabel. I know it must be terrible for her, what happened to her grandfather."

Tess stepped farther into the living room. This was the home Lourdes and Dominic had shared, which she'd kept in the divorce. No wonder Dominic was such a neatnik, his home sparsely decorated. The decor here was busy with painted furniture, brass lamps, embellished mirrors and framed school photos of the children.

"Your tree is lovely," said Tess. It was a noble fir, at least ten feet tall, dripping with lights and ornaments of all sorts.

"The kids and I decorated. We always go over the top with the tree."

For a moment, Tess felt a wave of nostalgia, sweeping her back to her childhood Christmases in Dublin with Nana. It was often just the two of them, with Shannon away at work, but they made it cozy with cream scones from the neighborhood bakery, spiced tea, carols playing on the stereo.

As an adult, Tess practiced rigorous Christmas avoidance. She attended a few parties, but prior to the holiday she took off for someplace like Thailand or Mumbai, where Christmas was just another day. Often her mother would meet her somewhere and the two of them would exchange gifts and go out to dinner, and that would be that. She told herself Christmas was overrated. Families got together, and there was awkwardness and squabbling. Invariably someone had too much to drink and someone else got her feelings hurt, a gift didn't fit or failed to please. There was an overabundance of food, especially sweets, a feeling of uncomfortable excess. A family holiday was never really the warm and fuzzy time it was cracked up to be.

In the deepest part of herself, she didn't believe any of that. But she had to tell herself so just to keep from wanting something she couldn't have.

Maybe this year, things would be different. She had Isabel. She'd been told the party at Bella Vista was not to be missed. Everyone on the estate gathered for a Christmas Eve feast. Father Tom would stop by on his way to celebrate midnight mass to offer a blessing. Tess knew the traditions would have a deeper meaning this year, with everyone's hearts yearning for Magnus to heal.

"I'll get you a glass of wine." Lourdes went to the kitchen. "I'll get us both a glass."

"I don't…" Tess changed her mind. "On the other hand, I'd like that."

Listening to the clinking of glass in the other room, she

blinked and looked at the Christmas tree. Other people's Christmas trees had always held a peculiar fascination for her. She and Nana used to keep it simple—a few choice bone china ornaments, glittery balls, fairy lights and a few treasures from Things Forgotten. Lourdes's tree was far more elaborate, covered in gold ornaments, mostly flashy glass bulbs. On the lower, sturdier branches hung the heavier ornaments, some made of pottery or carved wood or resin. There were a few doughy-looking creations that had probably been crafted by children through the years.

A light sparkled over the burnished golden curve of a Christmas ball. Frowning, she bent down to inspect the flash that had caught her eye. The ornament was shaped like a large, shiny egg. She didn't breathe, didn't move a muscle. Reaching through the branches of the tree, she unhooked the golden ball.

Instantly she knew—this was a glass bulb, painted gold from the inside. Pretty, but hardly the treasure she was looking for. Feeling foolish, she looked for a place to rehang the bauble. She found a spot down low, amid the homespun carvings and school projects. She paused to look at one, a framed Polaroid photo showing a beautiful little girl with dark hair and large, dark eyes, a laughing mouth. She sat at the knee of a handsome man with a moustache; Tess recognized Carlos from her research. As she reached in toward the trunk of the tree, the needles of the fir tree brushed over her arm. The back of her hand brushed something heavy, hanging amid humble ornaments on the lowest branch of the tree, beside a thick clay imprint of a child's hand and a moss-clad nativity scene.

It was weighty, its finish a dull yellow. As she lifted it toward her, she stopped breathing again. Working gingerly, she unhooked the object and freed it from the lighted branches. This time, there was no mistake.

The egg was slightly larger than she'd imagined it. And infinitely, immeasurably more elaborate. Clad in a basket of the most delicate gold filigree, its surface was tarnished by time and neglect.

Holy mother of God. She was holding the treasure in her hand. The golden surface felt warm and alive with stories. Simply cradling it between her palms transported her. She freed the delicate latch and opened it to find the interior filled with Christmas candy.

"I didn't ask if you prefer red or white," said Lourdes, coming into the room with two glasses of wine on a tray. "I'm guessing white for you."

Tess composed herself and straightened up, dusting herself off. She kept her face completely impassive. "White's fine," she said. "Thank you." She knew what she had to do. This was her job, separating people from their treasures. It was common to her experience to find artifacts where they didn't belong. Her task was to put things right. But never had the stakes been higher.

She closed and latched the egg and held it by the slender wire attached to it, causing it to slowly turn. The sensation gave her the shivers. "Do you know where this came from?"

Lourdes took a gulp of wine. "It's been around for decades. After my father died, my mother found it in a box of my father's things, carnival prizes he'd won, lottery ticket stubs, other Christmas ornaments, toys he meant to give me but never did. It was probably with all his other things." She handed Tess a glass of wine.

"Cheers." Tess had done stranger things than clink glasses with her boyfriend's ex-wife, but she couldn't remember when. "Actually, this piece is what I came to ask you about. Isabel's been looking for it. I believe—and this comes from a lot of research—this belonged to Erik Johansen."

Lourdes laughed and took a drink of wine. "God, you are a piece of work. It's not enough that you're dating my husband…"

Ex-husband, Tess thought.

"But now you want to take away a trinket that was left to me by my father?"

"I'm trying to help out my sister and Magnus, that's all." Tess had brought only two photographs with her, both taken at Bella Vista during Erik's lifetime, both showing the egg on display with both Erik and Magnus present. "I trace heirlooms as a job. It originally belonged to Magnus. He brought it from the old country after the war. It went missing, so it's kind of a miracle to find it. Having it again would mean the world to Isabel."

Lourdes finished her wine and refilled her glass. "Maybe it would mean the world to me."

"Would it?"

"I barely remember my father. It's nice having something that belonged to him."

"Isabel and I never knew ours, either." Tess kept a poker face. Softball or hardball, she asked herself. Lourdes was a lawyer. She was probably smart as a whip. If she had the first inkling of the egg's value, she'd never surrender it.

"Look, I'll be frank," Tess said. "Isabel is having an incredibly hard time and reclaiming a family heirloom will help her. It still belongs to Magnus Johansen. Restoring a piece of family history to Isabel would be such a kindness."

"And if I refuse?"

Tess wanted to avoid any hint of drama. She could provide provenance that would make Lourdes's father look like a thief, but she didn't want to use that as leverage. "If you refuse," she said, "you won't be the person your kids think you are. They adore and admire their mom."

Lourdes's gaze flickered, and she took a hurried sip of wine. Tess carefully replaced the egg. She avoided looking at it.

Lourdes poured herself another glass of wine and took a seat on the sofa. "It seems to me," she said slowly, "we've each got something the other wants." Lourdes crossed one leg over the other and twirled her foot.

"I'm not sure I understand. I don't want anything from you. I was just suggesting it would be a kindness to Isabel if you were to restore the ornament to her."

"I'm not going to mince words. You know as well as I do that you're the only thing standing in the way of me and Dominic reconciling."

Tess felt bad for her, worse still for Dominic and the children. Recalling the loneliness and isolation of growing up without a family, she wondered if she could put herself in the way of this broken family's attempt to repair itself. "I'm not in the way," she said quietly.

"He is the father of my children. We're a family. You have no right to interfere with that. Let's agree that you can give Isabel the Christmas ornament, and you go back to wherever you came from."

Her flawed thinking was breathtaking, but Tess was not about to point that out. Lourdes was offering her a bargaining chip. Never mind that it was made of crazy.

"And if I refuse?" Tess deliberately echoed Lourdes.

"Then you're not the long-lost sister Isabel thinks you are. Oh, and by the way," Lourdes continued, "did Dominic tell you we're going to counseling?"

Tess felt as if she'd been punched in the gut. It must have shown on her face, because Lourdes gave a tiny smile. "Thought not. It's true, though. Ask him yourself." The woman was delusional. Yet she was also willing to make a deal.

Tess knew exactly what she had to do.

★ ★ ★

Tess went to the hospital. It only seemed right to bring the treasure straight to Magnus, who thought he'd lost the egg when he'd lost his son. When she got to his room, she found the doctor and two nurses clustered around the bed.

Her heart froze. Was she losing him?

"What's happening?" she demanded, pushing into the room. He looked the same. "Is something wrong?"

Dr. Hattori stepped back, adjusted his glasses. "We're upgrading his condition. There's been more reaction to stimuli."

"*Upgrading.* You mean he's waking up?"

"I'm seeing increased brain activity. There's eye movement and possibly some tracking."

"Have you called Isabel?"

"I left her a message." The doctor gave Tess a full report. The process could take days or even weeks, and the prognosis was far from certain. There was no way to predict the recovery. He might be in a vegetative state, or he could regain full functionality or anything in between.

"There is every reason to hope for a good outcome," the doctor said.

"What can I do?"

"What you've been doing all along. Talking and touching, staying close. He's lucky to have a granddaughter like you."

Tess felt a lump in her throat. "He has no idea. I mean he really, really has no idea."

Alone with Magnus, she rolled her chair close to the bed. "So I found it," she said to him. "Just like I told you I would. Hurry and wake up. I need to know what you know. Did you realize Erik had the egg? Did he just help himself to it? Did you realize it was then taken by Carlos?"

She took the egg from her bag. It was surreal, carrying a multimillion-dollar artifact around like it was a powder compact. "After I show you and Isabel, we'll want to go straight to the bank with this."

She placed the egg under the palm of his hand. She imagined that hand in younger years, holding the object, taking pride in the idea that it had been awarded to his grandfather for saving a precious young life.

"I had to make a deal in order to get this," she told Magnus. "Dominic's ex-wife gave it to me on condition that I take myself out of the picture. She's delusional if she thinks that is going to bring them back together, but of course I didn't tell her so. I do have to leave, though. Not just because of the deal I made, but because I don't…belong here."

She drew in a breath and realized her chest was aching. The rhythm of the pumps and monitors pulsed into the silence. "I didn't ever think anything would be this hard. I love him, Magnus. I've never felt this way before. I love his kids. I love his life. And yet I have to walk away. And it's tearing me up. I didn't know. I had absolutely no idea what real love feels like, what it could do to me. And now I have no idea what to do without it."

Freeing a tiny gold filigreed latch, she opened the egg. A half-melted candy cane fell out. "Lourdes had no idea what she was hanging on her tree, year in and year out," Tess said. "It was right in front of her the whole time." She put the egg back in her bag and sat in silence for a while.

Behind her grandfather's thin, closed eyelids, she could see movement. The doctors had cautioned her all along that Magnus was not simply going to leap out of his bed one day and take up where he'd left off. But that didn't keep her from hoping and dreaming that someday, they would meet face-to-face.

"I need to go," she said. "I have to show this to Isabel and then have a less fun conversation with Dominic." She took Magnus's hand and squeezed it.

"You squeezed back," she whispered. "I swear, I felt you do it. Do it again."

Nothing. But she refused to dismiss the feeling that he was somehow more present, the muscles of his face perhaps less slack, the position of his body more solid, as if someone was in charge.

Leaning down, she whispered, "See you soon," and drove back to Bella Vista.

Tess found Isabel up on a ladder at the roadside stand, detaching the sign from above the door. The old-world, hand-lettered sign read Bella Vista Fine Produce and according to Isabel, had hung in its place for more than fifty years. She looked adorable in faded overalls that were a couple of sizes too big, a hand-knit sweater and fingerless knitted gloves. Her breath made little clouds in the cold air.

Tess parked across the road by the mailbox. "Hey," she called.

"Hey, yourself." Isabel turned on the ladder to greet her.

"Be careful," Tess said. "Our family has bad luck with ladders." Hearing the words "our family" come out of her own mouth was surprising. "What are you doing?"

"I didn't want to leave this behind," Isabel said, indicating the enamel sign.

"Isabel—"

"I know you think I've been in denial about the foreclosure, but that's not true. I know exactly what's going to happen, and I know exactly what has to be done. I've got to start somewhere." She lowered the sign to the ground, then climbed down after it.

"Or not," said Tess. She crossed the road to Isabel and stepped into the abandoned shop. She remembered the day she'd met Dominic here, driven by a downpour. Had she fallen in love with him that day? Had it happened all at once, and she just hadn't recognized it?

Isabel followed her in. "I used to spend hours in here with my grandmother," she said. "The shop was her pet project. I wonder if it's a coincidence, that both our grandmothers kept shops."

"Dominic said it's in my blood."

"Maybe it is. After Bubbie got sick, Ernestina kept it up for a while, but it was never the same."

Tess set down her big handbag. "I just came from the hospital. Magnus is making progress."

"Really?" Isabel's face lit up. "Tell me everything."

"I had a little scare when I first showed up. There was a whole team all clustered around him. But it's good news. They're seeing increased activity." She explained what the doctor had told her.

"It would be a miracle if he got better. The Christmas miracle we're all praying for."

He seemed a long way from truly better, but there was no good reason to take her hope away. Especially now.

"There's something else," said Tess. "I went by the hospital because I wanted him to be the first to see this. You're the second." She moved to a counter-height table and took out the egg.

Isabel's breath caught. "Are. You. Kidding. Me." She shuddered as if a cold wave moved through her. "That's it? That's *it?*"

Tess laughed aloud at the expression on her sister's face. "Congratulations."

Isabel inspected every facet of the egg, her eyes soft with wonder. She held and touched it, set it down and regarded it from all angles. "You're amazing, Tess. My amazing sister. Tell me everything."

"My mom and I came up with a theory," she said.

"That's the first time I've heard you call her your mom."

Tess didn't want to let Isabel know about the deal she'd made. Not now, anyway. "Open it," she said to Isabel. "It needs a good cleaning, but it's just beautiful."

Isabel studied the gleaming inner surface. "So the angel fits right here."

"Yes."

"I'm freaking out. Are you freaking out?" Isabel laughed aloud. "So, now what? What on earth do we do next?"

"You need to be the one to decide."

"Oh, no. This is a family matter. You are family. We'll both decide."

"You have his power of attorney." Tess watched her sister's face, soft with sentiment and memories. She thought about her conversation with Miss Winther. It seemed so long ago. *If you'd trade memories for money then maybe you haven't made the right kind of memories.*

Isabel set the egg back into the nest of tissue paper. Her movements were brisk and efficient. "There's really no debate. You and I both know what this egg means to Grandfather."

TWENTY-EIGHT

Dominic used to look forward to his days off because it gave him time for what he really loved doing—making wine. Now he looked forward to it for a totally different reason—Tess. Still, there were chores to do. The kids were still asleep as he and the dogs headed out into the chill early morning. The Dude stayed on the porch, as usual, unwilling to leave while the children slept. Iggy raced through the heavy mist, weaving in and out of the rows in pursuit of some imaginary prey.

Winter in the vineyards was a secret and quiet time of the year, when the work of growing was hidden beneath the surface. The vines shut down for the season, but the trellises and soil needed attention. Patience and practice were required. There was something zenlike in the work of pruning and cultivating, and his mind wandered to its new favorite place— to Tess.

She had no idea what she meant to him. After all the drama with Lourdes, he thought he had given up on love. He believed he couldn't do it again, couldn't risk his heart by placing it into someone else's care.

Tess was proof that he could. He felt an overwhelming tenderness for her, this feisty, difficult, vulnerable woman. He had brought her kicking and screaming to Archangel, and he'd expected nothing but trouble from her. He'd gotten the trouble all right. He was in love again.

The thought made him grin like an idiot. Despite what had happened in the past, he wasn't cautious, or worried, or unsure. Despite the bleak, chilly weather, he was in a great mood. Today Isabel was going to teach him to make something called *pots de crème,* which apparently was about ninety-five percent chocolate and butter. He planned to serve it to Tess with a lush black Muscat made by his friend Xavier up at Misty Ridge. And then he had something important to ask her.

Charlie, the Johansens' German shepherd, appeared at the top of the ridge. A moment later, he came bounding down the slope toward Dominic, happily joining Iggy, scampering through the vineyards. Dominic peeled off his work gloves and looked around. If Charlie was in the vicinity, that meant Tess wasn't far behind. Lately the dog acted more like hers than Isabel's.

He spotted Tess walking toward the small arched bridge that spanned Angel Creek. She wore an embroidered jacket and a soft-looking scarf around her neck, and her hands were jammed into her pockets. Just the sight of her lifted his heart.

"Hey, you," he said, meeting her halfway on the bridge. He reached out to pull her against him, taking her soft face between his hands. "I was just thinking about you." The first touch of their lips was cool, quickly warming as they melded. It felt so damn good to kiss a woman he was in love with.

She pulled away and looked up at him. "I figured you were out doing chores."

"What's up? You've got that 'we need to talk' look."

"You have a good eye." She hesitated, and in that beat of time he felt a twist in his gut. This was not going to go well. "I found the egg."

His jaw unhinged. Then he gave a shout of laughter. "Wait, *what?* Seriously? Where the hell did you find it?"

"It's with Isabel now. And it appears to be exactly what we thought it was. *Exactly,* Dominic. It's perfect. And she needs to get it into a safety deposit box, because it's worth what we thought it was worth."

He picked her up and swung her around, laughing as his tension drained away. He'd been bracing himself for bad news.

"You're a genius, Tess. I swear, a bona fide genius. How the hell did you find it?"

"It was…mixed in with some Christmas decorations."

"Unbelievable. You're unbelievable."

"Well, about that." She stared at the ground. "I wanted to let you know, I'll be leaving."

His gut turned to stone. It wasn't the words she said but the intent behind them.

"You're not leaving," he stated.

"Of course I am," she said. "I never said I'd stay. We both knew from the start—"

"We didn't know shit from the start," he objected. "We both know now, the whole world is different."

"No, it's really not. Your life is here—your winemaking, your kids, your job, your home. As for me, I have a career, and plans. I work in the city and travel all the time. My next move will be to New York or London. It's what I do, and… I just can't stay here, Dominic. I…can't."

Each word she spoke hit him like a hammer blow. He hadn't

been looking for anything when he'd met her. In fact, he'd been trying to simplify his life, not complicate it with a head-strong woman. But something had happened. She made his heart new again, and he would never be the same.

"I'm asking you to stay," he said.

"You're asking me to give up the life I've built. Would you do the same for me? Would you uproot yourself and follow me?"

Ouch. "My custody agreement prohibits me from taking my kids that far from their mother."

She looked him in the eye. "You didn't tell me you and Lourdes were going to counseling."

"What the— Who the hell told you that?"

"Are you?"

"Yeah, but—"

"Kids need both parents," she said, her eyes chilly. "Dominic, we made a mistake. We never should have started anything—"

"Don't do this," he said simply.

"I have to. Better now than later, when we figure out it can't work."

"Better now?" he demanded. "Better than what?"

She was crying now. He'd never seen her cry before. "It was beautiful, my time here, with you," she said. "It was amazing, like a dream."

"Exactly. Then why the hell are you ending it?"

"I'm sorry. I have to go" was all she said.

TWENTY-NINE

"Just so you know," Tess murmured to Jude as they seated themselves on the "friends of the bride" side of the aisle, "showing up single at a wedding is one of my least favorite things to do."

"I'm wounded." Jude gave an exaggerated sniff. "Why can't I be your plus-one? Aren't I the one rescuing you from being parked at the leftovers table with the kids and awkward cousins?"

"I don't need rescuing." Her high-heeled pumps pinched already, and the ceremony hadn't even started.

"Fine, then I'll leave you to the mercy of the random friends and maiden aunts. And all those well-meaning matchmaking attempts."

"Stop it. This is Lydia's wedding. I'm going to be happy and look happy all day." She looked around at the venue—their favorite bar, the Top of the Mark, now festooned for the ceremony and reception.

"Yeah, good luck with that. There are any number of women here who would love to be seen on my arm."

"And some of them even have IQs in the double digits," she said.

"Very funny. FYI, the last woman I dated has a Ph.D. in medieval studies."

"That's probably why she's not dating you anymore."

"Hey," he said. "Just because you came back from the boonies with a broken heart doesn't mean you get to take it out on me."

She didn't even bother protesting. Ever since returning to San Francisco, she had felt like a misfit in her own life. It should have been a comfort to come back to her own world, to work and friends and the city, to her apartment and the life she knew. Instead, she carried around an ache of loss that showed no sign of getting better. *This,* she thought, *is why falling in love is such a terrible idea.* This hurt. This feeling that nothing in life will ever be bright again. Now she understood why loving a man was dangerous. When you fell as hard as she had, the landing was painful.

"Sorry," she said to Jude. "You're right. This is Lydia's day."

The wedding was a beautiful, joyous occasion. Nathan, the bridegroom, set the tone for the event when he got all choked up at his first glimpse of Lydia, walking up the aisle in a cloud of ivory silk chiffon. Tess felt a rush of tenderness for her friend, remembering the times they'd shared as roommates and confidantes, analyzing their Saturday night dates, and vowing to stay single forever, because it was so much fun. Back then, Tess hadn't known her own heart. Until recently, she hadn't realized that what she yearned for, what she craved above all else, could not be found at a loud party, or a hip coffeehouse, or working at a dream job. She wanted a deep sense of connection, she wanted to love without fear, and she wanted to know it could last forever. She considered it both a blessing and a curse that she had found it with Dominic Rossi.

Maybe one day she would find it in herself to be grateful for what she'd found with him, rather than filled with regrets over what she'd lost. Not today, though. Today, it was all she could do to let herself delight in Lydia's happiness. She could only imagine what it would be like to stand before friends and family in a beautiful dress, looking at a man looking at her, with all his love showing on his face.

Good for you, Lydia, she thought.

The weather was clear, the sun still out after the reception. She'd long since given up on the high-heeled pumps, swapping them for a pair of flip-flops she carried in her handbag. "Leaving already?" asked Neelie, her eyes sparkling from a few glasses of champagne.

"I'm going to walk home. Enjoy the sunshine while it's here."

"Take a piece of wedding cake." Neelie took her hand and towed her over to the table, where a server was boxing up generous portions. "No one's eating it, and it's delicious. Organic lemon."

A few minutes later, Tess found herself in the mirrored elevator, her heart speeding up as she remembered a night long ago, when she'd felt as if she were detaching from the world. She was a different person now. She knew what it was like to be connected...and she knew exactly what she'd given up.

It wasn't the deal she'd made with Lourdes Maldonado that had sent her packing. She could admit that now. That was simply a conveniently timed exit strategy. Deep down, she knew that what had sent her running for cover was her own lack of courage. She didn't believe she could dream and dare and risk everything, and she knew for certain she couldn't let herself be the one thing standing in the way of a family trying to heal itself.

Christmas had come and gone; she had spent the day with her mother in New York, where they'd both had business to do. Now she was back at work, weighing offers from both the New York and London offices, much to Jude's chagrin. Her job of finding and authenticating lost treasures was still interesting, but she found herself wanting more.

She decided to take the long way through the pretty streets of Nob Hill. She was in no hurry to get home.

There was a guy in Huntington Park with a "hungry, please help" sign and a little dog on a leash. She paused and wordlessly handed him the boxed wedding cake, which he acknowledged with a slight nod.

She left the park and headed down the hill, slowing down as she passed a rare empty retail space. She stepped back a few paces on the sidewalk to admire the shop front. It blended perfectly with the rest of the block, decked by moody-looking gaslights and hanging baskets trailing with ivy. This kind of retail space, in this Nob Hill location, didn't come up every day. It embodied the finest period architecture, with huge windows and tall ceilings, a classic iron front with bas-relief swags of leaves and embellishments, painted with enamel the satiny black of piano keys.

A sign advertised that the space was available for lease. With its vintage character of days gone by, it had the potential to be as beautiful as her nana's Things Forgotten. Tess would have poured her heart and soul into it and made it thrive. The impulse tempted her, made her imagine, just for a moment, taking another path. But she was missing the one thing that would make it happen—capital.

She regarded her image reflected in the window. She scarcely recognized the woman in the lime-green trench coat, her hair done in waves for the wedding. It was a day of rare sunshine but scant warmth. She looked healthier for sure, after decompressing from a stress she didn't even know she'd had. She was no longer a gaunt smoker who spent sleepless nights in a panic. She still felt adrift, but in the way of surrender rather than resistance. Before her sojourn in the far-off Sonoma town, amid the rich splendor of the apple orchards, she hadn't taken a sweet deep breath of pleasure in years. Being there had taught her to breathe again.

And coming back to the city taught her that there was no such thing as a life of unmitigated happiness. What she knew now was that life was made up of moments, and some of those moments were filled with joy, some with anger, some with sadness. The hope was that at the end of the day, there would be balance—the light and dark, sorrow and gladness.

Tess had to make peace with the fact that she had walked away from the one thing that could save her. Now she had to find a way to save herself. Her task was to survive this and move on, and in time, trusting for no good reason that the ache in her heart would heal. She used to think her life was about finding old treasure, relating its history and bringing it out to the world. All along, she was looking for something else; her obsession with secret histories had to do with all the unanswered questions about her family. The real treasure she'd found was at Bella Vista—family and friends, and the fact that her heart was open to a kind of love she hadn't known she was capable of. She had a sister who would always be part of her life. And if their prayers were answered, she would have Magnus, too.

Her phone made a soft chirruping sound, signaling a message. She checked the screen, frowning at the message marked Urgent.

"What the...?" Tess muttered. "What could she possibly want?"

★ ★ ★

"I must talk to you." Annelise Winther opened the door to her apartment. The place had not changed since Tess had brought the old lady the lavaliere last fall. It was tidy but a bit shabby, filled with the smell of something baking, just as Tess remembered. "I have something to give you." She bustled into the kitchen and handed over a small white cardboard box. "First, my lavender scones. I recall you like them."

Tess caught a whiff of butter, sugar and lavender. "They're wonderful." She didn't want to admit she'd given the original batch of scones to a homeless woman. She was mystified as to why Miss Winther would summon her to give her baked goods. "Thank you."

"And this," said Miss Winther, handing her a familiar-looking archival box. Inside lay the lavaliere Tess had restored to her. The winking facets of the pink stone and diamond baguettes still took her breath away. The day she'd brought the treasure to Miss Winther seemed like a lifetime ago.

Now Tess felt like apologizing to the old woman for pressuring her to auction it off. She finally understood what it meant, and why it was priceless. "I don't understand," she said. "Is there a problem with this piece?"

"On the contrary, I've discovered a solution for it at last. Do you know how stressful it is, keeping a jewel worth a fortune in my apartment or pocketbook?"

Tess smiled. "That's what safety deposit boxes are for."

"What is the point of having an object of beauty if you have to make an appointment to see it?"

"But I thought you intended to keep it."

"It is a privilege of old age to change one's mind. I'm giving the lavaliere to you. I don't need it, and I don't need the money, not after what that Tiffany tea service brought."

"You can't give this to me."

"I most certainly can. I have no...family." Her voice caught on the slight hesitation. "I'd like to give it to someone who understands its value, who will do something wonderful with it, and I expect you to sell the piece and create something vibrant with the proceeds." She handed Tess an envelope. "The legal counsel at your firm drew up a transfer claim. It's properly worded and notarized so there will never be a question about its provenance. I even made a digital video. It's yours, and you'd be a ninny not to take it."

"I'm not taking it. You should give this to a museum or donate the proceeds to a good cause. I don't need charity."

"No, but everyone can use a helping hand. You don't have to do everything alone, Theresa. You don't have to live your life alone."

The statement touched Tess in a tender spot. "You hardly know me."

She dropped the box into Tess's huge handbag. "My mother used to always tell me to embrace my dreams. If I can give you a chance to do so, then it's a gift to me, as well."

Tess stood there for a moment in a blur of confusion. "Miss Winther."

The old lady walked to the door and held it open. Her step was light, belying her age.

"Annelise!" Tess said.

The woman stopped and turned. "You won't make me change my mind."

"How did you know my name is Theresa?"

Miss Winther's face blanched. "I..."

Tess's stomach clenched. She thought about the framed needlework in Erik's room, the card in Magnus's hospital suite. "You're Erik Johansen's mother, aren't you?"

She made a fist and pressed it to her breast. "Erik...*who?*

That's preposterous. I'm sure I don't know what you're talking about."

"I found the records." Now Tess was bluffing, but she was also playing a very strong hunch. Every instinct she possessed was telling her that she might just be standing ten feet away from her grandmother. "It's all right," she said quietly. "You can tell me. I want to know." Annelise slowly closed the door. She returned to the parlor and sat down on a chintz settee. Feeling light-headed with a sense of unreality, Tess sat next to her.

The old woman lifted her hand and brushed Tess's cheek with the lightest of touches. The gesture took Tess back to the day they'd first met. Now she understood the sentiment behind the gesture.

"Oh, Theresa," said Annelise. "Times were so different then."

THIRTY

Now that she'd figured out the truth about Annelise Winther, Tess had no choice but to take her to see Magnus. The idea of returning to Archangel made her heart skip a beat, but it was from excitement, not panic. During the long drive from the city, Annelise talked nearly the whole time.

"People under siege tend to grow up fast or die," she said.

"You mean, in Copenhagen during the occupation."

"Yes. Although there were no official battles fought in Denmark, everyone, even the youngest of us, felt embattled. There was the constant pressure of keeping secrets and staying out of trouble. I was no exception, even as young as I was when it all started. Even though there was no active fighting, there were casualties. I remember seeing men who'd had a limb blown off by a bomb or mortar in some distant theater where the fighting raged. And in some way I felt just like them, someone who had lost a vital part of herself, whose entire future had been changed in a single moment. My missing family was like that phantom limb. I knew where it was supposed to be. I could *feel* it, but it was gone."

"Listen, if this is hard to talk about—"

"It's hard, but it should be talked about. Magnus's accident was a horrible reminder that we're fragile, we mortals."

"How long have you known him?"

"I met Magnus for the first time the day my parents were taken away. He was just a boy, a few years older than me, but I believe he was already working for the Holger Danske—the Resistance. He spirited me away by boat to Helsingør—the place Shakespeare fans know as Elsinore, where my grandmother lived."

"Did Magnus stay there with you?"

"No. I didn't see him again until a few years later." She took a handkerchief from her purse and briefly dabbed at her eyes. Then, with exceeding care, she folded the handkerchief in her lap. "I was flung out of childhood by the delivery of a telegram. After my parents were arrested, I was taken to live with my grandmother when the message arrived."

"The telegram," said Tess, keeping her eyes on the road, though she wanted to look at Miss Winther. Annelise.

"It was a mechanically produced telegram on extremely thin paper, as if the murder of my parents didn't warrant a sheet of fine stationery. Of course it wasn't called murder. Officially, the cause of death was typhus. That moment, when we read the telegram, created a clear dividing line between my childhood and some other state, not adulthood…but in that moment, I turned into a different person, hardened and fearful. I had never felt such emotional pain. The horror of a family being torn apart…it is the worst kind of nightmare. That was when my childhood ended, thoroughly and completely, never to be regained. In normal times, that change for a girl might coincide with the gentle appearance of womanly curves. But these were not normal times."

"I'm so sorry," Tess said. "I don't know what else to say."

"When my grandmother died half a year later, I was sent to a church orphanage. I hated it there, and ran away as soon as I could escape. The trouble was, I had no place to go...except to find Magnus. In time, I joined the Resistance, because even though I'd lost everything, I dedicated myself to helping others avoid the terrors of German occupation."

"So you and Magnus worked together?"

"We did. There was a large group of us—all young, all angry and passionate as only the young can be. Ramon Maldonado was a member of that group. He'd been in the merchant marine, and threw in with the Resistance fighters out of a sense of adventure, at first. And then a sense of purpose."

"He was a long way from Archangel," said Tess. "Why would he be in Denmark, of all places?"

"A girl. When you're young and in love, you don't let something so small as a world war stop you. It didn't last, though. In those times, very little lasted. I'm not sure what happened. The Resistance got very busy in October of 1943, when the Germans instituted martial law. The Nazis ordered a roundup of all the Danish Jews, and we took part in the greatest rescue of the war. Nearly all of Denmark's eight thousand Jews were ferried to safety in Sweden. There was a very narrow strait between Helsingør and Sweden. The fishing boats sailed both day and night for two weeks."

"That's remarkable," said Tess. "It must have been so gratifying for you."

"It was. We were known as the Helsingør Sewing Club, organized by a man we knew only as Erling. All the Jews, except five hundred, were taken to safety."

SUSAN WIGGS

"And the five hundred," said Tess, feeling a chill. "Were they sent to Auschwitz?"

"Yes."

"So Eva was one of those."

"Yes," she said again. "Of the five hundred Danes at the camp, fifty-one were lost. All the others were rescued. By the time Denmark was liberated in 1945, Magnus and Ramon were more than just comrades in arms and coconspirators. They were best friends. Ramon gave us all a new life. In 1948, he arranged for all of us to come to California." She paused, watching out the window. "I had nowhere else to go. All I knew of America was what I saw in the movie pictures. It seemed like a dream to me. Eva and I became fast friends during that time." She paused again, watching the rolling dairy country pass by the window. "In America, life was perfect, except for one thing."

Tess scarcely breathed, waiting.

"There was only one Magnus," Annelise said with stark honesty, "and both of us were in love with him. We were all so young. Eva and I were still teenagers. I never told him the way I felt."

"Why not?"

"Appearances were everything back then," the old lady said, gazing out the window. "It's odd, isn't it, that we survived so much only to find we couldn't survive each other." She unfolded the handkerchief again, then refolded it. "Magnus chose based on who needed him more, and that was Eva. She'd always been fragile. And I kept my distance, though it was terribly hard."

Tess didn't say anything. Coming as she did from a line of independent women, she was in no position to judge anyone.

"As time passed, things between Magnus and Eva became strained. They wanted a child so very badly. And I... I wanted him so very badly. We lost ourselves in the situation. It was brief. I wanted it to last forever but I knew it had to end. Then I discovered I was pregnant."

Tess tried to picture what the situation had been like, so long ago. Annelise—alone, pregnant, scandalized. Magnus and Eva, yearning.

"I came out of the fog and realized the answer was right there before me," Annelise continued. "I had nearly destroyed their marriage. There was no way to undo the damage. But I could save the child we'd made by giving him a family, a beautiful life. I wish Erik had been in the world longer, but wishes are sometimes not enough."

A long silence passed. Winery gardens, gorgeous even in winter, flowed past the car windows. "Thank you for telling me this," Tess said. "It means a lot to me." She was amazed at how her simple question had opened a floodgate of memories. Annelise, Eva and Magnus had become intertwined during the war years. They had suffered unspeakable losses, had fought and faced danger, ultimately escaping to a new life.

But America, for all its opportunity, had not been a panacea after all. There was still struggle, still tragedy, still acts committed in the heat of passion and reconciled with cold precision. Annelise seemed almost relieved to talk about it.

"I have one more question," Tess said as she took the winding county road toward Archangel. "After Eva passed away, did you and Magnus ever see each other?"

"No," said Annelise. "We talked on the telephone. It's funny, at our age, we acted as if we had all the time in the world. It was only when I saw you on the History Channel program that I began to think it was time to try to make things right."

When they arrived at the medical center, Annelise paused at the front door and placed her hand on Tess's arm. "I lost the love of my life because I was too cowardly to declare myself. Make all the mistakes you need to in life, but try not to make that one, Theresa."

She took her hand away and moved with a brisk eagerness that belied her age. She didn't even hesitate in the doorway of Magnus's suite, but strode right to his bedside. Tess knew she would be forever haunted by the expression on Annelise's face—a mixture of awe, regret, tenderness and love. She sank into a chair and took hold of Magnus's hand as if it were the most precious of artifacts, and lifted it to her cheek. She whispered something in Danish, and though Tess didn't understand, she felt shivers course down her spine.

The love emanating from the old woman was as unmistakable as the sun breaking through the clouds. Love, Tess realized, didn't always take a predictable course. Time and circumstances could batter away at it, like waves on a rocky shore, but for some people, love never died.

With all her heart, Tess knew she was one of those people, too. She couldn't turn off her feelings for Dominic, not even after walking away. Maybe the lesson to be learned here was that the price of letting someone into her heart was the pain of letting go. Or maybe the even harder work of holding on, no matter what the risk.

Annelise turned to Tess and switched to English. "I'd like to sit with him for a while, if that's all right."

The anxiety Tess had felt upon first coming here had belonged to a different person, someone who was alone and uncertain, scared to jump into life. Now, as she wended her way along the highway to the turnoff, she simply felt a sense of bittersweet nostalgia, as if she were coming home.

Isabel still hadn't done anything about the egg. At one time, Tess would have declared the decision a no-brainer, but now she was not so certain. Perhaps it was time for Bella Vista to pass into someone else's hands, after all.

The old roadside market still stood suspended in time, its homey wraparound porch seeming to be waiting for the springtime. She wondered if the future owner of Bella Vista, whoever that might be, would ever do something with the place.

Isabel rushed out of the house to greet her. Their embrace felt natural and comforting. "I missed you," Tess said.

"Same here. Come on in. We've got a lot to talk about. Where's...? What do we even call her? Miss Winther? Annelise?"

"She's with Magnus. She's anxious to meet you, too."

"In the meantime," Isabel said, on autopilot as she put out tea and lemon bars, "we need to talk about the egg."

Tess smiled. "You know me well."

"You weren't going to sit through a bunch of small talk." She went to the freezer and took out an ornate case, a redwood box carved by Magnus. "I didn't get a safe deposit box for it. I took your advice and stored it with the walnut pesto." Setting the box on the table, she opened it up. The egg gleamed on a pillow of white satin.

"I don't want you to feel pressured, Isabel," Tess said. "I used to be focused on separating people from their treasures, but I get it now. The egg belongs to Magnus and it's a part of you. The decision to keep it or sell it is in your hands." Tess felt good about saying it aloud. She wouldn't blame her sentimental, impractical sister if she felt that keeping the egg would keep her closer to Magnus.

"It's one of the most beautiful things I've ever seen," said Isabel. "It's amazing to imagine Grandfather keeping it with him throughout the war, and after. It's followed him through all of his days. I've thought and thought about it. There's no price to be put on a man's life, is there?"

"I'm not sure what you're getting at, Isabel."

She closed the box and pushed it across the table. "I'd like you to sell it to the highest bidder."

Tess nearly choked on a lemon bar. "Wait…what? You're selling it?"

"Didn't you estimate it'll fetch twenty million?"

"I did. Jude thinks it could go higher."

"Then of course we should sell it."

"Isabel—"

"The egg is not the treasure. The real value is… It's this." She opened her arms to encompass the room. "Us, Tess, and what we've found together. That's what I think, anyway. I've thought long and hard about this, and selling the egg is exactly what we should do. We can pay off Grandfather's debt and get the payroll straightened out, and you'll have whatever you need to have the life you want."

The life I want can't be bought with money, thought Tess. "What about you, Isabel? What are you going to do for yourself?"

Her face lit up as she folded her arms on the table. "How does this sound to you? The Bella Vista Cooking School."

"You want to start a cooking school?"

"Crazy, right? You were my inspiration for that, Tess. It'll be a working farm and culinary school. I'll have my beehives after all. I can convert the bedrooms to guest quarters, and turn it into a destination for people who need to get away and learn something new."

"That could have described me, when I first came here," Tess admitted. She pictured the place filled with people who wanted to learn more about the earthly delights of food and the pleasure of preparing it well. "It *is* crazy. And you're going to be fabulous."

They strolled outside together into the freshening breeze that was just beginning to smell of springtime. Almost reflexively, Tess checked her phone before remembering that she didn't get a signal here.

"Maybe if the auction goes well, I'll put in a cell phone tower," Isabel said.

"Don't you dare."

"Kidding."

Tess looked around, envisioning what the trees would look like in blossom. They walked along in silence for a bit. The auction was going to be the firm's biggest event of the year. Tess wondered why she wasn't more excited about that. Maybe the excitement would sink in later.

"You haven't asked about him," Isabel said.

Tess's stomach dropped. "And I don't intend to."

"You should," Isabel insisted.

"It's none of my bus—"

"She left," Isabel said. "Lourdes. She moved to Petaluma. Jake Camden did, too, although I have no idea if they're together. A lot of things have changed for Dominic. He, um— he was fired from the bank."

Her stomach dropped. "What?"

"He broke some kind of rule, or did something wrong— for us, Tess. For Grandfather and Bella Vista. He committed some kind of technical foul to defer the foreclosure, and they fired him."

"Oh, God. It was about the egg," she said with sudden clarity. "He classified it as an unrecovered asset, something like that."

"Go see him, Tess. If you don't, you'll always wonder."

Tess regarded her, aghast. Go see him and say...what? "I'm scared," she admitted.

"People don't die of fright," Isabel reminded her. "My older, wiser sister once told me that."

It was mid-afternoon on a weekday, but Isabel had said Dominic would be at home, probably working in the winery or vineyard. Tess drove too fast over the gravel road to his place, determined to get there before she lost her nerve. She kept hearing Annelise's voice in her head, reminding her to live this day, and love like there was no tomorrow.

As she got out of the car, she saw Dominic coming toward her, and her heart seized. She was not over him. She would never be over him.

He looked...different. Gone were the banker's suit and wingtip shoes, the frown of worry between his eyes. She noticed something else there, though. A deep hurt, one she recognized. One she had caused.

"Hey," she said.

"Hey, yourself." He stood firm, impassive.

"Do you have time to talk?"

"I've got nothing but time. I'm unemployed."

"Isabel told me about the bank, and I'm sorry about that. I know you put your job at risk for us. If I'd realized it could get you fired, I wouldn't have let you do it."

He shrugged. "It was the nudge I needed. Nudged me right into irresponsibility and unemployment. Right into doing what I should have been doing all along."

"I wish you'd called, Dominic. I wish you'd told me what was going on."

"Why would I call you, Tess? You walked away."

"I had to leave. You have a family with her, Dominic—"

"And we'll always have that."

"She told me you were going to counseling."

"For Trini. Did she tell you it was to help Trini at school?"

"I assumed it was to reunite your family."

"I tried to explain it to you that last day, but you didn't listen. I wanted you, Tess. I thought you wanted me."

"You thought?" She didn't know whether to laugh or cry. "You *thought?* Did I not make it obvious enough?"

"You walked away," he reminded her again.

She weighed all the possible facts she could reveal here, and settled on the raw, painful truth. "I was scared. And then you took down my walls, Dominic, and everything you see here—it's all me. It's all I have, far from perfect, but it's all yours, if you'll have me. Every minute I've been gone, I've missed you. I love your life, your kids, your dogs—and you. I love you." She looked at him, and her heart sped up. "I'm still scared, but I won't hide anymore. No more running. No more secrets." She took a breath. "I... I stole a shirt."

"What?"

"I stole one of your shirts, a soft, faded denim one that smells like you, and I sleep with it every night and I've been afraid to wash it because I don't want to lose you."

For a moment, he looked angry or maybe baffled, but then he laughed softly. "Tess. Why steal my shirt when you can have the whole guy?"

Part Ten

... • ...

BAKED HOT CHOCOLATE

It's crucial to use the best quality chocolate you can find. Don't put anything in this dessert you wouldn't eat directly. And don't overbake. You want a delicate crust on top of a warm, silken interior.

9 ounces of dark semi-sweet chocolate, chopped

6 tablespoons unsalted butter, cut into cubes

4 eggs

¼ cup sugar

whipped cream or vanilla ice cream to taste

Preheat oven to 350 degrees. Arrange six small ovenproof mugs or custard cups in a baking pan.

Melt the chocolate and butter together in a double boiler set over barely simmering water. Whisk until smooth and set aside.

Whisk eggs and sugar together in a mixing bowl, then set the bowl over simmering water and stir constantly until warm to the touch.

Remove from heat. Beat egg mixture with an electric mixer until light and fluffy. Fold egg mixture into chocolate mixture.

Spoon the batter into cups. Add enough hot water to baking pan to come halfway up sides of cups. Bake until the tops lose their glossy finish, about fifteen minutes.

Serve warm or at room temperature with a scoop of ice cream or dollop of whipped cream that has been lightly sweetened and spiked with Cointreau.

(Source: Adapted from a recipe by Heidi Friedlander, former pastry chef of the Cleveland bistro Moxie)

EPILOGUE

The mariachi band came to the grand opening of the shop. The refurbished building looked as fresh as a new bride, hung with flower baskets filled with May-blooming lilies and vines. Rose blossoms were scattered artfully on the lawn and walkways, their bright tones reflected in the polished windows.

As the festivities ramped up, Tess was nearly giddy with excitement. The shop, once the place where Eva Johansen sold produce from the orchards, was now Tess's very own domain. She had poured her heart and soul into transforming Eva's place into her own. When she was ordering the sign that would arch over the front door, she had made a last-minute adjustment. Instead of calling the place Things Forgotten like her grandmother's place in Dublin, she decided to rename it Things Remembered.

Everyone came to check out Archangel's newest establishment and to wish Tess well. Even her friends from the city had come—Neelie, the newlyweds Lydia and Nathan, and

Jude, trying hard to maintain his edge of cynicism amid the music, the food and wine. There were pavilions set up outside the shop for the band and the food, and a big area of the parking lot was kept clear for dancing.

Tess was startled by the arrival of a black town car, sending up a rooster tail of dust as it pulled into the parking area. "Excuse me," she said, her stomach tightening in anticipation as she headed for the car.

"Oh, baby, I hope I didn't miss the festivities," Shannon said, exiting the town car on a swirl of colorful scarves, an oversize handbag on her arm.

There were a hundred things Tess could say to that, but she let go of her exasperation and hugged her mother close. "You're just in time, Mom."

"That's wonderful," said Shannon. "I'm so excited for you, Tess."

"That makes two of us. Come on, there's someone I want you to meet." Tess took her mother's hand and led her to the front of the building.

The VIP of the day was Magnus Johansen. He was in a wheelchair and could only be up a short time at a stretch, but he was getting stronger every day. Just as the doctor had predicted, he'd emerged gradually from the coma. Tess liked to think the main turning point had occurred when Annelise had visited him, taking his hand and speaking in Danish, sitting with him for hours.

"Magnus," said Tess, putting a hand on his shoulder. "My mother's here. Shannon Delaney."

The old man looked up, dignified with his snowy froth of hair and the new shirt Isabel had given him. His lap was covered by a plaid woolen blanket. "I'm glad to meet you," he said, extending his hand.

Shannon and Tess sat with him for a few minutes. "Erik told me about you," he said.

"I didn't know that."

"I wish I'd listened better. I'm sorry."

"There's no need to apologize," said Shannon.

"He didn't take the egg," Magnus said.

"What?" both Tess and her mother asked in unison.

"Erik," Magnus explained. "He didn't take the egg. My son was far from perfect, as are we all. But he was no thief. I sent him to sell it. That was the last I saw of my son—and the treasure."

Tess leaned forward and placed a soft kiss on his cheek. "Thank you for telling us."

"Now everything is as it should be," Magnus said. As Tess rose to resume her hostess duties, he reached for her hand one more time. "I dreamed of you," he said. "When I was in the hospital, I dreamed of the day you'd come to Bella Vista. But this…" He gestured at the colorful gathering, the beautifully restored shop with its freshly painted sign. "It's better than I could have dreamed."

Her heart was full as she posed for pictures in front of the new shop. There was so much more of Tess here, objects that represented her taste and her values, but it wasn't just her. Isabel's jams, sauces and baked goods were offered, and she'd promised jars of honey from next year's harvest. The gorgeous rare wines of Angel Creek Winery were featured—of course. There were some fine antiques, but they were mixed in with vintage items, as well—time-worn enamelware, vintage glassware, handmade soaps and candles, crafts from local artisans, anything that caught Tess's fancy. Things Remembered already felt like home to her, a place filled with history and meaning for the Johansens, and now for Tess, as well. She thought her grandmothers, Nana and Eva, would approve. She knew for certain that Annelise did; she was a frequent visitor to Archangel, spending most of her time in quiet devotion to Magnus. She never failed to lift his spirits, and some of her best rummage-sale finds were now for sale in the shop.

The delicate chords of the vihuela heralded the mariachis' signature song, "Cielito Lindo," and nearly everyone danced. These days, she saw everything through a gauzy dream of happiness. It was Dominic's doing. She had completely changed her life for him, and her every instinct told her she was finally on the right path. When he arrived with his kids, she felt a flood of emotion that underscored those instincts.

"Listen," he said, "I need to talk to you. I know you've got a lot going on today, but it's making me crazy to wait." He took her hand and led her into the shop, which was closed off to the public until the ribbon cutting. Everything inside had been restored and arranged, the antiques and collectibles beautifully curated on shelves, the local produce, including Isabel's preserves and Angel Creek wine, displayed in abundance. In the center of the place, as grand as a church organ, sat Nana's desk, from where she had presided over Things Forgotten in Dublin. Tess ran her hand across the top of the massive piece, suddenly filled with memories. Nana had never really left her.

"The first time I set foot in your apartment," Dominic said, "I knew I was going to fall in love with you."

"Really?" Her heart skipped a beat. "I was so embarrassed. The place was a mess. I was a mess."

"True," he said, "but that didn't stop me. Maybe it was the way you kept your files in the fridge, or the panties drying on a lampshade." He laughed at her expression, then turned serious. "It was just…you, Tess. I liked everything about you. I could see your heart in the things you collected and surrounded yourself with."

"Other people's treasures," she said softly.

"I loved that, and I loved the fact that you kept your grandmother's desk."

"She'd be so happy for me today," Tess said.

He brought her over by the old iron stove, now restored to a fresh gleam and decked with cut flowers. "This," he said, "is when I knew for sure I loved you. Right here, the day of the storm."

"You made a fire. I loved that day, too. And I loved you. I wish I'd told you then."

"You can tell me now." He took a ring from his shirt pocket and slipped it on her finger. The chill, bright platinum immediately warmed, and the diamond winked in the sunlight through the window. "Your grandfather gave me the diamond," Dominic said. "I had it made from a tie tack his wife gave him as an anniversary gift one year. Marry me, Tess." He lifted her left hand to his lips. "Say you'll marry me."

She couldn't speak, but she knew her heart was in her eyes when she looked up at Dominic. He bent and brushed his lips to her temple. "Okay, how about this. Stomp your foot once for yes, and twice for—"

"Yes," she said on a rush of joy. "How could it be anything but yes?" They shared a long kiss, and she felt the world shift—invisibly, inexorably.

Arm in arm, they walked outside together. "Ah, Tess. It's going to be so good."

"It already is," she said. "But what about—"

Trini and Antonio hurried toward them, their faces lit with curiosity.

"Something tells me they already know," said Dominic.

"Did you do it, Dad? Did you pop the question?" Trini demanded.

"Actually, I—"

"I knew it!" Trini said, throwing her arms around Tess. "I totally knew it!"

Tess looked at Antonio over his sister's head. "We wanted you guys to be the first to know. Are you okay with this?"

"Does it mean you're gonna move in?"

"Yes, after we get married."

"Where's the ring?" Trini grabbed both her hands. "Gosh, that's a really pretty ring. Can I tell people, Dad? Can I?"

"Sure, you can." He tousled Antonio's hair. "You want to go help spread the news?"

He took off, and within moments, literally, Tess and Dominic were inundated with well-wishers. She caught his eye as he submitted to the backslapping and high-fiving, and mouthed the words, *I'm going to love it here.*

Whether he understood her or not, she couldn't tell, but he looked ridiculously happy as he opened a jeroboam of his best wine.

As the wine was being poured, Tess spied Isabel through the crowd, and when their gazes met, they made their way toward each other, jostling past friends and neighbors. Isabel looked so beautiful to Tess just then, her face shining with delight. She looked like...*family.* "When?" she demanded, pulling Tess into a hug.

Tess pulled back. "Just now. I swear, I didn't see it coming. I wished for it, of course. Dreamed of it, but...he took me totally by surprise. I think I'm in shock. And so happy, Isabel. I never thought I could be this happy."

"It's only the beginning," said Isabel. "And it'll only get better from here."

Tess extended her hand to her sister. They held fast to one another as they headed toward the dancing crowd, aglow in the golden light of late afternoon, surrounded by the bright sounds of music and laughter.

★ ★ ★ ★ ★

ACKNOWLEDGMENTS

I've been blessed with a fantastic publishing team—my editor, Margaret O'Neill Marbury and her assistant Giselle Regus, and also Meg Ruley and Annelise Robey of the Jane Rotrosen Agency. Thank you for your expertise, your kindness and humor, and for making business a pleasure, time and time again.

I also need to thank my fellow writers—Elsa Watson, Sheila Roberts, Lois Faye Dyer, Kate Breslin and Anjali Banerjee. Ladies, there are no words. I'll just leave it at that.

A very special thank-you to Bob and Fay Krokower and the irrepressible Charlie for your generosity to P.A.W.S. and your kindness to pets in need.

THE
APPLE
ORCHARD

SUSAN WIGGS

Reader's Guide

mira

1. The author uses nonlinear story structure (present day interspersed with scenes from the past) for several of her books. Here, she takes us back to WWII Denmark where we see Magnus Johansen as a young boy. Can the past, particularly one's ancestry, influence the present? What are some examples of this in the book?

2. How would you feel if someone told you had a half sister you never knew about? Neither Tess nor Isabel ever had the chance to meet their father, Erik. Do you think this paternal tie is what pulls them together, or do you think the bonds of sisterhood go much deeper than a shared father?

3. Tess and Isabel couldn't be more different. One is a brash, deal-making, world-weary redhead who can't slow down and pursues lots of seemingly superficial friendships, and the other is a calm brunette who'd rather stay at Bella Vista creating farm-to-table meals with her extended family than venture out. This picture would certainly support the theory of nurture vs. nature. Yet, if

you look more closely, you'll find that the two sisters have more in common than meets the eye. What characteristics do they share?

4. The main character, Tess Delaney, is a provenance expert. She has an uncanny ability to find things, valuable things, from the past. At one point Tess even says, "I guess you could say finding treasure is in my blood." When she finds the pink topaz lavaliere necklace that belongs to Annelise Winther—a necklace that could allow Annelise to live in the lap of luxury for the rest of her days—she's disappointed that Annelise will not sell the necklace, but she's not *devastated*. Is there some part of Tess that wishes she had such a powerful connection to someone that no amount of money could replace it?

5. When did you know that Dominic Rossi was the right man for Tess? Was it right away, when he brushes the powdered sugar from the doughnut off her nose at work, or in the E.R., when he stays in the waiting room to help out Tess, a near-stranger? Or was there another moment?

6. Tess is very tightly wound. Why do you think she's so keyed up all of the time? She's very controlled in certain aspects of her life, but appears to have no control or organization at all over other parts. Sometimes people create their own obstacles to happiness, whether it's out of a belief that they don't deserve happiness or because they're just not ready to be happy. Have you ever felt this way?

7. As writer Elin Hilderbrand says of this book, "The most storied of fruits is done incredible justice here... *The Apple Orchard* is sweet, crisp and juicy." The apple has been a symbol of temptation, it has been known to keep one healthy and it's the thing to give when currying a

teacher's favor. How does the author bring the themes of temptation, health and seeking acceptance into the book?

8. At the beginning of the story, Tess doesn't appear to have a maternal bone in her body. And yet she's surprisingly comfortable around Dominic's kids. Do you think Tess will be a good stepmother and mother?

9. The author writes about the German occupation of Denmark during WWII, in particular the resistance movement known as the Holger Danske. Nearly 8,000 Jews found safe harbor thanks to Danish citizens like the fictional Magnus Johansen. Were you aware that such heroic efforts were taking place during that time? The more serious subject matter helps to put the struggles and conflicts of the present-day story into perspective. Did you enjoy how the author uses a historical event to frame a fictional narrative?

10. Susan Wiggs is an animal lover who has three dogs at present. In this story, Dominic has rescued a dog, Charlie. Do you think pet owners are more compassionate people? Would this be an instant check on the list of "things to look for in a partner" for you?

*Turn the page for a sneak peek
at the next book in the Bella Vista Chronicles,*

The Beekeeper's Ball,

in paperback from MIRA

Isabel dressed in a softly gathered skirt, sandals and a gauzy, loose-fitting blouse, light and comfortable in the warm weather. Her dark heavy curls—a legacy from the mother she'd never known—would dry in the sunshine today. Spring was in full bloom, and she had tons to do, starting with supervising the workers who were fixing a pergola over the new section of the patio, which had been expanded to make way for guests.

With its central fountain, wrought iron chairs and café tables with cobalt-blue majolica tile, the open-air space would be a gathering place—first for Tess and Dominic's wedding guests, and later, starting in the fall, for people who came to attend the cooking school. Isabel wanted it to be as beautiful and inviting as a vintage California hacienda, and she'd planned the project down to the last golden limestone paver.

This had always been a private home, but this summer it

would be opened to the world. The estate had lain in slumber like an enchanted kingdom, and now it was finally waking up, opening its embrace to new energy. New life.

Yet despite all the details that needed attending to, her mind kept flitting to Cormac O'Neill. She reminded herself that his business was with her grandfather, not her. A biography. Why hadn't Grandfather told her about this?

On her way down to the kitchen, she paused on the landing, which featured a wall-sized mirror. For some reason, she flashed on a bit from the article she'd seen in the waiting room—*Wear something sexy.* It just wasn't her style. She favored clothes that were long, loose and drapey. *Concealing.* The most formfitting garment she owned was her chef's apron. Sometimes she wished she had her sister's natural eye for fashion, but when Isabel tried for that, she felt self-conscious, like a kid playing at dress up. She hadn't even settled on her maid-of-honor dress.

Tess was at the kitchen counter, gazing out the window and eating a wedge of bee sting cake, cream filled and glossy with a crust of honeyed almonds. "If you don't quit feeding me like this," Tess scolded, "I'm never going to fit into my wedding dress."

"That was for the workmen," Isabel said. She'd quickly learned that construction guys needed baked goods to keep them at peak performance.

Tess shook back her glossy red hair. She had been growing it long in order to wear it up on her wedding day. "Couldn't resist. Sorry. So where have you been all morning?"

"Dealing with your friend Cormac O'Neill."

Tess brightened. "Oh! He's here?"

All glorious six-foot-something of him. "He got stung by bees and had an allergic reaction, so I took him to the clinic in town."

"Oh, my gosh. Is he—"

"He'll be fine. He says he's here to work on Grandfather's biography. Do you know anything about that?"

"Sure." Tess paged through her wedding notebook, which was stuffed with lists and clippings of flowers, food and decor.

"Why didn't you tell me about this project?" With a twinge of irritation, Isabel studied her sister. In one short year, they'd grown close, though at times there were moments of tension. Like now. In some areas, they were still finding their way.

"We just got word yesterday that Mac's available."

Mac. Like the truck.

"I would have told you, but it's been a whirlwind around here, and you've had enough on your plate, helping me with the wedding and getting the place ready for the cooking school. The plan came together really fast. Mac wasn't available, and suddenly he was, so I jumped at the chance. Magnus's story begs to be written, and Cormac O'Neill is the perfect one to do it."

"You should have checked with me."

"You're right. Look, if having him here is going to be a problem, we can find someplace else for him. He could stay at Dominic's."

"Your fiancé doesn't need a houseguest. He's already got half of Southern Italy coming for the wedding. It's fine for this guy to stay for a while. Lord knows, we've got nothing but room." She looked around the kitchen, a big bright space where she'd grown up learning to cook at her grandmother's side. "That's not what I'm worried about. Does Grandfather want his life story out there for all the world to know?"

"That's the point, isn't it? But he wants it done right, and that's where Mac comes in." Tess unceremoniously licked the crumbs from her plate. "Holy cow, that's delicious. The workmen are never going to leave. You keep feeding them like this, and they'll perform miracles. Can we have this for the wedding breakfast? God, I'm obsessed, aren't I?"

"You're the bride. You are supposed to be obsessed with your wedding."

"Okay, but you get to tell me if I'm unbearable."

Isabel was excited for Tess and Dominic and his kids, but sometimes, when she lay awake at night, she felt an unbidden curl of envy. Tess made love look easy, while Isabel hadn't had a date in years. She knew she needed to take down her walls, but how did someone do that?

She batted away the thought. "Don't try to change the subject. Cormac O'Neill."

"You're going to be glad he's the one to document Magnus's life. Our grandfather has a unique story. An important one. It's not just family pride, Iz. He was a key player in the Danish Resistance. There were eight thousand Jews in Denmark during the German occupation, and Magnus's group helped rescue seventy-five hundred of them. It's a rare bright spot in the middle of the darkest of times. Most of all, it's something Magnus wants."

Isabel tucked a damp stray curl behind her ear and looked out the window. From one side of the kitchen, she could see the rows of trees, some of the stock decades old. The blossoms of springtime were flurrying down as the new fruit emerged, a tangible sign of renewal. She loved Bella Vista, loved the rhythm of the seasons. She was lucky to be a part of it.

"Yes," she said quietly. "Grandfather did say that." Neither sister stated the obvious—that their grandfather wasn't getting any younger. "So tell me about this guy."

"He's written award-winning nonfiction," Tess said. "He's won all kinds of literary prizes. He already has a publisher on board—assuming the project gets done. Anyway, the impor-

tant thing is, he's here with us now, and I think he'll be perfect for Magnus."

"Where is he going to stay?" Isabel asked.

"I thought we'd put him in Erik's room."

Erik—their father. He had died before either of them was
born, leaving their separate mothers both pregnant and alone,
unaware of each other. Over the past year, Isabel and Tess had
spent hours speculating about the situation, but frustratingly,
had never been able to figure out what had driven Erik to do
the things he'd done.

"Why Erik's room?" asked Isabel.

"Because it's available, and he doesn't need anything fancy.
I thought Erik's room would be a good choice. The history,
you know? If he's going to do a thorough job, Mac needs to
be wrapped into the family."

The idea made Isabel distinctly uncomfortable. "Suppose
we don't want to wrap him into the family?"

"Our grandfather wants it. I swear, it'll be fine. Just fine."
Tess put her dishes in the sink, then poured herself a cup of
coffee and took a sip. She never seemed to be completely still,
physically or mentally. She was always thinking, planning,
doing. She had the kind of energy that made caffeine jumpy.
"I'm really sorry, Iz. Don't be mad, okay?"

"I never get mad," said Isabel.

"I know. It's freaky. I'm about to become a stepmom to two
school-age kids, so I need to take lessons from you on how to
be mellow about things."

Isabel flashed on Calvin Sharpe, and she felt anything but
mellow. "Hey, off the subject, but did you attend the last
Chamber of Commerce meeting?"

"Yep. I'm a card-carrying member. They're going to fea-
ture Things Remembered on the Chamber website in December. Cool, huh?"

"Very cool. And, um, was there any talk of that new restaurant coming in? It was in the newsletter…"

"Yeah, I think it's kind of a big deal. Some famous chef… Cleavon or Calvin…?"

"Calvin Sharpe. A TV chef." Isabel kept her face neutral. *You never get mad.* Great, just great.

"Yeah, that's the one. Super good-looking, and he had an entourage with him. I remember now—he's calling the new place CalSharpe's. So, you know this guy?"

"He was an instructor at the culinary institute when I went there, years ago."

"And? What's he like?"

"Like a guy who thinks the sun rises every morning just to hear him crow," Isabel said. "But he can cook. And it appears he's got a restaurant empire going." She didn't want to talk about it anymore. She'd already given him too much space in her head. "Anyway. Back to the other guy—Cormac O'Neill. You call him Mac."

Tess grabbed her arm and pulled her toward the lounge room. "Come here," she said. "Let me show you something."

She led the way to the big room, which had already been refurbished for the cooking school. It was light and airy with freshly whitewashed plaster walls and tall ceilings, filled with cookbooks and old furniture and Bubbie's baby grand piano. When Isabel was growing up, the rolling ladder against the tall built-in bookcases had been her stairway to a different world. That was what books had offered her—all the voyages she wanted, to different realms. Even as a tiny girl, she'd been the consummate armchair traveler, seeing the world from the safety of her own home.

Now she was a steward of this place. For her, Bella Vista lived and breathed with the essence of life, representing security and permanence in a world that had not always been kind to her. Her mission was to revive the place, resuscitate it after the hard times. Her grandfather's accident last year had shaken Isabel's foundations. Magnus was a father figure and besides Tess, her only family.

Isabel still loved to pore over photographs of castles on the Rhein, Ayers Rock in Australia, Italy's Amalfi coast. Sometimes, gazing at the pictures, she would feel a yearning deep in her stomach. Yet when it came to actually traveling to those places, something always made her balk. To her, adventure was always more appealing within the pages of a travelogue.

Tess pulled a stack of new-looking books from a shelf and set them on the lid of the piano. "I met Mac for the first time when I was working in Krakow. I was tracing the origin of some paintings that had been hidden by the Nazis, and he was doing an article on restoring Nazi plunder. I'm actually a footnote in one of his books." She flipped open a thick volume called *Behind the Iron Curtain*. "He talks about the Krakow treasure here."

Isabel felt a surge of admiration for her sister. They had grown up separately, in completely different circumstances, Isabel at Bella Vista, and Tess traveling the world with her mother, a museum acquisitions expert. Isabel could easily picture Tess examining old artifacts, ferreting out the truth about them. She'd had a high-level position finding lost treasures and researching their origins at an auction house in the Bay Area. In fact, her expertise had been instrumental in saving Bella Vista from bankruptcy.

But along with the estate's reversal of fortune came a good deal of unwanted attention. She very much doubted Cormac O'Neill would have anything to do with her grandfather if not for the stories Tess had uncovered in her research. And then there was the lawsuit…brought by Archangel's most wily lawyer, a woman named Lourdes Maldonado. She was a neighbor and friend—*former* friend—who was suddenly looking for some kind of settlement.

"You've had such an amazing career," she said, pushing aside the troubling thought. "Do you miss it?"

"Every once in a while, yeah. I did have a good job in the city.

"It was great for a long time. But I found something better here." Tess's face softened, as it always did when she thought of her fiancé. "I know, I'm ridiculous. Honestly, Iz, I never knew love could feel this way. You'll see, one of these days. When the right guy comes along."

"Not holding my breath," Isabel said.

"Not even for *this* guy?" Tess handed her the Iron Curtain book.

Isabel took it from her and turned it over in her hands. She studied the author photo on the back. It was an extremely cleaned up version of the grubby, swearing traveler covered in beestings. "Oh, my."

The Beekeeper's Ball
by New York Times *bestselling author Susan Wiggs,*
available now wherever MIRA Books are sold!